Alice Teale is Missing

Alice Teale is Missing

HOWARD LINSKEY

PENGUIN BOOKS

PENGUIN BOOKS

UK | USA | Canada | Ireland | Australia
India | New Zealand | South Africa

Penguin Books is part of the Penguin Random House group of companies
whose addresses can be found at global.penguinrandomhouse.com.

First published in Penguin Books 2019
001

Set in 12.5/14.75 pt Garamond MT Std
Typeset by Jouve (UK), Milton Keynes
Printed and bound in Great Britain by Clays Ltd, Elcograf S.p.A.

A CIP catalogue record for this book is available from the British Library

ISBN: 978–1–405–93332–2

www.greenpenguin.co.uk

MIX
Paper from
responsible sources
FSC® C018179

Penguin Random House is committed to a
sustainable future for our business, our readers
and our planet. This book is made from Forest
Stewardship Council® certified paper.

This one is for my wonderful daughter, Erin,
who makes everything worthwhile

You had to wear gloves, always, otherwise they would catch you. The sender knew that. It made the whole exercise more difficult, though, because it deadened the sensation in the fingertips and it was harder to turn the individual pages of the journal, so it was a slow and frustrating process.

The surgical gloves had been a better idea. They were thinner and it was much easier to turn each page then read the words written there.

The sender devoured them.

Some of them were truly shocking. How did the girl know all this? She was like a spy.

There were words on the pages that frightened the sender and others that exhilarated or teased with their promise of forbidden knowledge. There were passages of text filled with love for others and writing so cruel and mean-spirited it was hard to imagine they were written by the same person, let alone a teenage girl.

Parts of the journal were true, the sender knew this, but there were other sections that were impossible to verify and some that had to be little more than wild speculation.

What was needed here was a passage that could be sent to the right person, a page or two that would have sufficient impact, like striking a match. Something that would burn this whole town down.

It took some considerable time to find the right words, but worthwhile things took effort. You only got out of life what you were prepared to put into it.

Eventually, the solution was obvious.

Begin at the end.

The final entry.

The sender made a decision then and pressed a hand against one side of the opened journal, trapping it against the table so that the pages couldn't move. Taking hold of the opposite page firmly, they tore it free. The page gave way surprisingly easily and came out cleanly. Heart thumping, the sender re-read it once more and experienced the excitement of knowing it was about to trigger a series of events no one could ignore. There would be further pages from the journal that could follow after, but the first one was the most important. Time could be taken, then, to read through it all again and tease out the right extracts to share.

All the sender had to do now was put this first extract in an envelope and help it on its way.

Then the game could start.

The Journal of Alice Teale

Every word I have written here is true, but I've changed the names to protect the guilty. There are a lot of guilty people. It's a town full of secrets. I can't *out* everybody.

I'm guilty, too. I've done some very bad things. I've hurt people, I've been immoral, by most people's standards, but mostly I am guilty of not seeing what was right in front of me. It should have been so obvious because it was there all the time. I have been entirely blind.

Until now.

Everything has changed. Now I can see it all clearly, view things exactly as they really are, with no secrets, lies or pretence. It's all been stripped away, and nothing will ever be the same again. The old Alice Teale is dead. She is gone for ever, along with her stupid doubts and fears and all the secrets she has carried around with her for so long. What remains of her is not going to take it any more. I want everything out in the open.

Not yet, though. There's something I need first.

Keep your sharp tongue in check, Alice, for once in your stupid bloody life, and carry on for just a little while longer, acting out all the parts, like you've always done.

Daughter, sister, girlfriend, friend.

But you've not been very good at any of those lately.

Worker, pupil . . . Little Miss Perfect.

But it's all unravelling now.

Virgin, good girl, ice queen, geek.
Hot babe, slut, disgusting freak!

Who cares what they think of you, Alice? None of that matters now.

It's all over.

At least, it will be.

Soon.

I

Six days ago

The girl left the school by the main entrance, which was why Miss Pearce saw her leave. Her vantage point was the first-floor staff-room window. Normally, this would have been a busy and noisy spot, with younger pupils shoving and shoulder-charging each other as they bottlenecked through the doors and were finally forced out by sheer weight of numbers, but school had been over for hours now. Only a handful of kids remained, finishing off the numerous sporting activities and after-school clubs Collemby Comprehensive School had become known for under its strict but progressive headteacher, who believed that education was not confined to regular school hours or mere academic qualifications. 'We are not only training young people to pass exams,' he would remind his staff earnestly, 'we are preparing them for life.'

Was it still a bit late for a kid to be leaving, even if she was a sixth-former? It was quite light, with the summer almost here; a little more than a month to go before they broke up for six glorious weeks of holiday. The PE teacher glanced at her watch. Almost nine o'clock; the activities she'd presided over had finished half an hour ago. She had only stayed behind herself because she knew she'd never make it to the bus stop in time and couldn't face standing there for an hour waiting for the next one. She had gone up to the empty staff room, flicked on the kettle and phoned Rob, her fiancé, to ask if he could come and pick her up. He hadn't sounded too happy about that. 'I'm tired, too, Jessica,' he'd told her, 'it's been a long day,' but he'd eventually agreed to drive out and get her, albeit with bad grace.

He must have taken his time leaving their flat because there was still no sign of him and she had drunk most of her tea. Jessica Pearce watched the road from the big window to make sure she didn't miss him. As she waited, she remembered the promise he had made when they first got together. 'I would do anything for you,' he'd assured her. *'Anything.'* Now, seven years on, it seemed a fifteen-minute drive was too much trouble. She wondered if this was how everyone ended up once they'd got beyond the dating stage and moved in together?

She looked back at the girl. You could tell it was Alice Teale, even from the back and this vantage point. The sixth-former was a distinctive figure with her trademark hooded Oasis-style green parka and floppy red shoulder-bag.

Alice Teale was a girl you would notice, even when you were a straight woman like Jessica. The boys certainly noticed Alice. They were queueing up for her. The girl's face was ridiculously pretty and she had an almost equine grace about her when she walked, though, just as she thought that, Jessica noticed the teenager stumble slightly, possibly under the weight of the bag.

Further thoughts on Alice Teale were broken by the sight of two cars that passed each other. One of them was driven by Simon Nash, the young drama teacher. Simon had squeezed his frame into his car and pulled out of the car park then driven away towards the town, just as Rob suddenly appeared, heading in the opposite direction, towards the school, in his silver Fiat, which he slowed almost to a halt before guiding it across the road and in through the entrance to the school car park.

Jessica Pearce bent to grab her bag.

She turned back to the window in time to see Rob walking on to the long, straight path that led to the school, just as Alice Teale reached the far end of it. They might have collided with each other if he hadn't stepped out of her way. Silly girl had her head down and probably wasn't looking where she was going.

Jessica Pearce waved then and Rob looked up, caught her eye, but did not return the wave. Instead, he stopped in his tracks, so she knew he had no intention of wasting any more time by walking into the building.

In her haste to meet him she forgot all about Alice, who must have passed between the retirement cottages that lay just beyond the school's boundary, as she could no longer be seen.

No one knew it at the time but that glimpse Miss Pearce had of the sixth-former would be the last recorded sighting of the girl, before the word went out the next day.

Alice Teale was missing.

Alice Teale was gone.

2

DC Beth Winter tried to leave quietly and discreetly without anyone noticing, but it was a forlorn hope. Anne Hudson spotted her as she finished clearing the last items from her desk, dropping them without ceremony into a plastic bag. If only Beth had been a bit quicker, she could have been out of there, avoiding the inquisition that was heading her way.

Anne was a fellow fast-tracker from the direct-entry scheme, which meant that she, like Beth, had never walked the beat or spent a working day in uniform. Instead, they had both joined the Northumbria police force as detectives – trainee ones, at any rate – and had endured a two-year training programme before finally passing the National Investigator's exam. On the face of it, they had something in common. They were female, of roughly the same age and background and both yet to prove themselves on a major case. That's how it worked on direct entry: you had to earn your place investigating minor crimes as part of your probation. That time was coming to an end and they were both eager to get out and join a squad working on something bigger than burglaries on the industrial estate. There had been three of them to begin with, but Peter Kennedy had already been nabbed by an undermanned DI. He was a good candidate and a nice bloke, but Beth knew she was every bit as good as him and was disappointed, though not surprised, that the only male in their intake had been the first to be snapped up.

'I heard your news,' said Anne. 'Transferred to DCI Everleigh's squad. Well done you!' That last bit was a little too loud and the smile forced.

'Thanks . . . erm . . . they must be desperate.' If Beth thought self-deprecation was going to get her off the hook, she was mistaken.

'I suppose it's only a missing person,' Anne said slyly.

'It could be a murder' – Beth couldn't help but rise to it – 'they think.'

'Who does?'

'Everleigh and his people, apparently.'

'They haven't found a body.'

'Not yet,' said Beth. 'You seem to know a lot about it?' she added, meaning that Anne obviously wanted to be the one added to DCI Everleigh's squad.

Anne ignored this. 'Still, it's good news for you, a chance to shine. You'll be great . . .'

'Thank you.'

'. . . if you can cope with you-know-who.'

The bombshell. There was always going to be one from Anne. This must be it.

'Sorry?'

'His DS?' She said that as if a) it was obvious and b) Beth must have forgotten who this mysterious DS was.

Beth thought for a second. How could she answer this in a way that would completely ruin Anne's fun? Pretend she knew who the other girl was referring to and laugh off the man's foibles? If she did, she might run the risk of belatedly learning she was about to work with a serial groper. Alternatively, Beth could ask Anne outright what she was talking about, which would make her seem less than clued up – never a good look for a detective, especially a new one. Anne would love that. Instead, she went for the middle ground.

'Which one?' she asked.

'You mean you don't know?' replied Anne. She was obviously loving this. Well, let her enjoy her tiny victory. Anne wasn't the one being transferred to a real case. Soon Beth might be on the trail of a murderer while her mean-spirited colleague would be back investigating the industrial-estate burglaries.

'I've only just heard I'm going to be working for Everleigh,' Beth said, as sweetly as possible. 'I haven't had time to find out who else is working for him.'

'Call yourself a detective,' trilled Anne, and Beth wanted to thump her, right there and then, in headquarters, and in the face, but she told herself not to react. 'You'll be seeing a lot more of his DS than you will of DCI Everleigh,' she added. 'You do know that's how it works, right?'

Beth lost patience then. 'I know how it works, Anne. If you know the DS I'll be paired with, then why don't you just tell me? I know you're dying to.'

'All right, Grumpy' – that smile again, the one that allowed Anne to pretend she was only teasing and not being bitchy because she was jealous – 'but brace yourself.' She took a breath. 'You've got DS Black.' And when Beth didn't react, because she didn't know the man at all, Anne added, 'DS *Lucas* Black,' and she tilted her head to one side then surveyed her colleague, looking for some sort of recognition, as if Beth had accidentally slept with the bloke at the last Christmas party then completely forgotten about him.

'I don't really know him,' conceded Beth. There were dozens of detective sergeants in the Northumbria police force, for God's sake.

'Well, he's a nightmare.'

'In what way?' She wanted to add, *Spit it out, woman!*

'Can't believe you haven't heard . . .'

'Look, Anne, whatever it is, it can't be that bad or he wouldn't still be employed here. If he's a bit handsy, I'll deal with it – I'll report him or break one of his fingers. Whatever else it could be, I'll manage. So, you know, don't worry about me.'

When Anne replied this time, her tone was mock-casual. 'Oh, okay, whatever you say, Beth. I'm sure it'll all be fine. It's just, you know, Lucas Black has . . .' She exhaled then, delaying the pleasure of her answer. 'How can I put this? . . . Actually killed someone, that's all.'

3

'What do you mean, he's killed someone?' asked Beth, but she didn't get an answer.

Instead, their boss shouted across the room at her colleague, 'DC Hudson, stop gassing and get back on those burglaries! They won't solve themselves.' DI Curran was a man who seemed to resent the very presence of direct entrants in his squad, almost as much as the low-level crimes he was tasked to investigate these days, now that his career had seemingly plateaued. Only a few days ago, Beth had personally witnessed him getting very drunk at a fellow DI's retirement do. He had stood in the beer garden loudly telling everyone that DI Monaghan was 'a lucky bastard because he wouldn't have to put up with any more shit'. Not that he was bitter, of course.

He turned to Beth then. 'And DC Winter?'

'Yes, sir?'

'Why are you still here?' he asked wearily. 'I mean, if you don't want to go and do this missing-persons case, we can always keep you . . .'

'On my way now, sir.' And she was, but when she glanced back at Anne, who was busying herself with a phone call, it was her words that stayed with Beth.

'Come in, DC Winter,' ordered DCI Everleigh. He'd seen her approach his open office door and was, thankfully, expecting her. He was young for a detective chief inspector and Beth had heard he was both ambitious and on the rise. This was her first actual interaction with the man, though, and she was keen not to blow it.

'Welcome to the team.' He smiled at her.

'Thank you, sir.'

'Have you met DS Black?' He gestured towards a tall, stocky man with dark hair who was standing in front of him. He was in his late thirties or perhaps early forties, and he stared back at Beth without making any effort to welcome her. So, this was the apparently infamous DS Black. Beth confirmed they hadn't met before but that she was pleased to be working with him now. Oddly, he still said nothing, as if he either couldn't be bothered with pleasantries or didn't see any value in them; instead, he dipped his head for the merest second to acknowledge her presence then turned back to the DCI. In the briefest of pauses, she couldn't help but think again about what Anne had said.

'You and DS Black will be taking over a case in Colemby,' Everleigh told her. Beth had heard of the Northumbrian town, but she had been brought up south of Newcastle, on the other side of the river, and had no memory of even having driven through the place before. 'DI Fraser has elected to take early retirement.'

'Why?' asked Black. 'What has he done?'

Everleigh shot him an angry look. 'He hasn't done anything. For God's sake, Black, not everyone here is bent, you know.'

Black didn't react to this telling-off. 'The girl hasn't been missing all that long,' he explained. 'You wouldn't have given Fraser the case if you knew he was planning to take early retirement, so it's sudden.' Even Beth knew that detectives who abruptly elected to take early retirement were often escaping investigations into their misconduct, which would cease if they were no longer serving police officers. It was an unwritten rule that, if you went early and quietly, no further action would be taken against you, unless you'd done something very serious indeed.

Though Everleigh didn't contradict the logic of DS Black's argument, he didn't appear impressed by it either. 'He wasn't planning to leave,' said the DCI, 'he was offered a package. Our new chief constable has been tasked with major cost savings and that includes manpower, as always.'

Was there no end to these cuts? There seemed to be a leaving do every week and it was always seasoned detectives who were going, because the force wanted them and their more generous salaries off the books. No one seemed to be replacing them, though.

'We're encouraging voluntary redundancy. They're trying to get people out ASAP, so they get an offer and either go straight away or it's immediately withdrawn. The package is a generous one, if you are the right age and have served enough time. Fraser is a family man with a grandkid. It makes perfect sense for him, but that leaves us with a gap on the Alice Teale case.'

'You want me to take over from DI Fraser?' asked DS Black.

'Until your own DI gets back, yes.'

'And do we know when that will be, sir?'

'No,' admitted the DCI. 'That's . . . open-ended.'

'So, it's me and DC Winter here.' He sounded unimpressed. 'Anyone else?'

'Fraser had a couple of DCs. I'll keep them on it, but you are on point on this one, as it were.'

'Four of us, including a complete novice?' He didn't look at Beth, but he didn't have to. He didn't seem to give a damn that she was standing there in the room when he said it. 'This could be a murder,' Black reminded the DCI.

'And it could just as easily be a runaway. There is no body. She may very well be shacked up with a new boyfriend somewhere.'

'Still —'

Black was interrupted by the DCI's raised palm before he could object further. 'Frankly, there's no one else' — he made it sound as if Black and Winter were the last two kids picked for games at school — 'but I know you'll get a result.'

'Your faith is touching, sir.' Black's tone was unchallengingly neutral but his words were still scathing.

Everleigh chose to ignore this and turned to Beth. 'Thoughts, DC Winter?'

'Er . . . just that I'm looking forward to proving myself, sir, and . . . er . . .'

'And er . . . what?' The DCI didn't appear to appreciate her hesitation.

'What do we know about this girl, Alice . . . ?'

'Teale.' He really did look irritated now. He obviously expected her to remember the name he had mentioned. Everleigh made a point of slowly spelling it for her, as if she were a slow learner. Beth nodded when he had finished, as if she were grateful for his time, while secretly deciding that her new boss was a bit of a twat.

He continued, unabated: 'Alice Teale is seventeen and has been gone for several days now. She was last seen leaving her after-school club on Friday evening, but she failed to reach her home. DI Fraser has been unable to uncover any obvious reason or motive for her disappearance, aside from a somewhat tangled private and home life.'

It seemed that was all they were going to get from the DCI.

'Do we get a briefing from Fraser before he goes?' asked Black.

'If you don't hang about. He has one day left. Get down to Collemby. Fraser's set up a major-incident room in the town hall there. You'll need to notify the parents that you and DC Winter are now heading up the investigation. Their details are in here.'

He handed Black a slim file on the case.

'And DS Black . . .' Was that a supportive half-smile on the DCI's face or a grimace? 'Be aware that I've already vouched for you to those on high, so don't let me down.'

The big man took large strides and Beth struggled to keep up. She was almost jogging as they reached the lift together. Black didn't seem inclined to say anything, so she thought she'd better break the ice, but what could she say to him?

So, is it true you killed someone?

Possibly not the best opening gambit, so instead she settled on, 'I just wanted to say, I know you'd prefer someone with more experience but I'm really grateful for the opportunity to join the team.'

'I'm not the one giving you the opportunity. DCI Everleigh is.'

'Still . . .' And she couldn't think of anything else to say, until she recalled the mention of his detective inspector. 'Your DI is away at the moment?' she asked, hoping that might draw some sort of response from him.

'He won't be back in a hurry.'

'Why? What happened?'

Black sighed, then: 'He had a breakdown.' He gave her a withering look. 'Do you want all the details?'

They rode in excruciating silence after that until finally there was a ping and the lift doors opened.

The Journal of Alice Teale

I love this journal. Love, love, LOVE it! Best gift ever!

There, I finally wrote something inside it, and a little part of me is already regretting defacing its pristine pages. What could I write in here that's significant enough to justify its inclusion? Even so, I still feel like a character in a Jane Austen novel. It's so much cooler than all those electronic diaries online. You can actually pick this up, touch and hold it. It feels real.

And it has a lock. A small but sturdy little clasp with a key only I get to keep, which is just as well, because I don't intend to waste any of these precious pages on bullshit. This journal will hold the real and honest thoughts of Alice Teale or it will contain nothing at all, so you'd better not piss me off or you'll end up in here. Hah! This is my sacred place, to be filled with secrets but no lies.

I'll put my story ideas down in here, too, then I can work on them so they don't just swirl endlessly round and round in my head, going nowhere. I WILL be an author one day, and I am going to look back and say this was where it all began. They say that truth is stranger than fiction, and I won't have to look far for inspiration around here.

I love the cover! It's leather, I think, and I should

probably care that some animal has died for me, but I don't because it smells amazing.

And it has my name written through it, printed on every page. Love it!

Thanks for this, bro.

I love you, too.

4

Black drove an inexpensive Japanese car. Beth was expecting something bigger and flashier, like most of the other male detectives drove. She respected him a tiny bit more for not caring about it, or perhaps she was clutching at straws, desperately searching for a reason to like her gruff new partner.

'Where are we –?'

'Where do you think?' he interrupted.

'I was going to say, going *first*. I know we are going to Collemby, but to see DI Fraser or the parents?'

'I'd better prioritize DI Fraser before he leaves. When you're gone, you're gone. I don't think he'll appreciate it if I keep popping round with questions. Mentally, he's probably already on the golf course.'

'Okay,' she said, and waited.

'What?'

'You said *I*, not *we*,' Beth reminded him, 'so I'm waiting to hear what I'll be doing while you're being briefed by Fraser.'

'It's quicker this way,' he said. 'He briefs me then I brief you. I want you to go and see the parents.'

Great, thought Beth, so I get to explain that the man leading the investigation into the disappearance of their daughter has gone and we are starting all over again. At least he hadn't tried to convince her it was the cushier job.

'Read the case file now,' he continued. 'The quicker you grasp that nettle, the faster we can get on with it, and see what you can learn about Alice from the family while you're there. Meet me when you're done.'

He didn't say another word for at least three miles. She used that gap to read the flimsy file on Alice and her family, but the silence in the car was getting to her.

'What did Everleigh mean when he said you were on point?' she asked when she could take no more.

'It's an army phrase,' he said. 'It means the first man in a patrol, the one who leads it through hostile territory and is the most exposed so more likely to be shot. Sometimes the DCI likes to use military jargon.'

'Why?'

'Maybe it makes him sound more macho. Perhaps he thinks I'll respect him for it because I used to be in the army.' Was that what Anne Hudson had meant when she said Lucas Black had killed someone? He had been a soldier, so perhaps he'd shot somebody in Iraq or Afghanistan. Beth felt a little silly, now there was such an obvious explanation. 'Maybe he just likes the sound of his own voice.' He shrugged, as if it was of no consequence whatsoever.

'Don't like him much, do you?'

'Whether I like him or not is irrelevant. He's the DCI.'

'He must have done something right to reach that rank.'

'He has a degree in criminology, which he likes to refer to – a lot. One of the newspapers christened him "the thinking man's copper", which he pretends to be embarrassed about, but I reckon he secretly loves it. He's very aware of his public image and will be disproportionately aggrieved by anyone who undermines it. He wants to be chief constable one day, so God help anybody who gets in his way, including us.'

'Meaning we do what we are told?' It was a genuine query. She was finding his answers hard to interpret.

'Meaning we listen to what he has to say then use our discretion and initiative in the real world to solve the case. Look, we're not going to get any advice from Everleigh at ground level. He hasn't arrested anyone in years. Think of him as a politician, and try very hard not to piss him off, because he has the power to move us to some godforsaken corner of Northumbria Police from which we are unlikely ever to re-emerge. Got it?'

'Yeah,' she said.

'Good.'

'So, do you know this town, then?' she asked, deliberately changing the subject.

'Collemby? Of course.'

'I don't,' she admitted, and when it appeared this wasn't a strong enough hint: 'Could you tell me a bit about it, please? If you don't mind.'

'Not much to tell,' he said, and for a second she thought that was all she was getting. 'It's a typical, small Northumbrian town, around ten thousand people living there. It used to be known for its pit.' Then he said, 'Its coal mine.'

'I know what a pit is.'

'It also has an old railway station, but the railway is long gone.' His tone was brusque. 'There are some pubs, a few shops and a library. They have a market on Fridays. That's about it. It's not a tourist place like Seahouses or Tynemouth. You don't go to Collemby unless you have to.'

He flicked the indicator and started to turn off. 'And we are here.' He swung the car into a left turn and up a steep, winding hill that brought them into Collemby town centre. Beth took in a number of buildings, including a town hall with a large, white-stone war memorial and a market-place that doubled as a car park when, like today, there was no market. There was a tiny local library that had somehow survived the latest round of cuts, a working men's club, several pubs and a row of shops.

One pub in particular, which was almost opposite the town hall, caught her eye as he parked the car and they got out, because its ancient, rusty sign was swinging in the wind, making a jarring, squeaking sound.

'The Black Stallion?' she said.

'There used to be another pub here called the White Horse,' he said. 'Years ago, someone opened a new pub opposite and called it the Black Stallion.'

'Why?'

'Dunno – maybe to wind up the owner of the White Horse. Anyway, the two pubs were in direct competition for half a century or more, until the White Horse closed down and shut for good.'

'Leaving the Black Stallion as the clear winner.'

'Yes, except no one from Collemby ever calls it that.'

'What do they call it, then?'

'The Dirty Donkey.'

He pointed to a side street that led away from the market square. 'Head down there and make a right turn at the bottom of Neale Street, follow the road along for a bit until you see Neville Street on your left. The Teales live at number seven. Meet me back here when you're done.'

Yes, sir. She almost snapped to attention but thought better of mocking him.

She watched as Lucas Black started towards the town hall then went her own way along Neale Street.

DS Black could see that DI Fraser was still hard at work when he walked into the makeshift major-incident room at the town hall – hard at work entertaining his team, on his last day on the job, with stories of the old days. Fraser was halfway through an anecdote as Black entered the room, his voice animated – 'He's wearing these black shoes that have got – no word of a lie – a mirror shine on them. They were spotless . . .' – and there was laughter from his audience of two detective constables. They hadn't noticed Black yet. He crossed the room towards his table. DC Rodgers was the only one who could have seen him from this angle, but he either didn't notice Black or chose not to. Black knew him of old, so perhaps it was a calculated snub. Fraser continued: '. . . so the chief constable finally steps out of the building, thinking he's the absolute doggy's little bollocks, chin up, head held high, not a care in the bloody world' – he paused before the punchline – 'then he treads right in the middle of a steaming pile of horse shit.' The two DCs collapsed laughing at the image of the chief constable's spotless shoes tarnished with manure. 'But we've all got to stand there at attention, without reacting. He's trying to scrape it off on a clump of grass but that shit is clinging to his shoe like a jealous girlfriend and the smell . . .' DI Fraser stopped suddenly, noticed that Rodgers was look- ing at something, turned, evidently displeased that the merriment had been cut short. He realized DS Black was standing right behind him.

'So,' he said, 'Everleigh gave it to *you*?'

'You sound surprised.'

'I am,' he said, 'I'd have thought he'd put another DI on it, in case this turns out to be a biggie.' He meant a murder case and smiled a humourless smile. 'But then, your DI is still off, isn't he?'

'He is.'

'Any idea when he's due back? It's been a while.'

'No,' said Black, and the single word tersely communicated that he did not wish to discuss it further.

'Bit of a poisoned chalice. We've not been able to come up with anything much.'

'It's been a few days, right?' This was Black's way of pointing out that they'd had enough time to come up with something.

'We've not been idle,' flared Fraser. 'This is just a tea break.'

Black surveyed the number of dirty cups on the table and, since there were two for each man, it looked like the tea break had been going on for a while.

'The boys will be back out again afterwards,' he added.

'But not you?'

'It's my last day, DS Black. I've got paperwork to finish, then I am offski.'

'Congratulations.'

'I'm surprised you weren't interested in the package. You must have put in a few years by now?'

Black didn't answer.

'I thought, after what happened, you might be keen to

ride off into the sunset. No offence.' He was the kind of man who thought adding the words 'no offence' to his sentences made them less offensive. He was wrong about that.

'Can we talk about the case,' asked Black, 'since you're so keen to be off?'

'Sure. It's all in the file, though.' He handed over a larger file than the one the DCI had given Black earlier.

'It's never *all* in the file, Gavin, you know that.'

'Gavin?' he sniffed. 'You can call me that tomorrow, DS Black, but I'm still entitled to a "sir" until then. Rank has its privileges.'

Was this really what they were going to fall out over on Fraser's last day? A slip of the tongue from their earlier days, when they were both detective sergeants on a different team? Fraser's face was serious and Black was sorely tempted to tell him to fuck off. He knew the man would be too lazy to make a formal complaint with just a few hours to go. That wouldn't bring Alice Teale back, though, and he owed it to the girl to do this by the book.

'Apologies, Detective Inspector Fraser, old habits die hard. Now, if you would be good enough to spare me some of your valuable time to go through the case, I would be very grateful, sir.'

Fraser narrowed his eyes, as if carefully scrutinizing Black for any sign of mockery in his tone or demeanour, but he found none. Detective Constable Ferguson was smirking behind the DI now.

'Of course, lad. I'd be glad to. Now why don't you sit yourself down' – he patted the chair next to him, as if Black were a nine-year-old – 'and I'll tell you all about it.'

Black took the seat.

'What do you want to know?' asked Fraser.

'Everything.'

'Sure,' said Fraser. 'Put the kettle on again, will you, Rodgers? There's a good lad. Oh, and see if you can find Lucas here a biscuit.' He turned back to Black. 'Because *everything* is going to take a while.'

There were a couple of long residential streets full of two-up two-downs between Collemby Town Hall and the Teale family home. Beth decided to use the time productively while she walked, by taking out her mobile phone and doing a quick Web search on her new partner. On reflection, she was pretty sure Anne Hudson had been exaggerating to make Beth feel apprehensive. If Lucas Black really had killed someone, surely it must have been in combat with the army, not while serving in the police force, which was a wholly different proposition. In other words, Anne had been stirring it, her obvious motive jealousy because she had been passed over by DCI Everleigh in favour of Beth.

The Google search took a few moments and, at first, it didn't help. There was an American actor who shared the same name, so she amended her search by keying in the words 'police officer UK' after 'Lucas Black'.

The number of results that came up then stopped Beth in her tracks. There were dozens of newspaper articles about Black and they all appeared to be about the same incident, which had occurred seven years earlier. These weren't just local newspapers either. They were the big, heavy-hitting national tabloids. The first headline screamed at her.

Unarmed man gunned down by detective. The second read: Shot dead by police.

Oh Christ. Anne Hudson hadn't been exaggerating. Lucas Black really had killed a man. He had shot someone, and that someone hadn't even had a weapon. How the hell had that happened, and why was he still a detective? How come he wasn't out of the force or even languishing in a jail somewhere, serving life for murder?

Beth took a moment to look around her. The street was empty of people, so she stopped on the corner. She scrolled down until she found an article that covered the outcome of the case and began to read.

No action will be taken against a police officer who killed an unarmed man. The Crown Prosecution Service is refusing to prosecute Lucas Black, 31, who shot Rory Jordan, 44, in his garden, despite the victim being unarmed at the time. The Independent Police Complaints Commission investigated the shooting and criticized Detective Sergeant Black for acting rashly and inadvisedly, and for using excessive force. They concluded that he may have a case to answer for manslaughter. However, the CPS has ruled out prosecution, on the grounds that a jury would be unlikely to convict Black, due to a 'perceived threat' to the officer in question, even though the detective was some way from Mr Jordan and armed with a 9mm semi-automatic pistol, and that a prosecution would not be in the public interest.

Black, an authorized firearms officer, was called to Mr Jordan's home in Ashington, Northumbria, in November, to assist colleagues during a stand-off. It followed a report from a neighbour of a domestic disturbance involving an alleged assault on Jordan's wife and threats made against her and their nine-year-old daughter. Police surrounded the building and, when Rory Jordan left his house via its rear door, Black shot him in the chest. He died on the way to hospital.

In a statement from her solicitor, Jordan's widow, Carol, 38, said the killing of her husband was both unlawful and completely unnecessary. 'This policeman should be in prison for life for what he did to my husband. Nothing will bring Rory back, but it chills me to think that Detective Sergeant Black has got off scot-free when he is a clear and obvious danger to the public. He has ruined my life and my daughter's life but will go unpunished. Where is the justice in that?'

'Jesus Christ,' said Beth, closing the Web page on her phone abruptly, as if banishing the news. As she walked the final yards to Alice Teale's home, she tried to imagine any scenario where a detective could legally and morally justify gunning down an unarmed man outside his own home. She couldn't think of one.

5

Beth Winter experienced the full brunt of Alice Teale's father's frustration. 'He stood in front of me, right there' – and he pointed to the floor – 'where you are standing, and he told me' – he shook his head in disbelief – 'DI Fraser said, "Mr Teale, I shall not rest until we find your daughter," and now you're saying he's given up already!' He took a deep breath and went to his armchair then sat down heavily in it. Ronnie Teale was a big man who seemed to dwarf his wife, a slight woman who occupied a small corner of a floral-patterned sofa. Abigail Teale watched her husband carefully, as if she wasn't sure what he would do next. Their nineteen-year-old son, Daniel, stared down at the carpet.

They were all seated, while Beth stood there, feeling like an intruder.

'I thought at the time what a daft thing to say,' said Ronnie. '"I shall not rest" – of course you will. You have to sleep, you have to stop and eat. Bloody ridiculous. But I didn't think he'd just bail out like this.'

'I understand your frustration, Mr Teale . . .'

'Do you? I doubt it!'

'. . . but the force chose to offer DI Fraser early retirement, which he wasn't expecting when he agreed to the case. He had limited time to accept the offer.' Beth wasn't sure why she was defending DI Fraser, a man she had never met, then she realized she was doing it to spare the Teales' feelings. She wanted the family to believe they were committed to finding their daughter. 'I can assure you that the detective taking over is the best there is.' She desperately hoped they wouldn't do a Web search on him once they learned his name.

'You're just going to start again, is that it?'

That *was* it, but Beth didn't feel she could admit this. 'The work that has already been done will be invaluable, and we won't have to duplicate it,' she said. 'The most important thing is to make sure we are all fully focused on the search for Alice.'

'She's been missing for days, and not a trace of her,' said her father. 'Not since she left school that evening.' He frowned. 'Who leaves school at nine o'clock at night?' he asked. 'Bloody stupid!'

He got up out of his chair and walked to the window. He was like some big, wild animal trapped in a cage. Then he turned back to Beth.

'This is all my fault,' he said abruptly.

She waited for him to explain.

'This is all my fault,' he repeated. 'My fault.' But his reproachful look fell on Alice's mother.

'How is this your fault, Mr Teale?' she asked him.

'I should have kept a closer eye on her, instead of letting a teenage girl go out every night like that.'

His wife pursed her lips, as if she had been indirectly accused of permitting this while his back was turned. In a low voice that sounded full of meaning, Abigail Teale said, 'You kept a very close eye on her.'

'What's that supposed to mean?'

But Alice's mother said nothing. She just stared towards the back window, as if the answer she needed were written on the glass. Ronnie seemed to suddenly remember that Beth was there. 'Alice is always out, never at home.'

'And whose fault is that?' hissed her mother.

'Not mine!' He was angry again. 'I barely bloody saw her. If she wasn't doing after-school clubs, she was down that working men's club . . .'

'You told her to get a job,' Abigail reminded him, 'because money was tight.'

'And so it is, but does she have to work *there*?'

'Where else is she going to get a job round here?'

Beth got the impression that Abigail Teale rarely stood up to her husband, because the man seemed rattled by her defiance. This was not what Beth had been expecting. Why were they acting this way, particularly Alice's father? Instead of focusing on finding their missing daughter, they were arguing. It was bewildering.

'And even when she is at home, she's always up in her room, studying.'

'I thought you'd be glad of that,' Abigail said, and her husband shot her a look. 'At least she isn't lazy, at least she's trying to better herself.' And even though the comments were aimed at Alice's father, it was her brother's turn to shift uneasily in his seat, as if personally wounded by his mother's words. 'She can never do anything right.'

Ronnie seemed to get exasperated then, and turned back to Beth. 'I don't know what you want from us,' he told her. 'We've made statements, we've told you every-thing we know about that night – which is next to nothing, by the way. We've let your colleagues look all round our house and in Alice's room, we've given you the names of her friends, her work mates, her teachers. What else is there?'

'What do you think has happened to her, Mr Teale?' Beth asked him.

'How should I know?' he shouted at her. 'She's gone off somewhere, done something bloody stupid.'

'What kind of something?'

'Find her and you can fucking ask her!'

'Calm down, Ronnie,' his wife urged him quietly.

'Don't tell me what to do,' he snarled at his wife. 'Not anywhere' – he jabbed a finger – 'and never in my own house.' And he gave her a look of such venom Beth found it quite alarming.

'But what makes you think she's been stupid?' she asked.

'Because she's always doing daft things!'

'Please try and stay calm, Mr Teale. We need your help to find your daughter.'

'I don't know where she's gone.' He was wild-eyed, as if he had taken that comment personally. 'This has got nothing to do with me.'

'No one is saying that it has,' said Beth, wondering why he might have interpreted what she had said that way. 'In your statement, you said you were out at the pub when Alice went missing. Which one?'

He seemed to hesitate for a moment. 'I was . . .' he began, but then stopped.

'It was around nine o'clock,' she reminded him.

'I know what time it was,' he snapped. 'Just let me . . . I'd have probably been in the Dirty Donkey around about then.'

'The Black Stallion pub?' she clarified, noting that he had made his location and the timing of it a little vague.

'Yeah.'

'All night?'

He shook his head then realized she wanted more than that for an answer. 'It was Friday night,' he said. 'I called into a few places around town.'

'But you were definitely in the Black Stallion at nine o'clock?'

'Why are you asking me that?' He turned to his wife. 'Why is she asking me that?'

This wasn't going well, and Beth started to worry that her first attempt at securing an alibi might lead to the victim's father lodging an official complaint against her. She could imagine how Black would take that. Ronnie Teale's anger was blinding him. Beth needed the man to see that they were both on the same side, while at the same time trying to eliminate him from their inquiries. 'I'm just trying to place you on the night, Mr Teale. We'll be doing that with everyone.'

'I'm her bloody father, woman!' he shouted, jabbing a finger into his chest to make his point.

When Beth spoke she was deliberately calm. 'Then you'll understand that everything we do is designed to bring your daughter safely back to you.' She took a breath and turned to the man's son.

'What about you, Daniel?'

'Me?' He seemed surprised Beth even knew his name. 'I was in my room, messing around on my laptop.'

'You chat to anyone online?'

'A few people,' he said, and she figured that would be easy enough to verify.

'Do you have anything to add to your statement at all? It's been a few days, and you may have thought of something else?'

Daniel looked to his dad, as if seeking guidance or approval, but the older man's face betrayed no hint of what he might be thinking. The young man turned back to Beth. 'Me? No,' he said.

'I was wondering if you could tell me about some of Alice's gang?'

His father jumped in. 'Gang? She wasn't in a gang.'

'Her group of friends,' Beth clarified.

'You know what she means,' snapped Mrs Teale.

'What do you want to know?' asked Daniel.

'Who she hung out with, who she liked and disliked and who liked or disliked her, if anyone held any grudges against her or had argued with her, perhaps acted out of the ordinary, that kind of thing.'

'There was never any of that,' said her father before the boy could speak.

Beth was really tiring of his obstructive manner now. 'With respect, Mr Teale, how would you know?'

'I know my daughter.'

'But you said Alice was rarely at home and, when she was, she was usually in her room, studying,' Beth reminded him. 'If she did have a problem with someone at school, you might not have been aware of it.'

'So how is *he* going to know?'

Beth wondered why he was being so difficult. Did she really have to spell it out? 'Because Daniel is younger, goes to the same places and knows the same people.' She turned to Daniel. 'Also, I understand that you two are close. Maybe Alice told you something in passing that you thought at the time wasn't important but might prove significant now?'

The boy's eyes darted quickly between his father's face and Beth's. 'Maybe,' he admitted. 'But I can't think of anything.'

'What kind of "something"?' asked Ronnie.

'I don't know,' said Beth, 'but if Alice ran away, she obviously had her reasons and may have confided them to somebody. If someone abducted or harmed your daughter, something might have triggered it. I'm trying to find out everything I can about her, in case one snippet of information points us in the right direction. Is that all right?'

'Of course' – his tone was defensive – 'why wouldn't it be?'

'Then perhaps I could talk to Daniel on my own for a while?'

He looked as if he didn't like that idea, but his wife asked, 'Where's the harm in that?'

'Do what you like,' said Ronnie, then pulled the lounge door open with such force Beth wouldn't have been surprised if he had ripped it off its hinges. He walked into the tiny hallway and took a coat down from the wall hanger. 'I'm going for a pint.'

No one questioned this. Perhaps no one dared to.

Instead, they waited till they heard the sound of the front door opening then closing firmly behind him.

'He's gone,' said Alice's mother, as if they hadn't all just witnessed his departure. 'His daughter's missing and he's gone to the pub.' Beth noted she hadn't raised any objection before he left. Had she reached the limits of her defiance, or did she just want him out of her house?

'"I'm going for a pint."' Daniel mimicked his father, adding a sneering tone, and his mother did not chastise him for it. 'That's his answer to everything. He doesn't give a shit. He never has.' Beth didn't have any experience of dealing with worried parents of missing children, but she strongly suspected that Ronnie Teale's reaction was far from typical. At least Daniel was more talkative now his father had gone, but she still wanted to get the lad on his own.

'It's a nice day, Daniel,' said Beth. 'Why don't we go for a walk while we talk?'

6

'I give you *one* job, and you muck it up,' protested Fraser.

'Sorry, boss, we've run out.' Rodgers had failed his DI. He couldn't find a biscuit for Lucas.

'You can't get the staff these days.'

'Alice Teale,' Black said abruptly, trying to bring an end to the banter. 'What have you found out?'

'Not much,' said Fraser, and when the detective inspector realized how that made him sound: 'Not much *of significance*, but there's a lot of information and a ton of gossip.'

'Go on.'

'Events-wise, we have a reasonable idea of what happened. Alice Teale was last seen on her way home from an after-school club around nine p.m. on Friday. She set off from the school on foot. Sometimes she gets the bus and other times she walks, depending on the weather and how late it is. There are two buses an hour that go along her route. The school is at one end of the town and her home is two and a half miles away at the other. We've asked the drivers, and they reckon she never got on a bus. She's a very bonny lass, so they'd have remembered her.'

Black opened the file that was resting in his lap. There was a photograph of Alice Teale clipped to the first page. He had to agree with Fraser: Alice was strikingly pretty, with long, wavy brown hair, full red lips and bright green eyes.

Fraser continued, 'At first it was treated like any normal, run-of-the-mill disappearance. The uniforms assumed, like in the vast majority of cases, that she'd had a row with a boyfriend or was upset with her parents and expected her to show up sooner or later. Her family went out looking for her that night. When Alice didn't reappear in the morning, other people joined the search for her, retracing her route, knocking on the doors of her friends and classmates, asking questions, but there was no trace of her.'

'What about her phone?'

'Switched off,' he said. 'Or disposed of. We've not had a signal from it since she went missing, and she hasn't answered it.' Then he cautioned, 'Kids these days do know that you can trace people through their mobile phones if they're switched on. I blame the telly. She hasn't posted anything on social media either or used her debit card anywhere.'

'What do we know about Alice?' asked Black.

'She has a busy life for an almost-eighteen-year-old. Alice is deputy head girl, seemingly popular with her classmates and good at her studies, likely to go to a decent university, according to her teachers. She took part in a lot of extra-curricular activities, too.'

'What kind of activities?'

'Badminton, basketball, rambling, camera club, fundraising of various kinds for assorted charities and the sixth-form club, whatever that is.'

'Home life?' asked Black.

'Mum, dad and a brother,' said Fraser. 'He's a bit older, but they get on well, or so we're told. Dad's a bit of a weird one, but there's nothing obviously off there.'

'Does she have a boyfriend?'

'I was coming to that. Christopher Mullery – same age and school year as her – but he wasn't with her that night. He stayed in, said he had to study because he was slipping behind and was worried about his grades for university.'

'Do we believe that?' asked Black. 'A boy staying in on a Friday night instead of seeing his girlfriend?'

'He's the conscientious type, but it might be worth pressing him on it. His parents say he was in the house all evening, but *they* weren't, interestingly.'

'Where were they?'

'His father was down the working men's club and his mum nipped next door for a cup of tea with the neighbour.'

'How long for?'

'She said half an hour to an hour, but she's not entirely sure. She left Christopher revising in his room.'

'So he could have left the house and come back again without her knowing?'

'It's possible, and the timings do overlap. He was on his own when Alice was leaving the school and he doesn't live far away.'

'Wouldn't you want to go and meet your girlfriend on her way home if you'd been studying for hours?' wondered Black. 'Particularly if you live just around the corner?'

'You might,' agreed Fraser. 'And he sounds like the jealous type.' Then he added, 'Not without cause.'

'He liked to keep an eye on her?' asked Black. 'Was she messing him around?'

'Their relationship wasn't an easy one and they broke up for a while.'

'Teenagers are always breaking up and getting back together again,' said Black.

'But she went out with his best friend in between, which caused some ructions.'

'It would,' said Black, 'in a small town like this one. Can't be that many kids in the sixth form.'

'Fifty or so,' confirmed Fraser.

'And she went out with her boyfriend's best mate? Sounds like she was proving a point.'

'You'll have to ask him. Tony Douglas still lives in the town, but he dropped out of sixth form.'

'Because of Alice?'

'Because of the row caused by him and Alice and the fact she went back to her old boyfriend.'

'Anyone else we should know about?'

'A whole bunch of people,' confirmed Fraser. 'She worked in the working men's club as a pot lass, so there's the bar staff and the customers. Then there's the teachers, her classmates and friends – as well as her family, of course. We barely scratched the surface, so there's a lot of people to speak to. But I'm not telling you how to do your job.'

'You mentioned there was gossip,' Black reminded Fraser. 'What kind?'

'Every kind. Gossip about Alice, gossip about the family, speculation about her private life and what goes on up at that school after hours.' He made it sound like there was a wild party there every night. 'Then there's the town.' And when Black looked as if he required further explanation: 'This place, it's always been a funny area to police. There's bugger all here, so everyone is always into everyone else's business, which means you get all sorts of wild ideas doing the rounds. They've nothing better to do.'

'Are you saying that none of this' – he wanted to avoid the dismissive word 'gossip' again – 'speculation about Alice Teale is based on truth?'

'Oh, some of it will be, for sure, but which bits? That's the problem.' He nodded towards Black. 'That's *your* problem now,' as if Black needed the reminder.

'Okay, well, why don't you tell me what you've heard, however outlandish some of it might prove to be? Then I can evaluate it and make a judgement call.'

'"Evaluate it and make a judgement call"? Have you been on a course, Lucas?' And Fraser's DCs smirked again.

Black bridled at that. 'What's the matter? Too many syllables?'

There was anger in Fraser's eyes, but Black was getting annoyed, too. He'd eaten enough humble pie for one day. DI Fraser didn't like being put down, especially in front of his subordinates, but maybe he didn't like the look in Black's eyes either, because he chose not to respond.

'I'll start with the family, shall I?' he said tersely. 'We asked around. Her dad is a one-man ball of anger who likes to drink on his own, her mother is on pills for depression *and* anxiety.' He dipped his head, as if that last part was deeply significant. 'Wasn't that what your DI went off with?' Black didn't respond to the jibe. 'Oh, and she is *very* close to her brother.' He let that one sink in so Black could draw his own conclusion. 'And as well as the boyfriend and his best mate, there's a bloke at her part-time job who was sniffing round her.'

'Name?' asked Black, and Fraser looked blank but turned to Ferguson, who supplied it after checking his notebook.

'Ricky Madden, twenty-two, lives here in Collemby, barman at the club. One of the regulars there reckoned he took a proper shine to Alice but she turned him down without a thought.' *As is her right*, thought Black, because Fraser made it sound as if the girl was being unreasonable. 'Maybe he didn't take it well.'

'Have you spoken to Ricky?'

'Not yet.' Then he sounded defensive: 'We've only just learned of his existence, Lucas. We have been a bit busy.'

'Right.'

'Listen, my lads have been out knocking on doors since this girl was first reported missing. They've spoken to virtually everyone who knows her and we've been building up a picture of Alice Teale and her busy life.'

'What do you make of her, then?'

'She's very well known for such a young lass, which I put down to her looks.'

Of course you do, thought Black. *It couldn't be for any other reason, could it?*

'Do you think she ran away?' he asked.

'Maybe, but if she did, we don't know why. I mean, there's no obvious reason.'

'So it's starting to look like abduction. She hasn't been in touch with anyone, even though her face is all over the news and social media, but if someone has taken her, are we looking for a stranger or someone closer to home?'

'The uniforms started Operation Usual Suspects as soon as she'd been gone for forty-eight hours,' said Fraser.

This was a relatively new initiative from Northumbria Police and occurred whenever a child or vulnerable adult disappeared. Every known sex offender or criminal with a record of violence against females or children would be visited and made to account for their whereabouts, then asked if they would allow the police to check their homes. If they had no alibi or failed to cooperate, they would be hauled in for questioning. Most complied simply to avoid this. 'There was nothing,' continued Fraser, 'so, if this is the work of a stranger, then it's someone new who's just starting out.' He shook his head. 'But I don't think so. I reckon it's someone she knows.'

7

They talked as they walked the streets close to Daniel's home. There were no driveways or front gardens here, just rows of no-frills, functional houses. They were close to the front doors and windows of the terraced homes they passed, only net curtains preventing them from peering in. They walked at Daniel's pace, which was an unhurried amble, and made the most of the remnants of an uncharacteristic mini heatwave that had warmed the north-east for a week or more now. It was T-shirt weather, unusually early in the year.

'I didn't mean to,' said Daniel, 'but earlier, when you asked me what I was doing when Alice went missing, I kind of lied. I'm sorry.'

'You *kind of* lied?' she queried. 'Either you did or you didn't, Daniel. Where were you when Alice disappeared?'

'I didn't lie about that,' he protested. 'I was in my room, like I said.'

'Then what did you lie about?'

He sounded uncomfortable. 'I said I was chatting to people online, and I wasn't, not really.'

Which meant no one could vouch for him. 'Why did you lie?'

'Because my parents were there when you asked.'

'You weren't chatting,' Beth concluded. 'You were just surfing the Web?'

'Yeah.'

'Looking at what?'

He shrugged. 'Stuff.'

'Porn?' Was that what he meant?

'There was *some* porn, yes.'

'Well, Daniel,' she said. 'I don't think you are the first, but try to tell me the truth from here on in, will you?'

'I will,' he said. 'I promise.'

He seemed to loosen up then, as if the tension had been lifted when Beth hadn't judged him for his porn habit. 'How would you describe Alice's frame of mind?' she asked.

'You mean, lately? The same as always. I mean, Alice was stressed, but . . .'

'What was she stressed about?'

'Exams. What else?'

'Just exams? All kids her age worry about those. Was there anything else?'

'I don't know. Nothing major.'

'And you'd know?' asked Beth.

'What does that mean?' he snapped.

'We heard you were close so, if something was bothering her, then she might come to you about it.'

His tone softened. 'She would, usually.'

'But not this time.'

He thought for a moment. 'She *was* worried,' he admitted. 'About a number of things.' He started to count them off on his fingers. 'How she would do in her exams, would she get the grades she needed to get to uni and, if she did, would it be the right one? Would she fit in there, make friends and be happy? What was she going to do about her

46

boyfriend?' As he mentioned her boyfriend, he switched hands and started counting on the other one. 'She was worried about Mam and how Dad would be if she wasn't there any more. He has to take things out on someone. She was concerned about Grandad being lonely on his own. She worried about her friends, too, and whether they would be able to get where they wanted for uni ... Oh yeah, and she worries about me, bless her.' And he half smiled at that.

'Why does she worry about you?'

He was dismissive. 'I'm the family fuck-up. I messed up my A levels and I'm not sure where I go from here. She thought I should be taking life more seriously. She's a bit like Mam,' and he started to mimic his mother's voice: '"Why don't you get a proper job? When are you going to meet a nice girl?" They just want me to be happy, but I'm in no hurry. I've got a bar job in Newcastle. I'm doing okay.'

'You mentioned her boyfriend. Was she going to break up with him?'

He hesitated. 'She hadn't made her mind up about that.'

'But it was *on* her mind.'

'She didn't think long-distance relationships worked out.'

'Did he know Alice was thinking about finishing with him?'

'They discussed it – the future, I mean. I know he was very keen to keep on seeing her somehow. They had a big break-up last summer and he was gutted.'

'Tell me about that.'

'She was going out with Chris in the Lower Sixth and it got a bit intense, so he called it off. He said he wanted some time on his own over the holidays. She went along with it and started seeing someone else in the summer but kept it quiet to begin with.'

'Why?'

'Because it was his best mate. She knew him through Chris. They hung out together. Turned out Tony was the one who'd been encouraging Chris to let her go.'

'Because he wanted her instead?'

'Yeah,' said Daniel. 'Not cool.'

'What happened when Chris found out?'

'Big scene in the pub, which spilled out on to the car park.'

'A fight?'

He didn't make much of it. 'Some pushing and shoving, a lot of shouting.'

'With Alice in the middle?'

'I didn't see any of it. If I had, I would have banged their heads together.'

'What was the upshot?'

'Bad blood between the boys and a drama half the town was talking about for weeks.' He added dryly, 'Not much happens round here. We have to make our own entertainment.'

'Did she carry on seeing Tony?'

'For a while, but it burnt out over the summer.'

'And afterwards?'

'They all went back to sixth form. Alice patched it up with Chris and started seeing him again.'

'That must have been hard for Tony. He fell out with his best friend over a girl who ditched him, so he lost them both.'

'Almost everybody sided with Chris, so Tony dropped out.'

'He left sixth form because of Alice?'

'That's what he told everyone.'

'What's he doing these days?'

'Nothing,' said Daniel.

Then he has plenty of time to brood, thought Beth, on what his love for Alice cost him.

'Is Chris happy about the state of their relationship now, then?'

'I don't reckon Chris is ever happy about it. It's not like he walks round with a smile on his face while he's with her. I don't think he's good for her. Neither was Tony. She needs someone who doesn't try to control her all the time.'

'Could either of these controlling boyfriends have anything to do with her disappearance?'

He seemed conflicted. 'I would have said no, but I don't know why she's disappeared, so I can't rule anything out.'

'Was she sexually active?'

Daniel looked momentarily thrown by the directness of Beth's question then said, 'Yes.'

'With Chris?'

'Well, he is the one she's going out with.'

'And she wasn't seeing anyone else?'

'No. She had a boyfriend, they were having sex – so what? But there was no one else.'

'She'd have told you if she was?'

'Yeah.'

'But she wouldn't have told your dad.'

'God, no.'

'How would you describe your father?'

He thought for a second then said, 'Angry.'

'Angry? Is that it?' It seemed an accurate description.

'Everything makes him flare up, but he's losing control over me and my sister, and soon Alice will be off to uni . . .' He stopped short of finishing his sentence, perhaps realizing how absurd it sounded, given she was missing. 'I'll leave, too, when I can.' He seemed less sure of that.

'Did Alice make him angry?' asked Beth.

He nodded. 'All the time. I don't know how she stuck it.'

'Examples?'

'What she wore, where she went, how late she came back, the friends she knew, the boys she talked to.' He sighed. 'The way she spoke to him when she answered back, the way she looked at him when she didn't.'

'A hard man to please?'

'He's bad enough with me, but with Alice it's as if . . .'

'You can say it,' urged Beth.

'. . . as if he doesn't even like her.'

Beth could tell it had cost Daniel something to say that. Perhaps he felt disloyal or it was the first time he'd ever admitted this, even to himself. She wondered how best to frame her next question. She tried to sound casual. 'He ever really lose his temper with her?'

'Hit her, you mean?' Daniel shook his head. 'Not since she was a little kid.' And when Beth frowned at this he quickly added: 'A smack if she was naughty, nothing since then.' He straightened up. 'But he'd never hurt her. Don't go leaving here thinking he's somehow responsible for this, because he isn't.'

'You sound very sure of that, Daniel.'

'That's because I am.' His voice rose in protest.

Beth nodded to show she had taken the boy's views fully into account. She changed the subject.

'Would any of Alice's friends know if something else was bothering her?'

'Chloe and Kirstie are her closest mates.' He supplied surnames and the names of the streets they lived on. Beth dutifully noted them down.

'If you think of anything else that might give us any clue as to why she might suddenly take off —'

'There's her journal,' he blurted.

'She kept a journal?' Beth immediately wondered why no one had mentioned this before.

'I bought it for her,' Daniel explained. 'For her birthday. Alice has always been a writer. She wants to be an author one day. I reckon she could be, too. She's got a real way with words.'

'This could be important,' said Beth. 'If she was recording her thoughts prior to her disappearance.'

Daniel looked exasperated. 'I told the first police officer this when he came round, but he wasn't interested. He kept asking who she could have run off with.'

'Where is this journal?' Beth knew it could be vital. In the absence of the missing girl, this could be as near as they got to the inner workings of Alice Teale's mind. It might explain what had been going through it immediately before she went missing.

'They searched her room but didn't find it. I looked, too, but it wasn't there.'

'Would she have it with her?'

'It's probably in her bag. She didn't like to leave it lying around.'

'Because it was private? What did it look like?'

'It was about this big,' he said, miming its dimensions with his hands. 'A5, I think. It had a brown leather cover and they print your name all the way through it on the top of every page. "The Journal of Alice Teale". She loved that.'

'You ever read it?' asked Beth.

'It was private.'

'Sometimes people can't help themselves.'

'I would never do that. Anyway, it has a lock on it and she has the key.'

'If you do find this journal, then we obviously need to see it. It might shed some light on all of this.'

'I get it,' said the younger man impatiently, as if Beth thought he might be stupid.

'I mean it,' she insisted. 'We have to find this journal, Daniel.'

The Journal of Alice Teale

They all think I've got it nailed down, that it's so effortless and I just glide from place to place like I'm on castors – from home to school to job and all the extra-curricular stuff we are expected to do to bulk out a CV with nothing else on it – but they don't know the truth. They can't imagine what I've been going through. The pressure has been building up for so long now but soon everything will come crashing down and I know it's going to take me with it.

Until then I have to keep on pretending. I get to choose which role I'm going to play, but it always depends on the audience. Play the part, love, play the part, and hope that none of them ever really works you out. You've secrets none of them would believe.

You're disgusting.

You've known that for a while, but you don't care so much any more. Not now you know the truth about them.

Only *He* gets me. He can see right through me like I'm made of glass.

I can't tell him, though. He would know straight away that I'm not going to take this, because it feels like I have nothing left to lose.

God, I feel so empty. There is nothing left now.

I'm just a walking shadow.

8

Beth and Daniel walked in a loop that took them to the rear of the boy's house just as their talk reached a natural conclusion. A middle-aged man was standing by the back wall of the house next door, washing a car in his shirt-sleeves. Beth caught him staring at them and he looked away. Daniel didn't bother to greet him.

'Daniel, would you mind if I took a look at Alice's room?'

'It's already been searched,' he reminded her, 'but you can if you want.'

She didn't expect to find anything new in Alice's room but thought she might at least be able to build a clearer picture of the girl they were looking for.

Daniel led her through a paved backyard. There were a few potted plants to add colour and a wrought-iron table with some chairs by the rear window. The house was empty.

'Mam had to go to work,' he told her. 'No choice.' He meant financially, but Beth couldn't imagine how Mrs Teale could keep her mind on her job with her daughter still missing. Maybe it was even harder to sit around doing nothing, feeling helpless.

'Where does she work?'

'The minimart, on the tills and stacking shelves. It's a job.'

He led the way up the stairs, pointed to Alice's room, and

Beth opened the door. There was just enough space here for a single bed, a tall, thin wardrobe, a chest of drawers and a bedside cabinet. The room was cluttered with clothes. They were piled on the bed, including a discarded pair of jeans and a T-shirt that had been dropped there, next to a light blue scarf with stars on it and a couple of spaghetti-strap tops. It looked to Beth as if Alice had taste on a limited budget. She guessed that most of this stuff had been bought with her wages at the club; she doubted Alice got too many handouts from her dad. There were pairs of shoes and books on the floor, as well as handbags and some cushions that were supposed to be decorating the bed.

'Mam's always on at her to tidy the place.'

'Typical teenager,' observed Beth. 'Always in a hurry to be somewhere else.'

'My room's worse,' he admitted.

The room held all the necessities of a teenage girl's life, including a couple of hairbrushes, some scrunchies, lipsticks, cheap items of jewellery, scented candles and an incense burner with grey ash on it.

Beth picked up a camera body that was missing a lens and Daniel said, 'It got chipped when she dropped it at rambling club. It's old.' Beth put it back down then picked up another item, which had a familiar symbol on it. It was an old notebook with a pentacle embossed on its cover, and there was a pack of Tarot cards underneath it.

'That's not her journal,' said Daniel.

Beth opened the book and saw that notes had been written on several pages. 'She into this kind of thing?'

'For years.' He smiled. 'I blame *Charmed*. She watched all the reruns. What little girl doesn't want to be a witch?'

Beth read from the book: 'A spell to cast love?'

He laughed. 'Must have had a crush on someone who didn't notice her.'

'. . . a spell to enact revenge?'

'Yeah, well, she was only messing. That's old, too.' He meant the notebook.

'She use the Tarot cards on her friends?'

'Sometimes, I think,' he said. 'For a laugh.'

Beth put the notebook down and turned her attention to the posters on Alice Teale's wall. Some of them had slogans written on them. One said, 'I'm not perfect . . . but I'm close.' Another had the words 'Nasty Girl' written across the silhouette of a hot female dancer. Then there was a striking portrait of the famous Afghan girl wearing a red shawl, her piercing eyes staring intently into the lens of the camera. There was an old poster for *Trainspotting*, with the cast against an orange background, though Alice couldn't have been born when it was made, and a music poster featuring Benny Blanco.

'She's old school,' said Beth, and she pointed to a vinyl turntable with a pair of speakers on top of the chest of drawers.

'Alice likes anything retro,' he explained. 'Everybody does these days – old Nokia phones, proper cameras, paper journals, books, records. They're all big now.'

Beth understood. It was an antidote to spending virtually every waking minute online as they were growing up. Kids were craving authentic experiences, things they could touch and hold.

Beth leafed through a pile of second-hand LPs from the seventies and eighties: Tears for Fears, The Cure,

Siouxsie and the Banshees, The Human League, a faded copy of David Bowie's *Ziggy Stardust*. 'She likes the old ones, then?'

'They're cheap,' he explained. 'Most of them are from charity shops.'

Beth walked towards the window and peered out. Alice had a view of her neighbours' backyards and a set of allotments at the rear of her house. The neighbour was still standing there, absent-mindedly rubbing his car with a wash cloth. He didn't seem to be in any hurry.

'I'll go out the back door,' she told Daniel.

The wash cloth was moving half-heartedly, rubbing the same spot on his car, as Beth reached him.

'You're a detective,' said the man, as if Beth didn't already know this.

'I am.' Beth wasn't surprised. It was clear he wanted to talk to her. That was why he was hanging around, pretending to clean his car. She planned to ask him some questions of her own. Maybe he knew something.

'Any luck finding young Alice?'

'Not yet,' she said. 'You obviously know her?'

'I'm Bryan. The next-door neighbour,' he said, and Beth wondered if he might be enjoying that status around town. He didn't look too upset by her disappearance.

'Know the family well?'

'Er . . . quite well,' and Beth took that as a no. She couldn't imagine Ronnie Teale getting on with a busybody like this and Abigail probably kept herself to herself.

Beth could have left at that point, but killers often knew their victims and sometimes liked to talk to the

57

reporters or detectives who covered the cases they them-selves were involved in. They couldn't help it.

'Is there anything you can tell me about Alice that might be useful?' she offered. 'What did you make of her?'

'Nice lass,' he said a little hesitantly. 'Bit wild, perhaps.'

'Wild? In what way?'

'I heard she had a fair few boyfriends.' His tone bor-dered on disapproving. He lowered his voice then, even though the street was empty apart from them. 'She used to sunbathe, you know.'

'Right.'

'Making the most of the heatwave.' Bryan jerked his head towards the property next door. 'In the backyard.'

'Okay.'

'She'd be out there, with her books and stuff, studying and sunbathing,' he said, and when Beth just stared back at him, he added: 'In the nuddy.'

'She sunbathed naked?'

'In the afternoons, while her parents were out at work.'

'How do you know?'

'I saw her.'

Beth turned to survey the scene. 'But there's a big wall between your backyards.' Alice sunbathing nude might have been a little unusual, but she would have expected privacy in her own backyard.

'Well, I didn't see her from here,' he protested. 'I just happened to look out of my bedroom window and I saw her' – and he almost whispered it – 'with no clothes on.'

'And she did this more than once?'

'She did it a few times last summer and, again, more recently, when the weather turned warmer.'

'And you happened to glance out of your bedroom window each time?'

'Well, it's not a crime, is it? I'm allowed to look out of my own window.'

Beth looked up at the window in question. 'Where did she sunbathe? At the bottom of the yard?'

'Er, no, they have a table and chairs by their back window. The kind that lie flat if you adjust them.'

'And you could still see her from your bedroom window? You must have been standing on a chair.'

'What are you talking about? It's not my fault if she parades herself like that.' Beth said nothing and he became even more flustered. 'I'm not a bloody peeping Tom.'

No, of course not, thought Beth, but you did take an unhealthy interest in the attractive, naked teenager who lived next door, which might mean you know more about her than you're letting on. 'She doesn't care who sees her,' he went on. 'She never draws her bloody curtains.'

'How do you know she never draws her curtains?'

He looked flustered again. 'Because I have to come out here sometimes, don't I, to get to my shed or put the bins out.'

'Was that when you noticed her curtains weren't drawn?'

'They're always wide open.'

Beth realized that, with no houses behind hers, Alice Teale might have assumed no one would be able see into her bedroom. She also wondered how frequently Bryan liked to visit his shed in the evenings.

'So you will have seen Alice through her window,' she said. 'Often.'

'Not often,' he protested. 'Just on occasion when I was walking back through my yard. I'd sometimes catch a glimpse of her.'

'By accident, exactly.' Beth nodded because she didn't want him to clam up at this point. 'Ever see anyone else in the room with her?'

'She had music blaring out once, which was why I looked up – so I could see where it was coming from, you understand – and there was someone with her then.'

'Who was that?'

'It was another girl, and they were being daft together.'

'How do you mean?'

'I think they'd been drinking, and they were jumping about – dancing, I s'pose you'd call it – but it didn't look much like dancing to me, and the noise didn't sound much like music either.'

'One of her friends, then?' Beth wondered if it was Chloe, or perhaps Kirstie.

'Yes.'

'Ever see anyone else with her? A boy, maybe?' she asked him. 'Or a man? You might well have done, if you were working in your shed.'

'I did, once.' He lowered his head so that he didn't have to look the police officer in the eye when he said: 'There was this lad with her.'

'In her bedroom?'

'Aye, I noticed him because he had his shirt off.'

'Her boyfriend? He's the same age as her. Seventeen.'

'I've seen her boyfriend,' he said. 'This was a different bloke.'

'Was it?'

'He looked more like a man than a boy.'

'That's interesting.' Had Alice somehow smuggled an older man into her bedroom? 'How much older was he than her boyfriend?'

'Hard to say from where I was. A few years? I wasn't really looking.'

'But you noticed he was shirtless.'

'Yes, and there was no one else in the house then.'

'How can you be sure?'

'There were no lights on downstairs.'

He doesn't miss a trick, thought Beth. 'Would you recognize him if you saw him again?'

'Oh no,' he said. 'I just saw this bare torso and a flash of dark hair.'

Had he been mistaken? Did the boyfriend have dark hair?

'You saw Alice with this young man,' she said. 'Was she dressed?' The bluntness of Beth's question seemed to unsettle him.

'Not fully, no.'

'What was she wearing?'

'She was in her underwear, I think . . .' It was almost a stammer. 'Bra and pants – that sort of thing. That's what it looked like to me.'

'What colour bra and pants?' asked Beth innocently.

'What c——? What difference does it make?'

It didn't, but Beth was enjoying unsettling the man. He deserved it for his perving. 'Perhaps she was wearing the same ones when she disappeared.'

'From what I could see' – he was struggling to answer – 'it was a black bra.'

'Matching?'

'Eh?'

'Did the knickers match the bra?'

'I couldn't tell from that angle, could I?'

If that was true, Beth was surprised he hadn't used a stepladder to get a better look. 'And you only got the merest glimpse of her companion?' she probed. 'Dark hair and a flash of his torso,' Beth repeated. 'But not a good look at his face?'

'Not a good look, no,' said Bryan, 'but it definitely wasn't the boyfriend.'

Then who was Alice Teale's secret lover and, more importantly, was he responsible for her disappearance?

9

Moments before DI Fraser left both the incident room and the Northumbria police force, at one and the same time, he casually mentioned the press conference. When Black looked blank, he asked, 'Didn't Everleigh tell you? Well, there's no point in me doing it, is there? I can't go on the telly as the face of an investigation I'm no longer part of. No, it will have to be you.'

Black didn't like the sound of a televised press conference, but Fraser was right. If Black was leading the search for Alice Teale, then he should be the one appealing for help.

'Start with a prepared statement giving everyone the details, and make sure you know your stuff, in case any smartarse journalist lobs a tricky question at you.'

'When is it?'

Fraser made a show of looking at his watch. 'In a little under an hour.'

'Wait – what?'

When Beth Winter finally returned to the town hall, she found DS Black busily writing a statement to be read out at a press conference that was apparently only minutes away. She introduced herself to DC Rodgers. He was a gaunt man with a moustache and sweat marks on his shirt beneath both arms. She found herself automatically leaning back as she shook his hand. DC Ferguson shook her hand, too. He took her right hand in his, then placed his other hand on the outside of hers so that it was trapped between both of his as he shook it some more. 'Nice to meet you, pet,' he said, with heavy emphasis on the 'nice'. He stared at her intently and beamed at Beth as if she were the mail-order bride he had been waiting for.

It said something about Ferguson that Beth instantly felt more comfortable speaking to the man who had killed an unarmed civilian.

'Can I help at all?' she asked Black.

'How can you help?' he demanded, without looking up from the statement he was struggling to complete.

'I don't know. I was just . . .' *Trying to be sympathetic, but fuck you.*

'You can't do anything here so make yourself useful and go and see the boyfriend, will you?'

'Don't you want to hear what I found out at Alice Teale's home?'

He seemed conflicted then. He looked at his watch, sighed, pushed the statement he was writing to one side and said, 'Obviously, I want to hear it.'

She kept it factual and moved on whenever he grew impatient at what seemed to him to be an unsubstantiated opinion but, in the end, he listened while she told him everything she had learned.

'You don't like the dad, then,' he said, as if this were a case of Beth taking an irrational dislike to him and not merely an analysis of the man's unusual behaviour.

'He doesn't seem to like his daughter.' When Black opened his mouth to challenge that view, she quickly added: 'According to his own son.' Then she conceded, 'Though

64

Daniel doesn't think his father is responsible for her disappearance. I saw little actual concern or worry on the part of Ronnie Teale. He was frustrated, angry and basically unhelpful, bordering on obstructive. It wasn't the reaction of a man who is genuinely fearful for his daughter's life.' Black thought for a moment but didn't answer. 'I think there is something seriously wrong in that family, I really do.'

'What about his alibi? Does it stack up?'

She had been expecting him to ask. 'I checked it out on my way back here.'

'And?'

'The landlord of the Black Stallion wouldn't say that he wasn't there at nine o'clock but he couldn't say for sure that he was, and they don't have CCTV in there.'

'Hardly surprising. They've barely got glass in their windows. Okay, you've made your point. We'll keep him in mind.'

If they had been the kind of detectives you saw on TV, this would have been the moment when he might have said, *Good work, DC Winter,* in order to keep her motivated, but they weren't and he didn't. Instead, he just mumbled, 'That it?'

'No,' she said. That was not it. Beth told Black about the eyewitness who was convinced he had seen someone other than Alice's boyfriend in her bedroom with her. Even Black's face betrayed his interest.

'That could be significant,' he admitted when her account of the neighbour's sighting was done. He was about to turn his attention back to the unfinished statement for his press conference when he said, 'Anything else?'

'Yes,' she said, because she had saved the best bit till last. 'Alice Teale kept a journal.'

The Journal of Alice Teale

There are so many rules. I'm not even talking about the ones that are written down. Not the laws, or even the religious commandments, and certainly not all the school rules. There's way too many of them.

I'm thinking about the rules that aren't written down. The ones we are all just supposed to know. Morals, my mam would call them. Whenever some businessman or politician is caught doing something they shouldn't, she'll say, 'He's got no morals, that's his problem,' but what are morals? Our grandmothers were supposed to be virgins on their wedding nights, and if they weren't and there was a baby on the way, they were told they had to marry the guy. What choice did they have back then? I never used to think about it much when my nan told me stories of the old days, back in the fifties and sixties, but then I read a bit about it and realized what it must have been like. People were horrible to you if you were a single mum, if you were unmarried and having sex. If you were a white woman and you had a baby with a black man, they would call out at you in the street. Babies were given away, sold, by the Catholic Church in Ireland. If you go back just a bit further, women were locked up if they had too much sexual desire, but how much is too much? You had to pretend you didn't have any, I suppose, to be on the safe side.

This is all in books about life years ago. People read

these things, but I don't reckon they actually think about the girls who were affected, not really. They were only statistics, not real people with feelings, trying to live awful lives in a world that was supposedly full of morals. Nowadays, we are more liberal – you can use contraception, have an abortion, live with a boy without getting married to him, leave him when you choose, live with another girl, if that's what you prefer, even marry her; but just a few decades ago they'd have locked you up or driven you out and your own family would have been the first to slam the door in your face – because of morals. But morals change. We have different ones now, and I sometimes wonder if our grandkids will be as shocked by the restrictions on our lives as we are about the ones in the old days.

What if there were no morals at all? What if we were free to love and be loved by anyone we wanted? At least that would solve my little problem.

IO

Chris Mullery wasn't going into school at the moment. How could he, he asked Beth, with his girlfriend missing? He was worried sick, hadn't been able to eat, sleep or do anything. He had barely left his room since the news reached him, and the boy did genuinely look beside himself – but was he just a good actor? Beth reminded herself of all the murders of young girls she had read about and how often it turned out to be the boyfriend who was the guilty one. Usually, this was only discovered after his tearful appearance at the press conference, when he sobbed through an appeal for the safe return of the woman he'd killed.

Alice's boyfriend did have dark hair, so it was possible he could have been the shirtless man Bryan saw through her bedroom window, though he hadn't fully filled out yet and still looked like the teenager he clearly was. Chris was so pale Beth suggested they might go outside for a while so he could get some fresh air, and he agreed to accompany her to the garden. It would also separate them from Chris's mother, who had been hovering in the background since Beth arrived. She was virtually wringing her hands with concern over her boy, which was understandable enough under the circumstances, but Beth wanted to speak to Chris on his own.

As he walked out of the back door Chris picked up a bag of seeds and brought it with them.

'To feed the birds?' Beth asked.

'The squirrels,' he said. 'Some people don't like it, though.'

'Why not?'

'Because they are grey and a pest, supposedly, not the red ones everyone seems to love.' Then he said, 'But, personally, I'm against squirrel racism.' She could tell it was a joke he had used before, and his heart wasn't in it.

He poured a generous mound of seeds on to a bird table near the fence and retreated, then, instead of sitting down, they walked, slowly making circuits of the back garden together.

Beth eased into the conversation by asking the boy some simple questions she already knew most of the answers to, like where he and Alice went to school, what subjects they were studying and how long he had been going out with her. All this was in his first statement, taken by DC Ferguson, a suspiciously thin document that looked as if it had been done in a hurry at the outset of the investigation. It ended with the assertion that Chris had been at home on his own when his girlfriend vanished. Beth wanted to get the lad used to answering her questions before they tackled more contentious issues, like the lack of a real alibi.

'I was in all evening,' he assured her. 'Mam and Dad both went out, but I was still here when they got back.' When she pressed him on the time in between, he said, 'I was on my own. I'm sorry.' He meant he couldn't prove it.

'Weren't you tempted to go out and meet Alice?' she asked, keeping her tone neutral and avoiding the obvious

69

accusation in the words. 'The school's not far. I might have been if I had spent hours studying, particularly on a Friday night.'

He shook his head. 'She wouldn't have wanted me to.'

'Why not?' He shrugged, and it seemed it was the only answer she was going to get. 'Weren't you guys getting along?'

'It wasn't that. Alice is a very independent person and she doesn't like to be viewed as somebody's girlfriend. She likes alone-time.'

Good for her, thought Beth. 'How did you feel about that?'

'I don't own her. She can do what she likes. I'm there for her, always. We've already been through a lot.'

'Your break-up last year?'

'You know about that?' He seemed surprised.

'And her relationship with your best friend' – the boy looked sick then – 'short-lived as it was.'

'Yeah,' he said. 'That.'

'That must have been a really bad time for you,' Beth probed. 'When she started seeing Tony?'

'Yeah.' He avoided eye contact with her. The memory clearly hurt him, even now.

'But you patched it up?'

'We got back together. It was my fault, anyway.'

'Because you broke up with her before she started seeing Tony?'

'Yeah.'

'Still,' pressed Beth. 'Of all the people to start seeing . . . your best mate,' and when he didn't answer: 'Do you think she did that to hurt you?'

'No, I don't know. Maybe. No.'

'Which?' she asked softly.

'I know what you mean, but we all hung out together. I think she was upset when we broke up and he was the shoulder to cry on, wasn't he? Anyway, it didn't last.'

'You got back together instead.'

'Yeah.'

'And you forgave her?'

'What?' The question seemed to make him feel uncomfortable.

'I'm not saying she did anything wrong, but it must have bothered you when she became intimate with your closest friend. Some guys would have moved on, but you forgave her, obviously.'

'Yeah.' He mumbled it quietly.

'You *did* forgive her?' she pressed.

''Course.' He turned sullen then.

'Lately, though, things haven't been great.' She framed it as a statement, not a question, and he looked defensive.

'They have been,' he contradicted her. 'Just not the same.'

'In what way? Was she cooling off?' Would Chris concede that? Would he even admit it to himself?

'No.'

'We heard she might have been.'

Chris looked angry. 'Who told you that?'

'Is it true?'

There was another gap while she waited for Chris to admit it but, instead, he said, 'Her fucking brother. Was it him?'

'Was Alice cooling things down with you, Chris? Can you answer my question, please?'

71

'It was him, wasn't it? Fucking Daniel, jealous bastard. No, she wasn't cooling it with me.' He spat the word 'cooling' at her.

'Why would you say that?'

'Say what?'

'That her brother was jealous. Are you saying he was jealous of you?'

He looked guilty then, and said, 'Not jealous . . . Possessive, I mean, over-protective. That's what I meant. He was always . . .'

'Looking out for her?'

'Yeah, but too much, you know. She's seventeen, not eleven. She doesn't need her big brother any more. She's got me.'

'But they remain close?' asked Beth.

'I tell her, "Don't let him rule your life, just because he hasn't got one."'

'You think Daniel hasn't got a life?'

He seemed to realize he'd sounded harsh. 'All I meant was, he didn't do well at school, he works behind a bar and he hasn't got that many friends, or even a girlfriend. It's not much of a life, is it?'

'Okay,' she said. 'If Alice wasn't cooling it off with you, then why did you say things weren't the same? In what way?'

'I don't know. We used to spend all our free time together, we'd talk for hours, but there's a lot going on now – exams, her job at the club, all sorts of stuff.'

'Did you argue?'

'About what?'

'Her not being around quite as much.'

'We've always argued, but it doesn't mean anything. We're fine the next day. It's hard, you know, some days. It's like everything I do gets on her nerves. If I'm not there for her, she gets upset, but if I am there, it's like I'm an irritation. Alice can be moody, she admits it. That's why I didn't go and meet her after school that night. She told me she wants her own space.'

Beth knew it was likely that a young girl would want space for its own sake, but she might also need it for another reason.

'I have to ask you this, Chris,' she said, 'but is it possible she might have been spending that time with someone else?'

'What do you mean?' he asked, but she could tell he knew exactly what she meant.

'Alice has disappeared and our priority right now is finding her and getting her safely home. For that to happen, I need you to be very honest with me. Is there any way that Alice might have been seeing someone else?'

'No. No way,' he blurted, and he looked shocked and hurt even by the suggestion.

'Not someone else from school, somebody she worked with, or Tony?'

'No. Absolutely not. No chance. I would have known, and she wouldn't do that to me.'

'You're sure? She and Tony were definitely . . .'

'Over. Yes. She doesn't even speak to him any more, and there was no one else. Sure, guys are always hitting on her, but she doesn't let them . . .' He left the sentence unfinished.

'Okay, I get it.' She needed him to be calm, and he was

far from it. 'You guys were enough for each other. I'm sorry, I had to ask – we always have to ask.' That seemed to placate him. 'So when you wanted time alone together, where did you go? Here? Her place?'

He snorted. 'Not her place. Have you met her dad? No, my mum's cool with it, so we'd be in my room, here.'

'Never in hers?'

'No. Why do you ask?'

Because your girlfriend was seen in her bedroom, in her underwear, with another man. 'Because I have to build up a picture of Alice's life, her habits and movements.'

'Oh,' he said. 'I see.'

'Did she ever talk about running off, or anything like that?'

'Never. I mean, we both talked about being away one day – at uni, obviously, and then afterwards, in a job somewhere, and there aren't many of those around here. She never said she was going to actually run away, though.'

Beth chose that moment to bring up the subject of Alice's journal. 'Another thing her brother did for her,' he said, and his tone was distrustful.

'You knew about it, then?'

'She was always writing in it, but then she'd be like' – he mimed someone hastily snapping an invisible book shut – 'whenever I walked in the room. It was pathetic.'

'I guess she wanted to keep her private thoughts private,' said Beth.

'We weren't supposed to have any secrets,' he said. 'That was sort of the point, you know: openness, honesty – that kind of thing.' And his sarcastic tone betrayed just how annoyed he had been about the journal.

74

'She never let you read it?'

'Are you having a laugh?'

'What do you think she was writing about in it – if you had to make a guess?'

'Me, I suppose, among other things.'

'It wound you up?'

'Wouldn't it wind you up if your boyfriend wrote stuff about you in a journal but wouldn't let you see it? Wouldn't you want to know what he'd written?'

'I suppose I would.'

'Well, then.'

'Did you argue about it?'

'Yes.'

'But she carried on writing in it, anyway?'

'You can try arguing with Alice, but she never backs down. It's always her way or . . . Well, there is no other way.'

'You're saying she could be selfish?

'She's a complicated person. Alice can be so lovely, and she can also be so . . .' He settled on: 'Cold. If she doesn't agree with you, then she just won't listen to you, and there is no way you will ever change her mind.'

'She's headstrong,' offered Beth. 'Stubborn, even? That must be infuriating.'

'It is.'

'Yet you put up with it?'

'What can you do?' He shrugged. 'I love her.' And then he seemed to contemplate the girl and the way she made him feel because he suddenly said, 'Sometimes I wish I didn't.' He forced a laugh. 'I don't, really, it's just that she drives me crazy, and not always in a good way.'

They talked some more about Alice's friends and family and Chris gave similar answers to Daniel's. Beth was building up a clear picture of Alice's private life by now, but none of this was particularly new or likely to impress Lucas Black. Hopefully, he'd be too preoccupied with the outcome of his press conference.

'Did you notice anything else out of the ordinary recently? Anything at all in the way Alice talked or acted that made you think, *This isn't right?*'

'There was one thing.' As soon as he said it, he seemed to backtrack. 'It seemed weird at the time.' Chris looked reluctant to come to the point and Beth waited patiently for him to explain. 'A couple of weeks back, we were both at sixth-form club and I went looking for Alice, but I couldn't find her. I even went out on to the courts to see if she was watching her mates play netball, but she wasn't there. I went back down the side of the school building to go in again, and that's when I saw her.'

'Where was she?'

'On the roof.'

'Why would she go up there?'

'I don't know. It just seemed bizarre.'

'What did you do?'

'Called up to her, but she waved me away, so I went inside. There's a metal staircase that leads up to the door there. It's supposed to have an alarm on it, but someone set it off ages ago and they never reset it. As I reached it, she was coming back down.'

'What did she say?'

'I asked her why she had gone up on the roof, but she just said, "You can see everything from there." I told her she would get into trouble if anyone caught her, but she was dismissive and changed the subject. There's no reasoning with her when she's like that.'

'You didn't think she was harbouring any dark thoughts while she was up there?'

'About killing herself, you mean? God, no. It never even crossed my mind.'

'What about now?'

'Now? I don't know.'

'You didn't press her on her reasons for being there, then?' Beth couldn't understand why he wouldn't, particularly if Alice was being evasive.

'I told you,' he snapped. 'I tried, but she cut me off – just blanked me.' And then he said something that stayed with Beth afterwards: 'You don't understand what it's like for me. I do love Alice, completely, but sometimes, she can be a real bitch.'

The Journal of Alice Teale

I instinctively know how this is supposed to be. I am expected to put up with his inexperience, his clumsiness, his inability to work my body out. No one's told him what to do, so it's not his fault. I haven't. I wouldn't dare. Why can I summon up the courage to be naked next to him, to touch and be touched, yet say nothing to correct him when he is too quick, too rough or goes in the wrong direction? Because I'd rather die than speak to him about it, in case he thinks I'm some kind of sex-crazed slut demanding he satisfies me? That's it, I think. Are women trained from birth to be passive about these things, so that the man has to pretend he knows what he is doing, when he clearly doesn't, and I have to go along with it meekly? I think so.

Sometimes I close my eyes and an inner voice says to him, *You'll get nowhere like that*, but I don't even try to stop him. Instead, I just let him mess around down there like he's trying to fix something. Then I have to fake a mini climax, tell him how great it was and encourage him to get what he really wants before we can stop and he goes home. It was almost exactly the same with Tony, and I used to worry that it was me. I was doing it wrong, or feeling it wrong somehow, letting my own anxiety prevent me from enjoying something other girls take to so easily, if they're to be believed. But who's going to admit they don't really enjoy it with their boyfriend? Certainly not me. I'd feel like such a failure. I can't be the only one, surely.

I don't think there is anything wrong physically. I can nearly always sort myself out later. It must be all in my mind when he's with me, so is it my fault? Trouble is, when I'm lost in that moment later, on my own, it's not him I'm thinking about.

I I

Well, on the bright side, at least he had managed to go through the entire thing without saying the word 'fuck'. Other than that, it was hard to think of anything positive to say about the press conference and Black probably wouldn't bother to watch it on the late-evening news. He already knew how stiff and awkward he must have appeared and how he had so easily lapsed into that emotionless fact-speak police officers fall back on when they have to describe a murder or missing-persons case. The main thing was that the message was now out there. *Alice Teale is missing. I'm leading the investigation. Please help us to find her.*

'How did it go?' Beth asked him as she walked into the room, and he frowned at her.

'I survived.'

When it seemed that was all he was going to reveal, she said, 'I spoke to Chris Mullery.'

Black grabbed his coat. 'You can tell me on the way.'

'On the way where?'

'I want to walk where Alice walked,' he said, 'on the day she vanished.'

They pulled into the large empty car park, got out of Black's car and surveyed the school building. It was a lopsided, sixties-built, three-storey construction with

80

scaffolding covering around a third of it from floor to roof height to enable workmen to fix its crumbling façade. It was easy to see what work was needed. Most of the exterior was made up of coloured glass panels beneath large, grubby windows. Each floor had a different colour, with red panels on the ground floor, blue on the first and a garish yellow on the top. Whether you liked that look or not, and Beth didn't, it was undermined by the many broken panels that had been boarded up with wood or simply left empty, exposing the bare metal behind them. There were so many broken panels, Beth wondered if it was a rite of passage for pupils to smash one.

'It's a bit grim, isn't it?' observed Beth.

'None of the schools round here have been given any money for building projects for years, so they put these up instead.' Black drew her attention to a row of three small, flimsy buildings off to one side of the school on a raised portion of land close to its playing fields. 'Prefabs are supposed to be a temporary solution but these have probably been here for a decade.'

There were no signs of life in the main building, with lessons and after-school clubs long over, but Beth noticed something. She pointed to a window set back from the front of the school where the middle of the building curved inwards to form a U-shape.

'A light,' she said.

'In the U bend.'

'The what?'

He half smiled, and it was the first time Beth had seen him being anything other than completely serious. 'That's what the kids call it.'

How could he know that?

'Someone must have left it on.' But as she said that a shadow crossed the window. Somebody was moving around in there.

'Could be a cleaner or a caretaker,' he said, 'but there's no car in the car park. Let's have a nose round.'

They left their car and went down the side of the building nearest the prefabs so they could walk its perimeter. They passed the kitchens then a set of rear doors that opened out into a courtyard with a covered walkway that had presumably been built to keep out the cold. Judging by the wind that whistled through its numerous broken windows, this had been a forlorn hope.

'Look,' said Beth. She'd spotted a large green car parked by another side door, some way from the rear doors. It was partially obscured by a wall.

'That's an XJ,' said Black appreciatively, 'in racing green,' and they walked up to the car. 'Nice. Not the care-taker's, though. In fact, who can afford a Jag on a teacher's salary?'

'It's a few years old,' said Beth.

'Even so, the bodywork is gleaming. Somebody loves this car.' He took out his notebook and wrote down the registration number. 'And they're still working, even at this hour.'

There was nothing in the car that gave any clues to its ownership, so they left it to complete their tour of the school's perimeter. They passed a large gymnasium and a couple of offices before curving back round to the main doors.

A wide path led away from those thick wooden doors,

then diverged, one route leading you to the teachers' car park and the other a pedestrian walkway which went out of the grounds towards the two rows of pensioners' cottages. This was the last walk Alice had made before she disappeared.

'I don't understand how she could just vanish,' said Beth.

They were standing in front of the school but facing away from it, looking along the path Alice had taken. 'I keep thinking about it,' said Beth. 'Literally no one saw Alice after she walked down here. She had to have gone through the buildings there' – she pointed to a narrower path that split the rows of retirement cottages – 'but if she emerged, how come no one spotted her?'

Black didn't comment, but he was at least looking in the same direction.

'If she was snatched off the street, it's a main road, so surely someone would have seen it. It wasn't that late. If she'd screamed or struggled . . .'

'Perhaps she knew the man,' he said. 'Assuming it was a man.'

'It usually is,' she reminded him.

'How many murders have you worked?'

'None.' *And you know that already, you miserable bastard.* 'But I've read the stats. Women don't normally kill, and they very rarely murder other women, so it's probably a safe assumption that, if someone has abducted Alice, it's likely to be a man.'

'Never assume,' he told her. 'Look to the evidence, always.'

She sighed audibly.

'What?' he demanded.

'Nothing.'

They walked towards the pathway and considered Alice's route between the cottages. 'DI Fraser's team knocked on every door here. Nothing remotely sinister. It's all OAPs – a few former miners and their spouses. Alice's grandfather lives here and he didn't see her either. By nine o'clock, curtains would have been drawn and they would have been staring at their TVs. A girl could pass through unnoticed. I agree she probably wasn't snatched from the main road, but she could have been picked up by someone she knew. I doubt she would accept a lift from a stranger.'

'What about CCTV out front?'

'There's nothing,' he told her.

'Further down the road into town, then.' She thought back to her training. 'Can we log all the cars that went down the street around that time, get the reg numbers, talk to the owners to see if they all had a good reason to have been there at that time? If they can't account for their journey, or they know Alice . . .'

'There's no CCTV between here and Collemby town centre, and precious little once you get there.'

'Really?'

'You don't know Collemby,' he told her. 'It's like the land that time forgot. Towns in the north-east go one of two ways. If they have good transport links, with tourist attractions and gift shops, they can spend a bit of money to lure people in, but Collemby isn't Alnwick or Warkworth. The town has been going downhill for years. You don't invest in CCTV in a place like this. There are a few cameras on a couple of the shops and one outside the pub in the marketplace, but they point down so they can clock anyone up to no good outside their property. They're not aimed at the roads or at capturing car-reg plates.' He seemed irked that he had to explain this to her.

'Okay,' she said. 'I'm just trying to understand how no one has seen her at all since that night.'

'There have been numerous sightings,' he said, and that surprised Beth, 'just no credible ones. Her picture has been all over social media and in the national and local newspapers, as well as on the regional TV news bulletins, so we've had calls from the public. Some were nutters or attention-seekers; others said they were sure they had spotted her, but there are a lot of girls who look a bit like Alice . . . and we'll be inundated tomorrow.' He meant following the press conference.

'What if she's a runaway?'

'Her description has been issued to port authorities and airports in case she tries to leave the country, but she didn't take her passport, so that seems unlikely. Other forces have been notified and asked to look out for her.'

'Do you think she'll be okay? I know you don't like to assume, but you must have worked a few cases like this one.'

'I have,' he said. 'It doesn't look good.'

'Will we get anyone else to help us now it's been on national TV?'

'I doubt it. It's all about resources, or the lack of them. We currently have four separate ongoing suspicious-deaths inquiries, as well as two confirmed murders. They take precedence over missing-persons cases.'

'Because missing people usually turn up?'

'Normally, they are found or just come home again.'

'But you don't think this girl is just a missing person?'

'I don't know,' Black admitted. 'We're trained to classify missing-persons cases. We look for triggers. Does she have a reason to leave? Is she being abused at home, mentally or physically, or simply neglected? Does she have a history of depression, self-harm or a mental instability of some kind? None of that applies here.'

'Exam pressure, then?' offered Beth.

'She had an unconditional offer from one university and several conditional ones for grades she is likely to comfortably achieve. Her parents aren't the pushy kind. I don't think they even expected her to try and get into a uni.' Then he said, 'She could have had money worries, I suppose.'

'She lives pretty frugally,' said Beth, 'and has a part-time job.'

'What about her dad?' asked Black. 'Is he bad enough to run away from?'

'I'd be tempted, if I was her, but she was planning to leave for college anyway. Wouldn't she hang on for a few more months?'

'That would be the sensible move,' he agreed. 'But then what about this guy Alice's neighbour saw through her bedroom window? Could that have been her boyfriend or was it someone else?'

'It could have been him, but the neighbour said he looked older, and Chris told me they never went to her bedroom, only his, because he wanted to avoid bumping into Alice's father, which I can believe.'

'Then we need to find this mystery man,' he said. 'He could be the key.'

They returned to the car and Black drove them back to the city, dropping Beth at HQ so she could pick up her own vehicle from the otherwise almost-empty car park.

'I thought I'd take a look at her online presence,' she told him before she got out of his car. He didn't reply. She was starting to get used to the fact that he was a man of very few words and sometimes silence was as good as it got with him. She took it to mean he didn't think it was a terrible idea. 'See if she's on Facebook, Twitter, Instagram – all that.'

'It's late,' he reminded her, 'and I need you to meet me in Collemby in the morning. There's a lot of people to get round.' He meant there wouldn't be time.

'I'll do the social media tonight, and I'll give you a report in the morning.'

Again, silence. It would help if she had a clue what he was thinking. Was he impressed, unimpressed or didn't he give a damn? Did he think scanning Alice Teale's Facebook page was a waste of time?

Just when she thought he wasn't going to offer an opinion at all, he said, 'There probably won't be much there, not if it's public. If we can show probable cause, we can get a warrant to view her private messages on Facebook and Twitter. That's something we should explore in the morning.'

'But it won't do any harm if I have a look in the meantime.'

'Suit yourself.'

12

Was there anything more depressing than coming home to the cold, empty flat you used to share with the man you loved? If there was, Beth couldn't think of it right now. It was the same every night these days and the reason why she chose not to spend too much of her time here any more. She would have sold the place, if she had possessed the energy to put it on the market and keep it pristine enough for viewing. As it was, she barely felt energized enough to pick dirty clothes off the bedroom floor and keep a little food in the fridge. She opened it now to see what was in there.

Beth remembered a time when she used to cook proper meals every night – fresh food with real ingredients – but that was when she was cooking for two. It seemed pointless to go to that much effort when there was no one here to appreciate it. A microwaveable chilli con carne two days past its sell-by date looked the least worst option. She considered binning it, but there was no mould growing on it and she had nothing else in. Beef was safer than chicken, right? She slid off the cardboard sleeve, grabbed a small, sharp knife, stabbed the film as if it were her mortal enemy and popped it in the microwave. The four minutes needed to cook her meal was long enough to change into jogging bottoms and a baggy T-shirt then pour herself a large glass of white wine. She ate from a tray balanced on her knees and placed her laptop on the sofa next to her. This was where Jamie used to sit when they watched TV together, before he left Beth for *her*.

She quickly banished that thought in case it grew and festered. Before she knew it, she wouldn't be thinking about Alice Teale. Instead, she would be drunkenly stalking her ex-boyfriend on social media to see if there were any new photographs of Jamie with the girl who had ruined everything.

Don't think about it, Beth. Not now.

She took another swig of wine and realized she had almost finished her first glass before making any real inroads on the chilli. She set down the glass and googled 'Alice Teale'. She had to skip several newspaper reports on the girl's disappearance before she found what she was looking for. Alice was on Facebook and her page had a public setting. As she ate, Beth scrolled down the girl's timeline and immediately realized Alice had not updated her page in a long time. Beth knew young people were deserting Facebook in droves, mainly because their parents were on it, but judging by the dates of her most recent posting, it looked as if she had stepped away from it around the time she was dating Tony, her then ex-boyfriend's best friend. Had there been negative comments on here about that, or had she just wanted to lie low for a while?

Beth switched to Instagram and scrolled through dozens of pictures of Alice getting ready for nights out with friends, and others where the evening was in full swing. Kirstie and Chloe featured prominently. There were lots of photographs of Alice with Chris. Her life in the sixth form was also a regular topic and there were pictures from the various clubs she participated in, along with a number of photographs she had taken herself. There were shots of the countryside: rivers, fields and treelines, often with orange sunsets above them. Alice had made a point of noting the make and model of camera she had used to take these. Comments were numerous and largely supportive. There was nothing here that gave any hint of a grudge against the girl.

Beth switched to Twitter and followed Alice on it. Her presence here was less personal, more political. Alice had a social conscience. She was broadly left wing, which was no great surprise in the north-east and for someone her age, but she also supported causes dear to her heart, including animal welfare and gender equality, and there were retweets on sexual health, as well as campaigns for the eradication of various forms of cancer, 10k runs she had undertaken and, some way down, a picture of Alice standing with other young actors at what appeared to be the aftermath of a performance or rehearsal of a school play. She was on the side of the stage, looking to the left and slightly upwards. Alice was smiling and her gaze was almost adoring, but it wasn't directed at her boyfriend, who was also in the picture, at the other end of the group. Instead, she was beaming at a young man with brown hair at the centre of the photo who looked a little older than Alice – mid-twenties, perhaps. A teacher, thought Beth: he had to be.

A handsome bugger, too, and Alice clearly thought so, but had it been reciprocated? Judging by the smile he was flashing back at the beautiful young girl on the stage next to him that night, it was. Perhaps Chris had noticed this, too, which was why his face was like thunder.

13

No matter how late she stayed up the night before, Beth was nearly always awake long before the alarm. The first hint of sunlight against the curtains would be enough to break her sleep and begin the usual relentless round of over-thinking, starting with the realization that Jamie was gone and wasn't coming back, and moving on to a recap of all the reasons why.

Beth told herself to do the one thing that could banish those negative thoughts for a little while. Get up and out of her bed then go for a run in the park.

She ran three laps of the lake with only the ducks and a lone dog-walker for company before she came to a halt. Beth had spent her running time thinking about Alice Teale, the company the teenager had kept and just who might be responsible for her disappearance. The missing girl continued to dominate her thoughts while she showered, dressed, ate toast and drank a mug of coffee before climbing into her car. It was still absurdly early.

Black had asked Beth to drive herself to Collemby so she could meet him at the town hall that morning. She was not looking forward to this. He had been one of the reasons Beth had stayed up so late. After monitoring Alice Teale on social media, Beth had switched her attention to Lucas Black and read more of the coverage of the shooting incident which had left a man dead and her police partner castigated by the tabloids for his actions that day. Knowing that she had no choice but to work with Black, she had been searching for something – anything – that might explain why he had gunned down an unarmed civilian outside his own house. The closest she had found to this was a suggestion that he might have thought Rory Jordan was armed and had become confused in the dark. Was this possible? God, she hoped so, but it didn't seem very likely.

Beth had texted her fellow former trainee, Peter Kennedy, with an 'RU awake?' and when she got an instant reply in the affirmative, had asked him for a chat. Her mobile rang a moment later and, when she answered it, Peter was so full of congratulations, good wishes and curiosity about how it was going for her in the new role she found herself instantly forgiving him for being a man and leapfrogging her in the selection process.

They talked about the case and what he was working on, agreeing they should try and meet soon for a proper catch-up over lunch or, preferably, a beer. She noticed he avoided extending that invitation to Anne Hudson. Maybe he didn't like her either.

When they had talked for a while she said, 'Listen, Peter, I need a favour, if that's okay?'

'Sure,' he agreed, without even knowing what she was going to ask of him. Beth told him about Lucas Black and Peter admitted he had heard of the man but never met him. 'The guys in my squad probably know him, though.'

I'll bet they do.

Beth described the shooting incident. 'If you do hear anything about him, or if he should accidentally on purpose pop up in conversation, I'd be curious to know what other people think of him.'

'I suppose I could mention that my friend just joined his team and see what they say. No harm in that, is there?'

'Thanks, mate. No harm at all.'

Beth arrived at Collemby so early she thought the doors might not even be open yet, but they were. Black was already there, too, his car in the car park, and when she walked towards the major-incident room, she spotted him through one of the glass portholes on the double doors. He was sitting there, looking at something intently. Black was side-on to her, so he hadn't spotted Beth, but she had an uninterrupted view of him.

For some reason, she halted and didn't walk in right away. Instead, she peered through the window and watched him for a moment, as if that would help her to understand him.

'Are you coming in, or are you just going to stand there gawping?' He didn't even look up.

Flustered, Beth opened the door and walked into the room, wondering whether to apologize or bite back at him.

'Where are we off to today, then?' she asked instead.

'We'll split up again.' Beth's heart sank. How was she ever going to learn if she was always on her own? 'But first I have to go through all of this.' He indicated the pile of messages that had been placed there. 'It's the leads generated last night. I asked for them to be collated and brought here so I could hit them early.'

'I'll help you.'

He shook his head. 'It'll be quicker if I go through them on my own.'

Beth took that to mean he didn't trust her to sort the bogus calls from the genuine leads. 'I'll just put the kettle on, then, should I?' She hoped he would detect the sarcasm in her voice, but he said nothing so she went and did it anyway.

Beth came back with two mugs of instant coffee and handed him one. He actually thanked her, which was a surprise.

'When I'm done here, I'm going to see the embittered ex-boyfriend,' he said.

'Tony? How do we know he's embittered? Yesterday you told me never to assume.'

'I also told you to look to the evidence. Tony left school because of Alice and is currently doing bugger all, his prospects all but ruined, so there's a good chance he's not her biggest fan. You don't have to be a detective to work that out.'

He might have been correct, but that didn't make his tone any less exasperating. 'What do you want me to do?'

'Go and see Kirstie and Chloe.' He handed her the file full of statements so she could get the information she needed on Alice's two friends.

'I went through her social media last night,' she told him.

'But you didn't find anything.'

'How do you know?'

'If you had, you'd have told me by now,' he replied, as if she was a kid who couldn't wait before blurting out a new lead.

'There was one thing,' Beth told him, then realized she didn't have much and a man like Lucas Black was unlikely to be moved by it. 'It could be nothing.' He gave her a look of such irritation at her wavering that she felt the need to quickly plough on regardless. Beth told him about the photograph at the rehearsal and the beaming smile Alice Teale had given the young teacher. 'It seemed as if something might have passed between them, that's all.' When she had said it, it seemed so inconclusive, she fully expected to be shot down.

Instead, Black said, 'Okay, that's worth looking into,' and she assumed he was giving her permission to check it out or possibly even ordering her to get on with it.

Without explaining his change of heart, he took a sizeable number of the sightings and phone messages from the top of the large pile he was wading through and handed them to Beth. 'Here,' he said. 'It's a bit early to tackle Alice's mates. Go through some of those for me.' Maybe he trusted her after all.

They had been inundated with leads, sightings and theories about the girl's disappearance, all of which had to be read, analysed and prioritized, the more fanciful ones placed at the bottom of the heap, the conspiracy theories ignored and the dozen or so plausible callers put in a separate pile so that each one could be followed up on.

They had been at it for more than an hour when DC Ferguson and DC Rodgers finally arrived. Black pointedly looked at his watch and Rodgers said, 'Traffic's a bastard this morning.'

'You're just in time,' Black told them, handing Rodgers

the pile of vaguely plausible sightings, 'to follow up on this lot.'

'Okay,' said Ferguson, 'but I'll make us all a brew first.'

'Don't bother,' said Black. 'We're out of here.'

'Where are you going?' asked Rodgers, clearly irked by the exclusion.

'People to see,' said Black, and his dismissive tone made it clear how he felt about the other detectives and their late arrival.

As he marched across the car park, Beth struggled to stay alongside him. 'Do we have an issue with Ferguson and Rodgers?'

'You might. I don't,' he said, and when he reached his car he actually explained himself for once. 'I'll get something out of them, but they won't go the extra mile.'

'Time-servers?'

'You're keen and you work hard but this is your first real case. If fifteen years of shit-shovelling and cost-cutting means your family hardly sees you, maybe you won't be so motivated.'

He opened his car door and was about to leave her to it.

'You're still motivated.'

'I don't have a family,' he said, 'and I want to find Alice.'

14

Black still had a long list of people to talk to that day, but he had to start somewhere. The ex-boyfriend, who had lost his girl, his best mate and all his friends in one go, seemed like a good place to begin.

Tony's mother was not pleased to see the detective sergeant. 'My son didn't do anything wrong,' she said, her voice already sounding shrill, as if she had worked out that Tony might be quite high on the list of possible suspects in Alice's disappearance. 'That girl was single. She'd broken up with her boyfriend before he asked her out and he hasn't seen her in weeks.'

'It's all right,' Black assured her. 'Going out with your best friend's ex isn't a crime. I'm just here to have a word with your son, not arrest him.' *Unless he suddenly confesses to murder.*

He waited for her to admit him, but she said, 'He's in the garage.'

Tony's mother took Black round the side of the house. He expected to find the young lad working on something, but the double wooden doors of the old garage were firmly closed. She rapped on the doors with her knuckles. 'Tony, it's the police.' Was that a warning?

He didn't wait to find out. Black pulled open the nearest door.

The reason for her son's lack of response was immediately obvious. He was sprawled on an old sofa, his body motionless, and all Black could make out at first were the soles of his trainers, which protruded from one end because it wasn't long enough to accommodate his lanky frame. It took a moment for Black's eyes to adjust to the gloom but then he noticed that the boy's left arm was hanging down the front of the sofa, his hand trailing almost to the floor.

'Shit!' exclaimed Black, and moved quickly towards the boy, fearing the worst. He needn't have worried. The sight of a burly stranger bearing down on him caused Tony to stir and shout, 'What the fuck?'

'We knocked,' his mother protested, but then both she and Black noticed the headphones that had fallen from the boy's ears as he shot up from the sofa, a faint hiss coming from them as his music continued to play.

His mother managed to calm Tony down as she explained who Black was and why he was there, then she offered her son the chance to leave the gloomy garage and come inside, but he turned her down. 'I'm good in here,' he said. It sounded as if they'd had this conversation many times before.

She frowned at the makeshift room in her garage, which was lit by one bare electric bulb and a little veiled sunlight from a single dusty window. As well as the sofa, there was a rickety old coffee table which had three dirty mugs on it. His mother quickly scooped them up and left Black with Tony, who looked tired. Had he been sleeping, even as the music blared from his headphones?

Once Tony's mother had retreated, Black said, 'Nice place

you've got here,' and the boy gave him a withering look. 'No, I mean it. I'd have loved something like this when I was your age.' There was a dartboard on the far wall and an ageing stereo plugged into a socket. Cans of beer were stacked on the work bench next to it. 'Unfortunately, my dad had other ideas. He wanted to use our garage for his car, which was most unreasonable.' And he smiled at the lad, who was at least sitting up straight and taking notice of him.

'Where's the other one?' he asked Black as he reached into the old army jacket he was wearing and fished out a tin of tobacco, then opened it. The metal box contained a couple of hand-rolled cigarettes and a lighter.

'What other one?'

Tony put the cigarette into his mouth and lit it, inhaling deeply, then he threw his head back and exhaled. 'The bad cop.' He made a show of looking towards the open door. 'Is he running late?'

'We don't really do good cop, bad cop, son. I can be either or both. It depends.'

'On what?' the boy sneered.

'On how cooperative you are.'

The boy watched him for a while, as if he were gauging how serious Black was. 'And if I'm not cooperative. What then? You plant some drugs on me?'

Black sighed wearily. 'You know, that tends to only happen in films.'

'That's not what I've heard. I should just trust you, should I, because you're a police officer?'

'Why wouldn't you trust me, Tony? I'm trying to find out what happened to a young girl who has disappeared. I want to bring her back to her family.'

'You could twist something I said and lock me up for murder.'

'I never said she was dead.'

'You see.' His tone was triumphant. 'You're doing it already – twisting my words when I had nothing to do with any of it.'

'I'm not trying to trap anyone. You don't know me,' he conceded, 'but you do know Alice Teale and her family. I think you can imagine what they must be going through right now. You don't have to help me, Tony, but I was told you cared about her once. Perhaps I was misinformed.'

Black had chosen the right words. Tony's defiance ended immediately. The lad's lip quivered. 'I'm sorry,' he managed, and he had to put his hand to his eyes to hide the tears that were starting to form. It took a little while for him to calm down. Black waited while the boy kept repeating, 'I'm sorry.'

'That's all right, son. You take your time.'

Chloe had been given revision time. That's what the school were calling the flexible approach they were taking with Alice Teale's closest friends in the sixth form.

'I don't think they knew what to do with us,' admitted Chloe, who Beth found in the local library after the girl's mother had directed her there. It was a small building with a decent selection of books, but it wasn't the best environment for revision. The tables in the middle of the room were occupied by two pensioners reading, a middle-aged man who was researching something – probably his family tree, thought Beth – and another man nearby was being taught how to use the library's sole computer so that he could apply for a job. The coaching he was receiving from the librarian was loud enough to dominate the otherwise silent room. Chloe seemed to appreciate that this wasn't the best place to talk about Alice either. 'I was just about to stop for a coffee,' she told the detective.

'I'll buy you one,' said Beth, and the sixth-former closed her ring binder, stuffed it into her bag then followed Beth out of the library, across the car park and into Collemby's sole café, a gloomy, decidedly old-fashioned-looking place without a single other customer. They ordered coffee and Beth steered Chloe to the furthest corner from the counter, which placed them next to the café's window.

'You're one of Alice's closest friends,' Beth began.

'We grew up together, lived in the same street, been best friends since we were three years old.' She seemed proud of that fact. Chloe appeared a little nervous and awkward, but Beth reasoned she might be anxious around anyone, let alone a police officer. She spoke fast, almost blurting the words out, as if keen to make her point quickly, perhaps because she was used to being ignored. It probably didn't help that she spent much of her time with Alice Teale, who seemed to be constantly desired.

'If Alice had a secret, you might know about it.'

'I *would* know about it.' Then she qualified that: 'If anyone did.'

'And you don't know of any reason why Alice might have run away?'

'No.'

'But she did have secrets,' Beth persisted. 'I'm talking about her journal. According to her brother, she was always writing in it.'

'I know about her journal,' said Chloe, 'but she wouldn't write in it while other people were around and it was always locked.'

'She kept it with her, not at home?'

'In her bag,' she said, 'or her coat. She always wore a baggy green parka with these deep pockets.'

'So it's still on her,' said Beth, her hopes of finding any clues from it seemingly dashed. 'Chloe, do you know if anyone had a falling-out with Alice recently?'

'No. I mean, Alice and Chris used to argue, but it was just bickering.'

'What did they bicker about?'

'He used to get jealous,' she said, without expanding on it.

'Did Alice give him cause to be jealous?' Beth asked. 'In your opinion.'

There was a slight pause. 'Not deliberately, but Alice was friendly to everyone.'

'And that could be mistaken for flirting,' offered Beth, 'by an insecure boyfriend?'

When Chloe didn't contradict that, Beth moved on again.

'What about her home life? I understand things weren't always great there.'

'With her dad, not so much,' she agreed. 'With her mum, so-so, but she is very close to her grandad. He lives in one of the Aged Miners' cottages next to the school. She drops in all the time.'

Beth noticed she had missed someone out.

'And how are things with her brother?'

'Good,' said Chloe. 'Mostly.'

'But not always?'

'Daniel's a good guy, but he can be a bit controlling, too. Not on the same level as her dad, but he has a temper as well.'

'You ever see him lose that temper?'

'Daniel? No.' She must have reasoned that Beth would now assume she had nothing to back up her assertion about Daniel, so she added: 'But he got barred from the pub.'

'When was this?'

'A few weeks back.'

'What did he do to get barred?'

'Threw a drink in someone's face.'

'Was there an argument?' Beth asked. 'Or did he just march up to the bloke and chuck a pint at him?'

'He walked in, ordered a drink, took it over to the table and threw it,' said Chloe. 'And it wasn't another bloke. It was a girl.'

'Daniel Teale threw a drink in a girl's face?' This seemed both unlikely and bitterly ironic, considering Daniel's dismissal of his father as little more than an angry man. Had Beth misread him entirely? 'Why ever would he do that?'

'He just went a bit nuts.'

Beth Winter listened patiently then while Chloe breathlessly delivered the whole story of how Daniel had been barred from the Dirty Donkey for throwing the drink and now the landlord wouldn't let him back in. The incident had obviously been talked about by everyone in Chloe's social circle.

'Why would a boy like Daniel suddenly lose it like that? He must have had a reason.'

'He called her a load of names, too, then just walked out.'

Beth noticed the girl still hadn't answered the question. 'Did no one go after him? A girl gets a drink chucked in her face and nobody bats an eyelid?'

'I think her mates were in shock, and he's a big bloke. Plus, he was really angry.'

'And you've no idea what caused him to do that?'

She shook her head.

'Who would know? Kirstie?'

'She might. Kirstie knows all the gossip.'

'And where would I find her? Not in the library, obviously?'

Chloe laughed at the notion. 'She'll be at home watching TV, pretending to revise.'

Beth wondered whether Chloe had a low opinion of Kirstie or if they were simply competitors in the quest to be Alice Teale's BFF.

'You said Daniel called this girl names, in the pub? What did he call her?' asked Beth, and when Chloe looked a bit embarrassed the detective added, 'I probably hear worse every day in the canteen.'

'Well, he said she was a total C-word and he used the F-word a lot and he called her a bitch and a bastard, which is actually worse than it sounds, because she is – technically, I mean. She hasn't got a dad, and he would know that, so it was cruel.'

'Did he call her anything else?'

'A liar.'

'And what did he reckon she was lying about?'

'No idea, sorry.' Chloe said that quickly. Whether she

104

knew or not, it seemed she wasn't going to let on. Beth noticed she was absent-mindedly tugging a strand on her bag, straightening it out, letting it go then straightening it again, as if the action soothed her.

'You haven't mentioned the girl's name, the one he threw the drink at.'

'Oh, sorry. It was Sophie Mayhew.'

'And what did this Sophie Mayhew say or do when this awful thing happened to her in front of everyone?'

'I wasn't there.'

'No, you weren't,' said Beth, 'but the whole town must have been talking about it.'

'One of the bar staff threw Daniel out, then she went to the toilets to get cleaned up and went home.'

'Without saying anything to her friends? No explanation for what had happened to her, no harsh words about Daniel? Didn't she say anything to anyone?'

'She just said he was a fucking psycho.'

15

Tony didn't look like the kind of lad who would respond to an arm around the shoulder. Instead, Black waited till he had calmed down and asked, 'You miss her?', and the boy nodded forcefully. 'When was the last time you saw Alice?'

'Couple of weeks back.' He sniffed. 'I was with my mother. She was with *him*.'

'*Him* being her boyfriend, Chris?'

'Yeah.'

'Was anything said?'

'She just blanked me.' It was obvious how devastated he had been by that. 'I thought he was going to say something, but he just took her hand and steered her away. I felt about that tall.' And he showed Black a tiny gap between his thumb and forefinger.

'Your mother understand?'

He snorted. 'She just keeps telling me to forget her and get another girlfriend, like it's that simple.'

'But you can't forget Alice?'

'No. That's why I got upset. I want you to find her, too. Even if I never see her again, I want to know she's safe, that she's . . . alive.' He said the last word as if it was inconceivable Alice might not be.

Black thought it unlikely that this sensitive young man had murdered his ex-girlfriend but immediately told himself to ignore that inner voice. He had been wrong before now and first impressions could be misleading. Black knew how abruptly a teenage boy's feelings could switch from love and adoration to resentment and even hatred, particularly when he had been rejected.

'I have to ask where you were on the night Alice disappeared. She was last seen around nine o'clock in the evening.'

'I was here.'

'On your own?'

'Yeah.'

'You were sitting in the garage on a Friday night? You didn't feel like venturing out to the pub?'

'I don't go out.' He quickly added the word: 'Much.'

'In case you see her?'

'Or anyone else.'

'They all side with the other fella?' asked Black, and Tony nodded.

'You were the bad man who went off with his best friend's girl, is that it?' The boy didn't dispute this. 'But they'd broken up. She was fair game, wasn't she?'

By way of explanation, Tony said, 'We used to hang out all the time, Alice, Chris and me. I always thought she was really cool.'

'But he beat you to it?'

'Kind of. I ended up in the friend zone, but they were always arguing then making up and everything was really intense between them. It went on like that for ages. They weren't right for each other.' He seemed very sure about that. 'One night they had a blazing row about nothing, really, and he asked me what he should do.'

'And you said dump her?'

'I said perhaps they weren't good together. Maybe they should see how they felt if they were apart for a bit. He liked the sound of that.'

'So he finished with her. Were you planning to ask her out at that point?'

'No, I swear I wasn't.'

'But you had hopes . . .' Black began.

'That maybe one day . . .' Tony shrugged as he completed that thought.

'What happened?'

'As soon as he broke up with her she came around to see me. She was upset. I thought she was going to have a go at me for saying they weren't good together, but I don't think he'd told her, not by then. I put my arm round her and just listened at first. We talked for ages and I told her I thought he was stupid not to appreciate her because she was amazing, and we kissed.'

'That's how it began?' Tony nodded. 'How long before Chris found out?'

'In a town this size? Guess.'

'Not long.'

'First time we went to the pub together, his cousin spotted us, then it was all out in the open.'

'Did he go crazy?'

'I tried to explain I didn't break them up to get together with her, but he wasn't listening. He took a swing at me. He didn't believe me. No one did. I was the bad guy and he was the heartbroken one, even though he had dumped her. It didn't matter. Everyone was on his side.'

'But you had Alice,' said Black, 'so it was worth it?'

'It was.' He brightened for a moment.

'What happened?'

'I don't know. I really don't. I thought it was great, but she called it off.'

'Was it sudden?'

'I didn't see it coming,' Tony admitted.

'Did she give you a reason?'

'Just that it was all too intense and she couldn't handle it. She didn't want to be with anyone.' He snorted. 'A month later, she was back with him, like nothing had ever happened between us.'

'He took her back, and the friends did, too, I suppose?'

'I was the villain, wasn't I? I turned her head. He must have told her all about our little chat before he broke up with her, because she doesn't speak to me now.'

'How long were you seeing her?'

'A month.'

'But it feels longer.'

'Yeah.'

'What do you think has happened to her, Tony?'

'I don't know. It's all I can think about. Maybe she ran away.'

'From what? From Chris?'

'From him, from her old man, from all the pressure.'

'What pressure?'

'It was just something she said to me that night after Chris ditched her. She said she couldn't bear all the pressure she was under to be something she wasn't.'

'What did she think she had to be?'

'Perfect.'

The Journal of Alice Teale

I really hoped he would understand. That it would be a short, sharp break, a quick cutting of ties, hard but sudden, not a long-winded, drawn-out process like it became.

But Tony didn't get it at all, and totally wouldn't accept that we were done. There were tears, too, and what I can only describe as begging. Shit, I should have just ended it over the phone. Why would anyone want to stay with someone who didn't want them? I'll never understand that.

He kept asking me why, even though I'd already explained it. In the end, I had to leave. I didn't want to be there when his mam came home and found him in that state.

'Was it something I did?' he asked me for the umpteenth time as I was leaving.

I told him again that I just needed some space, because I couldn't breathe.

I told him it was my choice and I needed to do this, and he asked me if he didn't get a say in it.

'No,' I told him. 'You don't.'

That's when he called me a fucking bitch.

Those were his last words before I walked out of the door.

16

Chloe had been right about Kirstie. Beth could hear the TV even through the front door and she had to ring the doorbell then knock hard twice before the girl finally answered, looking flustered, her long hair wet and dripping water on to the shoulders of her T-shirt, as if she had dressed hurriedly when the doorbell went.

'I was drying my hair.' Was this an explanation for the late answering of the door or a rebuke because Beth had called at an inopportune time? Beth explained the reason for her visit and Kirstie looked genuinely upset at the mention of her friend's name. 'You've still not found her?'

'No,' said Beth, 'but we're doing everything we can.'

Kirstie offered to help if she could, and Beth asked if she could come in and ask a few questions. They went into the lounge and Kirstie turned off the television. The room was sparse and Beth was struck by the absence of the items you might normally find in someone's home. There were no books, no ornaments, no flowers, no paintings on the wall, only a cabinet with two small framed photographs on it. The first featured Kirstie with an older man who was presumably her father and a boy who Beth assumed must be her elder brother. The second showed the younger man in army uniform, holding a rifle, while on exercises somewhere hot. Beth instantly surmised that

Kirstie lived with her father and, for whatever reason, her mother was gone.

Once again, Beth took her time and began with questions about how long Kirstie had known Alice, their life in Collemby and the school. Kirstie was dismissive of the after-school activities, in particular the sixth-form club, which she described as lame. 'What do you like to do instead?' she asked the girl.

Kirstie shrugged. 'Come home. Who wants to hang out at school any longer than necessary?'

'So you were at home when Alice disappeared?'

'Yeah.'

'With a friend?' The girl shook her head. 'On your own, then? Watching TV and fighting your old man for the remote control, if your house is anything like mine was.'

'He was out, so I had the telly to myself.'

'What did you watch?'

Kirstie frowned at her, as if this was of no interest to anyone. She didn't realize that Beth was subtly establishing her alibi. 'Can't remember,' she said. 'The usual shite.' She rhymed off a list of soaps and reality TV she might have tuned into that night.

Beth gently steered the conversation round to talk of boyfriends. Kirstie didn't have one but thought Chris was okay. She was less keen on Tony. 'He took it all too seriously,' she said dismissively.

'Was there anyone else Alice fancied?'

'She used to say most of the boys in Collemby weren't worth crossing the road for. Why do you ask?'

'We heard Alice might have been seeing someone else, that's all.'

'Who?'

'We don't know. That's why I'm asking her friends.'

'Alice would never do that.'

'Because she had a boyfriend?'

'Yeah, so someone's stirring it.'

'Who would do that? Did Alice have enemies?'

'No, but people like to spread gossip, don't they?'

'Did Alice ever tell you about her drama group?'

'Sometimes. I'm not in it, though, so . . .' She meant it wouldn't be of much interest to her, hence why Alice didn't talk about it much.

'Did she ever mention any of the teachers who run it?' And when Kirstie looked blank, Beth said, 'I saw a picture of the drama class and there was quite a young teacher involved, looked like he was in his early to mid-twenties?'

'Oh, Mr Nash. He's lush.' She quickly added: 'For an older guy.'

'Alice seemed to think so, too, judging by the smile she was giving him in the photograph.'

'Everyone thinks he is good-looking, but we only look. Alice wouldn't cheat.'

Beth smiled at her. 'Not even if the guy was lush?'

Kirstie looked like a shocked maiden aunt. 'Of course not.'

'I was only joking,' Beth assured her.

'And anyway, he's got a fiancée,' said the girl, as if that were an end to the matter.

'Were there any other good-looking men in Alice's life she might have liked, even if she didn't do anything about them? Maybe they hit on her and she told you about it?'

'Ricky at the bar was always on at her to go out with him,' confirmed Kirstie. 'She told him she had a boyfriend, but it didn't stop him asking.'

'He was persistent, then,' asked Beth. 'Wouldn't take no for an answer?'

'Guys don't, do they?' she said wearily.

'You have a low opinion of them?'

'Only most of them,' she joked.

'What about Alice's brother?'

'Not my type, but he's okay, I suppose.'

'I'm guessing Sophie Mayhew would have a very low opinion of Daniel Teale.'

'Oh, her.' Kirstie raised her eyebrows. 'She would now, but she used to like him.'

'You mean she liked him as a person, or she fancied him?' asked Beth.

'She was definitely crushing on him.' This seemed like such an American expression Beth wondered if Kirstie had picked it up from the TV.

'He didn't feel the same way?'

'I don't know, but she certainly made it obvious.'

'So how did it go from that to him throwing a drink in her face?'

She hesitated and Beth urged her to go on. 'They went off together for a while on New Year's Eve.'

'What happened?'

'I don't know.'

'Come on, Kirstie.'

'I know she was after him that night, and they disappeared for ages, but after that she told everyone there was something not right about him.' She looked troubled then.

'And this stupid rumour started going around about Daniel and Alice.'

'What kind of rumour?'

'It was sick.'

'Tell me.'

She seemed reluctant but finally said, 'About him and Alice being more than just brother and sister.' Beth's eyes widened in shock. The rest of Kirstie's words came out in a rush. 'It was rubbish. They are close, but they're not . . .'

She couldn't even find the words. Instead, her face flushed and she looked down at her shoes.

'Okay, Kirstie,' said Beth. 'Where can I find this Sophie Mayhew?'

'What's this got to do with Alice's disappearance?'

Beth shrugged. 'Maybe nothing.'

'She'll be at work now, but in the pub later.'

'Which one?'

'The Dirty Donkey.' She corrected herself: 'I mean, the Black Stallion.'

'I know it.'

'She goes there every Friday and Saturday night, with the same old crowd from her school year.'

'Thanks for your help, Kirstie.'

'No problem. Anything at all — I mean it. If it will help you to bring Alice home.'

'There is one other thing you could do for me, if you don't mind?'

'Sure.'

'Give me all the goss.'

'About what?'

'Everything. Your school, for starters. We'll never get

to hear the truth about the place if I just ask the head-master, but I reckon you could give us the inside track.'

'What do you want to know?' She seemed hesitant now.

'I don't know. There must be some gossip – about the teachers as well as the pupils. I could spend all week taking statements from people there, but they might not tell me the truth. What I need is the word on the street from someone in the know.' This was designed to make Kirstie feel important, and it was the right approach.

'That's me, for sure. There's only one problem if you want all the gossip.'

'What's that?'

'Have you got all day?' She giggled. 'There's a lot of it. Collemby Comprehensive isn't like other schools.'

Beth smiled like they were two girls of equal age sharing confidences. 'What do you mean?'

'Virtually everyone there has done something they shouldn't have.' She laughed. 'And that's just the teachers.'

Beth folded her arms then said, 'And I bet you know all their secrets, Kirstie.'

The Journal of Alice Teale

Chloe and Kirstie.

Kirstie and Chloe.

What am I going to do with them?

One is needy, and the other one is . . .

I don't even need to write that down.

Kirstie and I both know Kirstie's little secret, and some secrets ought to stay that way until they are ready to be let out, so in consideration of Kirstie, my lips are sealed, which is kind of appropriate, really.

And then there's Chloe.

You have to love her.

No, really, you have to. Otherwise she'll let you know about it. If you haven't empathized and sympathized with her and prioritized her well-being, if you haven't called her, hugged her, picked her up, bigged her up or talked her down from whatever ledge she's metaphorically standing on, then woe betide you.

Oh God, I know I sound like a total bitch, even to myself, and I do love her, I really do, but the whole thing is so bloody exhausting. Yes, she does have a bit of a shit life with her mum and dad being the way they are and, yes, I know boys pretty much completely ignoring her has to be a bit of a brain-fuck so my oh sooo complicated love life must seem like a romantic adventure by comparison but, really, no, it isn't. It only looks that way from the outside, not when you're living it, and it's all relative, anyway. She'll find someone one day, she will, she's nice, most of the time, and fun. She's pretty when she smiles, which is almost never, but if she just made a bit of an effort. It's the endless pep talks I can't stand. I just don't have the energy any more. You think you've got problems, Chloe, but I'm here to tell you that you haven't, not really. Not compared to mine or others I could mention. I just wish I could say it to your face without you losing it completely.

I know depression is a thing and I'm not supposed to just say, 'Pull yourself together, woman,' but . . . PULL YOURSELF TOGETHER, WOMAN!

Phew, there, I've said it. Writing it down is very therapeutic. It's like shouting into the wind. No one can hear you, but it still makes you feel better somehow.

17

When Beth returned to the town hall there was no sign of
Ferguson or Rodgers but Black was on the phone to someone and he was calling that someone 'sir', so she assumed
it was DCI Everleigh. Black looked grim-faced, so she left
him to it and walked over to a table. She hung her bag
and jacket on a chair then spotted a large brown sealed
envelope lying face up on the table. It had the words
'DS LUCAS BLACK' written on it in capital letters with
black marker, so there wasn't even a clue in the handwrit-
ing. Either someone had placed it there while he was on
the phone, or he hadn't spotted the envelope when he
walked into the room.

Beth picked up the envelope just as Black groaned, and
she turned to see him looking completely exasperated as
he ended the call. Her questioning look at least solicited
an answer.

'Everleigh,' he said. 'I wanted to go up to the school to
speak to the head and Alice's teachers, but he's told me
to hold fire.'

'Why?'

'He wants to talk to the headteacher first.' When she
did not respond, Black explained, 'Collemby's head was
parachuted into the school a few years back when it was
failing, and he turned it around. Morgan, his name is,
and he's done it before. The press call him a super-head

because he advises other schools in the area. He's been in the papers, knows all the local politicians.'

'Friends in high places?'

'Including some very senior police officers, according to Everleigh.'

'I don't understand why that should prevent us from doing our job,' protested Beth. 'A girl has gone missing.'

'We seem to be the only people who suspect she might have come to harm. The school is playing it down, and so is Everleigh, who still thinks Alice will just walk back through her own front door, and you can bet he is parroting the view from on high. Everleigh wants to assure this super-head that our intentions are pure and that no one is suspecting anyone of anything.'

'Even though Alice might have been seeing one of her teachers?' she asked. 'Which wouldn't surprise me, from what I've been hearing about the school.'

'What actual evidence do we have of that?' he snapped. 'Beyond a photo of Alice smiling at a young teacher she may or may not have had a crush on and a vague report from a nosy neighbour about a man with a bare torso in her bedroom window, who, frankly, could have been anyone.'

When he said it like that, Beth had to admit it sounded weak. 'Kirstie told me that Collemby Comp is not like other schools. There's at least one teacher living with a former pupil and there are rumours about others.'

'Rumours are just that,' said Black. 'Rumours. What we need are facts.'

He seemed determined to pour cold water on everything. 'What do we do now, then?'

'We wait until we're given the go-ahead to speak to the teachers and, in the meantime, we explore other lines of inquiry.' It was then he noticed the envelope she was holding. 'What have you got there?'

Beth handed it to him. 'It was on the table.'

Black opened it, pulled out a folded piece of paper and started to read. Beth noticed the look on his face. It was somewhere between surprise and wonder.

'What is it?'

'Pages,' he said. 'From a journal.' And in case it wasn't entirely obvious: 'From *Alice Teale's* journal.'

'Oh my God.' Beth immediately went to his side to look at them too. 'Who sent them?'

He turned the now empty envelope upside down and gave it a shake to see if anything else fell out. There was no note, only the pages from Alice's journal. 'There's nothing here. It's an anonymous sender.' Like Beth, he was wondering who had sent these pages and why. One thing they could both agree on was that this was a hugely significant development. Black had already handled the pages as he pulled them from the envelope, but he placed them almost reverently face up on the nearest table so Beth could read the words as well without contaminating them further before he could get them forensically examined.

Each page had the words 'The Journal of Alice Teale' printed on it, just like Daniel had said.

'It looks genuine,' said Beth.

'If it isn't Alice's journal, then it's a particularly elaborate hoax by someone who knew about the original,' said Black. 'We'll get Forensics to look it over, but I'm thinking it's the real thing.' He scanned the pages. 'There's no date, so no way of knowing when she actually wrote this. And it's only a couple of pages.'

Beth pointed at the first words. 'So, line number one: *Every word I have written here is true, but I've changed the names to protect the guilty.*'

'That's a joke, right?' he told her. 'It's usually "I've changed the names to protect the *innocent*", so why does she want to protect the guilty?'

'Because there are too many of them,' said Beth, and she quoted Alice: '*I can't out everybody.*'

Black read a section aloud: '*I'm guilty, too. I've done some very bad things. I've hurt people, I've been immoral, by most people's standards, but mostly I am guilty of not seeing what was right in front of me. It should have been so obvious because it was there all the time. I have been entirely blind. Everything has changed. Now I can see it all clearly, view things exactly as they really are, with no secrets, lies or pretence. It's all been stripped away, and nothing will ever be the same again. The old Alice Teale is dead.*'

'Let's hope that isn't prophetic.'

Beth then read: '*She is gone for ever, along with her stupid doubts and fears and all the secrets she has carried around with her for so long. What remains of her is not going to take it any more. I want everything out in the open.*'

When they had finished reading the pages, Beth said, 'Wow.'

Black just muttered, 'Yeah,' but the way he said that single word left her in no doubt that he also appreciated the significance of the pages.

'And we have no idea who sent it?'

'There's no note or explanation, just a plain brown envelope with a local postmark.'

'The pages were torn out of her journal,' commented Beth, 'but who by? And why? I doubt it was Alice. I mean, why would she? It seems so personal.'

'It wouldn't be her,' Black agreed, 'but were these pages sent by a killer and, if so, why? To taunt us, maybe,' he suggested. 'Or to throw us off the scent?'

'What if it isn't a killer,' asked Beth, 'but someone who read the journal and wants him caught?'

'She carried it with her,' he reminded her. 'How could anyone get hold of it without being involved?'

'They found it? After she was taken?'

She looked down at the words again. 'But why these pages precisely, and not others or the whole thing? It's a bit enigmatic.'

'Deliberately so.' He added: 'It's like she is writing a partial truth but not giving us the whole picture in case anyone else gets hold of this. Alice couldn't have known she was going to disappear, but she did seem to realize she was on to something. The question is – what?'

'What secrets could a small-town teenage girl have that could be so important?'

'She's seen or heard something?' Black offered.

'Or experienced it herself.'

'Someone has done something terrible, and she knows about it but no one else does. Whoever it was, it must have come as a shock to her, because she berates herself for being so blind and not understanding it all until now.'

Beth nodded, and continued: '*Not yet, though. There's something I need first.*'

'What would she need?' Black wondered. 'Time? Help?'

'Proof?' suggested Beth.

'Yes,' he agreed. 'If she'd seen or experienced something, it would be her word against theirs. She would need proof, or no one would believe her.'

'This is the part I find most intriguing,' said Beth. '*Keep your sharp tongue in check, Alice, for once in your stupid bloody life, and carry on for just a little while longer, acting out all the parts, like you've always done.* God, she's so hard on herself.'

'But how she could possibly be all those contradictory things,' said Black. 'How can you be a virgin and a slut, an ice queen and a hot babe? I don't really get that.'

'She says it herself,' said Beth. 'She's playing a part when she's being each of those things. Acting it. Who she is depends upon the audience.'

'Then there's the last lines,' he reminded her. '*Who cares what they think of you, Alice? None of that matters now. It's all over. At least, it will be. Soon.*'

'Does that mean she's going to confront someone,' asked Beth, 'or . . .'

'End it all herself? *It's all over,*' he said again. '*At least it will be. Soon.* What if Alice was so disgusted with the world that what she actually needed was a way to leave it? If you read that entry through again, it sounds like a suicide note.'

Beth did just that before concluding, 'Yes, it does,' then she asked: 'But if Alice Teale really did kill herself, then how come we can't find her? And who sent these pages?'

18

In the short time they had been in the town hall, the sky had clouded over and it was now threatening to rain. The streets were narrow here and many of the buildings tall, which reduced the amount of light that shone down on to the grubby brickwork, when it shone at all. It left the whole town looking like it needed a thorough clean and gave Collemby a dark and foreboding look.

'There's something about the atmosphere here,' said Beth as they got into the car. 'Don't you think?'

'Not really.'

'You don't find it gloomy?'

'Well, yes, it *is* gloomy, but that's down to the Victorian architecture and the weather, not the town's atmosphere.'

'I don't think it's just that,' she muttered as he drove them out of the square. 'It feels . . .'

'What?'

'Different. I don't know. I realize it sounds stupid, but it's like there's a tension in the air.'

'You're right,' he said with conviction.

'Do you really think so?'

'Yes,' he said. 'It *does* sound stupid.'

There didn't seem any point in arguing with him further. 'Where are we going now?'

'I want to talk to this barman, Ricky,' he said, 'but he

won't be at the club yet, so there's time to follow up another lead. We got a call about a sighting of Alice Teale.'

'A recent one?' Could Alice still be alive? And why hadn't he mentioned this before?

'The call was recent but the sighting was a couple of weeks back,' he said. A young girl thought she saw Alice in a car down by the derelict railway station.'

'How old was the girl, and was she sure it was Alice?'

'Thirteen, and no. She wasn't a hundred per cent certain, but her older sister is in Alice's year so she does know her, at least by sight. She described the car as a big black one.'

'No make or model?'

'The kid doesn't know anything about cars, didn't even notice the badge as it went by. She said it was going too fast and almost knocked her and her dog over. Probably a young lad who doesn't know how to drive properly. It swerved out of their way and that was when she saw Alice, she thinks, in the front passenger seat, and she reckons she heard a bang.'

'Why would Alice be down at the derelict railway . . . Oh!' exclaimed Beth. 'It's a lovers' lane, isn't it?'

'A popular spot for courting couples,' said Black diplomatically.

'Does Alice's boyfriend drive a big black car?'

'Chris doesn't own a car. He does have a driving licence and his father lets him drive the family car, but it's dark grey.'

'It could look black in the dark,' said Beth. 'But Chris said his mum was cool about them getting together in his bedroom. Why would they need to go down to the railway station, when it's not private?'

'So, it wasn't Chris, then,' he speculated. 'It was your mystery man, the one in her bedroom.'

'I'd say that's more likely – and what if Chris found out? Sexual jealousy is one of the more common motives for murder, isn't it?'

'It is,' agreed Black. Then he recalled her words in the town hall before they had been distracted by the envelope. 'You said you'd heard things about the school. What kind of things?'

Beth was tempted to use Kirstie's phrase – 'Have you got all day?' – but knew Black would be unimpressed if she failed to stick to the facts. At least he was more interested in the rumours he'd been so dismissive of earlier. 'According to Kirstie, Collemby Comprehensive has a long and well-known history of inappropriate teacher behaviour and the head has struggled to clamp down on it.'

'What kind of behaviour?'

'At the lower end, affairs between married teachers, which complicates matters in the staff room –'

'And at the not so lower end?'

'I was coming to that.' She had barely drawn a breath before he interrupted. 'Relationships between male teachers and female pupils.'

'More than one?'

'Numerous, apparently, over the years.'

'Even though it's illegal and has been for years?'

'According to Kirstie, the teachers there used to consider it a perk of the job. Now that they can be sacked or even jailed for it, it's far less commonplace, but she claims it still goes on. It's just hidden.'

'And what about her mate? Was Alice involved with a teacher?'

'I asked,' said Beth, 'but she said, "No way." She was adamant Alice wasn't seeing anyone except Chris.'

'Then we're no further forward,' he said. 'All she gave us is gossip.'

'That's what I asked for,' protested Beth. 'And she did give us a couple of names. Alice's drama teacher is Simon Nash. He's young, supportive and good-looking. Kirstie reckons Alice really liked him, but not in *that* way. She did say he sometimes gave her lifts home after rehearsals. Then there is their English teacher, Mr Keech,' said Beth, 'who is openly living with a former Collemby pupil.'

'How does he get away with that?'

'He reckons their relationship started long after she left the school, and that's a grey area. She's nineteen.'

'And did it?'

'Kirstie says not and, apparently, it isn't his first offence. He's the bad boy of Collemby and the girls line up for him, so Kirstie says, but she claims that she and her friends can see right through him.'

'Then Alice is unlikely to have fallen for him,' said Black. 'Unless, of course, Kirstie is lying.'

'One girl made a complaint against him,' said Beth.

'What kind of complaint?'

'Indecent assault. He was accused of grabbing her breasts and the whole school heard about it.'

'What happened?'

'Nothing. The girl withdrew the complaint; it wasn't considered credible.'

'Interesting.'

When Beth had finished relating the 'goss' Chloe had provided, Black said, 'I see what she means when she says Collemby is not a normal school. And neither is the town from what I'm hearing.'

'Alice called it a town full of secrets.'

'It's also a town full of gossip, some of which might just be worth checking out.'

Black checked his watch then said, 'And I know the perfect place to start.'

The trail down to the abandoned railway station was little more than a rough track. It was wide enough for cars, but full of holes where the weather had worn the surface away, and Black's car bumped along.

'You would definitely need a reason to come down here,' said Beth, as she was bounced in her seat yet again.

'There used to be a standing joke in Collemby,' said Black, as he pulled the car over on to rough ground near the old railway line. 'If someone was having a fling with a girl, their mates would say, "He's just putting her on the train."'

'How romantic.' Again, Beth wondered how he had all this local knowledge and whether he had any past association with the town. It was obvious why couples would have chosen this location, though. It was set back from the town, it covered a large area, if you included its numerous outbuildings and sheds, it was bordered by woodland that had slowly encroached on the site over the years, and there were several places to discreetly park a car away from prying eyes.

They got out of the car and walked towards the station platforms. Beth surveyed the abandoned buildings. There was no evidence of structural damage, but they had evidently not been used in a long time. It crossed her mind that if you were looking for somewhere to hide a body one of these outbuildings might serve the purpose.

'Has anyone searched here?' she asked him.

'For signs of Alice? Fraser got the uniforms to take a look down here, but they're all boarded up and there were no signs of a break-in. You won't find Alice Teale down here.'

The place had the feel of a ghost town, and Beth asked, 'Why has it been left like this?'

'It's a strange tale,' he said. 'It started with a wealthy local man, Charles Denham, a descendant of the old mining family that invested in the colliery back in the 1800s. They made money hand over fist for nigh on a century, until the mines were nationalized by the government, not long after the Second World War. Denham sat on his fortune and didn't do much with it. He was the local eccentric. A wealthy old man with too much time and money, and he was looking for a project. When the mine closed he was outraged and when the branch line followed it he was incensed, so he arranged to buy the disused railway station, complete with the platforms and buildings.'

'What was he going to do with a station that had no railway?'

'Restore it to its former glory then run steam trains from one end of the county to the other.'

'An ambitious plan.'

'It never got off the ground, and he died a few years later, without an heir. The place has been in limbo ever since.'

'Why doesn't the council just knock it all down?'

'Because they don't own it. No one does, really. It's part of the unresolved estate of the man. Several relatives laid claim to his money, but it took a decade just to sort that out and nobody wanted this white elephant, so here it stands. Bizarre, isn't it?'

The sky was still overcast and the subdued light gave the station buildings and its platforms an eerie, almost silvery glow.

'You can walk the old line for miles,' Black told Beth as she followed him out of a central section where the tracks had once been, now flat land overgrown with grass and weeds, then they went up the ramp on to one of the platforms. It felt like they were stepping back in time. There was some graffiti, but if you closed your eyes you could almost imagine a train pulling in here.

They passed the window for the ticket office then went down the ramp on the other side, under a metal foot bridge which hung over what would have been the track to link the two platforms.

'What are you looking for?'

'The cause of the bang,' said Black.

The opposite platform had a section of ramp missing at its far end. It ended in an abrupt rectangular shape which jutted out then dropped a few feet, leaving it short of the ground. 'The edge of the platform must have crumbled away,' Black said, crossing the old line to take a closer look.

When Beth joined him there he was on his haunches looking at the ragged edge of the broken platform, then the long grass which grew next to it. 'The girl walking her dog said the car swerved to avoid her and she heard a bang. There are no scrape marks from a car's bodywork, but' – he parted some of the long grass – 'take a look.'

Beth bent to examine the ground below and she could see fragments of plastic on the ground. 'That could be pieces from a headlamp,' she said.

'If the car braked then swerved to avoid the girl' – he made that movement with his hand – 'its headlights would be roughly this height when it went across.' He brought his hand round till it hit the lowest point of the broken platform. 'If he stopped in time, he might smash a light but still be able to drive off.'

'You think it was someone in a hurry to get away from here because he didn't want to be seen with Alice?'

'*If* it was Alice,' he cautioned, 'and we don't know for sure that it was. At this stage, it's only a possible sighting, no more.'

'Might be worth checking the body shops, though there must be a hell of a lot of them around here.'

'I'll get someone down here,' he said, 'to bag up these bits.'

19

They got back to the town hall with the full intention of leaving it again as soon as they had checked for messages. It looked as if Ferguson and Rodgers had both gone home for the night, because the door to the major-incident room was locked. Black had to find his key to admit them. The first thing they noticed were the envelopes. There were three of them on the table Black usually worked from. When had they arrived and who had placed them there? Like the first envelope they had received, these were all large and brown with a local postmark and Lucas Black's name and rank on them in block capitals. He noticed from the postmarks that, although they had all arrived together, they had not been sent at the same time but over a period of three days, and he cursed the vagaries of the postal system.

Black opened each one carefully and upended them to allow the papers to gently fall on to the table without him having to touch them. Each envelope contained journal extracts, and Black wanted them to be examined by Forensics later, but they needed to read the words Alice had written now, before the pages were sent off. He used the blunt end of a pencil to separate the pages and position them on the table so each one could be scrutinized. There were seven extracts in total.

The first was innocuous enough, Alice detailing her

excitement at receiving the journal from her brother and stating that she loved him. Black wondered what the point was of sending that one? The second was more intriguing.

'*I'm just a walking shadow*?' Beth read. 'What does that mean?'

'It means she's depressed, doesn't it?' said Black. 'That's what it sounds like to me.'

'Could be,' Beth agreed. 'And who is *He*? The only one who gets her, the one who can see through her like she is made of glass?'

'Her teacher, her brother, a secret lover?' Black offered.

'It might be her brother,' said Beth, 'but why not say so?'

'Maybe she's embarrassed by how close they are because of all the gossip, or perhaps it's someone else entirely. Alice said she has a secret. Maybe this is it.'

'She's a bit dramatic, isn't she?' observed Beth.

Black shrugged. 'She's a teenager; they're all dramatic.'

'Are they?' she asked. 'Were you?'

'Judging by the number of rows I had with my old man, probably, yes. Everything is amplified at that age, isn't it, so it's all a big deal. Kids fall out with each other one day and are friends again the next. If you throw in relationships, which are nearly always overblown, then you end up with a drama.'

'I don't remember it being quite like that.'

'Youngsters are all daft, always have been. Look at *Romeo and Juliet*. He thought she was dead then he killed himself; she woke up and realized he was gone so she stabbed herself.'

'Oh my God,' blurted Beth.

'Don't tell me I've ruined it for you, Beth. Even I've seen it.'

'No, no!' she protested, waving her hand animatedly at him. 'It's Shakespeare!'

'I know it's Shakespeare. I might not be as educated as you are, but I'm familiar with *Romeo and Juliet*.'

'Not the play,' she almost shouted. 'The quote.' And when he obviously had no idea what she was talking about, she added: '*A walking shadow*. That's Shakespeare.'

'Oh,' he said, 'but not *Romeo and Juliet*?'

'No, it's *Macbeth*, I think,' and she took a breath while she tried to remember it before reciting: '"*Life's but a walking shadow, a poor player, That struts and frets his hour upon the stage And then is heard no more*." We studied it in English.'

She pointed to the paper with Alice's words on it. '*I'm just a walking shadow*,' she repeated, 'which comes just before "a poor player", meaning an actor. So, I think it means that *He* knows Alice is acting but she doesn't call herself an actor. It's as if it's a phrase they share, something they both understand.'

'Perhaps this is an older man who has taught her things, along with a bit of Shakespeare. The same person who is responsible for her disappearance, even.'

'She has English teachers,' she said, 'and Shakespeare will be on the curriculum. Plus, there is the young drama teacher.'

'We've narrowed it down, at least.'

'Unless I'm wrong,' Beth conceded, 'and it has no significance.'

'I think it is significant,' he said. 'I think it's their thing. She's been playing a part all this time and this is the one person she can reveal her true self to.' Black noticed Beth's face change then. 'What is it?'

'"A walking shadow" is Macbeth's speech, when he learns his wife is dead,' said Beth. 'And actually, she kills herself.'

'Another hint at suicide,' said Black.

They both fell silent for a time while they read the extract about morals and how changeable they were. When they reached the end Beth read aloud, '*What if there were no morals at all? What if we were free to love and be loved by anyone we wanted? At least that would solve my little problem.*'

'That backs up the idea that Alice Teale was seeing someone she shouldn't be,' said Black.

'Someone married, perhaps?' Beth wondered.

Their suspicions were heightened when the next extract was a damning critique of her sex life.

'This certainly supports the theory that she might have been seeing someone else,' said Beth. It would also provide Alice's boyfriend with an obvious motive.

The next extract was from the time when Alice acrimoniously broke up with Tony and he did not want to accept it. The significance of these words seemed clear: '*That's when he called me a fucking bitch. Those were his last words before I walked out of the door,*' recited Beth.

'He's angry,' said Black, 'but just how angry? Normal angry, or . . .?' Then he said: 'And who is sending these bloody extracts to us, and why?'

'They hint that Chris and Tony have a motive for making Alice disappear,' she said, 'so I think we can rule them both out as likely senders. Neither of them looks good here.'

Next, they read the extract that concerned Chloe and Kirstie.

'Bit harsh on her mates,' Beth observed once she'd finished. 'One of them, anyhow. I don't suppose Chloe would be too pleased if she read that about herself. Makes her sound like a drama queen.'

'Particularly if she has no inkling that that's how her best mate feels about her. It would be quite a betrayal.' Then he said: 'And what about the other girl, Kirstie? What's with the reference to *my lips are sealed*?' he said, almost to himself.

Beth picked up the paper again and read that passage aloud. '*Kirstie and I both know Kirstie's little secret, and some secrets ought to stay that way until they are ready to be let out, so in consideration of Kirstie, my lips are sealed, which is kind of appropriate, really.*' She looked up at Black. 'Why would that be *appropriate*?'

'You could go back and ask Kirstie?' he suggested.

'You think she'll tell me?'

'Doubtful, but it will be interesting to see if she tries to bluff or lie her way out of it.'

'It's very timely, this, isn't it?' observed Beth. 'The journal extracts landing in our laps so soon after we spoke to them?'

'So, the sender must know we've spoken to them both,' he said, 'or at the very least that we would be planning to speak to them because they are close to Alice.' They transferred their attention to the seventh and final extract, which once again referred to Alice's brother, Daniel.

The Journal of Alice Teale

Brother, I love you, and I'm sorry.

I know you only did what you did because of me.

Most girls hate their brothers. They think of them as gross, alien creatures, always getting in the way or telling them what to do. You were never like that, and I know you are always looking out for me and I do love you for it.

Remember when we were very little and Mam used to put us in the bath together on a Sunday night and there were always loads of bubbles? Afterwards, she would wrap us up in those massive towels that were almost as big as we were. She kept them on the hot radiators so we would be toasty and snug then tell us to get into our dressing gowns, and she would let us watch a DVD for an hour before we went off to bed. Dad was always out down the pub, and it felt so safe and warm, sitting on the sofa watching cartoons with you, with steaming mugs of hot chocolate. I was always really happy then.

There were the nights, years later, when I woke up terrified that someone was trying to get me. I never saw his face, but it was always the same man. I'd run out of my room and across the landing straight into yours; never to Mam and Dad, always to you.

It didn't matter how often it happened or how late it was, you never got mad at me. You always just pulled back the covers to let me in so I could snuggle up. You made me feel safe then, too. Always.

I think we are kind of special and that is why I cannot tell you my secret. Look what happened last time you heard something bad. You walked into the pub and threw a drink right in that bitch's face. I'm not saying she deserved it, though I won't claim she didn't. It is what it is, but if your intention was to kill the gossip and end the rumours about us, then, brother, I have to tell you: you blew it.

20

Beth had used the journey back to the town hall to describe everything else Kirstie had told her about Alice Teale's life, including the rumours about Alice and her brother, Daniel, so it was perhaps less of a surprise when Black asked her now:

'Do you think they were . . . ?'

'Having sex?' She almost didn't like to admit the possibility, having met Daniel, but she couldn't rule it out. 'Perhaps, or maybe she is writing the truth – he made her feel safe.'

'But is it a partial truth? They used to have baths together.'

'*When we were very little,*' she reminded him. 'That happens, doesn't it?'

'What about *then there were the nights, years later* . . . ?' He set down the paper. 'She basically crawled into bed with him whenever she had a nightmare, which sounds like it was pretty often. I'm guessing he had a single bed. They must have been packed in pretty tight and, well, if they were older, and it sounds like they were, something might have happened.'

'It might,' she admitted, and immediately Beth thought of the bare torso Alice's neighbour had seen through her bedroom window. Could that have been Daniel? 'But how will we ever know?'

'We could ask him,' he told her, 'but he's never going to admit it, is he?'

'And it doesn't mean he is any more likely to have harmed Alice, either way.'

'It makes him suspect but not necessarily *a* suspect,' he said. 'I don't know what to think about this, to be honest, or even if it's credible.'

'What if someone found out about it?' she asked. 'Proof, I mean, not just gossip?'

'Would it make them go after Alice or Daniel?' he wondered aloud, clearly thinking of blackmail. 'And how would Daniel react if they did?'

'Sophie Mayhew thinks Daniel is a psycho, but he did throw a drink in her face.'

'You said she would be in the pub tonight, so let's go and talk to her about him.' Then he added pointedly: 'Unless there's somewhere you'd rather be?'

'No, I'm good.' She hoped he would leave it at that and not question why she had no plans of her own.

'Okay, then,' he said. 'And let's speak to this barman who worked with Alice at the club.'

'The one who won't take no for an answer?'

'That's the fella.'

'Do you think his persistence eventually paid off?' asked Beth.

He considered this. 'He *could* be the man in her window, or . . .'

'Perhaps he didn't take rejection well.' She completed the sentence for him.

'Someone in this town is responsible for Alice's disappearance,' he said. 'Maybe it's him.'

*

The working men's club was dead at this hour. It had just opened up again for the evening and only a couple of hardcore regulars were in there, dotted around a large room with numerous empty tables.

'Is it always this quiet?' Black asked the young barman.

'No, it'll fill up, but not for an hour.'

'In that case, you'll be able to spare some time to talk to us,' said Black, and he showed the lad his ID. 'Ricky, is it?'

Ricky looked worried then, but Black didn't read too much into it. People often acted as if they had a guilty conscience around the police. Beth suggested they take a table close to the bar but away from customers, and Ricky sat down with them. The barman was a skinny but good-looking young man, and he had dark hair, too. Could his have been the torso in the window?

'You work with Alice Teale, behind the bar?'

'I work with Alice Teale, but not behind the bar,' he said. 'She's too young. Alice is our pot lass, and she hoovers up at the end.'

'But you work with her,' insisted Black, because the distinction was unimportant to him. 'You saw her two or three times a week here?'

'On the busy nights, yeah.'

'So that's two or three nights a week?' Black repeated.

'Thursday, Friday and Saturday night we get busy,' he said, 'but she doesn't work Fridays.' Black knew Friday was the one night Alice could hang out with her friends at the school. 'There's another lass who does it then. I barely see Alice, to be honest. She turns up at eight and starts going around the room, brings back the empty glasses and wipes down the tables.'

'What is she like?'

'How do you mean?'

Black sighed. 'I mean, what . . . is . . . she . . . like?' And he locked eyes with the man.

The barman shrugged. 'She's all right. A canny lass, I suppose. I don't have that much to do with her.'

'But you must have a bit of interaction with her,' said Beth, 'if she brings dirty glasses back to the bar?'

'Yeah, but that was about it.'

'You didn't speak to her?' said Black.

'Not really.'

He gave Ricky a look that conveyed his disbelief. 'In all the time she worked here, you never exchanged a word, not one?'

'I might have said, "Alice, can you get me a few clean pint pots?" or "Alice, can you wipe those tables down for me, pet?"'

'And that was it?'

'Pretty much.'

'She meant nothing to you?'

His eyes narrowed then, as if Black were trying to trap him. 'I didn't say she meant nothing to me. Christ, I hope you find her, and she presumably means something to someone.'

'Just not to you?'

'I didn't really have an opinion about her.'

'That's funny. I thought you did,' said Black. 'You didn't want her, then?'

Black watched him closely to see if the comment hit home. It did.

'What?' he managed.

143

'I thought you wanted Alice Teale.'

'Why would you think that?' The words came out in a rush.

'Because you said so,' said Black reasonably. 'To her, regularly.'

'When you were asking her out,' Beth reminded him, 'which you kept doing, even though she turned you down, because she already had a boyfriend.'

'Who said that?'

'Alice did,' said Black. 'Indirectly. She told her friends, and they told us.'

'That was just a bit of a laugh.'

'Was it?'

'Yeah.'

'So, you didn't actually want her to go out with you at all?'

'I asked her out, sure, but she's a bonny lass.' He shrugged, as if to imply that he asked out every pretty girl he met, and maybe he did.

'Then why did you tell us you barely spoke to her?' asked Beth.

Ricky's eyes darted from Beth to Black, as if he were weighing them both up. 'I didn't want to get in any trouble.'

'Why would admitting you asked a girl out get you into trouble, Ricky?' asked Black. 'If you'd told us the truth, you'd have been fine, but you just lied to police officers, which makes me worry.'

Ricky opened his mouth to answer but, before he could, one of his customers tapped a pound coin on the bar to attract his attention. He was holding his empty pint glass expectantly. 'You know which pump it is,' snapped Ricky. 'Help yourself and leave the money on the bar. Can't you see I'm helping the police?'

'Helping them, are you?' the old man replied archly as he went behind the bar. 'That's nice of you.'

Ricky looked angry then, but he turned away from the old man just as Beth asked, 'Why did you keep on at her, Ricky, when she'd made it clear she didn't want to know?'

'She might have *said* no,' he explained, 'but I could tell she was interested.'

'So, "no" doesn't always mean "no", then?' asked Beth.

'Yes,' he said quickly. 'No, that's not what I meant. "No" does mean "no" but I didn't think she was all that into her boyfriend.'

'How do you know?' asked Black.

'I could tell she was keen on me,' he said. 'At least, I thought she was.'

'There you go again, Ricky,' said Black, 'not taking no for an answer. That's what people have been saying about you.'

'Which people?'

'Never you mind.'

'I haven't done anything,' he protested.

'You sure about that?' asked Black. 'You don't sound like someone who takes rejection too well.'

'She didn't reject me, she just wasn't interested right there and then, and I had a bit of competition, didn't I?'

'Her boyfriend?' asked Beth.

'Not him.'

'Who, then?' demanded Black.

He didn't answer at first, then he finally settled on: 'Lots of people.'

'So, lots of people wanted to go out with her,' Beth confirmed, 'but was she seeing someone else?'

He looked quickly round the room and lowered his voice to ensure he wasn't overheard.

'Maybe. I don't know.'

'Or are you just saying that because it was really you, Ricky?' asked Black.

'No.' He shook his head.

'You said she was interested,' Beth reminded him, 'and you kept on asking her.'

'I thought she was,' he said. 'At first.'

'You ever go back to her house?'

'No.'

'So you've never been in her bedroom?' Beth persisted.

'How could I, if I've never been to her house?' he protested.

'It's a small town, Ricky,' said Black. 'People talk, especially in bars. If she was seeing another guy, you might have heard something.'

'Yeah, *if* she was seeing another guy.'

'What's that supposed to mean?'

'Nothing.'

'You know something,' Black told him. 'I know you do.'

For a moment it looked as if he was about to weaken, and Beth waited for him to reveal something, but he seemed reluctant to say it out loud in the bar. When he finally spoke his voice was low but firm. 'I don't know anything about it, all right?' Then he clammed up.

To Beth's surprise, Black actually smiled at the barman then. 'Okay, Ricky,' he said. 'But if we find out you're lying, we're going to be straight back round here looking for you.'

It was darker outside when they were finally finished with Ricky, the whole of Collemby made greyer thanks to a covering of black clouds. Rain made the pavements shine.

'Looks like our sunny days are finally over,' said Beth.

'Let's try the Dirty Donkey,' said Black. 'Hopefully, Sophie Mayhew will be there by now and we can talk to her at the scene of the crime, so to speak.' He meant the drink that had been thrown into her face by Alice Teale's brother, and, though they were obviously focusing on that, it was the rumours involving Daniel and Alice and what light Sophie could shed on these that were of most interest to them. Beth didn't know what to think. It still seemed far-fetched, but hadn't Ricky just said that he had 'competition' for Alice, and not just from her boyfriend?

They crossed the car park towards the pub and Beth said, 'Is this really the best way to interview someone?'

'You get more out of people in an informal environment,' Black told her. 'They let their guard down in pubs and talk to you like a normal person. If you haul them to the station for questioning under caution, they get apprehensive and clam up. Also, solicitors complicate matters.' As if anticipating her fears, he said, 'We're not really questioning Sophie about the disappearance of Alice Teale, just asking her about the incident with Daniel so we can learn a bit more about him.'

'But' she began hesitantly, 'in front of her friends?'

'I especially want her friends to be there.' But he didn't tell her why. 'Come on. I'm buying.'

'Wait, aren't we on duty?'

'At this hour? We're just going for a drink and having a chat with the locals, if anyone asks.'

21

The Black Stallion was always busy on a Friday night. You could tell by the number of bar staff and how used they were to calmly serving large numbers of people.

Beth and Black ordered drinks and, while they waited for them, Beth scanned the room for Sophie. She'd checked her pictures on Instagram and knew what the girl looked like. Sophie wore a lot of black clothing and dark eye make-up. She was one of those unsmiling young girls who looked almost permanently defiant.

'She's not here yet,' Beth told him.

'Let's hope this isn't the one night of the year she chooses not to show.'

'Worst-case scenario – you've got a pint in your hand and intelligent company.'

He pretended to look around. 'Where?'

'That was very nearly a joke.'

At that point, an older member of the bar staff walked by. He saw Black and said, 'All right?', like he knew the detective. When he was gone, Beth gave Black a quizzical look, but he just shrugged, as if he didn't know why the man had bothered to greet him.

Beth noticed something then. 'I think those might be her mates,' she said, jerking her head slightly to the far corner of the bar. They certainly looked familiar, from what she had seen of Sophie's social media pics, which had a number of group shots.

'Great. They're here, and she isn't.'

They took a table at the other end of the room which gave them a view of the far corner, where Sophie's friends had congregated.

'Did that bloke know you?' she asked.

He shook his head then immediately changed the subject. 'Doesn't it bother you, being out in Collemby on a Friday night? Haven't you got a million better things to do?'

It was her turn to evade the question. 'I don't have a family either,' she said, 'and I also want to find Alice.'

He took another sip, then said, 'Yeah, well, don't want it too much.' Was he warning her not to be too devastated if the girl turned up dead?

Black looked at his watch again so she said, 'Second time you've done that. Got a hot date?'

'No,' he said quickly. 'I promised a friend I'd drop something off for him.'

'Okay.'

'But I can do that afterwards.' Then, to Beth's amazement, he said, 'You can come if you like. There'll be food.'

Beth hesitated. Normally, she would have welcomed the opportunity to break down the barrier of formality between her and a new colleague, but she felt uncomfortable at the thought of eating with someone who had gunned down a civilian.

'Well,' Beth said, after a pause that she belatedly realized was far too lengthy, 'I do like food.'

They had nearly finished their drinks when the rear

door of the pub opened and a girl with a Goth look about her walked in and was greeted by the group of mates in the corner. One of them let her take his seat and he went to the bar to get her a drink. Beth and Black got up and walked over. They introduced themselves to Sophie and the group of girls and boys sipping cider and beer. Beth thought they might not want to talk to two detectives about Alice's disappearance, but it seemed it was the only topic of conversation, judging by the animated way they asked questions or offered up theories they'd heard, most of which seemed little more than wild rumour.

'Is it true she was pregnant?' asked one of the girls, and Beth wondered if there was any substance to her question.

'Not that we're aware of,' she told the girl. 'Where did you hear that?'

'Oh, just around.' The girl seemed to shrink into her seat then, as if she were worried they thought she knew something they didn't.

It took a while for them to settle down and listen to Beth. She noticed how Black hung back and let her do most of the talking. Did he think a young woman would be more likely to get some answers from these kids than a burly man in middle age?

Beth asked if they had noticed anything strange or out of the ordinary in Alice's life. That was enough to get the reaction she was looking for.

'You should start with her brother,' said the girl who had asked if Alice was pregnant. The way she said it made it clear she felt there was something very wrong with him.

'Why do you say that?'

'He's not right, is he? In the head, I mean.'

Beth noticed one of the girl's friends look down then, and another looked away, as if they either didn't agree with that assessment or thought it a harsh one under the circumstances; his sister was missing, after all. 'What makes you say that?' she asked.

'He threw a drink in my friend's face.' She jerked her head at Sophie.

'Where was this?' asked Beth, as if she didn't know already.

'Here,' confirmed Sophie.

'When?'

'A couple of weeks back.'

Beth nodded slowly. 'So he threw a drink at you' – the girl nodded – 'for no reason?'

She looked sheepish. 'He *thought* he had a reason, but he didn't, not really.' Some of the fire seemed to have gone out of her already.

'What reason did he think he had?'

'Said I'd been talking about him behind his back, and I never.'

'He was wrong about that, then?' Beth wasn't expecting her to admit it. 'What did he think you'd been saying?'

'Stuff about him and his sister.'

'What kind of stuff?'

'That they were creepy together and not like a normal brother and sister.'

'I see,' said Beth. 'And were they creepy together?'

Before Sophie could answer, the other girl cut in to back up her friend. 'They were always hugging and touching each other, if that's what you mean.'

152

'They were tactile?' asked Beth.

'Yeah, but it was more than that, and they told each other everything.' She snorted. 'I don't tell my brother anything,' she said, but no one laughed. The others were looking everywhere but at her, Sophie or the two detectives. There was an absence of solidarity here now. Beth could feel it.

'They didn't have a normal brother–sister relationship, then?' asked Beth, her tone neutral.

'It didn't look normal,' Sophie mumbled.

'Sorry?' Beth was deliberately challenging the girl to say it clearly.

'It didn't *look* normal,' she almost shouted.

'Did anyone else think that?' Beth glanced at the other teenagers, but no one looked back at her. Sophie quickly interjected.

'Lots of people.'

'How do you know?'

She shrugged. 'People talk. We all did, about them.'

'Oh, so you *did* talk about him and his sister, then? Just now, you said you didn't.'

She folded her arms defensively. 'I meant, I wasn't the only one.'

'But he heard you were one of the people talking about him and Alice,' said Beth, and Sophie didn't contradict this. 'You'd been saying that his relationship with his sister wasn't a normal one . . . meaning it was sexual.'

'I never said that!' Sophie looked panicked.

'You didn't have to. You said it wasn't normal. You were implying they had an unnatural relationship. Strongly implying it, in fact.'

153

'I never said . . .' she began, and her eyes darted from right to left, looking for support, but none came, not even from the girl who'd interrupted before. 'I never meant that.'

'What was this rumour doing the rounds about them, then? Specifically, I mean.'

'What rumour?' Everyone's eyes were averted now, so Beth knew they understood that there was a specific story about the Teale siblings.

'Gossip everyone heard that made people believe there was something not quite right about Alice and Daniel? A couple of public hugs and a few shared confidences wouldn't lead anyone to believe they were more than just close. It was something else. I can easily find out, so you might as well tell me.'

Sophie looked towards her friends, but no one gave her any clues as to the wisdom of telling Beth the truth or not, so she began tentatively. 'Well, the story was that Alice caught him.' And she looked as if she didn't want to go on.

'Doing what?'

'She came home early one day and he was alone in his room.' The girl who had been sticking up for Sophie actually let out a gasp, then, that was part nervous laughter, part embarrassment. Beth ignored her.

'What was he doing in his room?'

'I think you can guess.' She rolled her eyes in a knowing, jaded way.

'You're implying he was masturbating and Alice walked in on him. That would be embarrassing for them both, but it doesn't mean anything.'

'Yeah, but . . .'

'What? Come on, Sophie, out with it. You've obviously

discussed this before with your mates. They all know about it, I can tell, and we don't embarrass easily.'

'All right,' she said. 'If you want to hear the truth, she didn't leave.'

'She stayed in the room?'

'Yeah.' She sniggered. 'And she – you know – gave him a hand.'

A couple of her friends lost control then and began sniggering.

Until that point, Beth had been trying to keep an open mind regarding the gossip about Alice and Daniel's unnatural relationship. It sounded messed up, but she supposed it could actually have been true. Sophie's description of what supposedly happened between them ended those thoughts instantly. 'Right,' said Beth dryly. 'Sounds plausible.'

Black cut in then, his tone blunt. 'You saw it, did you?' he asked Sophie. 'You were there, too?'

'Eh?' The girl looked panicked. ''Course not.'

'Then how do you know about it?'

'Word got round. Someone told someone and, soon, everyone knew. That's how we heard.'

'Okay, Sophie, explain this to me, then,' Black demanded. 'How did word get round? Who would tell anyone about that, if it actually happened? Would Daniel tell someone? Doubt it. Would Alice mention it to one of her friends? No chance. So, if not them, then who?' The girl did not answer. 'Was it you? I think it was.'

'It wasn't me,' said Sophie, but she looked incredibly guilty. It hadn't taken long for Black to completely undermine her. A few well-chosen questions from an experienced interrogator and Sophie Mayhew's credibility was hanging by a thread.

Beth knew just what to ask the girl next. 'What happened on New Year's Eve, Sophie?'

'What?'

'You went off with Daniel, didn't you?'

'No, I never –'

'Yes, you did,' said one of her friends, almost without thinking, and turned to Beth. 'They were gone for ages.'

'You really wanted him,' said Beth. 'That's what we were told.'

She didn't deny it. 'Yeah, well, I thought he was cool, but that was before I knew how weird he was.'

'You mean, on New Year's Eve, he told you that little story about his sister?'

''Course not!'

'So how did you know he was weird?'

'He just was. He acted strange.'

'Did he act strange when he turned you down, Sophie, was that it?' asked Beth. 'Or were you hurt because he never called you afterwards?'

'No.' She looked completely panicked now. 'Who's been saying that?'

'It's pretty obvious,' Beth told her. 'And it explains why you would make up a sick story like that to get your own back. '"What's the worst thing I can say about him?" Was that what you asked yourself, or were you just jealous because he actually loved his sister but didn't care about you?'

'That wasn't it. I never liked him that much, even then.'

Another voice chipped in then, a girl from the other

end of the table, speaking for the first time. 'You told me you did.' And it sounded true, because it was said with just the right amount of conviction, even relish.

'I never.' But Sophie's protest was weak.

'Who told you that sick rumour about Daniel and his sister?' Black was addressing them all. 'Was it this one?' He jerked his head towards Sophie; he didn't even want to use her name.

A couple of them nodded, and one or two of them mumbled that it had been. They were hanging Sophie out to dry.

'It wasn't me that started it.'

'Of course it was,' said Black.

'I just passed on what I was told.'

'Who told it to you, then?'

'I can't remember.'

'How convenient. I've been doing this for a long time, Sophie, and I know a made-up story when I hear one. This was just juicy enough to go around a small town in days.'

The girl looked like she wanted to be anywhere but there. 'Daniel knew it was you straight away, didn't he? That's why he threw that drink in your face,' he told the shocked girl, and the others stared at Sophie, as if truly seeing her for the first time.

'*I'd* have thrown a drink in her face,' Beth told Black as they exited the pub a moment later.

They were halfway across the market square and heading for Black's car when a man suddenly emerged from the working men's club and came towards them at speed. It was Ricky. He'd obviously seen them both go into the

Dirty Donkey and had been looking out for them ever since. It was a short jog, but he was out of condition and breathless when he reached Beth and Lucas. He opened his mouth to speak, but all that came out at first was a gasp.

'You got something to tell us, Ricky?' Black feigned surprise.

'I didn't want to say anything in there,' he managed, and he jerked his thumb back at the club. 'Too many nosy buggers.'

'Out with it, then,' urged Black.

'It's not what you think. You've got it all wrong about her,' he said. 'Alice, I mean.'

'If you've got something to tell us, then say it. Hints aren't helpful.'

'All right,' he said after a moment. 'You're barking up the wrong tree. She wasn't really interested in guys. I thought she was, but it turns out she wasn't.'

'She has a boyfriend, Ricky,' Beth reminded him.

'Yeah, I wonder why.' His tone was sarcastic. 'Maybe to deflect attention?'

'From what?'

'From what she really liked.'

'Oh God,' said Black. 'You're one of those blokes, aren't you? You think you're God's gift to women and, if one of them doesn't fancy you, then she must be a lesbian. I knew guys like you existed. I've just never met one – till now.'

He flushed then. 'I'm not making this up,' he blustered. 'Alice Teale is a dyke. She's on the other bus.'

'Bullshit,' said Black.

'It's not bullshit, and if you don't believe me, then ask that friend of hers.'

'Chloe?' asked Beth.

'No, the other one,' he said. 'The fit one – and what a bloody waste that is.'

'Alice Teale is not in a relationship with Kirstie,' said Beth scornfully. 'No one has told us that.'

'How come they kissed, then?'

Black gave Ricky a disbelieving look.

'I saw it!'

'You saw Alice kissing Kirstie?'

'Yeah.'

'But a kiss doesn't always mean . . .' Beth began.

'This wasn't a peck on the cheek. It was a full-on snog.'

'And you actually saw this?' said Black. 'How? Were you peeping in through her window?'

'It wasn't just me. A bunch of us saw them, and it was the kind of kiss you can't fake.'

Until that point, it had never crossed Beth's mind that, if Alice Teale was really seeing someone else, it might be a woman. In her journal she talked about a '*He*' not a 'her', and Alice's neighbour had clearly seen a man's torso, not a woman's, through her bedroom window, but there was something about the certainty in Ricky's manner that made her feel she couldn't entirely dismiss that notion now. Was this why Alice found her boyfriend so unsatisfying? She preferred girls? Was there one more secret Alice Teale had been keeping from the world, and how, if at all, was this linked to the girl's disappearance?

'Where exactly was this, Ricky?' asked Beth.

He pointed back the way they had come. 'The pub you've just been in.'

22

'Well,' said Black as they watched Ricky walk back into the working men's club, 'I wasn't expecting that.'

'*My lips are sealed*,' said Beth.

'What?'

'That's what Alice said about Kirstie's secret, in the journal, remember? *My lips are sealed, which is kind of appropriate, really*,' she recited. 'She must have been talking about their kiss.'

'She must have been,' conceded Black, who was taken aback by the notion of Alice Teale and Kirstie being more than just friends.

'We'd better speak to Kirstie again.'

'Yes.' Black looked at his watch. 'But not now. It'll keep. You in a hurry to get back?' he asked, once they were in his car.

To an empty flat? Of course not.

'No, and you promised me food.'

'Okay,' he said. 'I have to pick something up first.' *Could he be any more vague?* 'But it's on the way.'

Anything to avoid another omelette or microwaved jacket potato. 'And you can guarantee food?'

'Yes.'

'Then I'm in.'

*

He drove them to a tiny former fishing town and weaved through the streets until he found the road he was looking for. He parked by a broken street lamp and said, 'Wait here.'

Beth watched as Black left the car, walked a few yards down the street then turned and climbed some steps towards a large building that had been converted into apartments. If she leaned to one side and craned her neck, she could just make out his profile through a gap in the bushes. What was he up to? He rang the bell and the door was answered by another man, who left Black standing on the step. Moments later, he returned with a large cardboard box, which he set down on the step. Black disappeared from view for a moment while he bent down, presumably to examine the contents. Seconds later, satisfied, he reached into his pocket, took out his wallet and paid the man with a small bundle of notes. Beth leaned back into a more normal position in time to see him re-emerge, carrying the box, which he put in the boot before joining her in the car.

Without explanation, he drove away.

'What's in the box?' she asked.

'Cocaine,' he said. 'Ninety per cent pure, finest Bolivian and, if you don't squeal, I'll give you a slice of the action.'

'You never should have given up the stand-up comedy,' she said dryly.

Their destination turned out to be three ancient railway carriages that had been linked together on an isolated plot of land high up by the side of a main road overlooking the Northumbrian coastline. The carriages were freshly painted and had been lovingly restored, lights glowed inside them and there were tiny curtains in the windows. There was a prefab office nearby, a static caravan off to one side, and a sign at the edge of the gravel car park explained that the 'Sidings Diner' was opening soon.

Black carried the box up the steps of the first railway carriage and Beth followed him. He rapped on the door and a woman in her early thirties answered. 'Lucas!' she exclaimed brightly. Was there another side to her grumpy colleague, and a parallel universe in which people were actually pleased to see this man? The woman noticed her then. 'And you brought a friend.'

'This is my colleague, Beth.' He emphasized the word 'colleague' to forestall any notion that she was a friend.

'Hi, I'm Gemma.' She stretched past Black to briefly shake Beth's hand. 'Come in, both of you.'

They walked in on a cosy, almost-finished scene, tables standing ready to be laid for dinner. The original seats had been taken out of the carriages and the space this made had been used to create an American-style diner, complete with framed vintage posters of US adverts and an ancient jukebox in one corner. A man in his mid-thirties was standing on a small stool while he worked to rewire a light in the ceiling of the carriage. 'Lucas, how are you doing, mate?' He stepped down from the stool and came towards them. 'You're a bit early, though. The opening isn't till next week.'

'I know. I brought you something for *that*.' And he nodded towards the jukebox. He set the cardboard box down on the floor and then told Beth, 'Adam and Gemma are responsible for this . . .'

'Monstrosity?' Adam laughed and Gemma clasped his hand.

'Don't talk about our baby like that,' she mock-scolded him.

'What've you got in the box?' Adam sounded like an excitable child and he bent to examine its contents. 'Seven-inch records,' he noted approvingly. 'And they're already dinked!'

'Dinked?' asked Beth.

'The holes in the middle are enlarged so they can be played on a jukebox,' explained Adam. 'Where did you get all these?'

'I scoured dozens of record stores across the region till I had enough.'

'Really?' asked Gemma, impressed.

'No,' he laughed. 'I bought them all off eBay from some guy down the road who didn't know what he was sitting on. Got the lot for thirty-five quid.'

'Thirty-five? There's got to be . . .' Adam was flicking through the classic vinyl singles animatedly.

'Two hundred,' said Lucas. 'I didn't count them, but I know where he lives, so . . .'

' "River Deep – Mountain High" . . . "Hotel California" . . . "Waterloo Sunset" . . .' Each title made him more excited. 'Pay the man, Gemma!'

'Of course.'

Black shook his head. 'A housewarming present.' Then he corrected himself: 'A diner-warming present.'

'Thank you,' said Adam.

'Stay for dinner at least, please, both of you. I'll make a bowl of chilli.'

This was the food he had promised Beth, but now, for Gemma's benefit, he acted surprised. 'Well,' he said, 'if you're sure it's no trouble.'

They ate in the carriage, to the sound of classic sixties and seventies soul songs coming from the old jukebox. That, and the subdued lighting, gave the diner a mellow vibe, or maybe it was the wine. Gemma insisted on topping up Beth. 'Why not,' she told her, 'if Lucas is driving?'

'Why not indeed?'

'Are you both on this Alice Teale case?' asked Gemma.

'We saw you on the news, Lucas,' explained Adam. 'Your press conference.'

'Yeah, we're both on it.'

'It's terrible. Are you going to get someone for it?' Adam asked them. 'I mean, I know you can't really talk about it, but . . .'

'If someone has abducted her, or harmed her, then yes, we'll get them.'

Adam seemed confused. 'Well, what other explanation could there be?'

'She might have run off,' said Black. 'People do some-times.'

'But you don't believe that,' said Adam. 'I can tell.'

Black shrugged in a non-committal way, but Adam was warming to the subject. 'Did she have a boyfriend? I bet it was the boyfriend.' Adam didn't seem to have picked up on the fact that Black wasn't keen to discuss it.

'Adam,' warned Gemma.

'What? It often is,' he protested. 'What do you think, Beth?'

And when all eyes turned to her, Beth said, 'I think . . . this chilli is great,' and Gemma laughed. 'And I love your diner.'

'Then you must come to the opening,' Gemma assured her. 'Right, Lucas?'

'Er,' was all he managed.

'Oh no,' said Beth. 'Lucas might want to bring someone else.'

'That'll be the day,' said Gemma.

Adam instantly started singing 'That'll Be the Day' by Buddy Holly, then he stopped and wondered out loud, 'Do we have that one, do you think?' He meant in the pile of 45s Black had brought him. 'You should defin itely come, Beth. You two might be the only ones who do.'

'He's such a pessimist!' said Gemma. 'But yes, do come, please.'

'Thanks.' Beth was won over by their enthusiasm. 'I will.'

It was a balmy night now the rain had cleared, so after dinner they went outside to admire the view from the back of the diner. You could hear the sound of the waves as the North Sea crashed against the rocks far below. Black peered down at them and said, 'You are insured, right? In case of erosion.'

'Very funny,' said Adam, and they moved closer to the edge. Gemma hung back and chatted to Beth as they walked round the rest of the site.

'It's starting to feel very real,' she said.

'How long have you been working on it?'

'Oh, ages. We've dreamed about it since we first met,

pretty much. Now, that dream is close to coming true, and I should feel excited but, actually, I'm completely terrified in case it bombs.'

'It'll do really well.'

'God, I hope so,' said Gemma. 'What about you? Did you always want to be a police officer?'

'Not always,' admitted Beth. 'But when I graduated I realized I didn't like the idea of an office job. I think I wanted . . .' She wasn't sure how to finish the sentence.

'To make a difference?'

'Maybe. I don't know. God, I sound like an airhead.'

'You can't be if you made it through college and now you're a detective. Your folks must be proud.'

'Not really.'

Gemma clasped her hand to her mouth. 'Please tell me you have parents!' She meant she would be mortified if they were dead.

'One of each,' said Beth, 'I just meant they're not too happy I'm in the police.'

'Why ever not?'

'Mum worries I might be killed in the line of duty. She reads the newspaper and frets. For Dad, it's different. He's opposed to it ideologically.'

'Really?'

'Yeah. He's a politics lecturer and has always thought the police were a politically motivated tool of the right used to suppress the working classes.' She shook her head at this idiocy. 'Though he still called them when we were burgled, funnily enough.'

'Disowned you, has he?'

'Not quite, but when I see them I don't talk about work.'

'That's a shame. Do you enjoy the job?' Beth nodded. 'And what about working with Lucas?'

How could she answer that one honestly? For a moment Beth wondered what her father would have made of Lucas Black. The former army man would be the personification of everything her dad loathed about the force. Beth herself still hadn't worked the man out. Clearly, he was human, he had at least two friends and was well thought of by them, but how could she reconcile that with him having killed a man? She wanted to answer Gemma's question about Lucas with some of her own, but that might not end well. Gemma would obviously be on his side and might take exception to being questioned, so Beth chickened out. 'It's great,' she said, with as much enthusiasm as she could fake.

'Really?' Gemma sounded surprised. 'I hated him at first.' And they both laughed in shock at this admission. 'I did. I thought he was a huge grump and, when he wasn't all moody, he was basically silent.'

'I get that a lot,' said Beth.

'It takes a while to get to know him. He's been treated pretty poorly in the past.' And when Beth said nothing, she went on, 'By his ex and the job.'

'Were he and Adam in the army together?' Beth jerked her head towards the two men, who were deep in conversation and walking surprisingly close to the cliff edge.

Gemma laughed. 'God, no. Adam wouldn't last five minutes in the army. They played five-a-side football together and used to get a beer afterwards. It was months before Adam even found out Lucas was a detective. I don't think he trusts many people.' Gemma seemed to

167

care about Black's well-being. 'Lucas has too much time to sit on his own thinking about how things should have worked out. He's been a great friend to Adam and me, though. Those jukebox records,' she said. 'Just perfect, and I don't know anyone else who would have gone to the trouble to get them but made out it was no trouble at all.'

'Then, thanks to you, I've seen his good side,' said Beth.

'He does have one.' Gemma grinned. 'He just keeps it well hidden.'

The Journal of Alice Teale

Ever been close to the edge of a cliff or the top of a tall building and had a sudden urge to throw yourself off it, knowing you could end it all in only a few seconds? I have.

Haven't we all?

The French have a phrase for it (*Quelle surprise!*). They call it *l'appel du vide*, which means 'the call of the void'.

I sometimes feel the void is beckoning me. Late at night, when I think about cutting myself and actually go so far as to take a knife from the kitchen; one of the long ones with a serrated blade. I lie on my bed, roll up my sleeve and press the teeth of the knife right next to the skin, then I wonder what it would feel like to draw that knife across my arm. I contemplate the deep wound it would make and how dark the blood would be, whether it would seep or pump out and if the pain would be enough to blot out everything else I am feeling. I don't want to feel anything any more, because it's all too much.

Then common sense kicks in and I start thinking about practical things, like not being able to control how deep the teeth cut into me or how I could hit a big vein, possibly even an artery; my knowledge of human biology is so insufficient, I'm sure I wouldn't be able to miss them. I contemplate how it would feel to see my blood pumping out right in front of me and the helplessness I'd experience if I couldn't stop it. Imagine bleeding out and dying on your bed because you'd had another bad day and just wanted to stop yourself thinking about it. I wonder if that's ever happened to anyone? Bound to have, I reckon. How many so-called suicides were really just anxious teenagers who accidentally went a bit too far and couldn't stop what they had started?

So I go back down to the kitchen, put the knife away then pour myself a drink instead. That helps to make the pain go away, too, and it takes a hell of a lot longer to kill you.

23

It was no great surprise to find another envelope on his desk. Black read the words from Alice's journal on the wisdom of cutting herself then handed the page to Beth as soon as she arrived at the major-incident room.

As Beth read the entry, he handed her another half-page. 'This arrived at the same time.' It contained only a few words, written in a jittery, urgent scrawl.

He stayed silent as Beth read the words aloud.

'*Yesterday I went to the roof. It's higher than it seems from the ground, but everything seems scarier when you're looking down, doesn't it? You could climb out on to all that wobbly scaffolding. If you could just hold your nerve, then it would work.*' She looked up at Black before finishing: '*I just need the courage to see it through.*'

She commented, 'That's a pretty clear indication of Alice Teale's state of mind. She didn't do it, obviously, not from the school roof, but it reads like a suicide note, or the precursor to one. She had been up on the roof, too,' she recalled. 'Chris told me he had to call her down.' Then she said, 'I'm itching to get into that school. Her teachers must know something about Alice.'

'Particularly the young one who has been giving her lifts,' he agreed. 'It's strange, though, isn't it? No one has said she suffered from depression or exhibited any suicidal tendencies. But the pressure she was under to be' he shrugged – '"perfect", as Tony put it, was getting to her.

She told him that, and her notes about playing lots of parts and acting them all out does show that her mind was troubled.'

'She felt she was living a lie,' said Beth. 'Maybe the pressure did become too great and she seriously entertained the idea of ending it all.' They contemplated this for a moment. 'But if she did, then why haven't we found a body?'

'That's the big question,' he said. 'And we won't answer it sitting round here. Come on.'

'Where are we heading?'

'I've been thinking about the Teale family,' said Black, 'and how things don't seem quite right with them, particularly Alice's father. We already know he has a temper, and his alibi isn't cast-iron. Now we find Alice has been thinking about self-harming and throwing herself off a roof. That's a bit extreme, and maybe the issues start at home.'

'It's possible,' said Beth cautiously. 'Ronnie Teale's wife and son aren't his biggest fans, but they don't suspect him of involvement in Alice's disappearance. Even Daniel said he would never hurt Alice.'

'Maybe he's too close to the problem,' said Black. 'But there's one member of the Teale family we haven't spoken to yet.'

'The grandfather.'

'He lives in one of those cottages right by the school. He didn't see Alice on the day she disappeared, but I do want to speak to him about his son-in-law.'

'And you said "I" again,' she observed, and when he didn't explain further, she said, 'Which means you want me to ask Kirstie about that kiss.'

*

Alice Teale's grandfather, Stan, was close to Alice, and she had to have walked right by his home just before she disappeared.

The cottages were just yards from the school, in two long, neat rows. Black scanned the doors until he found the right one. He knocked, but there was no answer, so he went around the back. The little cottage had a sizeable garden to its rear and Alice's grandfather was busy tending it. Black called the man's name and he turned around. The detective introduced himself and told him why he was here. 'Bloody hell, son,' he said. 'Don't do that to me. I thought you'd come with bad news.'

'I'm sorry,' said Black, 'but if we don't tell people who we are right from the off, they tend to get upset later.'

'Aye, I bet they do.' Black wondered if the old man shared the inherent distrust of the police he always seemed to detect in former mining communities.

'Would it be okay if I had a chat with you about your granddaughter?' he asked.

'Howay in,' said the old man. 'I'll put the kettle on.'

Once the tea was made, Stan brought Black outside again and they sat on two rickety kitchen chairs on the patio, looking out at the garden. 'Nice spot you have here,' said the detective. 'It catches the light.'

'Anyone can have one of these cottages, you know,' the old man said dryly. 'All you have to do is join a very long waiting list and try not to pop your clogs in the meantime.'

'I'm sure you earned it.'

'I was brought up to work hard and bring a wage home

to my family. I did that until my daughter grew up then got married, and I thought I'd have a few years with my Ivy before God called me' – he was staring straight ahead and not betraying any emotion – 'but he took her instead. Now I'm on my own, my daughter doesn't pop round much, on account of her job and tending to her own family. I've got my garden and I've got my granddaughter. If God takes her from me as well, I swear I'll burn his church to the ground.'

Black decided to deflect him from that thought. 'You don't see much of your grandson, then?'

'He's a man,' he said, in excuse for the lack of contact. 'They're always off out doing things, aren't they? I would be, too, if I still had the energy. Women are more caring.'

'Not all of them,' observed Black. 'But your granddaughter obviously is. How often does she pop in?'

'Every couple of days. Sometimes she comes up specially, but mostly it's a look in on me after school. We have a cup of tea and a biscuit before she heads home.'

'She didn't call in on the night she went missing?'

'No.' He shook his head. Perhaps he was thinking that, if only she had, Alice might still be here.

'And you didn't see her walk by?'

'I was watching the telly in the front room.' He meant he couldn't have seen the path at the back of the cottages as his lounge window faced the other way. 'I didn't think she'd be there that late, otherwise I'd have left the back door open. That's what I usually do, so she knows I'm in.'

It seemed a quaint idea to leave a back door open, but Stan probably didn't have that much to steal and he was still a formidable-looking man. He might be old, thought Black, but you wouldn't want to mess with him.

'She popped in a lot,' confirmed Black, 'even though she was busy elsewhere, with her job and school activities? She must have very little free time.'

'It's hectic, I think, what with her studying and all.'

'They must hardly see her at home.' Black dropped the observation in lightly, and the old man made a dismissive noise through his teeth.

'Her fatha's a . . .' And whatever word he was about to use was lost when he went off on a tangent. 'Don't get me wrong, he'll be worried sick about Alice – he loves her, I'm certain of that, but . . .'

'He gives her a hard time?'

'I was a strict father, and I make no apology for that. My daughter has manners and knows how to behave in company. When she was little, she'd get a smack if she played up, so I'm not one to criticize another man for scolding his daughter when it's needed.'

'But it's not always needed?'

'She can barely breathe, man!' Black was startled by the ferocity of the statement. A bird had flown from the bushes at the suddenness of the outburst. 'She could never do anything right. I used to say to her when she was small, "You must have done something to cause it," but after a while I realized he was never happy, no matter what she did. It's always wrong.'

'You ever intervene?'

'You can't, can you? Another man's family,' he explained.

'Your family, too,' Black reminded him, but he knew the old man didn't view it that way.

'If he'd been hitting her or my daughter, then he'd have got a good hiding, but this was just words.'

Just words. Black contemplated that for a moment and wondered at the impact words might have on a girl like Alice, then Stan continued, 'I saw him down the club once and bought him a pint. I tried to raise it with him, gentle, like, but I didn't get very far.'

'He tell you to mind your own business?'

'In so many words. He said he was responsible for his daughter until she was married and somebody else's problem. That's how he described her, as a problem. Then he said, "No one ever told you how to raise Abigail," meaning that I shouldn't tell him how to bring up Alice.'

Ronnie had chosen the best way to silence his father-in-law, by invoking the outmoded right of a man to run his house and order his family around as he saw fit.

'Do you think there was anything more to it?' asked Black tentatively. 'Anything going on inside the house, I mean. Was it just controlling, unforgiving behaviour from her father or something' – he was choosing his words carefully now – 'worse?'

'Worse? Like what?'

'I don't know.' But Black could tell the old man knew what he was inferring, because he looked alarmed.

'Don't you go reading too much into what I just said. Ronnie can be a bit of a bully and I might not like him all that much, but Alice is his daughter and he would never lay a hand on her like that.'

'Good,' said Black quickly, as if he were able to immediately dismiss the notion and move on, though he reasoned that if something more sinister was going on in

Alice's home, then Stan wasn't likely to know too much about it. Alice could have confided in him, but then her grandfather would likely have ended up brawling with her father in the street. She would have known that and probably done anything she could to avoid it.

They sat in silence for a while until Black asked him, 'Where do you think she is?'

'I haven't a clue, son. That's your job, isn't it?' His tone softened then. 'I genuinely do not know where my granddaughter is, and it is breaking my heart.' He had to make an effort to compose himself before continuing: 'Do you think I wouldn't be out there now looking for her if she'd run off with some young bloke and I knew who it was? 'Course I would.'

'Okay.'

'Just find her and bring her home.'

Black drained his cup of tea. 'You didn't see anyone else kicking about that night around the time she came out of school? That boyfriend of hers, or a stranger, perhaps?'

'I didn't see her boyfriend or anybody who wouldn't normally be here, but I wasn't out back when she was last seen.'

'Did you see anyone at all that night, either leaving the school or milling around outside it?'

'Evie from next door,' he said helplessly, knowing this would be of no use to the detective. 'I saw Archie Thorogood on his way back from fishing, and Dolly got dropped off by her daughter – she'd been for her tea and I saw Happy Harry.' He said that last bit as if Black would know who he meant.

'Happy Harry?' The old man nodded. 'Does this chap have a surname?'

'Must do,' he said. 'But I don't know what it is. He was round the back.'

'Okay. What was he doing round the back?'

'He was on the cadge, like always.' Then he said: 'He's soft in the head. That's why they call him Happy Harry, 'cos he's happy just plodding round. You see him all over town, begging. Some folk are daft enough to give him money, but he spends it all on booze.'

'He's an alcoholic?' asked Black.

'He begs in the marketplace in the morning and round here in the evening, so what do you think? Don't know where he gets the booze from, since he's been barred out of every pub in town. He'll ask the old wifies round here for summat – food or money or a cup of tea in that manky old flask he carries.'

'Did he knock on your door that night?'

'No,' he said. 'He was fishing inside the bins.'

'He was looking in the rubbish bins?'

'He's always doing it.'

'How can I find this Happy Harry?'

'He'll be wandering around the town,' he said. 'Why do you care about him?'

'He might have seen something if he was hanging round the back of your house.'

The old man seemed to consider this a reasonable assumption. 'Maybe,' he said. 'If you can get any sense out of him.'

'Have you seen him since that night?'

'Now you come to mention it, no, I haven't.'

'Where does he bed down? In the town?'

'No.' He shook his head. 'He wouldn't be safe when the

pubs turn out. There're some mad young buggers in this town. They'd probably set him alight.'

'So where, then?'

'No idea,' he said. 'It's not as if he has an address.'

Black got to his feet and thanked the man. A breeze went through the back gardens then, and it carried a rank smell. Alice's grandfather must have smelled it, too, because he said, 'That's Billy on the corner,' then added: 'Well, not him, his garden. He's obsessed with his bloody roses, piles loads of manure by them and swears it makes all the difference.'

'And does it?' asked Black.

'Must do. He grows a bonny rose,' conceded the old man. 'Trouble is, his whole garden smells of shite.' He shook his head again, at the idiocy of that. 'And you know what they say about shitting on your own doorstep.'

24

Kirstie didn't seem thrilled to find Beth standing there when she opened the door.

'Hello, Kirstie, I was wondering if I could have another word with you.' As Beth said this, the sound of hammering from the lounge reached her.

'My dad's laying a new carpet.'

'I was hoping for a chat in private.'

Was Kirstie surprised? She didn't look it. 'We can talk in my room,' she said, and trudged up the stairs while Beth followed.

Once inside her room, Kirstie sat on the bed and left Beth standing. She looked around and saw an old wicker chair next to the wardrobe. 'Can I?' she asked.

'It's a free country.'

Beth dragged the chair over to the end of Kirstie's bed and sat down.

'We've been speaking to a number of people about Alice' – Beth didn't mention Ricky at this point – 'and we learned a little more about her personal life.'

'Why are you so interested in her personal life?'

'We are looking for reasons why she might have run off, or, if she's been taken by someone, who it might be. In cases like this, it's often someone close to the' – she almost said 'victim' – 'missing person who is responsible.'

Beth had intended to set the scene. She'd planned to go

for a gentle, gradual build-up about Alice Teale's boy-friend and her ex-boyfriend, plus anyone else she might have taken an interest in. Only then was she going to try to ease the question of Kirstie's feelings for Alice, and whether they were reciprocated, into the conversation. But something made her abandon that tactic. Perhaps it was the girl's defensiveness that made her want to unsettle Kirstie into revealing something.

'Tell me about the kiss,' she said, and waited to see if Kirstie knew what she meant. Would she deny it ever happened?

'Oh, that.' Kirstie laughed it away, but without humour. 'You heard about it then? It seemed like a good idea at the time, but we were wasted. We'd been on the tequila at my house while we were getting ready. You know what they say about tequila – "One tequila, two tequila, three tequila, floor."' And she brought the palm of her hand down on to the bed to mimic someone hitting that floor.

'Then you went to the pub?'

Kirstie just nodded. 'It's a lot cheaper to get hammered before you go.'

'So whose idea was it? To kiss, I mean, not to drink a lot of tequila.'

'Hers.' Was it Beth's imagination or had Kirstie said that just a little too quickly and too brightly?

'And she just planted a kiss on you in front of a bunch of people in the bar.'

'Yeah – well, no.'

'Which?'

'When I said it was her idea, it wasn't Alice who suggested it, but it wasn't me either. She just went along with it. We'd been drinking for ages and having a really good laugh, but we started getting attention from some of the older guys in the pub. They thought they had a chance with us and we couldn't get rid of them. Then one of them called us a couple of dykes.'

'How did you react to that?'

'I was annoyed and I wanted them to leave us alone.'

'But not Alice?' Beth probed.

'Alice didn't like it either, but she handled it differently. She started to take the piss, putting her arm round my shoulder, giving me a hug – that sort of thing – and I went along with it for a laugh. It was just a silly thing.' She seemed embarrassed now. 'The clingier we got with each other, the more they liked it. I can't really explain it now – we were so bloody drunk and we were draped over each other – but all of a sudden it was like we were the centre of their attention, as if we were on stage or something, and they were loving it. They started cheering us.'

'So you kissed?'

'Someone shouted out, "Kiss her!" I just shook my head, but Alice, she was even more wasted than me, she just said, "What do we get if we do?" The blokes started promising us drinks, and if they were stupid enough to buy them . . .' She shrugged as if it was no big deal. 'Someone bought us both a drink then said, "You have to kiss now," and Alice kissed me and I kissed her, but it was only on the cheek. They wanted us to kiss on the lips, so Alice said, "Two more drinks, then." I thought they'd be pissed off, but another bloke bought the next two, and they were all saying how long the kiss had to last and everything or we wouldn't get the drinks.

'Like I said, it was stupid, but you had to be there. Right then, with them buying the drinks, it felt like we were winning, you know, like we'd turned the tables on these idiots. They were paying for our night out because they were getting off on something so stupid. Blokes round here are all the same.'

'They're like that everywhere,' Beth confirmed. 'So they bought more drinks and you kissed on the lips. Was that it?'

She shook her head and looked away from Beth while she finished the story. 'One of them offered to buy more drinks if we snogged – full on, you know.' And she shrugged again.

'We both said no. I'd struggled to finish the drinks we had, but another guy slapped a fiver down on the table as if that was enough to get us to do it. Alice just laughed at him, but he put down another fiver, and so did his mate. They'd all just been paid, so they were flush. There was sixty quid on the table and they were telling us what we had to do to earn it.' She shook her head again. 'If I'd have been sober, I'd have told them where to go. Alice would have, too – she's the biggest feminist I know, but for some reason . . .'

'You were caught up in the moment?'

'There's a bunch of guys treating us like we're goddesses or something. They said we had to snog for three minutes and we could have the money.'

'Alice was hammered. She shouts out, "Money first, then we snog," and she grabbed it. I didn't know if she was serious or was going to run off with the cash. I was a bit scared in case it turned nasty, but they all started cheering and egging us on. She just laughed and winked at me. She's, like, "It's sixty quid, girl!" She stuffed the money in her jacket pocket and the men were all chanting, "Oi, oi, oi!" at us. She stood me up straight and planted a kiss on my lips, and I went along with it.'

'For three minutes?'

'Yeah. It was a very long three minutes. They were timing us, and we didn't want to stop in case they tried to take the money off us.'

'So, she kissed you and you kissed her back and it was a . . . full-on snog, as you called it.'

'That was the bet.'

'And you won the bet.'

'Yeah, they counted down the last twenty seconds, then this massive cheer went up and the men were all happy. We broke off and it all calmed down at last.'

'What did you do then? Did you stay in the pub?'

'God, no. I was too embarrassed, and they wanted us to do more stuff. The guys were trying to make us stay, shouting out about grabbing each other's tits and that. We left sharpish.'

'What time was that?'

'I don't know. We were wrecked.'

'But it was before closing time.'

'Oh, yeah, well before then. I'd say about ten o'clock. We'd been drinking since five o'clock, so we didn't want any more.'

'Where did you go then?'

'Home.'

'Your home or Alice's?'

'Mine.' Her voice was a little quieter now.

'Anyone else in that night?'

'My dad goes out on a Saturday night. He's got a woman in Rothbury. My mum died eight years ago and my brother's away in the army.'

'So you had the place to yourself?'

'Yeah.' Kirstie seemed tense. Beth noticed a slight strain in her voice, and her posture altered as she sat up more stiffly.

'What did you do? Drink more?'

'I had some cheap wine in the fridge.'

'You watch TV or just chat?'

'We played music and talked.'

'In the lounge?'

There was the briefest of pauses before Kirstie said, with as much casualness as she could muster, 'Here, in my room. I put some music on.'

'What did you talk about?' Beth was waiting for Kirstie to tell her to mind her own business and wondered why she hadn't yet.

'You know – stuff. Boys at school, the exams.'

'Didn't you talk about the night in the pub?' Beth contrived a laugh and widened her eyes. 'I think I would. You earned sixty quid just for kissing each other!'

'We couldn't believe how easy it was to get their money.'

'Was it easy?' Beth locked eyes with Kirstie to see if she would look away, but she didn't. 'Kissing your friend like that? Weren't you worried that it might make things awkward?'

'No, Alice isn't like that. She's a free spirit, and it was only a kiss.'

'A kiss with another girl, though, and a proper kiss

at that, for several minutes?' And when Kirstie didn't comment on that, Beth asked, 'How did it make you feel?'

'Afterwards?' asked Kirstie.

'During?'

'I don't know . . . it was a bit of a wild night. The blokes were all cheering, I was pleased we were going to get the money . . . but it was a bit strange.'

'Some girls would laugh that off, some would feel awkward afterwards, or mortified,' Beth offered casually, 'and some might want it to happen again, I suppose.'

'We were drunk,' she said softly. 'Who cares?'

Beth let that thought hang for a moment then said, 'How long did you and Alice stay in your room?'

'Not long,' Kirstie said quickly. 'Fifteen, maybe twenty minutes.'

'Then she left?'

'Yeah.'

'Where did she go? Another pub, or to see another friend?'

'Everywhere was shut by then, and she was really tired.'

'I thought the pubs had late licences round here?'

'They do.'

'It wasn't that late,' said Beth.

'Yeah, it was.'

'No, because you said you left the pub early, long before closing, around ten o'clock.'

'I think so.'

'Then – what? – a five-minute walk to your house?'

'Ten, maybe. We were swaying.'

'Then fifteen or twenty minutes at your house, so she'd

be on her way home by about half ten. Places would still be open for a long while after that.'

'We must have been talking longer than I thought, then,' said Kirstie, and Beth was convinced she'd caught her in a lie.

'You must have been,' she said.

'There's gaps in my memory. I told you. We'd been drinking since five.'

'That much drinking would finish me off, but then I'm a lightweight.'

Beth knew she wasn't really getting anywhere like this, but she was also convinced Kirstie wasn't being honest about that night. She realized the younger girl didn't know what she knew, particularly from the journal entry, so she decided to go out on a limb.

'You kissed her again, didn't you, Kirstie?' she asked abruptly, and the girl's eyes widened in panic. 'Here, in your room.'

'Who's been . . . ?' Kirstie looked confused and frightened.

'Telling me that?' asked Beth. 'You did, just now.'

'No, I never.'

'In a way, you did. You kissed your friend in the pub for three minutes then came back to your house,' Beth reminded her. 'Poured another drink, because maybe you didn't want the booze to wear off, then you both came upstairs and talked . . . for maybe a couple of hours.' She gave Kirstie a questioning look. 'But you told me it was only a few minutes.'

'I can barely remember the night, let alone the end of it.'

'You described the events at the pub in detail, Kirstie. You were aware enough to be able to pour some wine from the fridge and put music on, then, presumably you sat on your bed here together and talked about what had happened.'

'We were laughing about it, yeah.'

'Did you relive it?'

'Oh, please,' she protested.

'Why not? If you enjoyed the kiss, why not do it again when the guys weren't looking? It's not a crime, Kirstie. You love your friend.'

'Nothing happened.' She said it in a flat tone that led Beth to believe the exact opposite.

It was time to play the only card she had left. 'Alice said you had a secret.'

'What? When did she say that?' Poor Kirstie looked really worried then.

'We saw an entry from her journal.'

Beth had to concentrate hard to recall and recite the exact words from Alice's journal. *Kirstie and I both know Kirstie's little secret, and some secrets ought to stay that way until they are ready to be let out, so in consideration of Kirstie, my lips are sealed, which is kind of appropriate, really.*'

Kirstie looked as if she was about to burst into tears. She blinked and tried to compose herself.

'It's important that you tell me the truth, Kirstie, particularly if it has anything to do with Alice's disappearance.'

'It hasn't,' she said sharply.

'Then you'll be in the clear,' Beth assured her. 'But only if you tell me exactly what happened. Otherwise we'll think you have something to hide. No one here has the luxury of secrets any more, not when a young girl is missing.'

'She didn't run away because of me,' Kirstie said firmly. 'I didn't do anything, and I'm worried sick about her.'

'What happened that night, Kirstie?'

Kirstie took a cushion from the bed and pressed it against her body, wrapping her arms around it, as if for comfort. She looked like she would rather be anywhere but there right then and, when she recounted the events of the rest of that night to Beth, she did so listlessly.

'I was very drunk, so was Alice. I remember my mouth was dry and I didn't really want more booze but we had some wine anyway. We were laughing and Alice pulled a handful of crumpled fivers out of her pocket and she was, like, "Yay, we got paid." And I was, like, "We so did!" Alice gave me my share and I had to lean across her to put my share of the money down, and she said, "On the bed side cabinet, like a hooker." I said, "I'd be good at that," then I asked her if I was a better or worse kisser than Chris or Tony.'

'And what did she say?'

'Better than Tony, worse than Chris. She said Tony is all tongues, which is fine until you can't breathe. Then she said, "Chris used to be stiff-lipped like you, but I loosened him up and he's had a lot more practice. I told her it's not my fault I was stiff-lipped, I wasn't expecting it. And there was an audience. That I'm better than that, usually.

'She was all like, "So *you* say," practically daring me. It

189

was still a total laugh, so I pushed her on to her back on the bed and pretended to pin her down, then told her, "Prepare to be kissed."

'And she went along with it?'

'I didn't ask permission, but she didn't say or do anything to stop me. She was laughing.'

'So you kissed her?'

'Yeah.'

'And?'

'It seemed like the most natural thing in the world, and no one was more surprised by that than me. I opened my eyes to check, and her eyes were closed. That's how I knew Alice wanted it, too, so I kissed her properly. I mean, I couldn't believe this was actually happening.'

'But it felt right?'

Kirstie nodded. 'And it went on for the longest time.'

'What happened when it was over?'

'I said, "Now tell me I'm not as good as Chris," and I bent to kiss her again, but she suddenly sat up and said, "I don't want this," and then, "I've got to go." And she did. It was like a spell was broken.'

Beth could see that Kirstie's explanation of that evening had cost her a lot. She looked drained by the end of it.

'I'm not a . . .' Kirstie began, but halted. 'I'm not prejudiced, I'm just not a dyke. I don't normally . . .'

'I get it,' said Beth, trying to spare the girl, 'and I won't tell anyone – from the town, I mean.' She would have to inform Black, but that was different.

'Collemby is a very small place,' said Kirstie, and her agitation was obvious. 'Everyone knows everyone.' Her shoulders sagged. 'People don't just come out in little towns like this one, even if they *are* gay, and I'm definitely not. With Alice, it felt different . . .' And she faltered.

'I know,' said Beth, because she knew that, gay or straight, Kirstie was still trying to work it all out for herself and she didn't want to complicate the girl's life any further. 'If you could just tell me what happened between you and Alice afterwards.'

'I told you, she went home.'

'I meant later, in the days that followed. How was she with you?'

'She didn't mention it, and I didn't dare bring it up. We acted like it never happened or we were too drunk to remember, but we both knew what we did. I didn't force it and she didn't brush me away, not at first. I kissed her and she let me. She kissed me back, then all of a sudden . . .'

'Perhaps she was confused, too.' Then Beth remembered Alice's entries in her journal.

Kirstie and Chloe.
What am I going to do with them?
One is needy, and the other one is . . .
I don't even need to write that down.

It seemed likely that Alice hadn't wanted the kiss to mean anything at all but it had meant far more to Kirstie and that's why things had become awkward between them.

'You must have been hurt and confused?' Beth offered.

'I don't know,' she snapped. 'I'm not a lesbo, I just . . .'

'Love your friend?'

'Yeah.' She said it very softly.

'Did Alice avoid you afterwards?'

'No . . . a bit . . . It's hard to explain. We hung out with Chloe, but weren't alone much any more and she was always in a hurry to get going. I was worried our friendship was ruined.'

'How did you feel towards her then?'

'I felt a whole bunch of things at once. Embarrassed, confused, a bit pissed off with her.'

'You have a right to be angry,' offered Beth, and Kirstie immediately shot her a look.

'I didn't kill her!'

Beth was taken aback. 'Who said anything about killing anyone?'

'You think she might be dead,' protested Kirstie. 'And now you're acting like I'm the one who killed her, because of a stupid kiss!' She looked at Beth as if the detective had somehow conned her into revealing too much.

Kirstie flared then, and there was a hint of implied violence in the way her body stiffened and she jabbed a finger at Beth. 'I told you, we were drunk, and nobody better find out about any of it from you.' Beth almost recoiled at the fury in her eyes and the way her teeth suddenly bared. The mild girl Beth had felt sorry for moments earlier had transformed into a hurt, angry individual who looked like she might attack her.

'No one from the town will hear about it from me.'

'They'd better not,' she hissed, but Beth's reassuring words must have had a mollifying effect on the girl because her face lost its fury.

'I'm just trying to work out what was going through

Alice's mind when she disappeared, because it might help us to find her. That's all.'

'Really?' The girl sneered. 'Well, I think we've already established that the last thing going through Alice's mind then was me.'

25

Black had arranged to meet Beth in the town's lone café. She found him halfway through a bacon roll. The only other customers were two old ladies in a far corner, who were busy talking. 'You first,' he managed, despite a mouthful of bread and bacon. 'Any joy with Kirstie?'

'Oh, she told me plenty.' And Beth spent the next few minutes telling Black what had happened between Kirstie and Alice that night.

'Poor Kirstie,' he observed when he heard about the young girl's confusion.

'I'm surprised to hear you say that. I thought you'd think it was all a bit silly.'

'Unrequited love is a hard thing to cope with at that age.'

'I'm not sure if she's in love with her friend or just loves her *as* a friend. She's confused and hurt. You haven't met Kirstie, so you couldn't have noticed.'

'Noticed what?'

'Her hairstyle,' said Beth.

'What about it?'

'It's exactly the same as Alice's.'

'Interesting.'

'Perhaps Kirstie loves Alice, or just wants to be her.'

'Maybe. You don't think she's so obsessed with her friend, that she . . . ?'

'Could have killed Alice in a jealous rage, or to cover her embarrassment?' She recounted the darker ending to her conversation with the teenager.

He listened closely. 'She bared her fangs at you?'

'Almost literally – for a moment there, I thought she was going to swing at me . . . But do I think she murdered Alice? She doesn't have any kind of alibi. Kirstie claims she was at home on her own, watching soaps and reality TV, which is hard to prove or disprove. The way Alice treated her after their kiss was hurtful to her, so, at the very least, she can join our growing list of messed-up people in Alice's orbit,' concluded Beth. 'And we haven't even started on the school yet.'

'Everleigh gave me the go-ahead to go in there first thing on Monday,' he told her. 'We can question anyone who has had any dealings with Alice. The head has promised us full cooperation.'

'About time,' she said. 'I want to speak to him and the PE teacher, who was the last one to see Alice leave. Then there's the one who has flings with his pupils and the drama teacher she was smiling at in the photo. That's just for starters.'

'And we'll be able to do that, which is the good news, but otherwise, that's in short supply. Forensics have drawn a blank on the journal pages. Whoever is sending them knows what they're doing. They haven't left a trace on the pages, stamps or envelopes.'

'That's almost impressive,' Beth said begrudgingly. 'What about the fragments of headlamp down by the station?'

'Inconclusive so far. It's looking like more than one car

may have smashed into that broken platform. It will take them a while to sift through the pieces. And the warrants on social media proved fruitless, too. If Alice Teale was communicating with someone in a clandestine manner, she wasn't doing it that way.'

'It feels like one step forward and two back at the moment.'

'Do you want something to eat?' he asked her, now that he had finished his own breakfast.

'I'd love something, but there's no one here.' Beth hadn't seen a waitress since she walked in.

'That's my fault,' he said. 'She's out the back. Rita is a bit behind because of me. We had a long chat.'

'What about?'

'She's been working here for years and knows everybody in Collemby.'

'What did she tell you?'

'We talked about Alice, then we got on to the subject of her parents.'

'Did you find out why her dad is so angry all the time?'

'No,' he said, 'but I did hear a very interesting story about Ronnie and Abigail when they were young.'

'Tell me.'

'I will,' he said. 'But if it's true, I'm surprised her mum isn't the angry one.'

The waitress appeared then and they stopped discussing Alice's parents for a moment while Rita took Beth's order of a sausage sandwich and some tea. Rita left them to it and he started telling the story, and quite a story it was, too.

Beth soon realized that Lucas's casual chat to the

waitress in the café had yielded as much information as her lengthy interrogation of Kirstie.

'So, Alice Teale's dad walked out on the family?'

'When Alice's brother was tiny,' confirmed Lucas. 'Before she was even born. They'd only been married a year when he ran off with another woman.'

'He came back, though, eventually,' observed Beth.

'Within a few months. Begged her to take him back, by all accounts, and she relented. Alice was a product of that reunion.'

'She took him back,' mused Beth. 'Bet she never regretted that decision.'

'Life with him must have been an absolute barrel of laughs,' said Lucas, 'but being left on your own with a baby son when you've not been married long can't have been much fun either.'

'Particularly when your rat of a husband runs off with someone else. I wonder how she coped.' Then Beth noticed the gleam in Lucas's eye. 'You know, don't you?'

'Maybe.'

'She got herself a new man, didn't she? Tell me she did.'

'Kind of.'

'Kind of? She either had a new bloke or she didn't.'

'It wasn't that simple. You could say he was already taken.'

'He had a wife?'

'No,' said Black. 'He had a church.'

'Bloody hell,' said Beth. 'Are you serious?'

'I swear to God,' he deadpanned.

'No wonder Ronnie Teale is always angry, if his wife was cuddling up to the local vicar all those years ago. This case gets weirder by the hour – or are you going to tell me they're always like this?'

'No, not usually,' he said. 'I've been thinking about that. Alice Teale is not your typical runaway. Usually, if someone like that goes missing, they either turn up again pretty quickly or we find a body. When that happens, more often than not it's someone she's close to – her boyfriend or an ex. Being abducted and killed by a stranger is much rarer than people realize. In this case, we have no body, but no verified sightings of her either. The fact that she hasn't used her phone or drawn out any money means that, at best, someone must be helping or sheltering her, for whatever reason, but I don't think that's likely. If she has come to harm, we have a number of people who might have reason to do it. Her ex had his life derailed by Alice, and her current boyfriend has been described as both jealous and controlling. Her dad is like a bomb waiting to explode, and even her grandad confirms he was way too hard on Alice, which might have something to do with her thinking about self-harming. Her brother is nowhere near as volatile as her father but is capable of outbursts of temper. I think they were close, but probably not too close, since we know that Sophie Mayhew probably spread that rumour about them. We have a barman who doesn't like to hear the word "no" and teachers who don't seem to understand boundaries, as well as a mystery man, not her boyfriend, who might have been shirtless in Alice Teale's bedroom with her. Then there's Kirstie, who has an aggressive streak, too, and there's someone else I want to track down.' And he told her about the homeless man who had been hanging around the cottages.

'Why do I feel like we're going round in circles?' she asked him.

'Patience,' he said. 'This will all eventually unravel, and we'll see it for what it actually is.'

'But do we have the time for that? Alice has already been gone a while.'

'If I'm right,' he said, 'and I really hope I'm not, then it probably won't matter.'

'Why not?'

'Because I think Alice is already dead.'

Beth thought about this for a moment and said, 'Then let's hope you're wrong.'

Once they had eaten their meal, they went straight to the church, which was a short walk from the café. They passed a row of shops that told their own story of Collemby's demise. Around one in three had been closed for good, with only faded imprints of the lettering on old signs giving a clue to what they had sold when the town was more prosperous and able to support an array of stores. Now this particular street had only the minimart, where Alice Teale's mother worked, two fast-food takeaways either side of a boarded-up pub and a small bakery chain outlet.

'I called into the incident room before I went to the café,' said Black as they walked. 'There was another batch of phone-ins waiting for me.'

'Anything interesting?'

'Not much, but maybe something. A woman reported seeing a red car parked up a short way from the school. She said it was a sporty-looking model with blacked-out windows.'

'There were a number of cars parked along the road between the school and the town centre,' said Beth. 'What's special about this one?'

'It was parked across the lane that leads to the allotments, blocking it. She said it looked as if someone was waiting inside. It's worth checking on, because it's likely that Alice was picked up by someone not far from the school.'

'Without anyone noticing?'

'It only takes a moment to step into a car.'

They reached the parish church then, its doors open and inviting. A wooden A-framed sign, like the ones pubs use to advertise theme nights or meals, was positioned outside the door, welcoming worshippers with the phrase, 'Have you found Jesus?'

'Don't tell me he's gone missing, too,' muttered Black.

'Do you think this is going to work?' Beth asked uncertainly as they made to go in.

'Why not?' he asked her. 'We can't go to the school until Monday, anyway, so let's see what we can turn up here in the meantime. The more we know about the Teale family, the better.'

'We're going to ask the current vicar if the former vicar stepped over the line with a female parishioner? I always thought the default position of any church, whenever there's a whiff of scandal, is to immediately cover it up. It's been like that for hundreds of years.'

'You know why?' he asked. 'Because their whole world depends on faith – in God, in the Bible and particularly in those who deliver its message. If people start to lose that, they know their church is doomed.'

As they were about to walk into Collemby's parish church a gaggle of laughter rose up from the opened window of the church hall that was right next to it. Beth presented herself to a woman who was passing and asked for the vicar. 'I'll get him for you if you wait here,' she was told.

There was more laughter and raised voices from the hall, so Black walked back towards it. The sound of excitable elderly female voices came from the open window.

He turned back to Beth. 'You've got this, right?'

'What? Why? What are you going to do?'

'I'm going to leave you to it,' he said, 'because that sounds like a whist drive.'

'A what?' But Black slipped through the doors of the church hall without further explanation, just as the woman returned and beckoned Beth forward.

As she had predicted, Beth had a frustrating time with the vicar of the parish church, who had a politician's ability to use a lot of words to say very little. She eventually emerged with not much more than the date he had taken over the parish from his predecessor and a lecture on not taking local gossip seriously. Other than a tight-lipped acknowledgement that Alex McGregor had formerly been the vicar there and that Abigail Teale was indeed a parishioner, Beth received very little of substance. Frustrated, she gave up and left the vicar to it.

She was back outside when she heard the loud female voices again. They were so animated that, from the outside, they sounded like a gaggle of geese. Beth looked into the room, through the same window Black had chosen, and saw a dozen tables occupied by old ladies, who had come together in the church hall to play cards. They were chatting good-naturedly and in their midst was Lucas Black. Somehow, he had managed to talk himself on to a table and he was leaning in next to one of the old dears, perhaps offering her advice on which card to play next. What the hell was he doing?

A minute later he looked up, noticed Beth and gave her a thumbs-up. She had no idea what he was playing at, so he splayed his fingers to indicate he needed another five minutes. She nodded and went to wait for him in the car. It was another half an hour before he joined her.

'Sorry to keep you,' he said.

'This better be good.'

'I suspect you're wondering why I did that?' He sounded almost cheerful, which was unlike him.

'I'm wondering why you wasted all that time flirting with a bunch of old ladies.'

'Old ladies love to be flirted with,' he told her, 'and they are the very best source of information. What did you get out of the vicar?'

'Not much.'

'Thought so,' he said. 'He was worried about the reputation of his church, whereas my old ladies love a good gossip. All I had to do was ask them about the previous vicar, and I couldn't shut them up. When I threw in Abigail Teale's name, they were hardly able to contain themselves.'

'What did they tell you?'

'That she was *a one*.'

'A one what?'

'It's an expression. It means she wasn't quite a complete hussy, but she did throw herself at a man.'

'The vicar?'

'Yep, and apparently it was the talk of the diocese. She came in for guidance when her husband left her and became very close to the vicar. When she went back to her husband, the vicar left the parish.'

'What happened to him? The current vicar says he has no idea where he is now. I think he might be lying.'

'How very un-Christian of you. He's running a home-less shelter in Newcastle,' said Black. 'See how easy it is to get information when you help old ladies win at whist?'

'He didn't run away too far, then,' she said. 'Maybe we should look him up?'

'Alice Teale might not even be aware of the man's exist-ence, nor he of hers,' he said, 'but he might be able to shed some light on her messed-up family, and that alone has got to be worth the drive.'

26

The manager of the homeless shelter listened to Beth's explanation for their presence on his doorstep but seemed baffled as to how he could help them.

'I'm sorry, but did you say it's a girl that's missing?' Alex McGregor asked them. 'I'm afraid our shelter only takes in vulnerable male adults. Many of them have struggled with drug or alcohol dependency and it wouldn't be safe to house them alongside females. There is another shelter that takes in women, along with their children, if they have been the victim of domestic abuse. Young women without children are generally referred to a department of the local council, unless there are extenuating circumstances . . .'

'We didn't make it clear,' Beth said, even though he had interrupted her before she was finished, 'for which I apologize. We're not here to speak to you in your capacity as manager of this shelter.' His eyes narrowed in confusion. 'The missing girl is from Collemby. You used to be the vicar there.'

'Collemby? Right.' She could tell he was still perplexed.

'The girl's name is Alice,' said Lucas. 'Alice *Teale*.'

McGregor took this in without any outward sign of emotion. 'I see.' There was a long pause. 'Would you like a cup of tea?'

*

One of the shelter's volunteers made the tea for them, delivering it in old, slightly chipped mugs to a rickety desk in a bare office. McGregor moved some papers to one side for the tray and they each took a mug and sat on mismatched chairs which looked like they'd been donated. The man was dressed in blue jeans and a grey sweater. He may have been in his mid-forties now, but there was something still quite youthful, almost boyish, about his appearance.

When they were alone and the door was closed behind them, McGregor said, 'Collemby? God, I haven't been there for . . . It must be almost twenty years.'

'You left just over eighteen years ago,' confirmed Beth.

'That sounds about right.'

'You were the vicar there for around three years,' said Lucas.

'How do you know all this?' McGregor asked. 'Or perhaps I should be asking *why* do you know all this?'

'It's not like we had to read a file on you,' said Black. 'We just had a word with the vicar who took over from you. Your former parishioners filled in the gaps.'

There was a long pause then, during which McGregor waited for Black to add to this, and when he did not, he said, 'And what else did they tell you?'

'The reason you left Collemby,' said Black. 'Abigail Teale. Alice Teale's mother.'

McGregor blinked as if he were shocked. 'Abigail Teale was not the reason I left Collemby.' Then he seemed to think again. 'Not the main reason, at any rate.'

'But you did have an affair with her?'

'I'm sorry, but who has been saying that?'

'It wasn't an individual,' said Black. 'I think it is what is known as common knowledge, among the older parishioners, at least.'

'What passed between Abigail and myself is private, even if it is the subject of mean-spirited gossip.'

'You deny you were close to her,' asked Beth, 'even to the point where you were warned off by the dean?'

Again, a long pause while he was either attempting to compose himself or trying to find the right words. 'We were close, yes,' he admitted. 'She came to church regularly and sang in our choir. We became friendly.'

'She came to you,' said Black, 'for guidance.' Then he added the word: 'Initially.'

'Guidance?'

'Because her marriage was failing,' the detective reminded him. 'Her husband ran off with another woman, leaving her alone with her baby boy.'

'I don't think I should be speaking to you about confidential conversations I had with a parishioner, even if it was nearly twenty years ago.'

'Eighteen,' Black reminded him. 'Her husband eventually returned to patch up their marriage. She went back to him and, a few months later, you left the parish and the Church.'

'That is all factually correct,' said McGregor, 'but the inference is that I left because of her, and that simply isn't true.'

'Why else would you leave?'

'You're not going to say you lost your faith in God?' asked Beth.

He seemed to consider this for a while. 'I lost my faith in the Church.'

'Why?'

'I think that's my business, don't you?' He sighed. 'If you must know, I had a growing feeling that I wasn't doing any good. All we did was talk. Abigail was a case in point. You are correct that I was reprimanded for becoming too close to her, but only because I cared for her and her situation; also, there was a clash of interest.'

'How so?'

'In my capacity as the vicar, I was duty bound to advise her to do her utmost to repair her marriage and take her husband back.'

'And you wanted her for yourself?' asked Black.

He shook his head. 'I wanted her to leave him,' he said. 'But for herself, not for me.'

'Why?' asked Beth.

'Because Ronnie Teale was not a nice man and Abigail deserved better. That's the problem with dogma. Marriage has to be preserved at all costs, even when it becomes clear it's in everyone's best interest to move on. When I was resistant to the idea that she should return to a bully, the dean intervened and threatened to haul me up in front of the bishop. By then I think I had already had enough. I still believe in God, just not the Church. Now, I do what I can' – he gestured around him – 'and I am no longer constrained.'

He took a sip of his tea. 'I assume she is still with him, then – Ronnie Teale? You said they had a daughter.' He frowned. 'And she has gone missing?'

'They are still together and it's their daughter, Alice, who has disappeared. We're trying to find her,' explained Beth.

He nodded slowly then Black said, 'And we thought perhaps she might have turned up here.'

'Like I said, this shelter is men only.'

Black leaned forward in his chair and locked eyes with McGregor. 'We thought she might have come here looking for you.'

'Why ever would she do that?' he asked, though Beth could tell he knew the answer to that question already.

As soon as they were back in the car with the doors closed behind them, Beth let it out.

'Oh my God. Did you notice?'

'Yep,' said Lucas, as if it were obvious. 'There's a resemblance.'

'He looks like Alice Teale,' she said. 'Or I should say, *she* looks like him: same eye colour, nose, that bone structure, even down to the colour of his hair.'

'And there's the jewellery,' said Black, almost to himself.

'What jewellery?'

'When she went missing DI Fraser put out a description of the clothes Alice was wearing. It included a ring, gold stud earrings and there was also a gold cross on a chain that she wore around her neck. Her mother gave it to her. Abigail Teale was religious, but . . .'

'It has even more significance now,' said Beth, completing his thoughts for him.

'No wonder Ronnie hated her,' said Lucas. 'At least now we know the reason why Alice could never do anything right for Daddy.' Then he added: 'Because he suspects he isn't really her father.'

'You think he knows?' asked Beth.

'It would explain a lot. He was the one who walked out on Alice's mum and had the affair, then he chose to come back, probably when he heard his wife was spending a bit more time than normal at the local church. Maybe he listened to some gossip, so he returned and staked his claim on his wife and their marriage. Then, months later, Alice was born, but she almost certainly wasn't his. So, yeah, I think he knew. The question is whether he finally did something about it.'

Beth said, 'Actually, I wasn't talking about Ronnie Teale.'

'Oh,' said Lucas, and they both instinctively turned to look back at the shelter, where Alex McGregor now stood at the window, looking out at them. 'You mean, did *he* know? That's a very good question.'

'I think he does now,' said Beth.

27

When Beth's phone rang late that evening, she expected it to be Black with another query about the case but, instead, she heard the reassuringly familiar tones of Peter Kennedy.

'I did some asking around about DS Black.'

'That was good of you.' Familiarity with the man had made Beth a little calmer than she had been about working with Lucas Black, but she didn't want Peter to feel as if his efforts had been wasted.

'No problem and, don't worry, I didn't make it obvious. I just mentioned I had a friend who had joined his team. Believe me, that was enough.'

'What do you mean?'

'People weren't shy about voicing their opinions on DS Black.'

Beth sat up. 'What did they say about him?'

'That he was a loner and difficult, moody and unco-operative.'

Was that all? 'That does seem to sum him up, Peter, but I'm getting used to him.'

'Lucas Black is not a popular man,' Kennedy continued. 'No one likes working with the guy, and they say he has a right temper. They don't trust him, Beth.' He paused, then.

That was bad enough, but why did she get the impression Kennedy hadn't finished yet? If there was something else, she wanted him to spit it out, but it was his story to tell.

'And then there was the shooting.'

Oh, yes, the shooting.

'Did he tell you about that?' asked Kennedy.

'I haven't asked,' she admitted. 'And it's not something he's likely to volunteer as a topic of conversation.'

'You've read about it, though?' He meant online. 'How he claimed he thought the man was armed?'

'Yes.'

'The guy was carrying something that looked like a sawn-off shotgun. It was part of his statement,' Kennedy told her, 'but the victim was actually carrying a chair leg.'

'A chair leg?' she repeated. How could anyone mistake that for a weapon?

'Black claimed he thought the man's family was in danger so he shot the guy. I spoke to someone who was there that night. He said Black was like a robot. It was just *bang*. No hesitation. Right in the chest. He took that guy down so fast it was like an execution,' said Kennedy, and hearing it described like that made it far more real somehow. 'Then, afterwards, he never said a word about it. He was offered counselling but turned it down and just got on with his job like he didn't give a damn about that bloke.'

'Christ,' she hissed. She was working with a man who felt nothing, even when he had killed someone.

Perhaps Peter thought he had gone too far, because he

seemed to backtrack. 'Obviously, I wasn't there. It's just what they told me. Things like that must affect people in different ways, but it sounded pretty hardcore. He was in the army, though, wasn't he? Maybe he had killed before.'

Beth assumed Kennedy was saying this to explain Black's nonchalant approach to ending someone else's life. She didn't find any comfort in the idea that Black might have killed someone else.

Of all the people to end up working my first real case with, I end up with the cold-blooded killer.

Beth did not sleep at all well that night and, this time, she woke long before it was light. Once she was awake, her mind went back to the call from Peter Kennedy. She had hoped talking to him might calm some of her worries, but instead his comments about Black seemed to confirm her worst fears.

As Beth drove in that morning, she contemplated her options. She didn't want to carry on working with Lucas Black, but what choice did she have? She could go and see DCI Everleigh, of course, and demand to be taken off the case – but based on what? Rumours? Black had been officially cleared of wrongdoing. Everleigh would take a dim view if she dropped him in it by leaving an already undermanned team, and her career would be irreparably damaged before it had even begun. It wasn't even an option.

She decided to stick with it. Beth wanted to work this case and find Alice so she would have to try and put thoughts of Black's highly questionable past out of her mind until the case was concluded. Then she could review her situation. She told herself she would probably be moved to another squad after the case anyway. In the meantime, she would sit tight, keep her head down and try to just get on with the job.

28

The place couldn't have looked more different. The first time Beth had seen the building from the outside it had been at night and there had been barely a soul around. Now, on a Monday morning, hundreds of pupils were spilling from coaches parked outside the school or sauntering up the road from Collemby town centre at a snail's pace, as if trying to delay the inevitably dull day in full-time education for as long as humanly possible. Beth and Black watched them go in from their car. There wasn't much point fighting their way through the crowds. Beth couldn't bring herself to speak to Black, but he didn't seem to notice and was his usual silent self. She knew she would have to switch into professional mode once they entered the school but, right now, she was struggling to file away the thought that she was sitting next to a killer.

It was all over in five minutes. One moment, the last of the kids were pushing each other through the big double doors at the front of the school or filing into its numerous side exits; the next, there was absolute calm, with not a single person left outside the building, bar Beth and Lucas, who took the opportunity to walk unopposed into Collemby Comprehensive and request an audience with the headteacher.

*

Thanks to DCI Everleigh, Mr Morgan was expecting Beth and Lucas and he permitted them entry to his office, though he did not offer them any refreshment. If Beth had to pick one word to describe the man in front of her, she would have chosen 'serious'. The head was in his early fifties, wore the dark suit and tie of a middle manager, and his shoes looked as if they had been polished for an hour that morning. He wished them every success in their quest to find Alice but wasn't sure how he could help them.

'Were you in the building when Alice Teale disappeared?' asked Beth.

'I was, but I'm afraid I didn't see her leave the school. That was Miss Pearce, our PE teacher, who was in the staff room.'

'Do you often work that late?' asked Black.

'More than I'd like to. Friday is different, though. We encourage the sixth-formers to stay behind for A-level revision sessions, followed by sporting activities to help them unwind. I also have the DTs.'

Black instantly thought of delirium tremens, the symptoms displayed by acute alcoholics, but he didn't think those were the kind of DTs the head was talking about. 'The what?'

'Detention time,' Morgan explained. 'We deliberately schedule it on Friday evenings. We found that the kids who routinely misbehave don't care about normal detentions. If you schedule them for a slot when they would rather be somewhere else, however, such as Friday evenings or even Saturday mornings, it dramatically cuts the rate of offending. It's just one of my more radical ideas, which has helped to turn this school around.'

'And you've done that,' said Beth, 'from what we've heard. Truancy down, attendance up, bad behaviour down, exam results up. They're calling you a super-head. What's your secret?'

'Attention to detail in all things,' he said proudly. 'And we target the worst offenders remorselessly. I took the old New York City zero-tolerance approach to crime and adapted it to suit the needs of our school.'

'The Broken Windows model?' asked Black.

'That's the one,' said the head. 'It's been proven that if you stamp down hard on small misdemeanours like vandalism, graffiti or the dropping of litter, then larger crimes are less likely.'

'Crime rates fell in New York,' agreed Black, 'but how does that work in a school?'

'In exactly the same way. We also have a zero-tolerance approach to antisocial behaviour of any kind. We realized that twenty per cent of the pupils were responsible for eighty per cent of the bad behaviour. We were dealing with the same offenders time and time again, so we come down on them hard. The Friday-evening detentions have been a particularly effective deterrent.'

'So you were supervising the detentions when Alice left?' asked Beth.

'Yes.'

'That's pretty late, isn't it? If school turns out around three o'clock, you don't keep the kids back for six hours, surely?'

'No,' he said. 'We let them go home then bring them

back in for an hour or two at a pre-arranged slot, which is intended to cause maximum irritation to the culprit. These are serial offenders, with a history of dishonesty.'

'Ever have any reason to give Alice Teale a detention?' asked Black.

'Absolutely not.'

'Is Alice popular?' asked Beth.

'With teachers or classmates?' asked the head.

'Both.'

'From a teacher's perspective, I would say she is a good student who rarely, if ever, gives us any cause for concern, and she is deputy head girl,' he added approvingly. 'Among her fellow pupils, it's always hard to tell when you are the head of a school, but she seems well liked, though we did have an incident months ago.'

At that point there was a knock on the door and the school secretary walked in. 'Sorry, Mr Morgan, I need to collect the registers.' He nodded his assent.

'What kind of incident?' asked Beth.

'An act of vandalism.'

'Alice committed vandalism?' asked Beth. 'On school property?'

The headteacher glanced at the secretary, who was opening and closing drawers while looking for the registers. Her presence seemed to faze him. 'It's probably easier if I just show you.' He got out of his chair and gestured for them to follow.

They walked down the corridor and out through the side exit door that led to the spot where the green Jaguar was parked.

'This yours?' asked Black.

'Yes.'

'Nice.' He peered inside. 'And it's absolutely immaculate.'

'I have it valeted,' he said. 'Regularly.' Then he pointed. 'It's round here.' He led them around a corner, to a wall on a small outbuilding. 'It took the caretaker a devil of a time to scrub it off.'

Black and Beth moved closer to the greying red-brick wall and the marks that were still partially visible there. Black squinted at what remained of the lettering. Someone had written something on that wall in white spray paint and, despite the best efforts of the school caretaker, you could still just make out the outline of each of those faded letters and discern their meaning.

ALICE TEALE IS A SLAG

29

'You said this wasn't recent,' confirmed Beth as she surveyed the graffiti on the school wall.

'No, it was quite early into the new school year, in fact.'

'Why would someone do that?' she asked.

'Jealousy,' he explained. 'Teenage relationships are not always mature ones. From time to time, the school can be affected. This was one of those times.'

'Was Alice affected?'

'She was understandably upset, but we made a point of blocking off the area from the school body and the caretaker prioritized the removal of the graffiti.'

'Ever find out who did it?' Black was expecting that to be unlikely.

'The offender was identified and asked to leave the sixth form.'

'How did you find the culprit?' asked Beth.

'Alice had been involved with a classmate and, when the relationship ended, she began seeing a former boyfriend again. That was sufficient motive to put the boy who lost out under suspicion.'

'Tony,' said Black. 'Did he admit it?' In Tony's version of events, he had voluntarily dropped out of the sixth form because he couldn't stand to see Alice back with Chris. Had he instead been kicked out by the head for defacing the wall with this vengeful insult? If he'd lied about that, then what else was he keeping from Black?

'He was very dismissive at first, even though I had threatened him with possible expulsion. Then he told me he wanted to leave the sixth form anyway, and I thought it was for the best. I considered that to be the end of the matter.'

'Do you think he was definitely the one responsible?'

'Like I said, he admitted it,' said the head, as if that were proof enough. 'I would have been hard pressed to think of anyone else with sufficient motive. Shall we go back in?'

'It might be best to continue our discussion out here,' said Beth. 'I'd like to talk about an area of some sensitivity.'

'Go on.' The head made no further move to go back inside.

'Teacher–pupil relationships,' she said, and he looked uneasy.

'What kind of relationships?'

'The romantic kind,' said Beth, then added: 'The sexual kind.'

Morgan crossed his arms, a defensive posture. 'Who are you referring to?'

'A number of teachers over the years, apparently.'

'You've been listening to gossip, in other words.'

'Isn't it true that some male teachers have had relationships with female pupils?'

The headteacher paused. Black wondered if he was weighing up whether he could lie to a detective or perhaps evade the question, then he sighed and it was as if a dam had burst. 'Regrettably, there were some incidents in the past, long before I came here,' he admitted.

'And one or two currently.'

'Well, you might say that, but they are rather hard to prove.'

'And when they can be proven? Such as a former pupil living with her teacher?'

'If the girl in question has left the school, is over the age of eighteen and denies living with that teacher, then there isn't a great deal we can do.'

'Even when it is obvious the relationship must have begun when she was at the school, probably while still under the age of consent?'

'And how do we prove that? Unless a teacher is caught in a passionate embrace, they're going to deny everything and, in the majority of cases, so is the pupil.'

'What if they *were* caught?'

'That would be a different matter. It's serious misconduct for someone in a position of trust to have a relationship like that, even more so if the girl is under the age of consent. A teacher would be suspended then dismissed and most likely permanently struck off. We would also be sure to involve the police.'

'And yet there have been persistent rumours concerning particular teachers at Collemby having inappropriate relationships with pupils.'

'Rumours are one thing. Proof is very much another.'

'Has anyone ever been dismissed or struck off during your tenure as headteacher?'

The head was clearly growing exasperated with this line of questioning. 'No, but the burden of proof falls on the school and these situations are very hard to unravel. Do you know how many malicious allegations are made against teachers every year? They can ruin people's lives.'

He sighed. 'Look, I know who you are referring to. It's Mr Keech, isn't it?'

'Or "Keech the leech", as the pupils commonly refer to him,' said Beth. She had been fully briefed on this incident and others by Kirstie.

'I haven't heard that one before, but if the cap fits. Look, I don't like the situation any more than you do. It pains me far more, in fact, because this is my school, but I am tied by the law and the need for proof. I can promise you that all allegations of misconduct reported to me or any other member of staff are investigated thoroughly, but I can't simply fire a teacher because there is a whiff of something about them. The union would never let it go. Often it's little more than gossip.'

Beth was only too aware of the dangers of gossip and couldn't help but think of Alice and her brother.

'There was an allegation against Mr Keech, wasn't there?' she asked the headteacher. 'That he groped a former pupil.'

'You are aware of the allegation, but are you also aware of the accuser?'

'You didn't take it seriously?'

'I took it very seriously indeed. I involved the police at the earliest juncture, but this was clearly a malicious allegation.'

'You didn't believe it from the outset?'

'The girl in question has a long history of lying and deceitfulness. There had been multiple instances of truancy, she showed little academic ability or any sustained interest in lessons, aside from a repeated desire to disrupt them, and she has been arrested on more than one occasion for shoplifting. She did have some natural but quite basic writing ability, which Mr Keech attempted to encourage, to his credit. There is a feeling that her home life is troubled and, confidentially, some suspicion from social services that she may have been abused by a male member of her family, possibly by her father or her brother.'

'Mr Keech gave her tuition? Was this in class or on an extra-curricular basis?'

Beth's tone made it clear she was suspicious, and the headteacher picked up on it. 'He then took her, along with other members of his class, on theatre trips and allowed her to continue her writing in class when the school day was over, though I did caution him against that.'

'Why did you caution him?' she asked, 'if his motives were pure?'

'They were, I believe, but I questioned whether she might take advantage in some way.'

'You actually thought she might make a false accusation against him?'

He was cautious with his next words. 'My concerns were not as specific as that. I simply doubted whether she could be trusted. With hindsight, I was correct.'

'Why are you so certain that Mr Keech is blameless in this? Is it not possible that he might have actually done what he has been accused of doing?'

'It's not impossible but, having weighed up the evidence, I decided it was insufficient to take any further action.'

'You couldn't have weighed it up for long,' Beth reminded him. 'You dismissed it and immediately called the police on the girl. Is that really the way to encourage anyone with concerns about teachers at your school to come forward?'

'I'm sorry, but if you knew this girl you might feel differently about it. She was interviewed by the police, who came to the same conclusions regarding her reliability and likely motive.'

'Which was?'

'Money,' he said. 'In the form of compensation.'

'What did the police say to her?' asked Black.

'I wasn't in the room. I didn't want to influence them in any way.'

'But you must have,' he said, 'when you called them to say you had a malicious time-waster on your hands.'

He looked rattled then. 'I told them that that was my opinion on the matter but that they would obviously have to decide for themselves.'

'Based on her word versus that of a respectable headteacher,' Black said, almost to himself, 'what was the outcome?'

'She withdrew her allegation and admitted it never happened.'

'Did they interview the teacher?'

'They did, and they believed him.'

'Formally, under caution?' asked Black.

'That wasn't necessary.'

'Wasn't it? I don't know, I'm struggling here,' he said. 'A girl makes an allegation of sexual assault against one of your teachers and, because of her perceived character, it is instantly dismissed by her headteacher, who calls the police. They make it clear she probably won't be believed, so she retracts her story, which of course she would, under the circumstances.'

'I might not be Mr Keech's biggest fan – far from it – but this is the only allegation of that nature that has ever been levelled against him. I won't apologize for failing to think the worst of any members of my team. Now, I think we've probably finished here.'

'I'll tell you when we're finished,' said Black, 'if you don't mind.'

The head looked suitably chastened. Perhaps he was too used to being in charge; in any case, Black's tone soon changed his mind.

'I want to talk to this Mr Keech,' continued Black, 'and anyone else who had regular contact with Alice Teale.'

The headmaster nodded his head slightly to acknowledge his acceptance of this, but his face told Beth how uncomfortable he was to yield power in his domain.

'By all means, you can talk to Mr Keech,' said the head-teacher. 'He has a free period now, so he's probably marking in his form room, but don't expect him to open up to you.'

'Why not?'

The headteacher sighed, as if Keech were an ongoing cause of stress. 'He is not . . . how can I put this? . . . the most cooperative person you will ever meet. It would not be unreasonable to suggest he has issues with authority.'

'A thorn in your side, in other words?' asked Beth.

'When I try to implement something new, you can be sure he'll be in the vanguard of the resistance. Personally, I think he enjoys a good argument.'

'You don't like him much, then?' asked Black.

'Whether I like the man or not, I have to manage him.'

30

'Hates him, doesn't he?' said Beth when she was alone again with Black and walking down the corridor towards Keech's room.

'The head? Yes, he does.' Then he mimicked the head-teacher: '"I might not be Mr Keech's biggest fan." He really meant that Mr Keech is an arsehole.'

Beth had a scrap of paper with Keech's form-room number on it. 'These corridors go on for ever,' she said.

'Well, it's a big school.' Black's tone suggested that he was wondering what she had been expecting. 'They do bus people in from the surrounding area, not just the town.'

He said that as if she had forgotten it, and she was tempted to ask, *How am I supposed to know that?*, but thought better of it. *Keep your cool, Beth.* 'What did you make of the head?' She kept her voice low so that no one in any of the classrooms would overhear them.

'Apart from his arrogance and defensiveness, he was fine.'

Look who's talking.

They belatedly realized they were on the wrong floor and climbed to the next one, moving along it till they reached a block containing classrooms for the English and drama departments, the school library and, tucked away in the far corner, a room with the letters 'RLC' on its door.

'What does that stand for?' asked Beth.

'Resource Learning Centre.'

'How do you know that?'

Black drew her attention to a sign on the wall right by them directing students to various departments, the library and the resource learning centre with an arrow pointing towards the door in question.

'Oh,' she said.

'And you're a detective?'

Beth almost had to bite her lip but managed to ignore him. 'That's the room where all the detentions and exclusions happen,' she said. 'Kirstie reckoned everyone calls it the punishment block.'

Keech was in his form room. They could see him through the thin vertical glass panel in the centre of the door. There were exercise books on his desk, but he wasn't busy marking. Instead, he was leaning back in his chair, his feet up on his desk. He was dressed in a grey tracksuit, which seemed strange for an English teacher, and he was screwing up a piece of paper into a ball, which he then threw over his own shoulder in an exaggerated action so that it went up into the air in an arc behind him then bounced against the wall like a basketball and dropped into the waste-paper bin in the corner. Beth noticed that there were a number of scrunched-up bits of paper on the floor next to the bin where he had tried and failed to land his shots. He started to crumple up another piece as Beth knocked on his door.

Keech didn't seem remotely bothered to have been caught in the act. 'My new filing system,' he said, then waited for Black and Beth to explain their presence. Keech was no longer a young man, but he was far from old. He had a full head of dark hair with just a touch of grey that failed to dampen a slightly boyish look, despite the occasional line on his face. He peered at Beth with undisguised interest while she spoke, as if he were weighing up his chances with her. She immediately saw Keech as an ageing bad boy. An earlier generation might have described him as rakish, and she could easily see why impressionable young girls might find his self-confidence attractive.

'Run that by me again?' the teacher demanded when Beth told him why they were here. 'Am I a . . . what do you call it? . . . a "person of interest", or something?'

'At this stage in our inquiries we're talking to as many people as possible so we can build a picture of Alice's life and ascertain her final movements.'

'Well, no one knows her final movements after she left this building, since no one saw her after that. As for her life, I'm her English teacher, not her dad, so . . .' He made a gesture indicating helplessness, but it merely conveyed a lack of cooperation. The headteacher's words of warning had been no exaggeration.

'But you must have had some interaction with her,' Beth said, 'during lesson times and' – she locked eyes with him – 'perhaps on an extra-curricular basis?'

Keech immediately became defensive. 'I don't think I like your tone,' he told her, 'and I don't actually have to answer any of your questions at all, so I think I won't.'

Before Beth could answer him, Black intervened. 'That's correct. You don't have to answer our questions and I can assure you we walked in here without holding you under any kind of suspicion.'

'Good, then.' He seemed to think the matter was closed.

'Of course, if we walk out of the room now, I will have formed a very different view.'

'What do you mean?'

'Well, let's see, you have been hostile, evasive and have expressed no concern whatsoever about the well-being of a missing girl you've taught for several years. That's not normal.'

'I just don't like insinuations,' he countered.

'You've had experience of those?' asked Black, surveying the teacher coldly. 'Regarding the appropriateness of your relationships with pupils?'

'*Former* pupils,' Keech corrected him.

'There was the girl you used to live with,' said Beth. 'And the girl you live with now.' She turned to Black and said brightly, 'Funnily enough, they were former classmates, so he must have met them both at the same time.' This was more priceless information from Kirstie.

If he was wondering how Beth knew about his tangled private life, he didn't ask. 'Those relationships started long after they were pupils here. It's called serendipity.'

'We call it grooming,' said Lucas, 'and perhaps we should look into it more closely, once we've found Alice Teale.'

'What exactly do you want from me?' Keech demanded. 'I barely knew the girl. It's nothing to do with me.'

'No one is saying you are the cause of her disappearance,' said Beth, 'but we're trying to put all the pieces together and you may know something that helps us to do that, even if you don't realize it. If you were in the building on the night she disappeared, you might have seen something.'

'I was, and I didn't,' he said. 'And if you don't mind, I'm a bit busy.' He gestured to the pile of exercise books on his desk for marking. 'Even if you do mind, actually.'

Beth opened her mouth to continue the argument, but Black said, 'It's okay, Beth, we may as well go. It's entirely your call whether you talk to us today or not, Mr Keech.'

'It is,' he agreed.

'I'm sure my DCI won't mind speaking to you instead.' The teacher didn't look pleased at the idea of that. 'He likes to do everything by the book, though, so he'll more than likely interview you under caution. The detective chief inspector is very thorough, has been involved in several high-profile murder cases, tracked down paedophiles and rapists. They're talking of him as a future chief constable. He's that sharp.' Black smiled disarmingly. 'I think you'd like him.'

'Well, if he's that much of a high-flyer, he won't want to be wasting his time on me.' Black stayed silent and let Keech reel himself in. 'So what I'm saying is, if it will save him the trouble, you can go ahead and ask your questions now.'

'Thanks for your cooperation.'

31

'What exactly do you teach here, Mr Keech?' asked Black.

'I'm sure you know what I teach,' he said. 'English.'

'But you're wearing a tracksuit.'

'I help out with the sports teams. There are only three PE teachers. There should be four, but one of them is on long-term sick leave with stress.'

'That's very good of you,' said Black, who was surprised, because the headteacher had told them how uncooperative Keech was.

'I do my bit.'

'I understand you also teach ethics? How do you do that?'

'That's a module for some of the kids approaching the age where they have to make choices.'

'How old?'

'Fourteen, fifteen,' he said lightly.

'Could you explain to us what you meant by your lesson, "Morality is a construct".' This was another little gem Kirstie had provided.

'Why? Don't you understand the meaning of the word "construct"?'

'I understand it. I just want to know the point you were making to those impressionable, mostly female pupils.'

'They are not mostly female.'

'It's nearly seventy per cent girls, thirty per cent boys.'

At least it was according to Kirstie, and he didn't challenge that.

'Well, that's their choice, not a deliberate bias on my part. It clashes with a film course. Some of the boys want to be the next Spielberg or Scorsese.'

'Why do you think the girls do it, then?' asked Black. 'Instead of the film course, I mean.'

'Girls that age sometimes lack confidence, even behind a camera, and they are at a time in their life when they are making decisions that affect their future. I think some of them struggle with the advice they get from parents, relations or their friends. I try to open it up, so we discuss things, for example an ethical dilemma, then form our own conclusions. I'll ask them to tell me what they would do if it happened to them, for instance.'

'But you don't believe in a set morality?'

'How can I, when morality is such a moveable feast? Go back fifty years or so and you could be jailed for homosexuality, spurned by society if you had sex outside of wedlock, ostracized by your parents if you fell pregnant without a husband. Times have changed,' he went on, 'and morals have, thankfully, moved with them. Society is more tolerant, on the whole.'

It could have been an extract right out of Alice Teale's journal. Clearly, her view on the world had been influenced, at least in part, by his, but was this more than influence? Could it be evidence of grooming young girls to think the way he did?

'Society does still tend to frown on teachers who have sexual relationships with their pupils.'

'As I already explained,' he snapped, 'I am in a

consensual, committed, adult relationship with a woman who is over the age of eighteen, let alone the age of consent, and she lives with me. The fact that I used to teach her is irrelevant.'

'How is it irrelevant? You expect us to believe you never noticed her all the while she was going to your school? She may have even attended one of your "Morality is a Construct" lessons, you may have moulded her until the day you can blithely announce that, because she is over eighteen, it's all okay and there's nothing anyone can do about it?'

'You can think what you like, but none of this has anything whatsoever to do with Alice Teale.'

'But you taught her, too?' said Beth.

'I've taught hundreds of pupils. I'm not involved with . . .' He hesitated.

'All of them?' she asked.

'You know what I mean.'

'We are starting to suspect that she may have been involved with someone.'

'She had a boyfriend, or so I heard.'

'Someone else,' said Beth. 'Someone older, perhaps?'

'Well, it wasn't me.'

'Who was it, then?'

'I have no idea,' he snapped. 'Now are you finished, or are you going to continue your character assassination?'

'No one has any doubts about your character,' said Black.

Keech then brought an abrupt halt to the conversation and began to usher them from his classroom. Beth tried to raise the historic allegation against him, but he cut her off: 'That was a malicious accusation made by a disturbed young woman and it was thrown out. If you don't believe me, then ask your mates in the police.'

'We'll leave you to your marking, then,' Black told him. 'For now.'

Beth and Black waited for some of Alice's other teachers to have free periods or break times and interviewed them. One barely seemed to recall Alice at all, despite teaching her geography for more than a year. Beth got the impression he was one of those teachers who simply transmitted his learning, with little interaction between himself and the kids. Alice had a second English teacher, but he hadn't been around on the night she disappeared and kept confusing her with her friend Kirstie. Two more fruitless interviews followed, with teachers who expressed concern for Alice but claimed to have had no dealings with her outside of normal lessons and knew nothing about her home or private life.

'How many more have we got on the list?'

'There's Miss Pearce, who saw Alice walk away from the school,' said Beth. 'And of course Mr Nash, the drama teacher who directed the school plays she appeared in.'

'They are both key, so let's do one each to make sure we have enough time with them. Which one do you want?'

Beth was surprised to be given the choice. She sensed that Black wasn't as convinced as she was that the photo of Alice gazing at Nash was relevant, but since it had also been reported that he had given her lifts home, he still seemed a very plausible candidate to have been the shirtless man in Alice's room. 'I'll take Simon Nash,' she said.

*

Kirstie had described Mr Nash in gushing terms but this was not entirely restricted to his looks. She also said the drama teacher was 'young and kind of inspirational, unlike most of the teachers at Collemby Comp'. She also said he was 'minted'. Apparently, the teacher didn't really need to teach at all. He was engaged to the daughter of the heir to a bakery empire; a fortune founded on dozens of shops spread across the region, including the little branch in Collemby. If you bought a pasty for your lunch that day, there was a fifty per cent chance it was one of theirs. 'I don't know why he bothers to come in,' Kirstie had told Beth. 'I wouldn't, if I were him.'

Beth found him in the darkroom, which was attached to his own form room. She knew he ran the photography club, so it wasn't a surprise to see him in there. The door was open, and she could see Nash moving around; he appeared agitated. She paused for a moment at the classroom door to watch him without being seen. His back was to her and he was picking up boxes, peering behind them, replacing them then taking down others, lifting the lids and looking inside. He was doing this at a pace that showed he was keen to find something.

'Lost something?' she asked, and he jumped. 'Sorry,' she said.

'You startled me, that's all.' He seemed embarrassed. 'And yes, I'm looking for a camera,' he said. 'An old one, but still.'

'What does it look like?'

'It's a Canon AE-1; black plastic grip with a silver body. A nice bit of kit.'

Beth wondered why he hadn't asked who she was, but she pressed on regardless. 'Did someone take it?'

'I don't like to accuse anyone, but I can't find it anywhere. I do lend cameras out, but the students have to sign for them and bring them back without a scratch. Those are the rules.'

'Maybe someone borrowed it and forgot to put it in the book.'

'Hope so. The head is going mad about it. He signed off the funds for the camera club and blames me for being careless with our equipment.'

'Sounds like he isn't very tolerant of mistakes.'

'He's a good head, he really is – a great one, in fact – but he does let you know if you have let him down, and I'm one of the youngest teachers here, so . . .'

'You feel like a kid who's been told off in the head-teacher's office?'

He laughed. 'Exactly. It's silly, I know,' he said, then gave her a disarming smile. 'You'll be fine, though.'

He held out a hand to shake hers. That smile again. No wonder the girls liked him. He was about the same age as Beth and fully justified the description 'hot'. She resolved not to focus too closely on his good looks and to stick to the matter in hand.

'I'm Simon and you're Jane, right?'

'No,' she said. 'I'm Beth.'

'The new student teacher?' There was doubt in his voice now.

'No,' she admitted. 'I'm with the police and I'm here to talk to you about Alice Teale.'

32

For a teacher of physical education, Miss Pearce seemed quite slight, but she moved with the grace of a natural athlete. By the time Black had located her, she was walking away from the playing fields ahead of an exhausted-looking bunch of mud-caked teens she'd just been cajoling on the hockey pitch. Red faces were the norm among them, giving Black the impression that she drove her girls hard.

She saw Black coming and must have anticipated that his presence here might be about the missing schoolgirl, because she turned back and almost shrieked at the girls, 'Hit the showers! And that means *all* of you!'

No one gave her any lip or even groaned; they just trudged towards the changing rooms, one or two of them limping heavily.

'Miss Pearce, I'm Detective Sergeant Black and I'd like to talk to you about Alice Teale.'

'My office.' She nodded in the direction he should take. 'And call me Jessica, for Christ's sake. You're not thirteen.' It was a deliberate eschewing of formality but still said with a slightly bad grace, as if she shouldn't need to explain this to him.

Her office was little more than a cupboard with a desk and a shower built into a corner, the detritus of various sports littering the floor: a string bag full of netballs, a hockey stick, a stack of floats for the swimming pool.

'You were in school the night Alice went missing – the last to see her, in fact.'

'Yes,' she said, 'but I only saw her from a distance.'

'But it was definitely her?'

'It was definitely Alice. She had a green parka on, like Liam Gallagher's, and a big floppy bag. It was her all right.'

'Obviously you weren't able to tell what kind of mood she was in. She didn't look sad or angry – upset, maybe?'

'I couldn't see that from the staff-room window, but she seemed fine. She was just walking up the path away from the school. I was looking out for my fiancé, Rob, who was coming to pick me up. Otherwise, I wouldn't have seen her at all.'

'Was anyone else out there?'

'Not with her. She was walking on her own. The only other person I saw was Simon Nash, our drama teacher, squeezing into his car.' Black did not let on to Jessica Pearce that this was significant, but he made a mental note to let Beth know Simon Nash had left the school in his car just before Alice had walked away. 'As he drove off, Rob turned up, so I waved to him then quickly washed up my tea cup. By the time I looked back, Alice was gone.'

'Where do you think she went?'

'I assume she walked down the path between the cottages. There isn't really anywhere else to go from there.'

'You said you were in a hurry to meet Rob.'

'I didn't want to keep him waiting.'

'But you took the time to wash up a tea cup?'

'To avoid a telling-off from the head. Dirty cups are one of his bugbears.'

'What do you think about your headteacher?'

238

'In what way?'

'In any way.'

'He's all right, I suppose.'

'Only all right?'

'He runs a tight ship.'

'Is that code for "He's a bit of a bastard"?'

She smiled at that. 'I couldn't possibly . . .' She left the sentence deliberately unfinished.

'What about the culture here?' When she frowned her lack of understanding, he added: 'A number of teachers have had friendships or even relationships with students and former students.'

'I strongly disapprove of it. If it was up to me, they'd all be fired.'

'But it's not up to you.'

'No.'

'And the head hasn't clamped down on it. I know he's worried about the union and everything, but . . .'

She snorted. 'It's not the union that keeps him from acting against the teachers involved.'

'No? What is it, then?'

'Our headteacher has been happily married for a number of years and has three children, but there's something he would rather you didn't know.'

'He had an affair with a pupil?' asked Lucas.

'Well, sort of.'

'How do you mean?'

'He had an affair with a pupil years ago,' she said with a glint in her eye. 'And then he married her.'

'Mrs Morgan started out as a pupil in his school?' asked Black. 'No wonder he feels he can't intervene when it happens here. Does everyone know about this? I mean, how, if it was such a long time ago?'

'Teacher jungle drums.' She shrugged. 'Word gets around. There's always somebody who worked with someone who knows something.'

'The thing is, though I obviously don't approve of grown men courting then marrying their pupils, at least they seem to have made a life together,' said Black. 'The behaviour I'm referring to is quite different.'

'Mr Keech, you mean?' she said. 'He's the worst offender. He left his wife and kids ages ago; now he's a man in his forties, in a position of power, which makes any relationship unequal and wildly inappropriate. It makes me sick, quite frankly.'

'It's illegal, too.'

'If it can be proven that he started seeing them when they were pupils, yes.'

'What do you know about Alice?' Black asked her then. 'Any gossip in the staff room?'

She thought for a moment. 'Nothing much. She has a boyfriend. There was friction when one of his friends started seeing her instead, but that was some time ago.'

'When the wall was sprayed with her name?'

'Yes, but there hasn't been any problem since then.'

'No rows, tantrums or odd behaviour from Alice or anyone around her?' he asked.

She opened her mouth to answer, then stopped, frowned and considered this for a moment. 'Well, there was . . . It's probably nothing.' And she looked apologetic.

'Probably,' he told her, 'but it might be something, so I'd rather hear it than not.'

'Okay, well, I caught her up on the roof once.'

'The school roof?' So Chris wasn't the only one who'd seen Alice Teale up there. 'What was she doing?'

'I have no idea. It was odd. I did ask, and she said something about liking the view, but I think she was just being lippy.'

'And did you press her?'

'Not really. I don't know how used you are to dealing with teenagers. They all do strange things. I doubt she even knew the reason why she was up there herself. I just told her not to be so bloody stupid. I did say it was probably nothing.'

Simon Nash was obviously shocked to find he had been indulging in careless conversation with a detective, but he recovered and mumbled Beth an apology. They sat in chairs normally occupied by his form class.

'I understand you teach Alice Teale?'

'I used to,' he corrected her. 'When she took drama.'

'And she is involved in the school plays, which you direct.'

'Yes.'

'Is that why she stayed behind on the evening she disappeared?'

'No, she isn't in the new play. It's sixth-form club on a Friday evening. Most of them hang around for it. It's very informal and a great deal cheaper than the pub. It's also a . . .' He stopped himself abruptly. 'I was going to say *safe environment*, but that sounds ridiculous now.'

'Did you spend any time with her that night?'

'She's in the camera club, and I run that.'

'So you saw her that evening?'

'There wasn't a club meeting that night, but I don't mind if the kids want to use the darkroom, particularly sixth-formers, who we can trust with the equipment and the chemicals. They're less likely to burn the place down – or we hope so.'

'And they can do that unsupervised?'

'If they leave the place in a mess, they know I'll withdraw the privilege.'

'Why do you even have a darkroom?' she asked. 'Is it needed in a digital age?'

'We started with old, donated cameras and couldn't afford digital ones. My dad was into photography and I had his ancient SLR, which takes film, so I knew how to develop pictures and they let me set up the darkroom.'

'They?'

He corrected himself: 'The headteacher.'

'I'm surprised young people have the patience for it, when they all have cameras in their phones.'

'I was surprised, too,' he said, 'but they love it. You should see how enthusiastic they get when they use the chemicals to bring an image to life.'

Beth recalled Daniel telling her how Alice loved retro things. She began to understand the appeal of the darkroom to teenagers searching for authentic experiences.

'Did you help Alice in the darkroom that night?'

'I did for a while. She wanted to develop some photos of our rambling-club trip to Craster.'

'What kind of photos?'

'Trees, fields, a river, some shots of fellow ramblers.'

'Were they any good?'

'They were, actually. She has an eye for a picture. Not everyone does.'

'How long were you in the darkroom with her?'

'Difficult to say.'

'Please try.'

'Okay, well, maybe half an hour. Why do you ask?'

'Was anyone else in there with you?'

'Not that night, no.'

'And did she seem normal to you that evening?'

'I'd say so.'

'She didn't talk about where she might be going afterwards, or who with?'

'No, but then I don't really pry into the lives of my pupils and they rarely volunteer the information. Teenagers are pretty secretive.'

'So, what did you talk about, then?'

'Photography,' he said, as if that were obvious. 'Techniques for framing an image. And Alice wanted to know the difference between a telephoto lens and a zoom.'

To Beth this sounded like the kind of detailed explanation liars sometimes give, so she decided to test his knowledge. 'Which is?'

'Well, it's to do with focal length, which is variable on a zoom and determines the angle of view.'

'That's all you talked about – photography – the whole time?'

'I think there may have been some chat about the school play and how it was going.'

'But you said she wasn't in your latest play?'

'She maintained an interest. Alice wasn't in this one, but it was her choice, not mine.'

'Why?'

'The dreaded A levels. She didn't really have the time any more and I agreed she should concentrate on revision.'

'She has a very full life outside of school hours,' Beth observed. 'A part-time job, various clubs, a busy social life and, of course, relationships.'

'I think she had *a* relationship,' he said lightly. 'There's a boyfriend, isn't there?' He said this as if he were searching his memory, trying to recall something he was only vaguely aware of. Beth immediately felt he was lying, or at least trying not to admit that he knew all about it.

'Christopher Mullery,' he said finally. 'Nice lad.'

'The poor boy is worried sick.'

'Well, he would be.'

'She ever talk about her relationship with you at all?'

'She may have mentioned she had a boyfriend, but other than that . . .' He shook his head.

'What about her home life – her father, mother, brother?'

'Only vaguely.' When Beth stayed silent, he added: 'Occasional mentions of her father being cross with her if she got home late. I think he has a bit of a short fuse.'

'And she lived way over the other side of town, so the chances of her being back late would have been higher.'

'I suppose so.'

'Did you feel sorry for her?'

'She's hardly the first girl of her age to have a strict father, but I suppose I did a bit, yes.'

'Is that why you gave her lifts home?' asked Beth.

The question was like a grenade dropped right into the

middle of their conversation. She watched him closely while it went off. He looked as if he was trying to work out how she had heard about the lifts. 'That was only a few . . . A couple of times.'

'A couple?' she asked. 'Or a few? Just for the sake of clarity.'

He frowned as if he were trying to remember. 'I would say probably four times, in the course of an entire term. Look, I live in that direction. It's not much of a diversion to swing by her street on my way home. I didn't make a habit of it but, once or twice, after rehearsals for the last play, and a couple of times when she was working late in the darkroom, then yes, I did offer her a lift, and she accepted. I have a duty of care, as we all do.'

Beth nodded as if she understood and perhaps even agreed with his statement, then said, 'She's very pretty, Alice.'

She wondered if he might deny this or claim to have never noticed her looks, but instead, he said easily, 'She is.'

'You're a young man, Mr Nash, only a few years older than her. You probably have more in common with Alice than with some of the other teachers.'

'I enjoy her company and she *is* a pretty girl, but then I've known a lot of very attractive women in my time. You're not entirely unpresentable yourself, but I have managed to resist the temptation to make a pass at you, and you're not even my pupil. Alice is and it wouldn't be appropriate, even if I wasn't taken, which I am.'

'You have a partner?' asked Beth. She knew the answer already but didn't want to reveal how much she had learned from Kirstie.

'Fiancée.' He took out his wallet and opened it to show a picture of the two of them close up, laughing at someone else's wedding, an informal selfie of a perfect couple, their faces close together, almost touching. 'That's Karen.' Beth had to admit that his fiancée was stunning and easily on a par, looks-wise, with Alice Teale. She also looked several years older and more sophisticated than the missing girl.

'I hope that allays your suspicions.'

'Do you live with your fiancée?'

'Yes.'

'Did you tell her when you gave lifts to Alice Teale?'

There was a second's hesitation. 'I'm almost sure I will have done.'

'If I called her now, she'd confirm that?' asked Beth.

'Presumably. I'm pretty certain I would have mentioned it, but she's not the jealous type, so I imagine she barely took it in, and I can guarantee it won't have bothered her.'

'When's the wedding?'

'Next year. We're in no rush. Like I said, we already live together, so . . .'

'Congratulations.'

Simon Nash seemed more relaxed once he had proven the existence of his fiancée, but Beth kept coming with the questions.

'You didn't give Alice Teale a lift home on the night she disappeared. Why not?'

'I just didn't offer. Obviously, now, I wish I had. I keep thinking that, if I had just driven her home, she might be safe and well now, instead of . . .'

'Instead of?'

'Missing, obviously.'

'Why didn't you offer?'

'She didn't want a lift.'

'How do you know that if you didn't actually ask her?'

'She was keen to stay a little longer.'

'In the darkroom?'

'No, she had finished in the darkroom. I got the impression she had something else to do or someone to talk to.'

'Who?'

'I don't know,' he said. 'I cleared up and got my stuff together, then I went home.'

'Miss Pearce saw you leave the school from the staffroom window. She saw Alice leave, too, on foot, just moments after your car pulled away, so Alice didn't stay all that long.'

'No,' he said. 'She mustn't have done.'

His answers were calm and measured, betraying no sign of guilt or stress. There was no reason for Beth to be suspicious of the man and yet, for some reason, she was. She decided to keep at him. 'Is it normal for a teacher to give up his Friday evening to hang out with the sixth-formers?'

'It's not compulsory, but it gets you Brownie points from the head. He doesn't force you, but . . .'

'You feel obliged to?'

'There are teachers who don't get involved in anything, but I'm one of the newer ones.'

'Must be a pain, though, hanging out with a bunch of adolescents when you could be at home with your fiancée.'

'It comes with the job, and she accepts that.'

'How long did it take you to finish off after Alice left the darkroom?'

'A few minutes.'

'How many minutes?'

'Five, I suppose, and then I got changed.'

'You change your clothes to go home?'

'I wear sports gear at sixth-form club,' he said, 'for the badminton and basketball.'

'Do you shower as well?'

'Yes.'

'It would be a good twenty minutes or more, then, before you finally left.'

'And people saw me heading down to get changed and then afterwards, as I was leaving. You can check.'

'I will,' she said. 'And yet you and Alice still left at the same time.'

'If you say so.'

'I don't say so. A witness does. You were seen by the same person.'

'Miss Pearce. I know, you said.'

'She saw you drive off just as Alice was walking away.'

'Well, I didn't see her,' said Nash. 'Alice, I mean.' Beth now realized there was perhaps a twenty-minute window in Alice's evening that was unaccounted for, if he was telling the truth. 'I assumed she would have left by then.' He added: 'Was she hanging out with friends?'

'No one else saw her after she left the darkroom, only Miss Pearce, and she was the last person to see her.'

Simon Nash gave her a helpless look, as if he couldn't be of any further assistance with that. Was he being entirely honest with her, or was he more than just Alice's teacher? The thought of that made Beth recall the sighting of Alice in the big black car down by the railway station as it sped away.

'What car do you drive, Mr Nash?'

'I own a BMW 5 Series,' he said.

'Colour?'

'Blue.'

'Dark or light blue?'

'They call it Mediterranean blue,' he said. 'It's darkish.'

But was it dark enough to be mistaken for black at night, moving at speed between the platforms? At least she now knew he could not have been sitting in the parked red car that had been spotted between the cottages and the allotments.

'Nice car on a teacher's pay.' When Nash didn't answer, she added, 'I suppose Daddy bought it. Sorry, I mean Daddy-in-law.'

If he was rankled by her knowing or guessing that, he tried not to show it. 'It was a wedding gift,' he mumbled. 'He bought Karen a car, too.'

'But the wedding's not till next year?'

'He was pleased when we said we were going to get married.'

Beth couldn't imagine what it would be like to marry into such wealth and never have to worry about money again.

'One last thing. When you were driving away from the school, did you see anyone else hanging around there?'

When he answered he sounded hesitant. 'Not at first, no.'

'But you did see someone – is that what you're saying?'

'Further down the street, almost into the town. I saw him then.'

'Who?'

'Alice's boyfriend, Chris.'

'You saw Chris? Are you sure about that?' She needed to be certain because Chris had told everyone he hadn't left his house that night. If Nash was right about this, then the boy had lied to them. Alice was not seen again beyond the school perimeter, so it looked as if someone must have met her there. Maybe it was her boyfriend.

'It was only a glimpse as I drove by, but I'm pretty certain it was him.'

'What was he doing?'

'I assumed he was walking up to meet Alice. Sorry, is this significant? Should I have mentioned it earlier?'

Maybe you should have, thought Beth, *or perhaps it was perfect timing on your part, to leave me with that revelation about Chris just as I was drawing our interview to a close.* 'Thank you for your cooperation, Mr Nash.'

33

They tracked him down at a friend's house. Chris's mother
had told them he was studying there and strongly implied
she would rather he wasn't interrupted. It was as if she had
forgotten that a young girl – his girlfriend – was missing.
The other boy quickly offered to go up to his room so they
could speak to Chris privately in the lounge. He sat down
heavily on the sofa. 'What do you want?'

'We want to know why you lied, Chris,' Beth told
the boy.

'Lied? I didn't lie to you. Lied about what?'

'You said you didn't leave the house the night Alice disappeared,' Beth reminded him, 'but you did. You were
seen walking up the road towards the school.'

'Who saw me? Who *says* that they saw me?' he demanded,
and Beth noticed how quickly he had modified his answer,
though it was not quite quick enough.

'A credible witness,' Beth told him. 'And I suspect they
weren't the only one to see you. If I knocked on every door
between your house and the school, do you think I wouldn't
find at least one other person who saw you go by?'

Chris appeared to consider this and must have con
cluded the odds were against him.

'I'm sorry,' he said softly. 'I didn't mean to lie.'

'But you did, Chris,' said Black, 'and we'd like to know
why.'

'Why do you think?'

'You tell me.'

'I'm not an idiot,' he said. 'I watch TV, all those true-crime shows. The cops always think it's the husband or the boyfriend who's done it.'

'That's because it often is.'

'Yeah, well, not this time. When that detective, Ferguson, first came round, he was coming at me with all the questions like that.' He clicked his fingers three times in quick succession to denote the speed. 'I panicked a bit and I said I hadn't been up to the school. I knew I wasn't responsible for Alice disappearing and I figured she'd show up eventually. I just wanted him off my back.'

'You admit, then, that you did go up there?' asked Beth.

'I've just said, haven't I?'

'And you saw Alice?' she persisted.

'No,' he said vehemently. 'I couldn't find her, and I didn't want to hang around outside the school like a wallad.'

'A what?' asked Beth.

'An idiot.'

Beth wasn't even a decade older than Chris and his friends but sometimes even she couldn't understand them.

'Are you lying to us again, Chris?'

'No, no. Believe me, I'm not.'

Black shrugged. 'You lied before. Why should we believe you now?'

'I told you why I lied.'

'And I'm not convinced. You're saying you walked up on the off-chance?' asked Black.

'It's only a ten-minute walk,' Chris explained. 'I figured I'd see her coming the other way.'

'What if she got the bus?'

'Alice only gets one if it's raining or really dark. She likes to walk. It's safe if you stick to the main roads.'

'But you didn't see her,' asked Beth. She didn't know whether to believe him or not. Her frustration fed her anger towards the boy for wasting everyone's time. If he was lying about this, too, and they could prove it somehow, then Chris would be in big trouble. It would look more and more likely that, once again, it was the boyfriend who was responsible for the fate of a young girl. If Chris was telling the truth now, though, and he hadn't seen Alice on his way to the school, then the window in which she disappeared had to have been a very small one. 'What did you do?'

'I turned back and went home.'

'What time was this?'

'I don't know exactly, but it was around nine o'clock.'

'The same time Alice was seen leaving the school,' said Beth.

'Then she was later than usual.'

'Why would that be, do you think?'

'I don't know. Maybe she got talking to someone.'

'Who?'

'I dunno. I don't, really.'

'Why did you go up there? To hold her hand?' asked Black. 'Or was there some other reason?'

'Lately, she's been distant. I was worried. I wanted to talk to her about it.' Then he said, 'I wanted to talk to her about us.'

'You said she wasn't cooling things off.'

'I didn't think she was.' He corrected himself: 'I hoped she wasn't.'

'But you were worried she might be,' said Beth.

'I don't know.' When she gave him a questioning look, he admitted, 'A bit.'

'Were you worried about anything else, Chris?' she asked him.

'Like what?'

'That she might have been seeing someone else?'

'No.'

'You said that very quickly.'

'That's because it never crossed my mind.'

'You sure about that?' asked Black. 'She went off with your best friend.'

'We'd broken up, then. She wouldn't cheat on me.'

'How do you know that?'

He didn't give her a reason. 'Alice would *not* cheat on me.'

'Okay,' she said. 'Did you see anyone else up there?'

'Like who?'

'Anyone – friends, teachers, passers-by, anybody who looked out of the ordinary.'

'I didn't see anyone except an old bloke with a dog. There's nothing else up there except the cottages, the allotments and the school. You wouldn't go up there unless you were visiting someone.'

'No one hanging about just waiting?' asked Beth. 'Leaning on a fence or sitting in a parked car, maybe – someone who could have offered Alice a lift?' It still seemed the only way to explain her sudden disappearance.

He shook his head. 'There were some cars parked on the way up but nobody sitting in one, as far as I know.'

'What about right by the allotments?' asked Beth. 'Cast your mind back. Were there any cars there?'

He must have seen some urgency in her eyes, because he seemed to focus for a while, then he finally said, 'There was one car. I remember it was blocking the lane to the allotments, which was weird. I had to walk on the road to get by.'

'Are you sure there was no one in it?'

'I thought there wasn't, but it had dark windows.'

'Tinted ones?' He nodded. 'So you couldn't see in?'

'Yeah.'

'There might have been someone in it, then?' asked Black.

'I suppose there could have been.'

'What colour was this car, Chris?' asked Beth.

'Red.'

Beth and Black exchanged a look. The tip-off had been accurate and they both knew it could be a breakthrough. If Chris was telling the truth about not seeing Alice on the way up to the school, then she could have disappeared within yards of the school gate. Was the driver of the car responsible? Could Alice have even been in the car when Chris walked by it looking for her?

'Make and model?' demanded Black.

'It was one of those sporty cars, you know? Maybe a Mazda. I don't know.'

'An MX-5?' he asked.

'Maybe.' But they could tell he wasn't sure.

'Do you think you'll be able to track them down?' asked Chris.

'The owner of the car? Possibly, but it won't be easy without a make and model,' said Black pointedly.

'I'm not making it up,' said Chris. 'The car was there.'

'Then we'll find them,' said Beth. 'Maybe they saw something. Perhaps they saw Alice.'

And maybe they took her.

After catching Alice's boyfriend in a lie, it seemed a good time to confront her ex about his version of events. Tony had said he left the sixth form voluntarily. He hadn't mentioned spraying a spiteful message about Alice on the school wall for everyone to see. The boy would be easier to find, too, since he never went out and it was only a short drive to his house.

'What do you think?' Beth asked Black, following the interview with Chris.

'We'll put the word out that we are trying to trace a red, sporty-looking car that was seen parked by the entrance to the allotments. See if anyone admits it's theirs or reports someone else as the owner. It's frustrating, though, because hardly anyone saw anything. We still haven't traced Happy Harry, who is one of the few people who was definitely in the area around the time Alice left the school, but, since he is an alcoholic, he might not even remember what he saw that night. Even Chris didn't see him.'

'I meant, what do you think about Chris lying to us like that?'

'He lied to a police officer, which isn't good, but he's not the first to do that,' said Black, 'and Ferguson can be a bit intimidating. Maybe he's telling the truth – he lied because he panicked.'

'And if he isn't telling the truth?'

'If he did meet Alice from school, no one saw it, so nobody can contradict his version of events – so far, that is.'

'Let's say they did meet, though. Perhaps there was a row,' offered Beth, 'and it got out of hand.'

'He's the jealous type, so he lashed out?'

'Exactly.'

'There's just one problem with that theory, and it's the same one we keep coming up against.'

'There's no body?'

'Chris walked up there, and the land around the school has been searched. Could he really have killed her without anyone seeing? How would he remove the body from the scene without a car? He could hardly bury her with his bare hands.'

Beth agreed. 'It just doesn't add up.'

'I'm not saying Chris is in the clear, but there's not enough to make him a suspect.'

'Right now, if Nash can be believed, I'm more intrigued by the missing twenty minutes between Alice leaving the darkroom and walking away from the school,' said Beth. 'I want to know where she went, who she saw and what she did.'

34

At least Tony had finally emerged from the garage. He was standing on the front lawn, untangling the flex of a mower, when Black pulled up and asked if he could have another word. A woman with a child in a buggy was walking by on the other side of the road, and Tony looked uncomfortable. Perhaps she was a neighbour and he didn't want her to see him talking to the police, and it was obvious that's what they were, even in an unmarked car. The detective expected Tony to invite them back into the gloom of the garage, where it would be more private. Instead, he abandoned the mower on the lawn and climbed into the back of the car, sitting behind Beth.

'If you want to talk, drive,' he told the detective.

'Where to?'

He let out a big sigh. 'Anywhere but here.'

'Okay.' Black was happy enough to indulge the teenager if it would help him to open up. He did a three-point turn and steered the car out of the housing estate. As he drove, he introduced Beth, adding, 'She's the good cop you mentioned.'

Tony was leaning forward in the back seat so he could hear Black. 'Whatever.'

Black ignored the sullen tone and concentrated on putting some distance between Tony and his street before asking him about the graffiti. Instead he said, 'Your mother been nagging you to cut the lawn?'

'What's that got to do with anything? Leave my mother out of this.' The boy's tone was so sharp Black decided he'd had enough. The car wasn't going very fast, but he hit the brake so hard it came to an abrupt halt, startling Beth and pitching her forward. At least she was restrained by her seatbelt. Tony wasn't so fortunate and was thrown against the back of her seat. It wasn't hard enough to do him any damage, but he shouted in alarm. He was even more taken aback when Black rounded on him. 'Cut the attitude right now, Tony. We haven't got the time.'

'Okay,' he whined. 'There's no need to get . . .'

'To get what?'

Beth could understand why Tony would be too nervous to complete his sentence. The detective had lost his patience and was making sure the boy knew it.

'What do you want to ask me?' He was suddenly compliant.

Black simply glared at the boy, so Beth intervened, unclipping her seatbelt so she could turn and speak to Tony. 'Let's start with how you feel about Alice these days, Tony?'

'I will always care about Alice,' he responded. 'I loved her.'

'You don't *still* love her, then?'

'What would be the point?'

'We can't always help the way we feel about someone,' said Beth, 'even if they're with somebody else.'

'I don't see Alice any more. You can't love someone if you never have any contact with them. After a while, it just fades.'

'Why don't you see her any more? Did you cut off contact, or did she?'

When he did not immediately answer her, Black cut in: 'Was it because of the words you sprayed on the school wall?'

'For fuck's sake!' It was a cry of exasperation from the young man in the back seat. 'It was before that,' he admitted. 'She just didn't talk to me any more.'

'Is that why you did it?' asked Black. 'Or was it because she was back with her old boyfriend and you hated seeing it?'

'That must have really hurt,' said Beth when he didn't answer.

'Why'd she call it off with you, Tony? Did she get cold feet when people stopped talking to her? You didn't mind so much, did you? It was you and Alice against the world, wasn't it? You went out on a limb for her. When she dumped you and got back with Chris, it was all for nothing. They took her back, but they didn't take you back. Tony was the bad boy who got between Alice and Chris and stabbed his friend in the back.'

'They weren't really my friends anyway,' he said dismissively.

'But you thought they were,' Black reminded him. 'Until this happened. There you were, alone and dumped by the girl who had cost you everything, so you went up to the school with a can of spray paint and put a message on that wall.'

'If you say so.' He seemed too weary to either deny it or explain further.

'*You* said so,' Beth reminded him. 'You admitted it to the headteacher.'

'You've got all that anger and resentment in you and you want to express your innermost feelings,' said Black, 'so you got your can of paint and sprayed "Alice Teale is a slag" on the wall.'

'So what?'

'Was that honestly the best you could come up with? Calling the love of your young life a slag?'

'What do you want me to say?'

'I want you to convince me, Tony.'

'Convince you of what?'

'That you're not dangerous,' said Black. 'That you didn't let that anger get the better of you and make Alice disappear.'

'I would never do that.' He sounded appalled, but Black wasn't going to let him off the hook so easily.

'But she's a slag, Tony, you said so yourself, and what do young men like you want to do to slags, eh? Get even with them? Punish them? Make them pay for the way they make you feel? Was that it? Why shouldn't we make you our prime suspect, right now?'

'Because that's not why I sprayed the wall.'

'Then why did you do it?'

Tony just shrugged at that.

'And why admit it?' Beth's tone showed she was more surprised by this than the act itself. 'Why confess when there was no proof it was you? You could have lied.'

'You're pretty good at that,' said Black.

'I had my reasons,' he said, but then clammed up once more.

'And I think I know what they are,' said Beth. 'You didn't put that pathetic message up on the wall to get your own back on Alice,' she told him. 'I think you sprayed it there because you knew the head would make you leave. You wanted to be kicked out, didn't you, Tony?' When he didn't argue she continued: 'You hated every minute there once Alice got back with Chris. You had to put up with them hugging and kissing in the common room, whispering into each other's ears, holding hands in the corridor? Who would want to hang around after that?'

His resistance seemed to crumble then and, with apparent reluctance, he confirmed Beth's theory. 'My mam told me I had to keep going for another year, so I could sit the stupid A levels. When the head asked if I had sprayed the wall, I just said, "Yeah, sure, whatever," and he let me leave.' Tony looked like he might be about to start crying, but he managed to contain his emotion. 'It was either that or punch someone.'

'So you did it to get kicked out?' asked Black. 'I don't buy it.'

'It's true. If I'd just left, my mam would have made me go back there.'

'You're frightened of your own mam?' he asked.

'Not frightened, but she goes on and on at me and she never understands.'

'Why did you use that word "slag"?' asked Black. 'Was Alice seeing someone else?'

Tony looked at him as if he was an idiot. 'You know she was.'

'I meant someone other than Chris.'

'No.' Then he shook his head. 'I don't know, do I? I told

262

you I never saw her any more, except round school when she was glued to Chris. I sprayed the wall to get kicked out, like she said.' And he nodded towards Beth.

Black considered this for a moment then said, 'You're not in the clear, Tony. Not by a long shot. Now get out.'

The boy left the car and started to walk back to his house. When he was gone, Black started to drive again. 'What was that, then?' he asked Beth. 'Feminine intuition?'

'Just intuition,' she snapped. 'It was the only reason for him to fess up to it like that. He knew he'd be kicked out, and that's what he wanted.'

'Right,' said Black calmly. 'Well, the next time you think you know the reason why a suspect did something, tell me, not him.'

'What?'

'That might have been the reason he sprayed the wall, and it might not have been, but now, thanks to you, he has an excuse for it.' He quoted Tony's words back at her, '"I sprayed the wall to get kicked out, like she said."' Beth felt sick then because, whether she liked it or not, Black was right. She had just given Tony a way to explain his behaviour and he had taken it.

'I'm sorry,' she began. 'I just . . .' Then she stopped. What had she been doing? Guiding a suspect because she herself had not believed he was capable of harming his ex, showing Black how clever she was or just opening her mouth and speaking without considering the consequences? Maybe all three at once. All of a sudden, Beth felt incredibly stupid.

'I'm sorry,' she repeated, but Black didn't reply or even speak another word to her on the way back to the major-incident room.

35

In the end, there was no great fanfare when the news came. There never is. It began with a walker, one of the more adventurous types, the kind who likes to take the road less travelled, which was why he used a treacherous, eroded, long-neglected footpath directly overlooking the sea. He didn't seem to mind that he was inches from the edge or that the drop here was almost as high as Cullernose Point, the Northumbrian landmark near Craster he had passed a short time ago on his walk. It was a sunny morning, and the North Sea was calm for once, which was probably why he noticed her bobbing against the rocks, a bundle of wet rags going gently back and forth, trapped in a tiny inlet below him. He might have easily walked by without realizing it was a body, as she lay face down in the water, but one of her arms was outstretched and a milk-white hand was floating on the surface.

He didn't say anything because there was no one to hear him. Instead, he stood on the edge of the cliff, peering down intently to make sure he hadn't imagined it, that she wasn't some stag-do sex doll or shop-window mannequin which had been dropped over the edge for a joke. Then he would look foolish for wasting the authorities' time. But the hand looked authentic and so did the hair that floated out around her head, resting on the surface of the water like seaweed.

This was real. He turned abruptly and started to jog back down the path to get help.

A call was taken and then another, inquiries were made and, eventually, the right people for the job were located and despatched in a rubber boat; the body was retrieved and pulled on board then taken for examination.

An hour later Lucas Black picked up the ringing phone on his desk and took the call. He had been expecting it, but still.

Maybe she picked up on it from the expression on his face, but Beth quickly ended the call she was on. Black realized she was watching him. He asked all the relevant questions, wrote down details of time, location and the condition of the body, enquired about the post-mortem and finished by asking whether there was any doubt about the identity of the victim, bearing in mind there was trauma to the head and the body had been found in the sea. He was told the clothes matched, but it was the jewellery that was the clincher. No matter how mangled a face and body might become when subjected to brutal treatment then dumped in the sea, rings, necklaces and earrings remain largely undamaged. The local police had been able to check Black's detailed description of the missing seventeen-year old and confirmed that their body was wearing a gold necklace with a cross, two plain stud earrings and a ring that matched hers exactly.

Black didn't need to wait for formal identification on this one.

It was Alice.

He thanked the caller, replaced the receiver, looked up into Beth's grim face. 'They've found her.'

'I knew it was going to end this way,' said Beth helplessly, 'but I still had this hope at the back of my mind.'

'Like she was just going to turn up somehow?' asked Black.

'Yes. I know it was stupid.'

'I had it, too,' he confessed.

'I think we were all hoping for the best,' said Beth. 'I feel like I know her now.'

'That's it,' agreed Black. 'It's the journal, seeing her own words written down like that.'

'And the fact that she was so bloody young, with her whole life ahead of her.'

'Which always makes it worse. That, and not having all the answers.'

'Not yet, we don't,' said Beth, and there was a new determination in her tone.

Black obviously felt the same way. 'I want to get this bastard, whoever it is.'

'I can't imagine anyone being so cold-hearted.' She shook her head.

'I'll need to go and see the family,' he said.

Even though it was the last place she wanted to be, Beth said, 'I'll come with you. Her poor brother. He'll be devastated.'

'They all will,' said Black, though they were both wondering how Ronnie Teale would really feel about Alice's death.

*

She always knew this would be the worst part of the job, but nothing could have prepared Beth for the moment when Black broke the news of their daughter's death to the Teales. Abigail Teale let out a loud wail of despair, while her husband gripped her by the shoulders, squeezing her tightly, as if he could physically restrain her grief somehow, all the while saying, 'No, no, it can't be right, it can't be her.'

Daniel Teale bent double in his chair and buried his face in his hands, as if he didn't want anyone to see his grief, or perhaps he was blotting out the news, along with the rest of the world, while he wept for his sister, and Ronnie just kept on talking: 'No, no, no.' He was shaking his head, as if they had got this all completely wrong somehow. 'This isn't right,' he told them. 'That's not . . .' And for a moment Beth actually thought he was going to say *what I wanted*, but instead he just carried on denying the reality of the situation: 'No, you've made a mistake. She's all right. I know it.' Was this simply denial, or something more sinister? Beth was tempted to ask him what he meant by it, but this wasn't the time for an interrogation. Ronnie Teale always seemed to be on the verge of an explosion of rage or frustration but, today at least, it was justified. The hard questions could come later but, for now, both Beth and Black would leave the family to grieve.

The hour she spent at the Teales' home was the longest of Beth's life. She got home physically and mentally exhausted, drank an entire bottle of wine in less than two hours and still couldn't sleep.

The next day, other detectives and police officers started to show up, all of them reassigned from other ongoing investigations now that Alice Teale had been confirmed dead and the case officially designated a murder investigation. Beth counted twelve new detectives in the major-incident room, and she couldn't get near Black until he had finished briefing them all. Tasks were discussed and assigned and the extra manpower was backed up even further by the presence of additional uniformed officers who had been found from somewhere and sent to Collemby to assist with the legwork, which included going over old leads and conducting house-to-house inquiries all over the town.

DCI Everleigh oversaw everything from HQ, but everyone looked to Black to provide real guidance. He may have only been a DS, but he was the most senior man on the ground and had been there from the beginning of the investigation, so his word counted more than his rank. Confirmation of the girl's death brought a deluge of new leads from the public, who kept the phones ringing almost non-stop. All these potential leads had to be analysed and followed up. Beth already knew the vast majority would lead nowhere. It would mean long days of busy, often noisy activity, chasing leads until they hit dead ends then starting all over again.

When Black received the results of the post-mortem he called everyone together.

'There was blunt-force trauma to the head and face,' he told the assembled group, 'as well as multiple fractures, which you would expect if she was thrown from a height into the sea. There are rocks everywhere along that section of coastline,' he explained, 'but it wasn't the blunt force that killed her.'

'Then how did she die?' asked Beth.

'Alice was strangled,' he said. 'The pathologist doesn't want to go out on a limb on this one.' Then he added: 'They never do. He does think it's likely that some of the injuries to the face, head and body occurred before her death, while others are likely to have been caused by the rocks. In a way, we've been lucky, because strangulation cases don't always show outward signs, but this guy was thorough. He spotted characteristic abrasions on the skin around the neck, and petechiae.' Before she could ask him what that was, he explained: 'That's a tell-tale series of small red spots that appear on the skin, and they were still visible.'

'Even after she had been in the water, perhaps for several days?' asked DC Rodgers.

'The pathologist reckons she must have landed on the rocks then been pushed on to a ledge by the sea before she was spotted in the shallows of the sheltered cove, so the body was in a much better condition than it would have been if it had been dumped way out.' Black didn't need to add that this had minimized the damage caused by sea creatures.

'He thinks she might have been badly injured but still alive. Then, before she went into the water, someone finished her off.'

'Why would you beat someone severely around the head then strangle them?' asked Beth. 'Why not finish the job with whatever you were striking them with?'

'We don't know,' Black admitted.

'Where exactly was the body?' asked one of the new detectives.

'In a tiny inlet, close to Cullernose Point, not far from Craster.'

'Craster?' queried Beth.

'Do you know it?' he asked.

'I've been there,' said Beth, 'and so has Alice. She went there with the rambling club.'

'Simon Nash's rambling club?'

'Yes,' she said.

'How do you know that?'

'He told me.'

'Then why would he mention it?' asked Lucas, 'if he was guilty of dropping her body from a cliff near there? You immediately thought of him.'

'Perhaps that was someone's intention – to put Simon Nash in the frame by dumping Alice's body there.'

They worked long and late, putting in the hours until they were both tired but still reluctant to give up and go home. That was when Black remembered something. 'Shit,' he said. 'It's the diner's opening night.' He checked his watch. 'We'll be late, but we can still make it. Are you coming?'

'Do you want to go?' asked Beth.

'They're my friends,' he said, 'so, yes, but you don't have to.'

Beth thought of Gemma then, and her eager invitation, as well as her paranoia that no one would show up for the launch of her dream. 'I'd just forgotten about it,' she admitted, 'same as you, but yes, I can be there.'

'Great,' he said. 'To be honest, right now, I feel like I need a bloody drink.'

Beth had to admit that, despite her reservations about spending more time with Black than was strictly necessary, she really needed one, too.

36

The opening of the diner was a success. Virtually every-one who had been invited was there, the train carriages were packed, the drink flowed, the food arrived hot and on time and was devoured gratefully by hungry guests. They ate standing inside or, because it was another in a succession of warm nights, outside, so they could admire the view of the Northumbria coast. The local press were there, photographs were taken and most people, including Beth and Lucas, had had the sense to arrive and leave by taxi, so they could enjoy the wine all evening.

Beth made up for their lateness by buying flowers for Gemma on the way and Black got a bottle of champagne for the happy couple who had put so much work into their venture. Their hosts repaid them with effusive thanks, warm hugs and guest-of-honour status. Beth was begin-ning to really like them both and couldn't help but feel they deserved this success.

To Beth's shame, she couldn't recall the last time she'd had a proper night out; that wasn't an ageing detectives' leaving do. She mixed with the other guests and drank way more quickly than usual to combat her shyness and ease the stress of the previous days and found that this helped to take her mind away from the case, for a little while at least.

Eventually, the crowd thinned and she found herself

heading back to top up her glass at the same time as Lucas. She still didn't know how to take the man, or account for his actions, but he was the only one in the room she knew at all, apart from her hosts, and she was too tired to stay angry at him now. Perhaps the discovery of Alice Teale's body, along with the shared ordeal of breaking the news to her family, had brought them a little closer to a truce, at least in her eyes. With the simple wisdom of drink, Beth reasoned that Black had done what he'd done for whatever reason and that she would never learn the full truth, nor could she ever ask him about it, so she would tolerate his presence alongside her at the party. Despite everything, she had learned that he was a good detective, a diligent and hard-working man and that he actually cared about Alice Teale, which proved that he really did give a damn after all. They drank together, without talking about the case, and it was nice to simply forget about everything for a while.

The party broke up around midnight, but Black suggested that their taxi dropped them at a bar he knew that had a licence till 2 a.m. Somehow, Beth had enjoyed herself and was happy to continue with the drinking.

They were drunk by now, or at least Beth was, which she realized only when she stumbled slightly as she got out of the taxi, and she hoped to God Lucas was, too. Otherwise, it would be embarrassing in the morning.

Black commandeered a couple of stools so they could prop up the bar. They ordered more drinks and agreed it had been a good night. They talked for a while about the diner and other, more trivial things before Beth's curiosity finally got the better of her. If she hadn't been feeling more confident because of the effects of the booze, she would never have asked him. 'You know Collemby, don't you? From before, I mean?' She was sure he did. It was the way he knew the layout of the school, the story behind the name of the old pub, about the existence of the lovers' lane at the disused railway station – a barman had even said hello to him – so why wouldn't he just admit he was familiar with the place?

His whole body seemed to stiffen then, and he straightened on the bar stool. Oh God, he was about to go nuts and start shouting at her, ruining their evening and their barely functioning working relationship in one instant.

Instead, he said, 'It's nothing sinister.' At first it didn't appear that he was going to tell her anything more, but then he seemed to sag a little and made a sound that was almost a sigh. 'It's my ex-wife,' he conceded. 'She's from Collemby originally, so I do know the place. I used to go there years ago when we were both teenagers and dinosaurs roamed the Earth.'

'Then why didn't you just say?'

He drained the remnants of his drink before answering her. 'Because it was a very long time ago and I don't really like to think about it,' he told her quietly.

Beth hadn't been expecting that for an answer. Was Lucas Black really affected when he looked back on earlier, happier times, now that they were gone? It wasn't such a strange notion, she supposed. Wasn't everyone?

'Fair enough.'

'So, what's your story, Beth?' Black said that like he didn't want to continue with his.

She shrugged. 'I don't have one.'

'Everybody does,' he said. 'Some stories are more dramatic than others, I'll grant you, but we all have one.' She didn't respond, so he asked, 'Okay, do you have a boyfriend? Girlfriend? Partner? Significant other?'

'No one,' she said, then quickly added: 'At the moment.'

He didn't say anything further and, for some reason she couldn't quite explain, she said, 'There used to be. I lived with him.'

She didn't normally talk about her ex with anyone but her oldest, closest friends and, even then, it was never in the slightest bit cathartic. When they loyally attacked him on her behalf, she found herself defending him. The break-up had been her fault, she'd say, at least partially, at any rate, and they would often become infuriated with her for letting him off the hook so easily. He'd been the cheat, the rat, the one who left, not her, but it always seemed to come back to one thing for Beth. Why would he have done that if she hadn't been lacking in . . . something? She wasn't good enough.

'He bailed,' she said, and for some reason it was easier to tell Black this than she would have imagined. He'd told her about his own problematic love life after all, and at least his usual silence lacked judgement.

'He didn't just bail,' she admitted finally. 'He left me for my best friend.'

'Shit,' he said. 'That's awful.'

'It was,' she admitted, and she was about to give him the usual crap about picking herself up, dusting herself down and getting on with it, time healing wounds and maybe even *I'm glad I found out early on*, a line she had used with more than one friend, as if the pain were minimized because they weren't actually married, even though she'd always envisaged that, one day, they would be.

Instead she just said, 'It is.' Then she found herself confessing, 'It was a while ago, but a couple of weeks back I found out that she's pregnant and they're getting married.'

He looked straight ahead then, and it seemed he was about to say something profound. Instead, he raised a hand then a finger to gently draw the attention of the barman. Without asking her what she wanted he said, 'Two pints and two tequila slammers.'

'Like that's going to solve our problems.' But she said it wryly.

'It won't solve them,' he admitted, 'just make them seem less important.'

'I don't even remember how I'm supposed to do this,' she admitted when the barman handed them the slammers.

'Lick your hand,' he said. 'Like this.' And he did it to his own hand. Beth licked hers and he poured salt on to both. 'Lick the salt, skull the tequila then suck the lemon. One, two, go!' and they did. Beth licked the salt, winced, drank the tequila down in one go, coughed, then sucked the lemon and winced again. They both slammed their glasses down on the bar.

'God, that's revolting,' she said, though Black looked entirely unaffected.

'Cheers,' he said as he raised his pint.

Beth clinked glasses again and gratefully sipped her own beer because it took away the taste of the previous drink. A moment later they were somehow back on the topic of her ex.

'I suppose it was a bit like Chris and Tony, with Alice,' she offered. 'Only that makes me Tony. God, I'm the sad, desperate one,' she realized.

'It was nothing like it.' She was about to argue with him over that dismissive comment, but he went on: 'They were just teenagers; you were living with the guy. You thought he was the permanent one.' He took a sip of his pint. 'That's far worse.'

'Yeah,' she agreed. 'It is.'

'As for your ex-best friend.' He grew thoughtful. 'What a bitch. There aren't many rules left these days, but that's one of them. You don't touch your mate's other half. It's pretty simple.'

For some reason, it comforted Beth to hear this coming from someone who had not been directly involved in the messiest break-up imaginable. Nearly all Beth's friends had sided with her, though she was pretty sure some of them were torn and still in touch with *the bitch*, as they all now called her former best friend, and she couldn't help feeling that a lot of their supportive comments might be born out of pity for her. She often found herself wondering what they really thought. Had they seen it coming? Had they always imagined that Jamie would eventually leave her? Did they think he was out of her league? There was something nice about this virtual stranger's uncomplicated, male, simplistic view of things.

'Here's to your ex-best friend,' he said, raising a glass, and when she was confused by the gesture, he added: 'May her tits sag all the way down to her knees.'

Beth laughed and raised her glass to clink it against his. 'To saggy tits,' she agreed.

Of all the people to lighten the load of her troubles, she would have given very long odds a few days ago that this person might be Lucas. It didn't change much. She wasn't fine, things weren't going to be okay, but he had somehow made them temporarily bearable and that was enough for now.

'So, in the spirit of full disclosure, and since I know your story, what do you want to know about me?' he asked.

'Oh, nothing.'

'That's bull.'

'I mean, I probably know everything I need to know.'

He considered this for a moment. 'What do you know?'

Why did she feel like she was back on very dangerous ground, even though he seemed to be making light of this? She wanted to avoid the topic if she could, but something told her he would assume she was gossiping about him behind his back if she didn't just come out with it, so she ploughed on, carefully.

'Okay, you said you're ex-army?'

'I am.'

'But you left to join the police force.' Then she added: 'Obviously.'

'I left because my wife didn't want to be an army wife any more. I basically had a choice: leave or stay in the army and lose my marriage.'

'Then I'm sure you made the right choice.'

'Not really,' he said. 'She left me anyway, in the end.'

'I'm sorry.'

'Not your fault,' he said placidly. 'Not mine either – well, not entirely. It just didn't work out and it was a long while ago.'

'Do you miss it?'

'The wife or the army?' There was a twinkle in his eye when he said that and it made her laugh again, even though he had just indirectly described another woman as 'it'. Christ – Lucas Black made her laugh. Maybe he wasn't a compete android after all. 'I do miss her sometimes, but less often these days. I don't even know where she is.'

Beth tried to imagine what that must be like and realized that, one day, when she was older, she would be telling a very similar story about Jamie. It's not as if they kept in touch. How could they? It struck her then how you could stay friends with people for years, but if you broke up with someone you thought you were going to spend the rest of your life with, you might never see or hear from them again.

'I do miss the army,' he admitted. 'I felt like I was good at it, you know? I knew what I was doing.'

'You're good at this,' she offered.

'You don't actually mean that.'

'I do. I know we clashed a bit to begin with and, yes, I thought you were a miserable fucker' – he laughed at that description – 'but now I realize there's more to you than that.'

'Thanks.'

'You're not *just* a miserable fucker.'

To her surprise, he laughed quite hard at that, and it set off a bout of coughing. Was he shocked because the young female detective had used the F-word? He couldn't have been. He just liked the banter. Guys spoke to each other like that all the time, particularly in the army. Perhaps she had finally worked out how to speak fluent Lucas.

'So what else do you want to know?' he asked when his coughing had ceased.

'I don't need to know anything else about you, Lucas. Your life is none of my business.'

'I don't mind – really I don't. Gemma explained it to me.'

'What?'

'She said I ought to get to know you better. That you couldn't trust me if you didn't know me. She said it's a girl thing.'

She bridled at that. 'It's not a *girl* thing.'

He looked confused. 'Oh, she said it was. Sorry.'

'Maybe she thinks like that, but I don't. I don't want you to think of me as a girl.'

'I didn't mean it like that.'

'I know, and I appreciate you making the effort.' She softened then. It wasn't his fault he had been given advice from Gemma that didn't chime with her own feelings. 'Okay, then, where do you live?' she asked. He looked confused again, as if she were inviting herself back for coffee, and her face flushed. 'I mean, do you have a flat or a house?'

'Oh, I see. I kept the house. I mean, I bought her share when she . . .' He made a gesture with his hand that he must have thought symbolized his wife flying away. 'And before you ask, I live on my own.'

She thought it best not to go further down that route.

'Well, I know what car you drive, what beer you drink and the fact that you have two mad friends who've invested in a train-carriage diner, so that puts me way ahead of everyone else at HQ in the "what do you know about Lucas Black?" contest.'

'That's not saying a lot,' he said. 'What do they say about me? At HQ, I mean. I can guess, but I'd like to know.'

Oh God, what could she say? That he was a killer, possibly even a psycho, an ex-army man with hidden demons, perhaps caused by combat, and a temper that could flare at any moment? That he had shot down a man in cold blood in suspicious circumstances?

'They say you're an enigma.'

'Nice try, but they don't say that.'

She tried to look hurt, but could tell he was seeing right through her.

'They didn't say much, to be honest.'

'It's that bad, is it? I've often wondered. What did they tell you about me, really?'

'Honestly?' He nodded his assent, so she just blurted it out: 'That you had killed someone.'

37

There was a long pause before he responded, and Beth wondered if she had blown it.

'That does seem to define me round here. What did they tell you about it?'

'Nothing.' When he seemed sceptical, she said, 'Really. That was pretty much all I was told.' There was no way she was going to admit that she'd had a comprehensive briefing on it from Peter Kennedy. That would surely get his back up and, more than that, she wanted to hear Black's version of events. What would he tell her? Would it be anywhere close to the truth?

For a while he appeared to be contemplating whether to say anything at all. Finally, he told her, 'It was a few years back – a domestic hostage situation.' And all of a sudden Beth felt stone-cold sober, because she knew the importance of every word he was about to utter. 'I remember it was a cold, wet Friday night, the kind where you just want to stay in, lock your door, have a takeaway and a beer. The call came in that a man was holding his wife and daughter at gunpoint, threatening to kill them and himself. Someone even said a gunshot had already been reported from inside the house. The man had clearly lost it and there wasn't a lot of time for a coordinated response, so the word went out for any firearms-trained officers who could be deployed quickly to back up the uniforms in the area. I was one of them. You have to understand, it was a different world back then. These days, with all the terrorist alerts, we'd have a SWAT team on him in minutes. Anyway, I got down there quick-as. There's a guy on a loudhailer trying to talk this shouty man out of his house, asking him to at least free the kid, then his wife, but he's not listening. He sounds deranged and we can't even make out much of what he's saying. The wind didn't help. It was distorting his voice, but it sounded as if he was telling us to back off or he would kill everyone, then himself. It's a bad, confused situation, and it doesn't get any better when he goes back into his house and locks the door. I get ordered to go around the back, and I'm quietly hoping I won't be needed. There's three of us there, but I end up closest. I've got the rear wall of the property for cover and I'm aiming at the back door with a Glock.'

Beth couldn't take her eyes from him, but Black kept his gaze fixed ahead, staring at the optics behind the bar.

'With classic timing, he chose that moment to burst out of the back door with his wife and daughter. He's dragging the wife, who is screaming for help. The daughter, who is only about ten, is shouting, "Don't do it, Daddy!" and I think he's waving a gun. It's really dark at the back of the house, there's no lights and it's still pouring with rain, and I'm not sure, but it looks like a sawn-off shotgun. At this point I'm worried he's going to execute them both in the back garden right in front of me, and he obviously represents a clear and immediate danger to the family and us. I shout, "Armed police, don't move!" His reaction? To keep moving, and he's bellowing something about us police all being bastards. I shout, "Put down the weapon!", but he won't comply. It all happens very quickly then. He pushes his daughter down on to her knees in front of him and shoves his wife to one side. I see him removing those two obstacles to my line of fire, and then he swings the gun round and brings it up like he's about to shoot.' Black took a breath then. 'So I fired mine.'

He didn't say anything else for another minute, and all Beth could do was try to visualize the scenario. She realized she was holding her breath.

'The bullet hit him,' he said, and he still sounded surprised by that, even now. 'It struck him in the chest and he fell backwards on to the ground and sort of flailed there for a bit. I took a chance and went over the wall towards them. I was in the back garden and I got a closer look, all the while thinking, *Please don't get up again, or I'll have to finish you.* By this point, there's pandemonium. The guys behind me are shouting into their radios, I can hear the front door being kicked in, and the rest of the team burst through it and the guy on the ground is crying out in pain, the wife is sobbing and calling his name, but the worst of it is his daughter. She's hollering, "Daddy!" at the top of her voice. It's this high-pitched shriek, and one of the guys I'm with has to grab her to drag her away. The wife is bordering on hysterical because she can see it's a bad wound. The blood is' – he struggles to find the word and, when he does, his voice cracks a little – 'spreading all over the wet floor of the patio in amongst the rain. It's pretty clear he's probably not going to make it.' Then he said, 'And it turns out he doesn't. He died on the way to the hospital, but at this point he's still lying there in the rain, in a lot of pain and distress.'

He took a breath and kept his voice level. 'Then I saw the gun, only it wasn't a gun. The sawn-off shotgun, which I would have sworn on a stack of bibles I had seen, turned out to be a table leg.' He shook his head as if the explanation he was about to give was crazy, and maybe he thought it was, too. 'He pulled it off the kitchen table to threaten his family with when he started to properly lose it. So he's come out of his house armed with a table leg, but because I think he's waving a shotgun I shoot him and I kill him.'

'Oh my God,' she said quietly.

'And that's all there is to it, really.'

'What happened? To you, I mean?'

'I was suspended while the press ran a lot of stories about trigger-happy police firing on unarmed civilians, or at least ones who were armed only with a length of wood. Even the local MP questioned our professionalism and demanded a review of just who should be allowed to carry firearms and whether I was qualified enough. It was a year before I was exonerated, and even that was portrayed in the media as the police sticking up for one of their own. I can't say I blame them. The wife testified that the guy was mentally ill and no real threat to anyone. He would have come quietly, apparently, according to her.

'It was a shitstorm and I am an embarrassment. Everyone I knew kept their distance,' he concluded, 'and they still do.' He turned to face her then and said, 'So now you know.'

When he had finished, she didn't know what to say but, somehow, she managed, 'Lucas, I am so sorry.'

'Yeah,' he said. 'So am I.'

38

Like every big night out, it had seemed like a good idea at the time, the effects of the alcohol therapeutic after a stressful period. Now, though, Beth knew she would have to bury her feelings of nausea, as well as a splitting headache, and just get on with a hugely important day for the case. Getting out of bed had been a struggle and, for once, she would have gladly carried on sleeping, but guilt forced her to get up. She drank deeply from a bottle of water that she had no recollection of leaving on her bedside cabinet and immediately swallowed two ibuprofen, noticing she had carelessly dropped yesterday's clothes on the floor.

How pissed was I?

Beth experienced a few moments of dread while she relived the previous evening in her head until she could account for virtually all of it without experiencing a sense of shame. Beth had been pretty drunk when she and Lucas had finally parted, but they had gone their separate ways in different taxis without falling out. She had neither punched him nor kissed him, thank God, and the only vaguely embarrassing thing she could recall was an impromptu sharing of secrets. For some reason, she didn't feel in the slightest bit bothered about telling him how her ex had run off with her best friend. In return, he had provided her with such a frank, honest and affecting account of the shooting she now felt able to put an end to her worries about his integrity. It was an immense relief.

Somehow, she managed to get to Collemby at the same early hour as usual, but she was still feeling frail. Lucas Black was the only other one there at that time and he looked tired.

'Hangover breakfast?' he suggested as soon as Beth walked into the major-incident room, and she was grateful he was feeling the same way. They went straight to the café, which was busier than usual, with building-site workers in need of hearty food before the start of their day.

Black ordered two kill-or-cure fry-ups and mugs of coffee for them both then handed her the latest extracts from Alice Teale's journal, which had arrived with that morning's post.

The Journal of Alice Teale

Oh my God. OH MY GOD!

It isn't me. It wasn't my fault. All this time, I thought I was doing it wrong or that I'd numbed or damaged myself somehow when I was younger, but no. It just took the right person, someone who knew what they were doing, someone I felt so at ease with I could lose myself completely in the moment, so I didn't worry about how I looked or smelled or what I tasted like or how vulnerable I felt. All that time in Tony's garage and those sessions in Chris's bedroom and I never could. Not once.

All it took was a little while in the back of his car, with his light, insistent touch, and, I swear, I saw stars. My whole body shook. When I finally came down, I wanted to pass out. I was so relaxed I could have fallen asleep right there in his arms.

I'd have done anything for him then. Anything.

'Who do we think *He* is, then?' asked Black.

'She doesn't say,' said Beth. 'Except it *isn't* Chris or Tony. And why send us that bit now?' she asked, almost absent-mindedly.

'Alice's teacher used to drive her home,' said Black. 'But how many people knew that, and who knew that you have been talking to Simon Nash?'

'The whole school knew we were there, and I imagine a lot of people worked out who we were talking to.'

'And they would have told everybody else,' he agreed. 'But who knew about the lifts?'

'Kirstie told me,' she recalled, 'and she said the other girls teased Alice about it, so it must have been an open secret that Mr Nash drove her home after rehearsal sometimes.'

'That car park out front is wide open. Anyone could have looked out and seen her get into his car, but was it an entirely innocent arrangement? I thought Nash might be Alice's secret lover, too, but this arrived at the same time,' and he handed her the other extract.

The Journal of Alice Teale

He's bad, too. A real bad boy, and aren't we all supposed to love those? It's always the bad ones who get a girl's heart beating faster, the ones who make them risk it all, give up everything. At least, that's what happens in all the books and films. I wonder why? The films would be boring otherwise, I suppose. Perhaps real life is too dull for us without them, too. Maybe that's it.

But would I actually leave with him if he asked me?

Would I abandon everyone and run off with him somewhere, change our names so they can never find us, start again like we were two entirely different people and never go back? Never see my mam or dad again? What about my grandad?

Here's the thing. I'd do it in a heartbeat.

If *He* asked me, I'd say to hell with everybody else. They could think what they liked because it wouldn't matter any more.

Yeah, I'd do it.

If he asked me.

But he won't. I know that.

He is playing a part, too, and he's good at it, very good. He has to be. It's self-preservation, really. I don't reckon many people get to see the real man, the one beneath the surface. I might actually be the only one who has.

But I do think he loves me.

I do believe that.

39

'Doesn't mention her brother, does she?' Black observed when Beth had finished reading. 'Leaving him, I mean.'

'I think she knows he would forgive her, whatever she did with her life.'

'Even if she ran away with a total wrong'un? Perhaps,' he conceded, 'but who? The drama teacher, who is about to marry Little Miss Perfect? That might qualify as self-preservation, but is he really a bad boy? I'm not so sure. Maybe it's Keech, the womanizing English teacher who lives with a former pupil but wants Alice to be the next one in his life?'

'And I hate to say it, but he is attractive.' When Black's eyes widened at this, she said, '*I* don't fancy him – I think he's the personification of sleaze – but he is handsome, he's been around, and his only competition is a bunch of spotty teenage boys. For every girl who cringes when he's near them, there'll be another with a crush on him. I think it's complicated when you're that age, and he does keep getting the girls.'

'He does.' He hoped Alice Teale might have had more taste than that. 'But even Collemby School would fire him for having an affair with a seventeen-year-old pupil, and we would arrest him.'

'All the more reason to keep it secret,' said Beth.

'I spoke to the officer who investigated the allegation against him,' Black said. 'The one where he was accused of groping his pupil. It didn't get very far. The girl had a history of making false claims about a number of things.'

'What kind of things?'

'She said she'd had an accident in a department store, but CCTV proved she didn't actually fall down the stairs. She also claimed she'd been beaten up by a group of older girls but then withdrew the allegation.'

'That doesn't make it false,' said Beth. 'A lot of people change their minds about pressing charges against people who hurt them in case they hurt them again. There is a history of dishonesty, then, but that would make her the ideal target for an abuser, wouldn't it?'

'Yes,' said Black, 'which is why I didn't leave it there. As part of the initial investigation, Keech voluntarily submitted his CV so they could check up on his previous jobs, but when the girl retracted her story they didn't bother to find out why he had left any of those schools.'

He handed Beth a piece of paper with the schools' names typed on it and the dates Keech had worked at each one. 'He's moved around a bit, always in this region, nothing unusual at face value, no stays that look suspiciously short, and when he left it was always at the end of the year, not in the middle of term, as you might expect if he was sacked suddenly because of something he'd done with a pupil.'

Beth surveyed the list. It might be unusual for a teacher to work in six schools in a little over twenty years, but she told herself not to bend the facts to fit her theory that Keech was a bad man. If he had moved from place to place, he must have been able to provide references. Perhaps he got bored easily and needed new pupils or different challenges. Had he moved for family reasons, when he still had a family? You couldn't tell any of this simply by glancing at a list. Beth would need to dig deeper than that until she was satisfied.

'I'm on it,' she told Black.

Beth knew it would take all day to get around the schools that had employed Mr Keech and, right from the off, she wondered if it was a complete waste of time. The first school on the list was a dead end because the head and the office staff had no recollection of the man since they had all joined the school since his time there. They managed to find a teacher close to retirement who did remember Keech, but the details he could recall weren't all that helpful.

'Long-haired young chap, smoked a lot. I remember he drove a rusty old banger of a car.' He chuckled at the memory.

'But can you remember anything else about the man at all?' she asked him. 'How he interacted with the pupils?'

'God, no,' he said. 'Feels like a lifetime ago.'

'I suppose that does at least mean he wasn't involved in anything controversial or unusual, then?'

'Can't have been,' he said brightly, 'unless you count driving a car that looked like it had been welded together in metalwork class.'

The second school she visited was called St Margaret's and she was greeted with open hostility there. The deputy head was tight-lipped and defensive, as if the reputation of her entire school were being questioned. After a twenty-minute interview, Beth was assured there was absolutely nothing of any suspicious nature involving any of their teachers from that time.

Beth was going to press the point, but then she realized that Keech would have been newly married back then and perhaps less likely to have strayed at that point. Even if he had been chasing every girl in the school, they were hardly going to admit that now.

'You don't seem very willing to entertain the thought that Mr Keech might have been too close to some of his pupils?' Beth said, as a parting shot.

'Not when there was no evidence of any kind of impropriety,' she told Beth.

'Your primary concern being the school's reputation?'

'Of course.'

'Well, my main concern is finding the man who murdered a seventeen-year-old girl. There is ample evidence that Mr Keech has had inappropriate relations with pupils or former pupils, as it is common knowledge he has slept with at least two of them at his most recent school alone. If it turns out he has had anything to do with this girl's death, we will want to know if any other former pupils have been seduced or assaulted by him.' She finished with: 'It won't be possible to keep your school's name out of the newspapers then.'

She drew a complete blank at the third and fourth schools she visited, but at the fifth school they were at least passably cooperative and she was directed to a female former colleague who had worked with Keech in the

English department. Just when she thought she might be getting somewhere, the woman who worked on the reception desk came back with dispiriting news. 'I'm sorry,' she said, 'Miss Barton is away on the school's outward-bound trip to Devon. She'll be back in a few days. I could take a message,' she offered.

Beth wondered if there was any point, but decided to be thorough. She wrote down her contact details and handed them to the woman, who promised she would pass them on to Miss Barton upon her return, or if she phoned the school in the meantime.

On the drive home, Beth told herself there would likely be many wasted days like this one in her police career and she would just have to get used to it. It was never like this in the cop shows on TV.

It was late and the sun was setting when Beth walked into the major-incident room. Black waved at her to draw her attention while he was talking on the phone.

'That is good news,' he agreed with the caller, then glanced at his watch. 'No, we'll check it out now, before he breaks camp.'

When he had ended the call, he said, 'Grab your coat. All those new resources haven't been for nothing. We've finally found Happy Harry.'

40

He explained it all on the way. Happy Harry had been spotted by a farmer, who had been spoken to by a uniformed officer. He was one of many who had been asked to keep an eye out for the homeless man, who might have been one of the last people ever to see Alice Teale alive while he was rooting around in the bins. Though it was late, cold and raining, Black didn't want to delay the search or give the man any chance to leave the area.

'Aren't we supposed to call for back-up in situations like this?'

Black snorted. 'To question an old wino? You're joking, right? We'd never hear the last of it. No, we'll just have a look up there and see if we can find him, then bring him in.'

They drove out to the edge of the woods which bordered the farmland and parked their car in a layby next to a gate which led to a track that divided the woodland. 'This is it,' he told her, 'the lane where Harry was spotted.' They started to walk up the track together. Black had a torch, but there was still just enough light for them to see roughly where they were going, so he kept it switched off and in his pocket for now. Being out here like this as it was getting dark was eerie and Beth kept thinking she saw movement in the trees either side of them, until she peered more closely and realized it was just the fading light forming opaque shapes between branches. The lie of the land didn't help. To their left, the woodland was level with them, but on their right it fell away and the drop became longer and steeper as they went.

'Are you sure this is a good idea? How much do we know about this Harry? Is he really harmless?'

'Mostly,' he said quietly.

'What does that mean?' It didn't sound good.

'I asked around,' he explained. 'He's been begging for booze money in Collemby and the surrounding villages for years.'

'That it?' For some reason, she thought he knew more about the man than that but wasn't letting on.

'It's rumoured he might have been in the army once,' he said.

'Meaning he has actual training and knows how to kill people?' All of a sudden, being out here in the dark woods like this seemed a very bad idea.

'It was a long time ago' – he shrugged this off – 'and I'm with you, so it'll be fine.'

They walked in silence for a while and, as they trudged along the path, it grew darker still.

'It gets dark really quickly,' she said.

'It's the bloody trees,' said Black. 'They blot out what's left of the light.' But he didn't turn on the torch in case it signalled their presence to Harry.

'Five hundred yards' – he lowered his voice – 'that's what the farmer said. That's where he spotted Harry. One minute he was on the lane, the next he'd disappeared into the woods.' And so they walked the distance together, trying not to make any noise that might spook

Harry. It was impossible to be entirely quiet because the path had been layered with gravel and loose rocks that scrunched under their feet. Anyone could have heard them coming.

Sure enough, there was a flurry of movement from the trees up ahead and, when they looked towards the sound, they saw a figure break from cover and hare across the path ahead of them then disappear into the bushes. This didn't look like an old man. He was fast, astonishingly so for someone who spent all his days drinking. Only fear could have propelled him along like that.

Black cursed and set off after him, calling, 'Stay here!' to her over his shoulder. Even if she had wanted to go with him, Black covered the ground too fast and she was left trailing in his wake. He disappeared into the bushes after Harry.

Beth stopped where she was, stood, listened and waited. Nothing. When minutes had passed, she called, 'Lucas?', but there was no answer. 'Lucas!' Still no reply. 'For fuck's sake,' she hissed.

Beth heard a noise then and whirled round, but it was too late. The crashing sound was a figure charging from the bushes on the other side of the path but right by her. It smashed into her, sending her hurtling backwards off the raised lane, and she fell off the path and down the steep hill, hitting the ground hard then rolling over and over as her momentum took her through the bushes and down a long, muddy bank below. Beth's body had crashed against the ground with such force it knocked the wind out of her. She picked up speed, desperately trying to stop herself by grabbing at the ground with her hands and using her legs as a brake, but the drop was too steep. Her head hit an exposed tree root, stunning her, and something sharp scraped her cheek, drawing blood.

Beth had little choice but to let herself roll all the way down the hill and hope she landed safely at the bottom. She finally came to a halt with a bump, and the back of her head struck the ground hard. She gasped and moaned, then lay completely still while she attempted to work out how badly injured she was.

Beth's body ached and her head throbbed. She could feel cuts on her arms, legs and face, as well as areas where bruises would soon form, but she could flex her fingers, move her legs and tentatively raise her arms. Everything hurt like hell, but nothing was broken. She turned her head slightly and surveyed the bank she had just come down at speed. Her first thought was that it was a miracle she hadn't broken her neck, let alone anything else.

Then she wondered how the hell she was going to get back up that high, almost vertical, slippery bank. She turned her head to see what lay in the opposite direction so she could consider her options, and the problem of the bank went straight out of her mind. Now there was a more pressing concern. A dark shape in the undergrowth caught her eye and, at first, she thought it was her overwrought mind playing tricks on her, but then the shape moved and took a step in her direction.

The bulky presence was moving straight towards her. She tried to move away but pain shot through her body. She cried out in alarm and the figure kept coming right at her.

As it moved closer, she realized it was a filthy man

dressed in rags. A man with matted hair and a dirt-encrusted face. His wild eyes were full of fear and anger. He was getting closer and he was carrying a large knife.

A lot went through Beth's mind in the second or two it took the burly figure to bear down on her. By the time he was standing over her, his knife held in readiness, she knew he was Harry, the rough sleeper they were looking for, and, presumably, the man who had pushed her down the hill. She had fallen into a glade a dozen or so yards from the shelter he had constructed. She could just make it out in the background behind him.

She also realized from the look on his face how he viewed her – as a trespasser and a threat. She was trying to invade his territory, steal something from him, possibly take him away. Beth read all that in the man's enraged face.

She managed to slide herself back a yard or two, ignoring the pain. Before she could even sit up, he was towering over her, close enough for her to smell the stench on the man.

Without even rationally thinking about it, she blurted out, 'I'm Beth,' then held up a palm to fend him off. 'Please,' she urged him. 'Don't!'

Black was frustrated that Happy Harry had given him the slip. He turned and trudged back down the lane. It took him a while to reach the spot where Beth had been standing, and he didn't notice anything amiss apart from her absence. Hadn't he specifically told her to wait there?

Obviously, she had given up and trudged all the way back towards the gate and the car, so he set off to jog back that way himself.

41

Beth didn't even know if her words were registering with the man. He stared down at her intently as she continued to blurt out an explanation. 'Please, I'm sorry . . . I didn't mean to be here . . . I'll go.' And she managed to partially sit up, rolling over on to one elbow. His stance immediately altered and his arms went out wider, the knife in his hand. He was blocking her, preventing Beth from leaving.

'Let me go,' she pleaded. 'I'll get away from here.' Without taking her eyes from the knife for a second, she pushed the palm of her hand against the mud and levered herself into a standing position. If he wanted to strike, he would do it now, while she was off balance, at her most vulnerable. She anticipated the blow, but he did not lunge for her.

Instead, she could see the doubt and suspicion in his eyes as Beth got to her feet and tried to adopt the least threatening posture she could manage, bending low to look smaller and holding her hands out where he could see them so he would know she didn't have a weapon.

Their eyes locked then, and she wondered what madness lay behind his and whether it was strong enough for him to kill her out here in the woods without considering the consequences.

Beth took one tentative sideways step and, when he didn't try to stab her, she took another, then a third. He mimicked her movements, but only with small turns so he could continue to face her. She couldn't run back up the hill and she needed clear ground ahead if she was going to get away from this madman.

Two more steps, and they were still facing each other but there was a way out behind Beth now. She knew, if she turned and ran away, he might give chase. She was injured and would not be as fast as normal, but fear and adrenaline would propel her. It was risky, but Beth made her decision then.

She turned on her heel and ran.

Heart pounding, legs pumping, Beth raced through the glade as fast as her battered body would allow. The ground was bumpy and uneven and at any second she expected to trip and fall, or that the man with the knife would catch up with her and stab her in the back. Fear drove her and she ran hard for a minute without looking back, dodging round trees, stumbling but righting herself once more then continuing forward until she risked a turn and a fleeting look behind her. Beth was convinced she would see him then, inches from her, with the knife raised, ready to strike, but all she saw was the outline of trees that were little more than shadows now.

He was gone.

Beth ran at an even pace, regularly glancing behind and to each side in case he'd stalked her by some other route, but there was no further sign of him. Each sound from the woods rattled her, every broken twig caused her to start.

She tried not to panic at the thought of him pursuing her and concentrated on working out exactly where she was. How far astray had she gone, and how could she get back to the road? Where the hell was bloody Lucas?

Keep going Beth, she told herself. *Ignore the pain and keep running.*

It seemed to take Beth an age, but at last she managed to circle back across rough ground until she could see the lane they had walked along up ahead of her. This gave her a burst of hope and she ran more quickly now, eager to get on to it because the going would be easier and the gap above it, between the canopy of trees, would allow more light to guide her way.

Beth half ran, half stumbled as she burst out of the trees and on to the path. She immediately collided hard with a big, dark shape that was coming along the lane at speed and she hit the ground once more, rolling on to her back and putting her arms up to her face in an act of self-preservation as the figure loomed over her. It was Harry, and this time he was going to stab her to death!

Then, the shape spoke.

It wasn't Harry. It was Lucas. She was not going to die.

'Bloody hell.' He sounded shocked at the sight of her dishevelled appearance. 'What the hell happened to you?'

'Christ, Lucas, you scared the crap out of me,' she told him as he took her hand and hauled her to her feet.

'Well, I'm sorry,' he said, 'but I didn't expect you to leap out of the trees at me like that.'

He clearly wanted an explanation, so she provided one, which included the fall, the knife and the shelter and ended with the words, 'I'm sorry, I lost him,' even though they both knew that wasn't strictly true. Beth assumed he would be disappointed with her for not tackling Harry when she had the chance.

She was surprised when he said, 'Not a good idea to try and disarm a man like that on your own. The main thing is you're safe. Now, do you think you can show me where this shelter is?'

Beth managed to lead Black back to the spot where she had been pushed into the bushes and down the hill. He shone his torch into the glade below and they could just make out the shelter, but there was no sign of life.

'Looks like he's taken off,' said Black, 'but at least we've found his home.' It seemed a strange word to describe the structure. 'Once it gets light, we shouldn't have too much difficulty tracking him down.'

'What happens now?'

He surveyed Beth, then asked, 'Are you sure you are okay?'

'I'm fine,' Beth assured him, though she was covered in cuts and bruises and in some pain.

'Okay,' he said. 'Then let's take a look.'

Black spotted a less treacherous route down the hill than the one Beth had been forced to take when she rolled heavily down it at speed, and they made their way slowly and carefully to the bottom, both keeping an eye out for any trace of the knife-wielding Harry as they went.

They did not expect to see Happy Harry sitting outside his shelter, but it was worth checking out his camp. He was, at the very least, a potential witness in the disappearance of Alice Teale and, judging by his violent reaction to Beth's presence in his camp, possibly even the cause of it.

Harry's shelter was as rudimentary as you'd expect of

any structure made from scrounged materials. There was plastic sheeting, secured over a section of tarpaulin, to provide some protection from the rain. The tarpaulin hung down to make a rear wall. Sections of wood and corrugated iron made it into a three-sided structure with an open front. The remnants of an extinguished fire were visible between a pile of stones, and there were empty cans of beans and soup outside, along with bottles of beer and vodka, discarded once they had been drained of their contents.

Black peered in and saw a sleeping bag. It was in a disgusting state, but at least Harry had something to sleep in. His bed was an old wooden pallet and the tiny shelter was filled with all kinds of stolen or donated things: a plate, an old saucepan, a couple of blankets, an ancient army kit bag.

Then Black's eyes settled something that was folded at the far end of the sleeping bag. Was Harry using this as a pillow?

The item looked new and in good condition. It was still relatively clean. Black squinted into the darkened shelter and realized it was a green parka with a fur-lined hood, like the one Alice Teale had been wearing on the night she disappeared.

While Black was still processing the likelihood of this being a coincidence, his eyes became fully accustomed to the gloom and he noticed another item hanging up by its straps at the rear of the shelter.

It was Alice Teale's big, floppy bag.

42

The next morning, even the water from the shower hurt, stinging Beth as it landed on bruised and scraped skin. She ached all over. At least it hadn't been for nothing, because Harry was now firmly at the centre of their investigation. Could there really be an innocent explanation for him having Alice Teale's coat and bag in his possession? It was looking more and more likely that he was the one responsible for her death. At the very least, he had to know something about it.

A forensic examination of the items they had retrieved might soon complete the picture, but there were precious few clues from the bag or Alice Teale's coat pockets. Crucially, her phone was still missing, as was the journal, but neither of them had expected that to be in Harry's filthy hands. The mystery of who was sending them the journal pages remained just that, and the other contents consisted of mundane items: toiletries, stationery and schoolbooks.

As always, when Beth walked into the major-incident room, Lucas Black was already there. Did the man never sleep?

'Have they had any luck tracking down Harry?' she asked.

'Not yet.'

His face betrayed his frustration, though Beth hadn't expected the rough-sleeping Harry to have been picked up while he still had the cover of darkness. 'He got hold of that bag and coat somehow, and maybe he killed for it. I want to find him before anyone else hears about it. If word gets out in the town, who knows what might happen.'

'You reckon people might try and harm him?'

'What do you think?'

It seemed likely, but she was surprised he was so concerned for Harry's well-being, until he added: 'We're not going to get much out of him if he's intercepted by an angry mob and beaten half to death.'

Other detectives and uniformed officers began to arrive then, and DS Black made sure they were all aware of the new developments in the case and the urgent need to find Harry. He was now priority number one.

Hearing this, Beth couldn't help but torture herself, thinking about the night before. Though she was relieved to have survived her encounter with him, Harry slipping through their fingers like that was a particularly cruel blow. She kept wondering what she could have done differently and whether she should have attempted to disarm him and bring the man in, but he was big, looked strong and could easily have ended her life there and then with his blade.

'We'll get him,' Black assured her, as if reading her mind. 'Then maybe we'll finally have some answers.'

'I hope so. It's been driving me crazy,' she admitted. 'This whole bloody case has. I keep thinking about the night when Alice vanished – that twenty-minute window beforehand and how she could just disappear like that when she walked between the cottages. I never really thought Harry was the answer, and I still don't understand how he could have got rid of Alice's body when he doesn't even have a vehicle. Even if he had access to one, I doubt he could have driven it in a straight line for long.'

'I've been going over that one, too,' Black admitted. 'On the one hand, how could he have Alice's stuff if he didn't take it from her or her body, but, like you say, he had no way of moving it more than a few yards on his own, let alone transporting it all the way to the coast. He doesn't strike me as the kind of man who has accomplices either.'

'Someone obviously did move her body, but how come no one saw them doing it? Just bad luck, I suppose. I thought that little red car might provide the answer, but no one has vouched for it or reported the driver since we put out the appeal. At one point, I thought Simon Nash or maybe Keech might have been waiting to pick her up outside the school, but neither of them drives a sporty little red car. Keech was seen on school premises after Alice left that night, and I checked his car. He drives a silver Astra.'

'And what about Nash?'

'A big blue Beemer,' she said. 'He told me when I interviewed him at the school.'

'That could be the car that was seen at the old station. It might look black in the darkness. We should check that out properly.'

'But it definitely wasn't the car parked by the side of the road,' she said. 'That was red, and much smaller.'

Something made Black focus on that for a moment and he became lost in his thoughts.

'Earth to Lucas,' she said, and he realized he'd been so engrossed he hadn't replied.

'The car parked by the allotments was small' – he frowned at his own observation – 'but the one Simon Nash drives is big?'

'Yes,' said Beth. He was stating the obvious now, and Beth looked at him as if he had received a sudden sharp blow to the head that had affected his reasoning. 'Why?'

'When I interviewed Jessica Pearce about what she saw from the staff-room window I was focusing on what she told me about Alice. I remember she said Nash pulled away just as her fiancé arrived, as Alice Teale was walking away.'

'Okay.'

'She said that Simon Nash had to squeeze into his car. Is he tall?'

'Above average, perhaps,' she said, 'but not very.'

'That doesn't sound like a big BMW to me.'

They both rose from their chairs at the same time and reached for their jackets. There was no need for communication between them. They both knew they were on their way to have another word with Simon Nash.

They got to the drama teacher's form room during a free period so they spoke to him alone in his empty classroom. He expressed his shock and deep distress at the terrible news about Alice. 'I can only imagine how awful it must be for her poor family,' he said.

Beth introduced Black then explained they had some follow-up questions about Alice Teale. Before the teacher could respond, Black said, 'Mostly, we want to know why you lied.'

'Lied about what?'

'Your car,' said Lucas. 'The one you were driving the

evening Alice Teale disappeared. You told my colleague here it was a big blue BMW 5 Series. In fact, you were driving a red Audi TT. Don't lie about it. We just checked with Miss Pearce. She remembered because of your height. She said you struggled to get into it.'

Simon Nash looked worried then. 'I suppose I might have been. I usually drive the Beemer, so I forgot.'

'Bullshit.'

'It's not bullshit. I do normally drive the BMW, but it had to go in for a repair and it must have been that day, now you mention it. My fiancée took it in to be fixed and I drove her car, which is an Audi TT and, yes, it is red. I remember now. I'm sorry. It wasn't my intention to mislead.'

'Oh, I think it was,' said Beth. 'And I think you knew why it would be of interest to the police if you were driving a red car rather than a black one.'

'I really don't understand.'

'Two witnesses saw a red car parked up by the allotments a short way from the school. It was described as sporty with tinted windows so you couldn't see in, just like your fiancée's Audi. They noticed it because it was blocking the lane and part of the path, so it looked as if someone was waiting inside. No one would leave their car blocking an access road like that.'

'There are a lot of red cars in the north-east of England,' Nash told them, and Black noticed he did not explicitly deny that he had parked the car there.

'All we have to do is show the witnesses the car, or even a picture of it, and they are going to identify it,' said Beth. 'Chris saw it on his way up to meet Alice. You said you saw him near the town when you sped by, but you were sitting in that car when he walked round it, and it was much nearer the school. You can't tell me there are lots of red Audi TT roadsters with tinted windows in this town. No one's going to believe that, least of all a jury.'

'A jury? I haven't done anything.'

'You'd be surprised to hear that criminals often say that,' responded Black dryly. 'Why did your own car need repairing?'

'I had a bit of a prang. It was very minor.'

'Where was the damage?'

'Only a headlamp.'

'Which one?'

He cleared his throat. 'Front passenger side. I scraped it.'

'How did you manage that?'

'I was driving too fast, okay? I'll admit that I'm not always the best driver.' Beth noticed he offered that up easily. In her experience, men rarely did that.

'I'm a bit baffled as to how you could have scraped the front passenger headlight and not the bodywork,' said Black.

'For some reason, the headlight took the brunt of it. It sort of exploded on impact.'

'What did you hit,' asked Lucas, 'when you scraped it?'

'I honestly can't remember.'

'You can't remember?' Black asked this as if he had never heard of anything so absurd. 'You scraped the headlight of the car your daddy-in-law paid for and it exploded, but you can't remember what on?'

'I think I blotted it out. I was embarrassed and a bit shocked. I didn't want him to know, so I figured I'd just fix the damage before he saw it.'

'Because he'd be angry?'

'Perhaps.'

'Or because he'd think less of you? You're marrying his daughter – wouldn't want him to think you couldn't handle a car properly.' Beth knew Black was goading the man, but Nash remained calm.

'I felt foolish. My other cars have been old bangers. This one really moves.'

'Handle well, don't they? Usually, I mean. That famous German engineering.'

'They do, but I did say I wasn't the world's best driver.'

'Still, I'm surprised you can't remember where you pranged it.'

'It was on a country bend,' he said. 'They all look alike to me. I must have hit the stone wall as I went around it.'

'So, you do remember?'

'I remember what happened more than I recall exactly where it occurred. Shock does that.'

'It's a big car, your Beemer?'

'Yes.'

'Alice Teale was spotted in a big black car a few weeks back. It sounded very like yours.'

He hesitated before answering: 'Well, mine is blue, and there are a lot of big cars in the world. I've already admitted that Alice has been in my car. I occasionally gave her lifts home.' He looked at Beth. 'I told you that.'

'You did admit *that*,' said Black, and he deliberately elongated the word 'that', 'but this witness saw a big car coming out of the old railway station at speed. She said you almost ran over her dog.'

'That wasn't me.' He looked shaken.

'Sorry,' said Lucas. 'Slip of the tongue. She said that the *as yet unidentified, young male driver* was travelling at speed and almost ran over her dog. He had to swerve to avoid it, then she heard a bang.' Black let that hang in the air for a while, then said, 'It sounds like that might have been a front passenger-side headlamp exploding against the edge of the old platform. What do you think?'

'It wasn't me,' he repeated.

'We've already been down there,' Black told him. 'We found the pieces. There were fragments of a headlamp on the ground by the platform. They were bagged up and taken in as evidence. If they are analysed and they match your car, then you'll have a lot of explaining to do, unless you admit it now.'

He said nothing to that. Beth took this to mean he had run out of answers or was desperately trying to think of new ones.

'You pulled up by the side of the road after you left the school that night, didn't you?' she accused him.

'Erm . . .' He frowned and shook his head, as if trying to clear it so he could remember. 'I *may* have . . .'

'You did,' said Black, 'and the car was seen by passers-by and you knew it. You panicked and pretended you were driving a Beemer instead.'

He deliberately looked away from Black then and focused on Beth. 'As I recall, you asked me what car I drove and, like I said, I own a BMW.'

'You knew I wasn't interested in the car you drive most of the time. I wanted to know about the car you were in that night. You lied to me, just as you're lying now. The only question is why.'

'Why what?' he stammered.

'Why are you lying? Why did you pull over shortly after leaving the school, just moments before Alice Teale disappeared?'

'I think to make a phone call, because I forgot to tell my fiancée I was on my way home.'

'She'd back that up, would she?' asked Beth. 'If we asked her?'

'Of course.'

'We'll call her and ask her in a minute, then,' said Lucas, 'but we'll be sure to check your mobile-phone records and, if it turns out you didn't make a call at that exact moment, then she will be prosecuted for perverting the course of justice. You get a year in prison for that, on average.' He turned to Beth. 'I suspect that might be the end of the engagement, and I don't think her daddy would be too forgiving.'

'Wait, I only said I *think* I made a call. I'm not one hundred per cent certain. Maybe that was another night.'

'You didn't make a call, did you?' asked Beth. 'You pulled over by the side of the road to wait for Alice.'

'No.' He shook his head violently, as if that would make any difference.

'You admitted you sometimes drove her home. It's on your way and a long walk for her when you don't,' said Beth, 'so why not take her home that night?'

'The headteacher doesn't like it. He spotted her getting into my car once in the car park and had a word with me about it the next day. He said it causes gossip.'

'So you never did it again?' asked Black abruptly.

'Mmmm.' Nash acted like he was trying to remember.

'Or were you just more careful about it?' asked Beth. 'Pulling over by the side of the road a few yards from the school so the head couldn't see you picking up your favourite girl, the one you'd taught for years, the girl who was in your plays, the one with the acting talent you nurtured? The pretty one?'

'It wasn't like that.' But his voice sounded so weak now they both began to think it must have been exactly like that.

'You pulled over across the lane by the allotments. You didn't mind blocking it because you knew Alice would be with you in a matter of moments,' said Beth. 'I think we can all agree that's what you did – unless you're covering for someone?'

'Covering for someone?' he repeated dumbly.

'Your fiancée,' she said.

'Maybe Miss Pearce was mistaken and it wasn't you behind the wheel that night.' Black knew it was a ludicrous notion, but he wanted to go along with Beth because she had thrown Nash off course. 'Perhaps she was the one waiting for Alice, but I wonder how she lured the girl into her car?'

'Did she tell Alice they needed to talk?' asked Beth, as if this was the most likely turn of events. 'Did she say she wanted a word with her about you?'

'No, that's ridiculous.'

'Well, if it wasn't you in the car that night, it must have been her behind those tinted windows. That's the only possible explanation.'

'Which makes her a murder suspect,' confirmed Black. 'I think we're done here, Beth. If Simon here is denying it was him, then we need to formally question his fiancée, under caution.' He turned back to the teacher. 'She'll need to engage a solicitor, but I'm sure her father will know some good ones.'

Beth and Black made as if to leave. The teacher looked aghast. 'Wait,' he said. 'Wait a minute . . .' Was he steeling himself to finally admit the truth? 'Please sit down . . .'

'We'll sit back down if you actually have something to tell us.'

'It was me.' His voice was very quiet now. 'I was in the car that night. I parked up by the allotments.'

'To wait for Alice?'

He nodded slowly, as if it were a supreme effort to do even that.

At last, thought Beth. 'I'd feel more comfortable if you said it out loud,' she told him.

'I was waiting for Alice,' he said. 'It was me in the car. There, I've said it. Now, please don't involve Karen in this. I'm begging you.'

Beth and Black exchanged a look. They had finally wrenched the truth from him, but not all of it. 'That depends,' said Beth.

'On what?'

'On whether you tell us everything,' said Lucas. 'Like what happened when she got in your car.'

'Where did you take her?' asked Beth. 'What did you do?'

It was Black who asked the key question: 'And why did you kill her?'

43

Simon Nash became almost frantic then. 'I didn't kill her,' he protested. 'I swear I didn't. I didn't do anything.'

'You must have,' said Black gently, as if he were coaxing the truth from a child. 'You were the last one to see her alive.'

'No, no, I wasn't.'

'Who was, then?' asked Beth. 'Where did you drop her off? If you're going to say you handed her over to someone else, then we're going to find that very hard to believe.'

'Particularly as you've been so intent on covering up your tracks. Stories don't get more suspicious than yours, Simon.'

'I didn't kill her,' he said again. 'I didn't even see her. I was waiting for her, yes, I admit that. I was going to run her home and we were going to have a talk on the way.' Then he looked at each of them in turn, as if imploring them to believe him. 'But she never got in the car.'

'She refused to go with you?' asked Beth.

'No! I never even saw her. I waited. I stayed there, way beyond the time she would have needed to get to me, but she never showed.'

'You'd agreed between you that she was going to come with you?' asked Lucas.

'Yes, in the darkroom I said I'd drive her home, and she agreed. We split up for twenty minutes so no one would notice. I said I wanted to talk to her, and she said she had something to tell me, too, so we arranged that I'd drive down the road and park up, then she would come to me, so no one would see.'

'And you went through all that subterfuge,' said Beth, 'but not because the headteacher disapproved. You did it because you were in a relationship.' When Nash looked as if he didn't want to admit it, she added: 'She wrote about you in her journal. It was pretty clear who she meant.'

The weight of the evidence seemed to overwhelm him then. 'Yes. I'd been seeing her for a while.'

'Years?' asked Lucas.

'God, no! Weeks.'

'I get it,' said Lucas. 'You were getting married, settling down. You'd have the young wife, the money, the lifestyle and the security you craved, but didn't you deserve one last fling with a beautiful, besotted young girl before you did it? Was that how you rationalized it?'

'In the beginning, yes.' He looked worn out then. 'That's exactly how I justified it.'

'So what happened? Were you about to call it off,' asked Beth, 'or planning to run away with her?'

'I don't know – neither. I just wanted to talk to her about us. I needed to know how she felt about me, because I didn't know how I felt about her any more. I was confused.'

'I bet you were,' said Lucas. 'That was quite a choice to make. Choose Alice and you lose everything, including your job, or stick with the fiancée, the cars, the house, the money. Tough call.'

'It wasn't like that.' He spoke in a very quiet voice.

'Because you loved her?' asked Beth.

'Yes,' he managed. 'I think I did.'

'And yet you still claim she didn't get in your car and drive away with you.'

'No, she didn't. I swear to God.'

'Let's keep Him out of it, shall we? So what did happen to her, then?'

'I don't know. I honestly don't. I've been going through hell ever since she disappeared, and then, when they found her' – he looked desolate – 'I couldn't even admit how I felt.'

'You could,' Black told him. 'You were just too much of a coward.'

'That's right,' Nash admitted. 'I was.'

'You hoped it would all go away and you could get on with your privileged life without a pause,' said Beth.

'Was that why you killed her?' asked Black. 'Was she going to tell the world about her secret lover? Was it all about to come crashing down around you? You had to shut her up, didn't you?'

'We know the truth now,' said Beth. 'You might as well admit it.'

'I swear to you, I didn't see her after I left the school.'

'But she left at the same time,' protested Beth, 'and disappeared after she walked between the cottages. Your car was a couple of hundred yards away, and you expect us to believe she vanished in that impossibly tiny window?'

'Yes,' he pleaded.

'You've lied before,' said Black reasonably. 'You've been lying all along, in fact. Why should we believe you now?'

'Because I'm not the killer, and that means there's a

madman still out there,' he said. 'I'm telling you, Alice did not get into my car that night.'

It was a pub night. They both agreed a drink was sorely needed after a day like this one. Simon Nash's partial confession, to his affair with Alice Teale at least, if not yet any involvement in her murder, had taken it out of both of them, not to mention the teacher.

Black bought the first round. 'There's something on your mind. I can tell.'

'I thought you might arrest him,' Beth told her colleague when he placed the drinks on the table. 'On suspicion of murder.'

'The evidence is a little flimsy at the moment, and he'll just keep on denying it. If we arrest him for that, the clock starts ticking and we have thirty-six hours to get enough to charge him or he walks.'

'We can ask for longer?'

'If we need longer, then we don't have a case,' he said. 'We'll wait till we have more on Nash than an affair with a pupil he didn't want the world to know about. That's enough to get him arrested and suspended but, really, it's all we have at the moment. A good defence lawyer would justify his lies and evasiveness on those grounds.'

'What have you told Everleigh?'

'The same, and he agrees. He'll let us run with it till we get more proof. DCI Everleigh is a great believer in means, motive and opportunity, and Nash had all three. He also thinks the most likely suspect is usually the one responsible. He's right about that, by the way.

Forensics will go through his car, and the one he borrowed from his fiancée. Maybe they'll come up with traces of Alice.'

'We already know she's been in his car,' said Beth.

'As a willing passenger, sure, and presumably she spent time on the back seat with him, but I'm more interested in the boot of that little red car, to see if he was the one transporting her body that night.'

'And the tyres,' she reminded him, 'to see if there are any traces that match the soil by the coastline.'

'They'll examine every inch of it.'

'Do you think Simon Nash murdered Alice?'

He didn't answer her directly. Instead, he said, 'You don't?'

'I don't know,' she replied honestly. 'Harry is still missing, and he had Alice's coat and bag.'

'He could have found them,' he said, 'though I am not sure how. He remains a suspect, along with Nash.'

'Simon Nash loved her, I think, improbable as that sounds.'

'A lot of women have been killed by men who professed to love them,' Black reminded her.

'But if he's telling the truth, they were thinking of a future together, so why would he kill her?'

'Lots of reasons,' said Black. 'One, he's lying, and they weren't planning a future together. Maybe he even wanted that, but she didn't. It's a lot to ask of a seventeen-year-old, to go off with an older man and pledge her whole life to him, no matter what the fallout. They were probably both happy enough for a while – forbidden fruit and all that – but if he fell in love with her, maybe she got cold feet.

If she panicked and wanted to end it, perhaps he became enraged and killed her.'

'Do you think that's what happened?'

'Well, it could have gone the other way. She might have wanted him to tell his fiancée. Maybe she threatened to do it for him. He had a lot to lose. He's saying he loved Alice, but he could have still viewed her as his last fling and now she was threatening to undo everything. That's a motive, right there.'

'Sounds a bit far-fetched to me.'

'Most murders do when you look at them closely,' said Black. 'You and I aren't wired like that, but other people will sometimes find the flimsiest pretext to kill, particularly when they feel threatened.'

'We'll know soon enough,' she said, 'when we get the forensics back from the car.'

44

Happy Harry couldn't stay missing for ever. He needed to eat, and very much needed to drink, which meant he was forced to beg. He was picked up in the next village along from Collemby, by an alert police patrol responding to Black's request to look out for the town's solitary rough sleeper, a man who was known by virtually everybody.

Black got Harry straight in for questioning, and soon regretted that decision. He should have had the man cleaned up first, because the smell of stale sweat, booze and urine clung to him, filling the air in the interrogation room.

Harry turned down the offer of legal representation. 'I speak for myself,' he rasped. 'I've done nowt.'

When Black pressed him on this, he continued to resist. 'You could be in a lot of trouble,' the detective said. 'You'll need a solicitor.'

'I speak for myself,' he repeated, louder this time. Black made a point of ensuring he was recorded discussing the absence of a solicitor, in case a lawyer came on board further down the line and tried to claim that his client had been coerced into a confession. Black asked Harry to confirm he understood he was waiving his right to a solicitor on the tape. 'Aye,' he said. 'I mean yes.'

'Do you know why you are here?' Black asked him.

'Because of the girl.'

'That's right, Harry, because of the girl.'

'I never did anything,' he protested. 'Honest.'

'But you saw her?'

'Aye, I saw her, like.'

'You were very probably the last person to see her,' Black told him, 'before she disappeared.'

'I didn't disappear her, if that's what you reckon.'

'What happened, then, Harry? Why don't you tell me in your own words?'

'I was frightened,' he said. 'I thought she was up to no good. You can't have that, can you?'

'Can't you?'

'Well, no.'

'But was she really up to no good, Harry?' Black was wondering if years of alcohol abuse had caused some form of psychosis or a schizophrenic episode in Harry. Had he really imagined Alice was up to no good on her way home after school?

'I thought she was, and that's why I did it.'

'You did it?'

'Yes, I admit it, but it didn't really hurt her.'

'Are you saying it was painless?' asked Black, wondering what *it* was in Harry's eyes.

'Aye.' He nodded his head vociferously.

'What did you do, Harry?' asked Black. They were surely near the end now; a confession was coming. 'What *exactly* did you do? Tell me, please.'

'I pulled my knife.'

'You stabbed her?' There was no mention of that in the post-mortem.

'No. I told you. I never hurt her.'

Realization began to dawn. 'Where was this, Harry? Behind the cottages near the school?'

'No, man,' he replied. 'In the woods.'

Black sighed. 'Not that girl, Harry, the other one.'

All that time Harry had thought Black was talking about Beth. Black took his time and carefully explained it all to Harry, who frowned at him as if he were trying to recollect events from long ago. When the detective had finished describing Alice and the fact that she had vanished around the time Harry had been seen near the Aged Miners' cottages that same evening, Harry said, 'I never saw her.'

'You didn't see her, you had no contact with her, you don't know anything about it?'

'No.'

'Would you mind explaining to me why you happen to have her coat and bag, then, Harry, because that's a bit mystifying.'

Black spent another hour with Harry, going through his account of that evening over and over, trying to catch the man out. He never did. The story always stayed the same.

'He says he never even saw her,' Black told Beth afterwards.

'Then how come he has her coat and bag?'

'Found them, or so he says.'

'Where?'

'There's a waste bin in the lane between the rows of Aged Miners' cottages. He was seen ferreting in the bins that evening, remember? Alice's grandfather told me that. He says that's where they were.'

'He claims they'd just been dumped in the bin?'

'Yeah. He thought it was his lucky day. He fished out the coat, and the bag was underneath it. They'd been stuffed in there. He took both items back to his den in the woods, figured he'd use a warm coat as extra bedding and thought there might be something of interest in the bag.'

'What was in it when he found it?'

'Stationery, make-up, a hairbrush, a can of anti-perspirant, some ring binders and Alice's purse.'

'Why would she dump all that in a waste bin, particularly her purse? It must have been the killer, mustn't it?'

'That's the bit I can't work out,' said Black. 'Alice wouldn't dump her coat and bag herself. But if she was snatched by someone in that alley or near it, surely she would struggle, shout or scream. Even if someone knocked her unconscious, why would they then pause to stuff her coat and bag into the bin? She was wearing the coat.'

'But you don't think Harry is responsible?' reasoned Beth.

'If he attacked Alice, killed her there or knocked her unconscious, what would he do with her body? He couldn't carry her off without anyone noticing, and he has no car.'

'He's telling the truth, then?' offered Beth.

'Possibly,' said Black. 'Though he claimed there was no money in the purse when he found it, and I'm sure that was a lie. The rest of his story sounded plausible, so I'm inclined to believe it.'

That evening, when Beth got home, she couldn't settle. Her restlessness drove her to an early-evening run through the park, despite her aches and pains. As she ran, random thoughts seemed to tumble through her mind, in no particular order. One minute she was thinking about Alice Teale and her short, tragic life; the next her thoughts drifted to Simon Nash and how his unknowing fiancée would have reacted once she learned he was having an affair with a seventeen-year-old pupil. That got Beth thinking about her own ex-boyfriend and how her whole future would now be entirely different without him. When Jamie did marry, have children then grow old, it would not be with Beth, as she had once imagined. Worse, it would be with *her*, and that thought made her run faster as she reached the lake. As she reached the end of her first lap, she focused her mind on poor Alice again and the mystery of her final moments before she was taken, beaten, strangled then her lifeless body thrown down on to the rocks. She pictured the girl lying there, and it was almost too much to bear. So, too, was the frustration of knowing they weren't quite there yet. It had taken them too long to pick up on the fact that Jessica Pearce had seen Simon Nash squeezing himself into a small car. What else had they missed? There was a nagging, gnawing thought that it was something that might be staring her right in the face and still she couldn't see it.

She ran harder then.

Go back, she thought, to the moments when Alice was last seen.

Pause, rewind, play, she told herself, as she recalled the words of the PE teacher then used them to imagine exactly what Jessica Pearce had seen when she looked out of that staff-room window and watched Alice walk away from the building.

There was something off about it. Beth knew it but she couldn't quite pin down what it was.

In her frustration, she ran even harder. As she powered forward, the exertion of running faster than normal made her regret wearing two layers on such a mild night. She was hot and sweating now, but she continued to run.

She was on her second lap around the lake when it hit her.

She ran back to her flat and was on the phone to Black before she had even showered. She could tell he was surprised; first that she'd called him, then by the breathlessness in her voice.

'Are you okay?' he asked.

'Yeah,' she panted. 'I've been thinking about what Jessica Pearce saw from the staff-room window, and a thought just struck me. The night Alice Teale disappeared was the same evening that DI Monaghan had his leaving do.'

'I didn't go to that.'

'He knew everyone. The pub was packed, but it didn't matter. It was so mild we sat outside in the beer garden. It was the hottest day of the year so far. More than twenty degrees.'

'That is uncharacteristically mild for the north-east of England.' Black couldn't help but wonder what she was getting at.

'But when Alice Teale left school that night she was still wearing her parka, with the hood pulled up.'

Black thought for a moment. 'I suppose she was fond of it, but you're right. It was very warm that day and she had a fair walk home.'

'Why didn't she carry it or stuff it inside her bag?'

'Teenagers can be strange about the things they wear.'

'Usually, they pride themselves on not wearing coats at all, especially round here.' She paused for a moment, thinking about it some more.

'What is it?'

'I think we should go and see Miss Pearce again,' she said, 'and ask her exactly what she saw that night.'

45

Rob managed to recover from the surprise of answering the door to two detectives and offered them tea. 'I've just boiled the kettle.' Jessica Pearce's fiancé wasted no time in making himself scarce, disappearing into the kitchen. While he was gone, the three of them sat at the dining table, which was wedged up against a wall with a large window, so they overlooked the tiny square below, which had flats on all sides. These were new-build apartments that had sprung up on a site that used to house a single pub and its car park. People were crammed in here, existing with very little space, on the first rung of the property ladder. There was just enough room for the table and three chairs, a sofa, a tiny coffee table and a TV. From what Beth could make out through the open door, the galley kitchen was even smaller. One person could cook in it, as long as no one tried to get by them.

'I'm sorry to bother you at home like this,' said Black, 'but we couldn't leave it.'

The teacher seemed sceptical that she could help them but said, 'Okay, so what did you want to ask me?'

'I'm not sure exactly,' he began, exchanging a look with Beth.

'Then how can I possibly help you?' She didn't bother to disguise her irritation, and Black saw a glimpse of the woman who snapped at her girls.

'What I mean is,' Black said, 'it depends on any explanation you can give for something strange that happened shortly after you witnessed Alice Teale walking away from the school.'

'I didn't see what happened after Alice walked away from school.' As she said this, her fiancé returned with a tray with mugs of tea, which he set down on the table. 'As she was going down the path, I saw Rob pull into the car park. I turned my attention to him. He got out of his car and walked towards the school. I waved, then I turned away to wash my tea cup. When I turned back, Rob was coming down the path and Alice was gone. She must have passed through the cut between the Aged Miners' cottages.'

'I can't believe I walked right past her,' said Rob, and he looked quite shaken by this realization.

'I told you that,' said Jessica.

'You told me you were the last to see her before I picked you up. I thought you meant moments before I got there. I didn't think you meant *just* as I got there.'

'Well, you saw her, too.' She rolled her eyes, as if her fiancé was an idiot. 'I'd have thought you'd have worked it out.'

'I saw a girl, yes.' It was his turn to get annoyed. 'But I thought the missing lass was older.'

'How could she be older?' His fiancée frowned at him and he looked as if he was about to continue the argument, but thought better of it in front of them.

'Wait,' Beth interjected. 'How old did you think Alice Teale was, Rob?'

He seemed a little distracted, like he didn't really want

to resume bickering with his fiancée. 'I don't know, seventeen or eighteen or something.'

'She was,' snapped Jessica.

'Whoa,' said Beth, and raised a hand to stop them arguing. 'Wait a moment. Rob, are you saying the girl you saw wasn't seventeen or eighteen?'

'No,' he said, 'she wasn't. The girl I saw was much younger.'

The tea went cold while they processed the new information they were receiving. They cross-examined him and his fiancée to get to the bottom of this discrepancy between their accounts of what had happened that night. It took a while to be absolutely certain of the order of events but, eventually, it became clear. Jessica Pearce had witnessed only one girl leaving the school late that evening and she was absolutely convinced it was Alice Teale who had walked down that path, right by her fiancé. Rob confirmed he hadn't seen anyone else apart from that same figure, but the girl he saw had been significantly younger than Alice.

When pushed, he offered, 'I'd say thirteen, or maybe fourteen, fifteen at the absolute most.' And when his fiancée gave him an angry look: 'You can frown at me all you like, love, but I'm telling you, she was never seventeen.'

He seemed so convinced that Black focused on the teacher. 'Can I just ask – and no one is doubting your genuinely held belief that the person you saw leaving that day was Alice – what was it that made you so sure it was her and not someone else?'

'It *was* her,' she said helplessly. 'I'd know her. I've known her for years – through PE lessons, netball teams, hockey teams, the sixth-form club and the school plays.'

'Okay,' he said. 'So you'd know her anywhere, but did you actually see her face that night? She was walking away from the building, wasn't she? Did she turn back towards you? Did she look up to the staff room and catch your eye?'

'Well, no.'

'Then how could you possibly know for sure that it was Alice?'

The question seemed to momentarily flummox Jessica Pearce and she had to take a moment to recollect. She finally offered: 'Because of what she was wearing,' then she said: 'Because she always wore it.'

'The coat?'

'She has this oversized green parka with a hood and she always carries that big, floppy bag on her shoulder.'

'So that's how you knew it was Alice?' asked Beth.

'Yes.'

'But it *could* have been someone else?' Black gently offered the possibility. 'Somebody who simply put Alice Teale's coat on, pulled the hood up over her head and made sure she had the girl's bag on her shoulder?'

'I . . .'

Beth could tell she was about to rebuff that idea as preposterous, but then she seemed to hesitate and give it some thought.

'I'd say it's more than likely,' said Beth, 'since Rob just said there's no way that girl was seventeen.' She could see the confusion in Miss Pearce's face. 'Wouldn't you?'

The PE teacher turned to her fiancé, and he gave her a

helpless look, as if to confirm he was not mistaken and couldn't go along with her account. It was clear he had been the only one to see the girl's face before she disappeared.

'I suppose . . .' It was a reluctant concession which went against her instincts, and perhaps she was worried this would make her seem like a liar in the eyes of the police.

'It's the explanation we've been searching for,' said Black, and he glanced at Beth. 'Why else would Happy Harry have found her coat and bag dumped in the bin like that, and how could Alice have vanished between the end of the path and Simon Nash's car? The only answer that makes any sense is that it wasn't Alice at all.'

'But why would someone do that?' asked Miss Pearce.

'They wanted everybody to think Alice walked away from the school that night,' said Beth. 'And she didn't.'

'That's right,' said Black. 'She never left.'

46

The headteacher was surprised to receive a delegation that morning. As well as Beth and Black, Miss Pearce was waiting for him and, for some reason he was yet to understand, her fiancé. Despite his bafflement, Mr Morgan let them into his office, where they explained the confusion surrounding the conflicting eyewitness accounts about Alice Teale.

It was soon clear that he didn't understand his role in any of this. 'I'm sorry, but how can I help you? I didn't see the poor girl leave.'

No one did, thought Beth, so perhaps Simon Nash really had been the last person to see her alive, but that still wouldn't explain the reason for Rob's sighting of a different girl in her coat. If Nash was telling the truth, there was still a twenty-minute gap in Alice Teale's final hour that was unexplained, and they needed Mr Morgan to help them account for those crucial missing minutes.

'Is there some pretext we could use to get all your pupils into the same place?' asked Lucas. 'The school hall, perhaps?'

'We could do that,' said Miss Pearce.

'I don't think it's a very practical idea to corral twelve hundred children together in one place,' muttered the headteacher. 'For health-and-safety reasons, we split our assemblies into smaller groups, because there are far too many pupils.'

'Do that, then,' said Black.

'And what will the pretext be?' he asked.

'That you need to talk to them about safety at school,' offered the PE teacher, 'in the context of what happened to poor Alice?' It struck Beth then that Alice Teale was likely to be known as 'poor Alice' from now on.

'Wouldn't that alarm them?' said Morgan.

'I don't think anything is likely to alarm them more than the murder of their fellow pupil,' said Beth.

'No. Of course,' he said. 'I'm sorry. You're absolutely right. We can certainly organize that for you.'

'Thank you,' said Black.

'If you want Rob here to look at the faces of every girl as they walk into the hall,' Morgan noted, 'it could cause a bit of a logjam in the corridors.'

'Let's admit them in class-sized groups, one at a time, then,' suggested the PE teacher. 'We bring out a class and get them to line up outside the hall for a few moments before letting them in. We can say we're also doing a uniform check. There're bound to be one or two girls in every class wearing hoop earrings or make-up.'

'Or with their skirts well above the knee,' the head conceded. 'It could work, I suppose.'

'While I'm berating them for uniform infractions, Rob could stand off to one side and take a good look at their faces. Maybe one of them will be the girl he thinks he saw.' Black noted her use of the words 'thinks he saw' and wondered if she was still sceptical, or perhaps a little resentful that her fiancé had undermined her story.

'Is Rob known here?' asked Black. 'By the students, I mean.'

'I don't think so. He picks me up sometimes if I'm very late, but they've usually all gone home by then.'

'So how will we explain his presence?' asked the headteacher.

'We won't,' Black told him. 'They'll assume he's with us.'

'Detective Constable Rob,' he said cheerfully, 'reporting for duty.' Jessica's fiancé seemed to like that idea.

'And what are we going to say about you' – the headteacher meant the police – 'if you're standing outside the school hall when they're waiting to file in?'

'What if I help Miss Pearce with her talk to the pupils about staying safe? Not walking home alone or accepting lifts from strangers, walking in well-lit areas, that kind of thing. Nothing they probably haven't heard before, but there is a murderer out there, so it won't do any harm for them to hear it again.'

'I suppose so, yes,' said the head, who seemed to be warming to the idea, now that his practical objections were being logically overruled.

'How soon can we arrange this?' asked Beth.

'I'll need to brief all of the heads of year then cascade this to each teacher. It's not a simple matter, but I think we can arrange it for tomorrow morning. Could we make it then, to avoid disruption?'

Beth expected Black to kick back on this and was surprised when he calmly accepted the delay. 'I suppose it can keep till then. And, as you said, there's no point in causing alarm.'

The head seemed energized by the task ahead. 'Good,

we'll work out a plan to get all the children out for the identity parade. Leave it with me. Thank you, Detective Sergeant.'

The next morning, there were girls of all heights, shapes and sizes lined up outside the school hall ready for their safety lecture, all of them dressed in the school's uniform of black skirt and blazer, with a red jumper and a silver-and-red tie with the school crest. The teachers ensured all the girls stood together, so Rob could ignore the boys, who were made to line up on the opposite side of the school hall's doors, where there was a more half-hearted attempt to ensure their shirts were tucked in and their ties weren't askew. They were boisterous and noisy, but at least they weren't in his line of vision.

As Miss Pearce had predicted, some of the girls wore contraband earrings or forbidden make-up and she was able to stall the first class, singling the offenders out for a telling-off. Beth and Black watched as she went along the lines and reminded the girls of the standards expected of them. DC Rodgers was there, too. Black must have asked him to come in as well and Beth wondered why he had felt the need to do that.

All the while, Rob stayed in the background, standing by the door of the school office, directly opposite the hall. The PE teacher looked towards her fiancé and he gave her a slight nod to indicate that he had seen everyone before the girls were allowed to file noisily into the hall. Another class would then be led to the door and the process would begin again.

Once the first batch had taken their seats, all eyes went

337

to Rob, who confirmed what they already knew, because he had not alerted Black. He had not recognized the girl.

Black and Miss Pearce went into the hall and gave a fifteen-minute talk to the pupils about keeping safe, then they answered questions before allowing them to go back to their lessons.

When the school bell rang after morning break, the second tranche of pupils were led towards the school hall. The process of delaying them with minor uniform infractions continued, then they all filed into the hall and everyone looked at Rob again. He seemed embarrassed, even a little panicked.

'I'm sorry. I . . . I didn't . . .'

Before he could go on, Black said, 'It's okay,' and cut him off to go and give the second talk. When that was over, they all reconvened in the head's office.

By then, Rob was even more apologetic. 'I'm really sorry,' he said. 'I feel so bad after you went to all that trouble, but I just didn't see her. I thought I would have spotted her – I was sure I would, in fact.'

'Don't worry,' said Black. 'I knew you wouldn't.'

'What?' asked Beth.

'It's not his fault,' Black explained. 'She wasn't there.'

'How do you know,' asked Beth, 'when we don't even know who *she* is?'

'Because someone tipped her off. Someone in this school told her not to come in today because there was going to be an ID parade.'

'That's a very serious allegation,' cautioned the headteacher.

'Yes,' agreed Black. 'It is.'

'So who knew about the ID parade?' asked the detective sergeant, and Beth was struck by how calm he was about their failure to find the girl. Had he expected this to happen and simply allowed it?

'Well,' said the headteacher, 'I had to tell the staff – obviously, I did. I mean, we had to prepare, so we could get all the pupils out of every class in the right order and at the correct time so, clearly, I had to tell them.'

'So any one of those teachers could have contacted that girl and told her not to attend school today?'

'I suppose so, but to what end?'

'To cover up their involvement in the death of Alice Teale,' said Black.

'But it won't work,' said Beth, 'because we can still find that girl.'

'There's a very simple way to do that,' said Black. 'We need to see today's school registers for each class then we can get the names of every girl who failed to attend.'

'I'll fetch Mrs Davenport,' said the headteacher, 'the school secretary.'

Mrs Davenport was called in then and sent to get the registers. She returned and set them down in piles. They went through them methodically. It took them a little while but, between them, they made relatively short work of the task.

'Eleven girls,' said Black, and he turned to the secretary again. 'How many of them phoned in?'

'I'll just go and check,' she said, and disappeared for a few moments. They sat in silence while they waited for her to bring the information. The secretary returned with an A4 notebook and said, 'Five.'

'Let's start with the girls who failed to call in, because the girl we are looking for won't want to draw attention to her absence.' Black turned to Rob and said, 'You can come with us,' then, to DC Rodgers: 'I'd like you to stay here.'

'Why?'

'Because I don't want anyone to leave this room while we're gone.'

'What?' blustered the headteacher. 'I've got a school to run.'

'Someone tipped off one of these girls, and that could happen again. If you stay here in this room with DC Rodgers, along with Miss Pearce and Mrs Davenport, I'll know that none of you are in a position to call anyone. That will rule you out if she disappears a second time.'

'I'm really not happy about this,' snapped the head.

'Your personal happiness is not my priority right now,' Black told him.

47

The first girl was holding a textbook when she answered the door. When she realized Black was a police officer she panicked and began to ramble about being behind in her GCSE revision, so she'd ducked out of school for a day to catch up. Black had to interrupt to calm her down, because he wasn't concerned about any of that. He looked at Rob, who shook his head, and they left the girl to her studying.

The second girl on their list seemed less bothered about her GCSEs, judging by her slightly dishevelled look as she answered the door, after some delay. Over her shoulder, Beth spotted a shirtless boy wandering around in the kitchen. She tried to explain she was poorly and had decided to convalesce at home, presumably with the help of her boyfriend. Once again, Rob signalled that this was not the girl and they left the amorous couple to their own devices.

They called on two more houses. One girl looked genuinely ill when she came to the door and even apologized for not phoning in. Rob once more indicated that she was not the pupil he had seen. The next girl wasn't in, but her mother was, and she went on a tirade about her daughter's apparent truancy. Black was assured she would get 'the bollocking of her life when I catch her'. They couldn't leave it at that, though, and he asked the mother to bring a photograph of the girl to the door so Rob could see it. He quickly ruled her out, and they left the mother to plan a suitable punishment for her errant daughter.

At the school, DC Rodgers, the head, Miss Pearce and the secretary had been sitting in the office since Beth and Black had left them there. DC Rodgers reached for his bag and took out a newspaper, which he began to read. The headteacher seemed to take this as his cue.

'This is ridiculous,' he told them all, 'I have work to do,' and he got to his feet.

'Don't,' Rodgers warned him.

The headteacher flared up. 'You can't stop me from leaving this room. What are you going to do, arrest me?'

'No,' Rodgers admitted, and went back to looking at his newspaper while he calmly answered the man. 'But DS Black asked you to stay in here, so you won't be suspected of tipping off a potential witness in a major criminal case. If you do leave this room, I'll be duty bound to report it to him. He may then suspect you of trying to pervert the course of justice.' He turned a page of his newspaper. 'You can get up to three years for that,' he said amiably, 'but it's your call.'

The headteacher watched Rodgers for a while, as if trying to gauge how serious he was, but the detective carried on reading.

The head sat back down.

The sixth girl didn't answer the door when they rang the bell. Black knocked as well in case it wasn't working, then he knocked again, louder this time. As he did this, Beth peered through the window and saw a flash of movement as a figure left the front room and disappeared into the kitchen.

'Round the back!' she called, and Black ran.

Black had to sprint past five houses before reaching the gable end of the terrace and rounding the corner, then he dashed to the rear of the houses, into a back street filled with wheelie bins awaiting collection. He'd been hoping to outpace the girl and meet her coming the other way, but his luck was out, because she had chosen to run the other way and he could just see her back as she ran as fast as she could in the opposite direction.

'Police!' he called, but she didn't stop. Black sprinted after her, but even from here he could tell she had too great a head start and was likely to reach the end of the back lane before he could catch up with her. He stared fixedly ahead as he powered after the girl, so he could see if she veered off to the left or right at the end and be less likely to lose her.

There were yards still between them and she was almost at the top of the lane when someone else came sharply into view. Anticipating the problem, Beth had run the other way and must have done so at an impressive speed, because she blocked the girl's progress now. The girl tried to swerve then dodge past her, but Beth stepped in her way and grabbed her. 'Got her!' Beth shouted to Black, but the girl struggled and they whirled round so that Beth was now behind Black and she and the girl were facing in the other direction, just as Rob came round the same corner.

Because he was directly opposite her and up close, he got a good look at the girl's face.

343

'It's her!' he called triumphantly, just as the girl lashed out, kicking him hard in the shins.

'Little bitch,' hissed Rob, and he hobbled away with a cut on his shin. He was limping and looked angry. Perhaps he no longer liked the idea of being a detective.

'Fuck off!' she told him, then she rounded on Beth. 'And *you* assaulted me,' she told Beth, 'grabbing me like that.'

'She grabbed you because you ran,' explained Black.

'I didn't know who you were.'

Black hit back, 'I called "Police!" at the top of my voice, Jennifer. I think you knew who we were.'

'I didn't hear you.' She didn't seem surprised that he knew her name. 'And don't call me Jennifer. It's Jenny.'

'Okay, Jenny, now I want you to get into the car and come back with me to HQ,' he told her. 'Then you can tell me why you missed the ID parade.'

'I didn't miss it deliberately,' she said, 'I was sick.'

'Yet you knew it was happening,' he said. 'How? The other pupils didn't, so who told you about it, Jenny? Who warned you not to come?'

She looked flustered to be caught out like that. 'I'm saying nowt,' she told him.

If Black thought that getting the girl out of Collemby and into police headquarters in Newcastle might in some way lead to her revealing more of the truth, he was soon to be disillusioned. For a lass who was barely fourteen, Jenny rebuffed his questions like a pro.

'That girl has been coached,' Black told Beth after a fruitless interview with Jenny and her appropriate adult, a social worker drafted in at the last minute to ensure the girl was treated according to her rights when no one was able to trace her mother, who Jenny said was 'in Spain' and could not be contacted.

'Is she refusing to speak to you?' asked Beth.

'She spoke to me,' said Black, 'eventually, but it's all denials. She said she didn't know about the ID parade, even though she'd already indicated she knew about it. She said she was off sick with a bad headache but it had cleared up by the time we arrived and she only ran away because she didn't know who we were.'

'What about Rob ID-ing her as the girl dressed in Alice Teale's gear?'

'She outright denies it. Jenny says it can't have been her and he must have it wrong, so it's his word against hers.' He shrugged to show how flimsy that argument was.

'But it obviously was her,' said Beth. 'She has guilt written all over her.'

'It was her all right,' said the detective, 'but proving it is another matter.'

'Does she admit being at the school that night?'

'She admits to being there after the school day was over but only because she had a detention, which she completed in the punishment block, before Alice Teale was supposedly seen leaving the building. That's the bit that's tucked away in the U-bend, set back in the middle of the school,' he said. 'It's basically the only part that doesn't have any scaffolding on it.'

As soon as he had said that to her, he seemed to reflect on his own words.

'What are you thinking?' she asked him.

'Nothing.' He dismissed it. 'There's something I want to check, that's all.'

Beth wanted to press him further on this, but at that point her mobile rang. The call was a distraction – an irritation, in fact. She wanted to stay focused on the matter in hand. They had Jenny, but she wasn't cooperating, and now Black had a hunch, but for some reason he wasn't sharing it with her, which rankled. Beth was tempted to ignore the call but thought it might be something important, so she answered.

The voice on the end of the line was unfamiliar. The woman introduced herself as Pamela Barton and for a moment the name meant nothing to Beth. The caller must have picked up on her hesitation because she said, '*You* called *me*.' Then she added: 'You left a message for me at the school.'

It finally dawned on Beth that this was the teacher who had worked with Keech at a previous school. She'd been away with the kids on an outward-bound holiday so Beth had left her mobile number with the school and more or less forgotten about it the moment she had driven away.

'Oh yes, Miss Barton. The reason for my call –'

'Mr Keech,' she interrupted, sounding testy. 'You said in your message.'

Beth didn't need this right now. The woman was obviously narked because Beth hadn't remembered her and wanted to press home the point. 'It's a routine inquiry,' she told her. Black was looking impatient so she gestured for him to go on and that she would catch him up, then turned her full attention to the call while Black sloped off to his desk. 'We've had a complaint against Mr Keech involving a pupil, and I wanted to ask if you had knowledge of anything similar occurring during the time you worked with him.'

'What kind of complaint?'

Beth chose her words carefully. She didn't want to lead the woman or guide her in any way towards turning something relatively minor into retrospective proof that Keech was something he wasn't, but she did want to be thorough. If a girl in one of Keech's classes had complained about him in the past or alleged she had been touched inappropriately, then it would obviously strengthen the credibility of a more recent accusation.

'No,' said Miss Barton, 'there was nothing like that at all,' and she went on to express her shock that the question had even been asked. Beth had to remind her that this was merely an allegation and had come from one girl, but it still had to be thoroughly investigated, even though, in reality, it probably hadn't been, thanks to neither the headmaster nor the police having taken it seriously from the outset.

'I see, well, yes, of course. I did find that Mr Keech was — how can I put this? — *close* to some of the girls, and perhaps a bit . . .'

'A bit what?'

'One hesitates to use the word "lecherous" . . .' But she did it just the same, thought Beth. 'He was a bit of a sleaze, but so many men are when they reach that age, aren't they? Perhaps it's the mid-life crisis or something. Some men buy a sports car or a motorbike, some try to bed every woman they meet.'

'Why did he leave? Was there a scandal of some kind?'

'No, nothing like that. I've been teaching for a very long time and every school has at least a couple of lechy male teachers who flirt with the girls and make inappropriate comments about them in the staff room. He wasn't that out of the ordinary.'

'Did he say why he decided to go?'

'I don't remember his reasons. Maybe he just wanted a change.'

'Maybe.' Beth's frustration was growing. She had been convinced that if she just spent the time making enquiries at Keech's former schools, something incriminating would come up. Now, here she was, talking to a woman who had known him before he left for Collemby, and even she could offer nothing more than the fact that he was a bit of a sleaze. Beth would have to concede the obvious truth. She'd drawn a complete blank. She needed to end this conversation abruptly and catch up with Black, who looked ready to leave without her.

'Perhaps the head promised him something better in his new role,' Miss Barton said matter-of-factly.

'His current head, do you mean?'

'Yes.' Then she added, 'Well, they knew each other from before.'

'Did they?'

'Yes,' she said. 'I'm sure they worked together. I think that was one of the reasons he was so keen to be off.'

'Wait a second, you're saying that Mr Keech and Mr Morgan worked together previously – that the headteacher of his current school had dealings with Keech before?'

'Yes, I'm sure they did,' she replied. 'I thought that was the main reason Keech left.'

Beth collared Black on the way to the lift. They walked there together and rode down to the ground floor while she told him all about the call.

'This could be big,' she told him. 'When we spoke to Morgan, he gave us the impression he would happily fire Keech for his indiscretions and, at best, that he disapproved of – possibly even actively disliked – him. Now it turns out that not only did he appoint the man, he knew him of old.'

'That *is* interesting,' Black conceded. 'He did act as if Keech was someone who'd been there long before him, an irritant he had inherited and couldn't get rid of. If Keech was as uncooperative as he said, then why take him on in the first place?'

'And I don't think a man like Keech would suddenly start having flings with female pupils when he arrived at Collemby. Pamela Barton said he was close to some of his girls and a bit lechy. I don't think she realized how close. Behaviour like that is probably ingrained.'

'This needs checking. Find out what year Morgan became head and when Keech started at Collemby, but do it discreetly,' he warned. 'I don't want them to know we're on to them.'

'Leave it with me.'

She was about to go back into the building when he said, 'Do it later. I need you to do something for me now.'

'What?'

'Be my lookout.'

'What? Where?'

'At the school.'

'We're going back to the school?' she asked.

'Exactly.'

48

Black didn't say a word on the drive over to Collemby School.

'Are you going to tell me what we're going there for?'

'There's something I want to check out,' he told her.

'You said that,' she reminded him, 'but didn't enlighten me any further, so why the big mystery?'

'Because it might be nothing.'

They got out of the car, and Black moved purposefully towards the building, with Beth following him doubtfully down the main pathway towards the front doors, which, as expected, were locked. There was no sign of life anywhere in the building. Just before they reached them, Black veered off and took the path to the side of the building. They walked past the scaffolding that covered a good section of it. The lowest sections were blocked behind a temporary wooden construction which covered them. There was a rudimentary door and Black tried it, but it was locked to prevent anyone messing about on the scaffolding.

'What are we doing?' she asked. 'Forget that – what are *you* doing?'

'I want to take a look at something,' he said.

'The scaffolding?'

'The roof,' he said. 'Alice Teale went up on it at least twice, remember?'

'Of course I remember.'

'Why would she do that?'

'I don't know,' she said. 'Any ideas?'

'No.' He didn't enlighten her further. 'But we still have that twenty-minute window that's unaccounted for.'

'If Simon Nash is telling the truth,' she reminded him.

'And if he is, Alice must have been somewhere.'

They walked quickly down the side of the building and reached the spot at the rear where the headteacher usually parked his Jaguar. It was empty now.

'Don't we need a warrant?'

'Nope.'

Beth felt uneasy. 'Please tell me we're not breaking into the school?'

'Technically, I'm not,' he assured her, and took off his jacket then handed it to her for safekeeping.

'Technically? What does that mean?' But Black was too busy looking up at the wooden slats, which formed a cage that encased what looked to Beth like an old water tank that was stuck to the side of the building. There were small gaps between the planks and he seemed to be evaluating them. When he failed to give her an answer, she asked, 'What do you want to look at?'

'The view,' he said, then he smiled at her and began to climb.

Black wedged his toes between the gaps in the wooden slats and levered himself upwards, then grabbed the highest point of the wooden cage and pulled himself higher. Seconds later he was standing on top of the water tank and surveying the gap between it and the school roof, which was directly above, perhaps thirty feet from the ground below him.

'You'll never get up there . . .' But before she had even finished her sentence Black took a couple of steps back, followed by a running jump at the wall, his front foot hitting it and propelling him upwards so his hands could grasp the ledge above him. He managed to grab it with both hands and hold on. With a slight grunt of exertion, he pulled his body upwards and positioned one elbow on to the ledge, then the other, and from that point it was a simple matter to get on to the roof.

He got to his feet, turned and looked down at her.

'What are you doing?'

'Alice Teale went up on the roof at least twice. Chris saw her up there, and Jessica Pearce, who said Alice gave her reason for being there as *the view*.'

'You said she thought Alice was being cheeky.'

'And maybe she was,' he conceded, 'but perhaps she wasn't. I want to see what she was looking at.'

'Okay, but don't be too long. I feel like your accomplice.'

'No one could spot me up here,' he told her. 'Except the old biddies in the Aged Miners' cottages, and I'd be surprised if they can see beyond the backs of their gardens. Just give me a shout if anyone comes.'

'Okay.' She started to walk back round the side of the building. As Black turned away, he heard her call, 'Be careful up there.'

'It's nice to know you care.'

He couldn't see her any more but heard her shout back, 'I haven't got time to do your work as well as mine.'

Black looked at the roof. It seemed sturdy enough. The surface had been covered with thick sheets of felt that had been stuck down firmly, and nothing gave when he trod on it. If he just avoided stepping on to the glass skylights that were dotted about, he would be fine.

From where he was standing, it was still light enough to see the view from the rear of the building, which consisted of little more than a couple of old school outbuildings and one of its playing fields, which had goal posts at either end. A barbed-wire fence marked its boundary and there were some fields beyond, but there wasn't much to see here.

Black turned back and walked to the front of the building. As he crossed the roof, he noted he was on a lower section that was level with the third floor, so there was a sizeable wall to his right. From here, he could tell that the higher section of the roof was less inviting. It was sloping and had roof tiles that didn't look stable, along with an assortment of obstacles in the form of Velux windows, television aerials, air vents and heating ducts. Black couldn't imagine Alice Teale scrambling around up there, so he would restrict his exploration to the section of the roof he was already standing on.

When he reached the front of the school he stood close to the edge and gazed out at the view. Beneath him and to his right was the main path leading from the front door, which meant the staff room had to be right next to him, but he couldn't see into it without stepping off the roof on to the rickety scaffolding, and he didn't fancy that because the drop, if he slipped and fell, was considerable.

He followed the path with his eyes till it veered off towards the car park and the road beside it. Beyond the road was another large expanse of fields that stretched for miles. It wasn't a bad view, but not so spectacular that it warranted a climb on to the roof, and he was almost certain that was not what Alice had been talking about, so he transferred his attention to the Aged Miners' cottages.

He wondered if Alice could have seen something from the roof that alarmed her. Had she then confronted someone about it? Could she see her grandfather's house from here? Black squinted. Just.

Maybe Alice had better eyesight than he did, but he could only make out the buildings, their doors and windows. He couldn't see inside them from here.

An old lady was standing in her garden looking towards the school and it was then that a thought struck him. Alice would have been able to see if someone went into one of the cottages, probably even be able to tell who they were. Was that what she had meant by 'the view'?

'What did you see, Alice?' he asked himself quietly. 'What grabbed your eye?'

He glanced off to his left, but all he could see was more playing fields and a netball court enclosed by a tall wire-mesh fence. There was nothing else here, so it had to be the cottages, surely.

Unless.

Black took a look at the side of the building to his right. It was here that the scaffolding started, and it went all along the front of the building till it took a sudden left turn then went inwards where the school formed its uneven U-shape. He didn't want to do it. The scaffolding looked unstable and was designed to accommodate nerveless, experienced men who were used to working at heights. His first instinct was to climb back down, but he had to do this.

'Christ,' he muttered as he reached out and placed a hand against the cold metal of the scaffolding pole. He grasped it firmly and, trying not to look down, stepped off the side of the building. For a moment, there was nothing but air between Black and the ground below. With a slight jump, he landed with his left foot on the wooden scaffold, wrapping both arms round the pole and holding on for dear life.

Below him, Beth called out in alarm, 'Lucas!'

He eased his body round the pole until both feet were on the scaffolding. There was no wooden cage this high up, just open spaces between the poles that he could easily fall through if he tripped or grew careless.

'I'm fine,' he lied.

Black inched his way gingerly around the scaffold, keeping as much distance as possible from the edge. He stopped by the first window he reached, went down low and peered in. The staff room was, of course, empty and there wasn't much to see, just a few chairs and battered sofas, along with a table that held a kettle and a dozen mugs stacked up on it.

Black went further and passed three more classrooms before he reached the end. He checked each one, but they were almost uniform in their blandness, with rows of tables and chairs, a few books on the shelves and a black-board on the wall.

This was going to be a waste of time, he realized that now, but he kept going until he reached the corner of the school then took a right turn and walked further along the scaffolding, which wobbled alarmingly and became springier at this point. He hoped this bit hadn't been put together by a careless apprentice, or they would be scraping him off the pavement later.

At least here some of the front sections were lightly protected by sheets of tarpaulin that hung down and were tied in place, reducing the risk of falling, but not every section was covered. Black walked past three sections of scaffolding with tarpaulin over them until he reached a place where it was open once more and he could look out at a spot to the rear of the U-bend where the windows of the school were close enough to peer into again.

It hit him then, suddenly and in a rush, and he almost lost his balance in the exhilaration he felt at that moment. Grabbing the scaffolding pole to ensure he did not fall, Black steadied himself and looked more closely at the sight which greeted him.

'Oh my God,' he said quietly, because now he understood what Alice Teale had been doing up here and what she had been talking about when she mentioned the view.

49

Beth watched as Black carefully climbed down from the roof and felt relieved when his feet touched the ground again.

'Anything?' she asked him.

'Not much,' he said, 'at first. It's just fields at the back, and a similar view at the front, apart from the cottages. Then I realized that just because Miss Pearce and Chris both saw Alice on the section of roof I was standing on, it doesn't mean that is the view she was referring to. From there, you can climb on to the scaffolding and go right round that part of the building. Most of the time, you're shielded from view by its height and some pieces of tarp that cover the walkway, and very few people out front are facing the building, particularly when all the kids have gone home.'

'You reckon Alice went on to the scaffolding. Why?'

'Because you can follow it round into that bit the kids call the U-bend. If you do that, you get a bird's-eye view into a row of classrooms.'

'Which ones?'

'That's the interesting bit,' he said. 'The library, the drama room, the English teachers' rooms and, if you go right to the edge, the room they call the punishment block, where all the bollockings and detentions happen.'

'You think she was spying on something going on in one of those rooms?'

'What else could be of interest to her up there? The view from the roof? No, there's nothing there. If she was suicidal, she wouldn't throw herself from that height. I was scared of falling, but it's survivable. It's not high enough to be sure it would kill you. The only thing of any interest up there is the scaffolding and the view it gives you, and I think that's where Alice was, during that crucial time between the darkroom and the point when Jessica Pearce saw who she thought was Alice leaving the school.'

'She saw something up there that mattered,' deduced Beth. 'Something that led to her death. You think that's her big secret? But what is it, and how will we ever know?'

'That's the problem. She's no longer around, so we can only guess what it might be, but one of the teachers must have done something pretty bad. She guessed, or found out about it somehow, but needed to see it with her own eyes to fully believe it.'

'Alice Teale was killed for a reason,' said Beth, 'and you might just have found that reason.'

'But we don't have any proof.' His tone betrayed his frustration.

'Proof!' said Beth, and her eyes widened. 'Remember when we read the first page of her journal? *There's something I need first.* That's what she wrote, and we both agreed it was proof.'

'We did.'

'But simply seeing something isn't proof. You can't just tell people you saw something when it's your word against someone else's.'

'What are you getting at?'

'The camera,' said Beth. 'I didn't think it was significant, but a camera went missing from the darkroom. Simon Nash told me about it. Alice's own camera was broken. Daniel showed me it in her room. Nash also said Alice had been asking him the difference between telephoto and zoom lenses.'

'You would need one,' he told her. 'No ordinary phone camera would do the trick from up there. Alice took the camera,' he concluded. 'She must have. She went up on to the scaffolding with it, looked into one of those rooms and saw what was going on.'

'Then she took a picture,' said Beth. 'There's her proof.'

Black took a deep breath as they both let that sink in. 'But where's the camera now?' he asked.

'If someone caught Alice and killed her, then they took the camera and destroyed it,' Beth offered. 'That would explain why we can't find it.'

He thought for a moment. 'I don't think so. Put yourself in their shoes and ask yourself what you would do. You've caught Alice, you've killed her and you're going to have to dispose of the body. That's your prime concern, and nothing else matters right then.' He started speaking slowly, as if he was beginning to put the pieces together. Beth wondered where he was going with this. 'If you saw her with the camera, if you found it, you wouldn't try to destroy it, would you? If it's one of those old ones that need film – all you'd have to do is open the back and pull out the roll. It would be destroyed as soon as light hit it, or you could burn it later. That's far easier than trying to smash the camera and get rid of the pieces. Without the film, it's no use to anyone as evidence. You could just put it back or say you'd found it lying around somewhere and some kid or other would get the blame for being careless.'

'I've been along every inch of that scaffolding,' he added. 'There's no nook or ledge big enough for her to hide a camera.'

'Then where could it be?' asked Beth and, suddenly, it hit her. 'They didn't see the camera!' She almost shouted it.

'What do you mean?'

She became animated then, talking in a rush. 'Alice is on the scaffolding and sees what she sees. She takes a picture, maybe several, and the person she's photographing doesn't spot her, not then.' She held up a finger as if she were thinking it through bit by bit. Black listened without interrupting. 'She puts the camera away and makes to leave. Did the killer see her then, but only then? Was it her movement that alerted him, and he came after her, but he didn't know about the camera?'

'Her bag,' said Lucas. 'It was in her bloody bag!'

'It was,' said Beth, 'but it isn't now.'

'Harry,' said Lucas. 'We need to get to Harry.'

50

Happy Harry was unrecognizable. He was clean and shaven and dressed in hand-me-down clothes that actually fitted him: trousers, shirt and a cardigan. He'd even had a haircut and, aside from some blemishes on his face, he looked like any normal man might. He even seemed sober. His short time at Alex McGregor's shelter had obviously been good for him. It was the logical solution to the problem of what to do with the homeless man, and at least now he was easier to locate, particularly after dark.

'I like it here,' he told them when they asked him how he was. 'They feed you and they let you have hot tea.' He held up his mug to show them this unimaginable luxury. 'It's better than the streets and warmer than the woods.' Beth realized how luxurious a bed indoors must have seemed to Harry. 'Thanks for putting a word in for me.'

'No problem,' said Black. McGregor's shelter was a better option for Harry than sleeping rough, and it meant they knew where he was and could find him again easily if there were further developments in the case. They were glad of their decision now.

Beth explained why they needed to speak to him again. She promised him that his place at the hostel and any future help he had been offered to keep him off the streets permanently was not in jeopardy: 'But only if you tell us the truth now.' And he nodded eagerly along to that.

It was Black's turn then. They had prearranged their approach. Beth would be kind then Black would come in and play the bad guy.

'Of course, if we find out later that you've lied or held out on us, then that's a very different matter. That would be serious, Harry' – the homeless man looked alarmed – 'and we would have to review your situation here.'

'Review?' he asked them uncertainly.

'Which is why we're going to give you this chance to clear the air and get everything out in the open,' Beth told him, 'because there is one important thing you haven't told us.'

'Maybe you were worried you'd get into more trouble,' Black said.

'I didn't do anything,' said Harry, but his guilty face betrayed him and Black knew they were on the right lines.

'The camera, Harry,' he said. 'Tell us what you did with the camera.'

Kevin Brown complained a lot, even after they showed him their warrant cards. The shopkeeper couldn't understand why they were there, knocking on his door so insistently at such a late hour, or why they needed him to leave his apartment to open up the shop so they could inspect its contents.

'It's late,' he said, as if they didn't know this. 'We're closed. Why can't you wait till the morning?'

'This won't wait till the morning,' explained Beth, her patience quickly reaching its limit, 'and you live *above* your shop! We're not asking you to drive across town.'

He greeted this statement with a sigh and a muttered

curse but made no further objection as he went back into his flat to grab the keys to the shop below.

The shabby little shop was right at the far end of the town and not a great distance from Alice Teale's own home. The faded sign outside still claimed the place to be a newsagent's, but that had closed down long ago and he hadn't bothered to put up a new one. It was obvious from the window that he was trading in second-hand goods which he had picked up for a pittance from desperate people who were strapped for cash and looking to get a few quid by flogging everything from tumble dryers to vacuum cleaners. The front window was jam-packed with vases and ornaments, old coffee tables, lampshades, an ancient battered chest of drawers and a paraffin heater.

He opened the front door and let them in while they explained what they were looking for. 'I get a lot of cameras,' he said, making it sound like dozens crossed his counter every day.

Beth went over to the glass-fronted cabinet, also for sale, which housed half a dozen cameras, as well as other electrical goods, an ancient TV game and an early-eighties computer.

'Did you buy one from Harry?' asked Black.

'Harry who?'

'Everyone in Collemby knows Harry,' Black told him. 'He's not someone you'd forget. Has he been in here recently with a camera for sale?'

'Not that I recollect.' The man's posture stiffened. He must have assumed that Harry had stolen the camera from someone, even as he paid the homeless man for it. Beth and Lucas's presence in his shop had confirmed that suspicion.

'It's here,' called Beth, and she turned away from the cabinet: 'Canon AE-1, black plastic grip with a silver body.'

'Oh, er, I'm not sure about that,' he stammered. 'I think we've had that one for a while.'

'Then why does it have "CCS" on it?' She pointed at the identifying white markings. 'For Collemby Comprehensive School.'

'Eh?' he said innocently, and walked over to survey the camera with mock-incredulity. 'Well, that *is* strange. I've not noticed that before.'

'Just hand it over,' said Lucas, and when the shop owner seemed reluctant: 'Or we'll take you in.'

The man saw sense then and nodded at the locked glass cabinet. 'I'll just get the key.'

He took a while to locate the right key but, eventually, while Beth and Black waited impatiently for him, he re-emerged and walked over to the cabinet, tried the key in the lock and opened it then reached inside for the camera. He handed it to Beth and she checked it.

She looked up at Lucas. 'There's film in here.'

There was no one at police HQ who could develop old-fashioned 35mm film at that hour, so Black kept the camera and they reconvened the next morning. Black knew a technician who was old enough to recall a pre-digital age and they accosted him as soon as he arrived. He explained the urgency of the situation and urged the man to take great care.

He needn't have worried that there might be a lack of enthusiasm. 'Oh, wow, actual film, like from the Ark,' he enthused. 'I haven't seen a roll of film in a camera in I don't know how long, but it's years.'

'You do know how to do this, right?'

'Of course,' he said. 'That's how I started out. Don't worry, you're in good hands here, mate.'

'I hope so,' said Black. 'And, if you don't mind, I'll wait till you're done.'

The technician looked as if he was going to advise against that, but when he saw the look on Black's face he relented. 'I'll be a while,' he said. 'I'll have to nip out and get some developer. You might want to get yourself a cup of tea. I'll come and get you as soon as I'm finished.' Then he said, 'I promise. What are you expecting to find, anyway?'

'I don't know.'

Black could tell the man did not believe he had no idea what was on the roll. The technician didn't challenge him, though, he simply said, 'It must be important.'

'It is,' Black assured him. 'A girl died for it.'

They went to Black's desk at HQ and the first thing he noticed was a large envelope resting on the keyboard by his computer. He opened it then said, 'It's the forensic results on the car Simon Nash was driving that night.' He looked accusingly around the room. 'You would have thought someone might have called me,' he said, loud enough for everyone to hear, and Beth noticed how they all studiously ignored him.

Black read through the report then briefed her. 'It's clean. No fibres, no blood or bodily fluids of any kind that link the inside of the car to Alice and, more importantly, no trace of her body in the boot. No trace of her anywhere, in fact.'

'Perhaps even Nash baulked at the idea of sex with a secret lover in his fiancée's car?' offered Beth.

'Either way, it looks like he may have been telling the truth about that night.'

'The part about her not getting in his car, perhaps,' she said, 'but he might still have been the last one to see her alive in the school.'

'If he killed her there, why would he then park his car a few yards away?'

Beth had no idea but suggested, 'Shock, maybe? At the realization of what he had done. Maybe he had to pull over to process it?'

'Perhaps.' But he sounded doubtful. 'And his room is one of the ones that can be overlooked from the scaffolding.'

Whatever else he might have been about to add was lost when the phone rang. Black answered the call, listened for a moment and his face betrayed anxiety at what he was being told. Beth could only wait until he had finished and hung up before she could learn more.

'It's the Teales,' he told her grimly. 'Ronnie Teale has been arrested.'

'What for?'

'Assault occasioning actual bodily harm.'

So, Ronnie Teale had finally exploded on someone.

Before she could ask who the unfortunate victim was, Black filled in the gaps, 'And Abigail Teale is in hospital.'

Black looked conflicted then. She knew his main focus was on the photographs and that he wouldn't want to leave here until they had been developed and he'd seen the results, but she wanted to check on Abigail, both on her well-being and also to get her side of the story before Ronnie could influence it.

'I'll go,' she told him.

Side-on, Abigail looked okay. She was sitting up in bed, propped up by pillows, fully conscious and seemingly unharmed. It was only when Beth drew level with the foot of her bed and saw the damage to the other side of the woman's face that she realized the extent of her injuries. Her left side was badly bruised, her eye swollen so badly it was completely closed, but that wasn't the worst of it. The half-dozen stitches that ran from her forehead to her temple told the story of what must have been a gaping wound before they patched Abigail up.

Beth gasped, 'Oh my God, Mrs Teale, what happened?'

'I fell,' she said flatly.

It was a while before Beth could answer her calmly, 'You're saying he didn't hit you?'

Abigail took even longer with her response. 'He *did* hit me,' she admitted, 'and then I fell. Hit my head on the edge of the coffee table.'

At least she hadn't lied about being hit by Ronnie Teale. Surely now she would kick the man out or leave him.

'We can help you, Abigail,' Beth said. 'We can make sure Ronnie never –'

The woman interrupted her. 'It was my fault.'

'No,' said Beth. 'It wasn't. Women often say that, but –'

'I know they do, and I know why they say it,' said Abigail. 'They make excuses for their men, but this time it's true.'

'How could this be your fault?'

'Because I told him he was the reason Alice was dead.'

'Wait – what did you say?' Had Abigail learned something new about her daughter's death? 'Why is Alice dead because of him?'

'I said it was all his fault.'

'What did he do? Abigail, if Ronnie is in any way responsible for what happened to Alice, then you must tell me.' *And tell me now before we arrest the wrong guy for it.* 'If you know something, then you must say, for Alice's sake and your own.'

'No.' She shook her head then winced at the pain this caused her. 'You don't understand. Ronnie didn't kill her and it wasn't his fault. I just said that it was.'

Beth was confused. 'Why would you say that,' she asked, 'if it wasn't true?'

'Because I was angry about the way he was with her all those years and I wanted to hurt him.' Then she said, 'And then he hurt me. So, really, it *was* my fault and he only hit me once.'

'Hard enough to cause that,' said Beth, and she pointed to the side of her own face to indicate the damage he had done with that one hefty blow.

'It looks worse than it is.'

'You have to leave him.'

'And go where? Do what?' snapped Abigail. 'With no proper job, no money and no home?'

'Then kick him out. Get a restraining order. Your face

is all the proof you need. We're on your side. We'll charge him with assault.'

'You think I'd like you to put my husband in prison? We just lost our daughter and you want to put *him* in jail? He's all I've got.'

'You are lucky to be alive, Abigail. If you stay with him, how do you know this won't happen again?'

'Because I won't ever be cruel enough to accuse him of being the cause of his own daughter's death, that's why.'

Beth listened to Abigail's argument with mounting frustration at the thought of the woman going back to this one-man ball of rage. She might not have many more options, but surely one of them was more palatable than living the rest of her life with Ronnie.

Beth had one last card to play and she reasoned she had nothing to lose. 'I have to ask you this, Abigail,' she began, and the woman regarded her closely. 'Was Ronnie Alice's father?'

Abigail's shoulder seemed to sag and, for a moment, Beth was convinced the woman was about to tell her everything. Then she gave Beth a look of complete disgust and said, 'You bitch. How dare you? I just lost her,' and stared at Beth in disbelief. 'I lost my little girl, and you come here and say you're on my side then ask me that? What's wrong with you? Get out,' she said, then screamed: 'Get out!'

Beth flinched at the ferocity of the woman's cry and left the ward without a word.

Black didn't know what to do with himself while the film was being developed, so he took the technician's advice.

He went to the canteen for a mug of coffee and sat quietly on his own in the corner, lost in his thoughts, while silently praying there would be something of significance on that roll of film which might lead him and Beth to the killer. What if there was nothing, though? They'd be no further forward. What if the images were blurred or the identities of the people in the pictures inconclusive? What if they were completely mistaken and all they were going to get back were a few snapshots of Alice and her friends on one of their rambles in the countryside? Black was snapped from his thoughts by a loud crash as a young man working in the canteen dropped a stack of dirty plates on the floor and smashed them. There were a couple of mock-cheers from policemen who were eating there and some swearing from someone behind the scenes who was unamused by the boy's clumsiness. There was a sole cry of 'Sack the juggler!' from a comedian who must have assumed no one had heard that before. Black glanced at his tea. The contents of the mug had gone cold and he realized he hadn't drunk a single drop.

'Mind if I join you?'

He looked up to find Beth standing there in front of him.

'How did it go at the hospital?'

She pulled out a chair and sat down opposite him. 'Not well.' She told him about Abigail Teale's reaction to the assault by Ronnie and Beth's suggestion that she should leave the man.

'I've seen that a lot, and it never gets any easier. You tried,' he told her, 'and sometimes that's all you can do. Maybe when she's had time to process it . . .' But they both knew Abigail Teale was unlikely to change her mind.

Beth checked the time on her phone. 'How long has it been?' she asked.

'Long enough.'

'I hope your guy doesn't muck it up.'

'He won't,' Black assured her, though he wasn't entirely certain of that himself. His contact was more used to a digital age and an examination of close-up crime-scene photos, not shots taken on an old film camera by a school-girl from an obscure vantage point. 'Let's hope Alice Teale had a good eye and a steady hand.'

More time passed, and they were beginning to wonder what was keeping the man. 'Has something gone wrong, do you think?' asked Beth.

'Christ!' Black blurted in exasperation, and it was loud enough for those at the next table to turn and glance at him questioningly before resuming their conversation. He made Beth jump as well, but she realized it was frustra-tion, not anger at her question. 'Where is he?'

It was an entirely rhetorical question, but Beth looked around and found that she was able to answer it.

'Here he is.' They both got to their feet.

The technician was carrying a large brown envelope which contained the results of his work. It seemed to take him an age to walk through the tables and chairs to reach them. Beth and Black didn't take their eyes off him for a moment, both trying to read something in his expression-less features but finding nothing there. They'd know soon enough whether this was a waste of time or if there was gold in that envelope.

The technician handed the envelope to Lucas. 'Thanks,' said the detective sergeant, who was desperate now for any hint about its contents. 'I hope it was worth the effort.'

'Oh,' said the technician, 'I would say so,' but he gave them no further clue. 'See for yourself.'

They almost ran to the nearest empty room. As soon as they were inside and the door was closed behind them Black carefully opened the envelope and pulled out its contents. There were twelve prints in all. Black placed them face up, one at a time, on the table.

The first photograph made Beth's heart sink. The image showed a river running by a field. The second was of another rural scene with the same light and weather conditions, so it was more than likely taken on the same day. There were trees and more fields. The third showed two young people standing by a stile. They were dressed for outdoors activities, in durable jackets, and one of them wore walking boots.

'Bloody rambling club,' said Beth. 'Is that all this is?' Surely not, when the technician had already assured them it had been worth his effort. The fourth picture silenced her doubts. If the first three images had been captured by Alice, the latest one must have been taken by a friend. A group of three friends stood together: happy, smiling girls, bunched in close – Chloe, Kirstie and Alice. It was a great shot, perhaps taken by Simon Nash, and it showed every detail of their faces. They seemed so carefree, but that was all a lie – and now one of them was dead. A great sadness hit Beth then, along with the realization that Kirstie's and Chloe's lives would never be the same.

The fifth photograph snapped her out of it.

'What's that?' she asked Lucas.

'I can't make it out,' said Black.

'I think it's the edge of the inside of a bag. An accidental photograph while she was pulling it out in a hurry, maybe?'

'Looks like it,' he said.

Black placed the next photo face up on the table. The image was blurred, but it was definitely a shot of the windows of the school from the same vantage point Black had viewed them from the roof. He could make out three of the rooms he had peered at, including the library, the drama room, Keech's room and the punishment block. There were shadowy figures in each of them. It proved nothing by itself, but it meant they were definitely on the right track. Alice had been up on the scaffolding to take these pictures.

'I can't make anything out,' said Black. He was beginning to fear the pictures had been taken from too far away and the images would reveal nothing of any substance.

The next picture cured him of that fear. He placed it on the table and it was clear that Alice had managed to focus more clearly by zooming in on the relevant window. Both could make out two figures.

'That's the headteacher,' she said. 'But who is he speaking to?'

Black didn't reply, because the second figure was obscured by the window pane.

Beth didn't have to wait long for an answer. The next picture revealed the identity of the second figure.

'That's Keech,' she said.

'What's he doing in there with the head?'

'Another dressing-down?' asked Beth. 'In the punishment block?'

'Which is usually reserved for children,' said Black, just as the next image was placed on the table to reveal a third figure. It was young Jennifer.

'There's our proof she was with them in the room. That's what Alice was trying to photograph.'

The last three photographs revealed the truth. Neither of them spoke as Black placed the images on the table one at a time and the reason for Jenny's presence in the room became self-evident. There was absolute silence for a while until Beth, her voice cracking, said what they were both thinking. 'That's abuse.'

Black did not contradict her, because the images were plain enough. 'Keech is abusing that young girl,' she went on, 'right in front of the headteacher, and he's doing nothing, which means they're both in it together.'

'They always have been,' concluded Lucas. 'And they've been doing it for years.'

51

When they had finished examining the final photographs Black instinctively turned them over, as if banishing the damning images. Then he looked at Beth, who was in a state close to shock.

'This isn't going to be easy,' he told her, and she could tell he was shaken, too, 'but we owe it to Jenny . . . and to Alice . . . to make sure we do the right thing from now on, every step of the way, so we don't let these two evil bastards off the hook. Can you do that?'

'Of course,' she assured him. 'I'll stay professional.'

'Good. So now let's go over what we know,' he said. 'Alice took these photos, then she must have put the camera in her bag. At some point, Keech and Morgan realized she had seen them, so they killed her and took her body away from the school. They dressed Jenny in Alice's green parka then pulled the hood up over her head, knowing someone was bound to see her leave the school and they could throw everyone off the scent while they got Alice's body away from there.'

'And they put Alice's big floppy bag on Jenny's shoulder to complete the look,' said Beth. 'Not knowing that the camera, with the evidence Alice needed, was in the bottom of that bag.'

'Jenny played the part of Alice, but not for long,' added Black. 'As soon as she was clear of the school and thought no one was looking, she took the bag and the parka and stuffed them into the bin. Maybe she panicked. They would have been found when the uniforms first searched the area, but Harry came along and got to them first. He took the coat and the bag, found the camera in it then sold it for beer money. That's what we know – but what we don't know is just as important.'

'Like what exactly happened to Alice,' said Beth, 'and who killed her.'

'It has to be one of three people.'

'Three?'

'Keech, Morgan or Jenny.' And before Beth could protest, he assured her, 'I don't think it was Jenny. My money is obviously on the men, but which one? They both had a lot to lose if they were exposed.'

'Why would Jenny help them cover this up, though?' asked Beth. 'Why help your abusers at all?'

'It's complicated,' said Black. 'She was being abused, yes, but she probably didn't see it that way. I've seen this before.'

'You're not going to tell me she was willing,' said Beth accusingly, 'and so that makes it different?'

'No, I am not,' he shot back. 'With a girl that age, it's always abuse, but men like that are sly. They don't just take. I've seen it, Beth. They pay compliments and give out rewards in return for compliance: money, sweets, alcohol, drugs. Sometimes the victims get confused and think they're actually in love with their abusers, particularly if their home life is terrible. Her mother is in Spain, remember?' he said cynically. 'If no one has shown them any affection or given them anything before, then the abuse can look a lot like love to a confused and damaged young mind.

'It's how pimps recruit runaway girls straight off the bus to London. They don't offer them work as a prostitute, because they know most girls would turn that down. Instead they take them somewhere and buy them a burger and a Coke, offer them a place to crash for the night, listen to their sad stories and introduce them to other girls like them, make them feel loved and wanted. It's only later, when they're happy and settled, that they tell them they have to earn their keep by having sex with strangers. Often they don't realize they're being exploited until it's too late.'

'It would explain Jenny's complete lack of cooperation,' said Beth, 'but how do we get her to tell the truth?'

'I want *you* to try.' He spread his palms in a gesture of surrender. 'I have to recognize that you are likely to appear less threatening than me in her eyes.'

Beth was torn between her agreement on that and her confusion as to how best to get the truth out of Jenny. 'How do you think I should play this? What can I say to her that you haven't already tried?'

'I think you should show her the photographs.' And when Beth looked shaken by that he said, 'Tell her you know everything but you don't think any of it is her fault. If you lead her in the right direction, perhaps she'll implicate Keech, Morgan or both of them.'

'And if she doesn't?'

'I hate to say it, but there's one more tactic you could try.' He seemed reluctant to reveal it to her. 'It's a last resort.'

'I'm listening.'

'Tell her that I think *she* might have done it.'

'What?' Beth was shocked.

'Jenny has had dealings with the police before. Her default position will always be to lie or evade. You have to get her to feel she has something to lose if she won't tell us what happened. It's the carrot and the stick,' he explained. 'The carrot is that she'll be treated leniently, as a minor who was groomed and abused by adults. If she tells us what happened to Alice, the courts will likely treat her as a victim, not a conspirator, but that might not be enough.'

'You want me to tell an abused girl that my colleague thinks she might be a murderer?' Beth was genuinely shocked. 'What textbook told you to go down that route?'

'If it gets her to break free from her abusers and put them both behind bars, then I'll happily accuse her of the Hatton Garden heist.'

'We'll be slaughtered if this gets out.'

'Maybe.'

'But the end justifies the means, is that it?'

'If it's a choice between this and those two bastards walking free to abuse more young girls, then yes.'

'And you'll be able to live with that? You could sleep at night?'

'I don't really sleep anyway,' he told her.

Jenny was back in the police station, her appropriate adult by her side. Beth was about to walk into the room to conduct an interrogation that would make or break the case against Keech and Morgan. She was nervous, tense and terrified of adding any more demons to the number already undoubtedly swirling inside Jenny's young head.

'Just be strong,' Black told her. 'It's the only way.'

'I don't like this idea,' said Beth. 'She's the victim here.'

'She absolutely is,' agreed Lucas. 'She just doesn't know it. We have to find a way to get her to realize the truth, and that might involve shocking her. I'm certain she didn't kill Alice Teale, but she'll be able to tell us who did.'

'Maybe they both did,' said Beth.

'It's likely,' agreed Black. 'And our best bet with Keech and Morgan is to turn one against the other to see if they break.'

'At least we can agree on that.'

In the end, and to her immense relief, Beth didn't need to follow Lucas's suggestion about threatening Jenny with the status of prime suspect in the murder of Alice Teale so she would break ranks with her abusers.

A solicitor was also present, but things went fairly smoothly when he realized that Beth wanted the same thing he did, the release of his new client, who none of them actually suspected of murder. The photographic images left no one in the interview room in any doubt about the truth of the situation. Jennifer was a victim, not a criminal. She just had to be convinced to tell the truth, which she started to do once the evidence was placed in front of her.

'It's not what it looks like.' Her teak-hard veneer had been stripped away now. She was crying while she tried to defend the two men. 'I let them do it. They didn't force me. I let them do what they wanted.'

Beth had to fight the anger and nausea she was feeling

as she addressed the young girl in the calmest, gentlest voice she could muster. 'Okay, Jenny, I believe you, and you're certainly not in any trouble whatsoever, but it would be very helpful for me if I could understand what happened.'

'They said I was special,' sobbed the girl. 'They told me I was their special girl.'

Beth felt her own heart break a little then. Was that really all it took?

She spent an hour with Jenny before emerging to brief Black. By then, she felt completely exhausted.

'How did it go?'

'I didn't have to do it,' she said, and he knew she meant the accusation of murder.

'Good,' he said. 'What did she tell you?'

'Everything.'

Beth went through all the admissions that had seemed to flow from the girl once she had seen the photographs, the most shocking of which concerned the fate of Alice Teale.

'You were right,' she told Lucas. 'They saw Alice watching them from the scaffolding and they panicked. The men both ran out to try and stop her from talking about what she had seen, but Alice had to go back along that wobbly scaffolding, so they moved quicker than she did.'

'What happened?'

Beth's ashen face showed him she was coming to that, and he remained quiet so he could listen to her.

'Jenny says that Keech went up the staircase to the roof first, Morgan followed and she went up last. As she got to the top, she saw Keech sprinting towards Alice to try and grab her. She swears he was just trying to stop her from climbing down and exposing what had been going on, but she was running, he was running, and they came together at speed right on the edge of the building. He grabbed at her, but not strongly enough to hold on to her. She struggled to break free and, instead of restraining her' – Beth's mouth had gone dry and she struggled to complete the sentence – 'he somehow knocked her off the edge. She went over head first.'

Even though they both knew Alice Teale was dead and that she had to have been killed somehow, it was still a shock to hear it described like this. Now they were both able to fully visualize her fate and understand the blunt trauma to her head which had happened before her death. It sickened them.

'She's saying it was an accident,' he asked, 'or at least that Keech didn't intend to push her off the edge?'

Beth nodded. 'Jenny says she knew Alice had to be dead, even without seeing where she landed, because it was so high up there. She says she collapsed then and doesn't remember what was said to her at first, but Morgan ran around the back of the building.'

'His car was there,' said Black. 'How convenient.'

'Keech stayed with Jenny and somehow convinced her it was as much her fault as his. They were all in it together and she was still his special girl, so he would protect her from this. That's why she agreed to wear Alice's coat when Morgan came back with it and the shoulder bag. She walked off down the path and they all hoped someone would see her leave. Jessica Pearce did see her, but Jenny only saw Rob coming down the path. When he got a close look at her, she panicked. That's why she stuffed the coat and bag into the bin.'

'Until it was found by a grateful Harry,' said Black, 'complete with the camera and the film with the last pictures Alice took.'

'It's heartbreaking,' said Beth, 'to think that a young girl could die for that.'

'And another, even younger one would end up blaming herself. I've seen a lot of things in my time and I've questioned a lot of bad people, but what these men did ranks very high up with the worst of them. I know you must be exhausted . . .'

'I'm fine.'

'Then are you ready to question Keech now?' he asked her. 'Because I am.'

'Yes.'

'Let's nail the bastard.'

52

Keech caved in as soon as he was confronted with the photographic evidence. His shock helped. Until that moment, he hadn't even known of its existence. Jennifer's eyewitness testimony, that he had knocked Alice Teale from the roof, opened the flood gates and he admitted it all, but this was far from a complete confession to murder. It had all been an accident, apparently. As Black watched him spill the story, he knew what Keech was doing. The teacher understood he was in big trouble – his career over, his reputation ruined and jail time inevitable for the abuse of that young girl – but now he had entered a different world with even higher stakes, one in which he was trying to avoid the prospect of spending the rest of his life in prison.

Of course, he blamed Jennifer, who was no innocent in his eyes, even at her tender age. 'You don't imagine I was the first, do you?' he asked at one point, and Black had to forcibly restrain himself from smashing the man's face into the table, even in front of his solicitor.

Their relationship had been entirely consensual, he explained. Black had to remind him that, at Jennifer's age, it was irrelevant. 'Statutory rape is still rape,' he told Keech. Black also accused him of pushing Alice from the roof deliberately, murdering her, in effect, but he strongly denied this. It had been an accident. A tragedy. He had been trying to grab her and talk some sense into her but they collided and she fell. He had the nerve to tell the detective sergeant that he wished it had been him instead.

He admitted to persuading Jenny to wear Alice's coat when Morgan brought it back from her body. Jenny was tall for her age. She was virtually the same height as Alice, with similar-coloured hair, but Jenny shouldn't have panicked and ditched the coat. They didn't find out she had done that till much later, when it had already been retrieved by Harry, causing them all to panic, though that lessened as time passed and no one mentioned it.

Beth and Black listened to Keech's outpouring of regret, recrimination, remorse and self-justification. They recorded every word and allowed him to keep on burying himself and implicate Morgan, who he seemed to think had done the decent thing by helping him to dispose of the body of a girl who had been the victim of a tragic accident.

'Owning up to everything then,' he said, 'well, it wouldn't have brought poor Alice back.' He explained this as if he had recovered from the shock of the girl's death almost instantly, before rapidly going into self-preservation mode.

When he had finally finished, Black said, 'Thank you for that story, about Alice Teale and her unfortunate accident. There's just one problem with it.' And when Keech clearly didn't understand what he meant, Black explained, 'Alice Teale was still alive after she hit the ground. Her death wasn't caused by the fall. She might have lived if you had just called an ambulance.'

'No, that's not right,' protested Keech. 'She was dead.'

'You saw her?' asked Black. 'You checked her vital signs, just to be sure?'

'No,' he admitted, 'but Morgan did. He told us she was dead. He was certain.'

'Still alive,' countered Black, 'according to the pathologist. He confirmed that she didn't die in the fall.'

'But I don't understand . . .' sputtered Keech.

'I do. She was strangled, and that makes this a murder.'

Keech lost it then. He went on rambling his assurance that he didn't know anything about Alice surviving the fall, how he would have definitely called for an ambulance if he had only known she was still breathing, how he couldn't have seen the body because Morgan had scooped it up and placed it in the boot of his car then driven it away to Craster so he could throw it into the sea.

Finally, Keech must have realized what had really happened, and he turned on the headteacher completely.

'He must have been the one who killed her. It was Morgan,' he said, as if he had only just worked it out now. 'He must have done it. He killed Alice.'

'Thanks for that, Mr Keech,' said Black placidly, 'but I bet you a pound to a penny that he says it was you.'

In a way, Black was correct about Morgan and his likely denials of murder, but he would have lost his bet. When they interviewed the headteacher he did not try to claim that Keech had strangled Alice or that her fall from the rooftop was fatal or an accident. He tried an entirely different tactic, one that required a staggering amount of nerve. He denied any involvement in it whatsoever and told the detectives that if they thought he was even capable of such a thing, then they were completely deluded. Beth and Black were left with an impression of a man who had anticipated being dragged in for questioning one day, if anything went wrong. He must have practised his rebuttals until he could deliver them word-perfect, with just the right amount of incredulity and indignation to lend them authenticity. Even when confronted with the new photographic evidence, the testimony of Jenny and the partial confession of Keech, he didn't waver, not even for a second. It was a masterful performance.

Morgan didn't kill Alice. He had nothing to do with her death and he bridled at the suggestion, then he kicked back, hard. 'You think you have a case against me?' he asked, as if Beth and Black were crazy. 'Then prove it. Prove that I murdered Alice Teale. All you've got is the word of one mixed-up disgruntled young girl and a teacher with questionable morals who is desperate to shift attention away from himself. That blurred photograph proves nothing. Alice had a fall and bashed her face, or so you tell me, then someone strangled her. That is a tragedy, but I certainly wasn't the culprit and you have no evidence against me.'

'We'll find tiny traces of blood on the ground by your car,' said Beth, 'even if you can't see them.'

'Which might possibly prove she fell there, but not that I pushed her.'

'No, you didn't,' admitted Black. 'Keech did, and he admits that. He even thought he had killed her, though he claims it was an accident.'

Black could see in Morgan's eyes that he wanted to

contradict that, but how could he say it wasn't an accident when he wasn't supposed to know what had happened? Instead, he gave Black a sour look and let him continue.

'Keech says he thought Alice was dead when you put her in the boot of your car, but he didn't strangle her. You did, and he will testify that you did.'

'Of course he will, when he is the guilty party. He'll do anything to save his neck, but I'll deny everything. I wonder who will be believed.'

'We've seized your car,' said Black, and the headteacher did look momentarily troubled. 'He said Alice's body was put into your boot and you drove her away from the school. I know you had it valeted, but if any fibres remain, we'll find them. All it will take is a single hair from that poor girl's head, a tiny trace of blood from her broken face, and we've got you.'

'All that will prove is that he must have stolen my car.'

'Without you noticing? How long would he have needed it, to take her body from the school, drive out there, ditch her and get back to you?'

'I work very late. Everyone knows that. I wouldn't even have noticed if he had taken it for a while.'

'And the keys? How would he get those?'

'I have a tendency to leave them lying around,' he said airily, 'but I won't do that again. Go on,' the headteacher said. 'Charge me with murder and see how quickly the case collapses.'

'We have photographs of you watching while a young girl is abused in front of you.'

The headteacher fell silent then and folded his arms. It was time for his solicitor to earn his fees. 'It might have looked like that to you, Detective Sergeant, at first glance, but the viewpoint of the person who took those photographs is different from the one Mr Morgan had. His view of the incident was partially obstructed by a bookcase.'

'What?' Black was astonished at the downright nerve of the lie.

'It's true. Looking up at an angle, from his desk and a few yards –'

'It was about four feet away,' Black interrupted, but the solicitor continued unabated.

'All he could actually see was the girl's head and shoulders and Mr Keech standing directly behind her. He couldn't possibly see where the man's hands were.'

'No one will believe that.'

'I think a jury will,' said the solicitor, 'if you are foolish enough to pursue a prosecution against my client on such flimsy evidence.'

'Flimsy evidence! He was right there in the room!'

'And would have intervened if he had realized what Mr Keech was doing, but there is no evidence of that and the girl didn't indicate she was in any kind of distress.'

'Because they had groomed her.'

'Mr Keech possibly had, but not my client,' the solicitor explained in a reasonable tone, 'who has an entirely unblemished reputation and is a pillar of the community.'

'Yes, he is, isn't he? What perfect cover. So Keech abused her, right in front of his own headteacher, with only a low shelf full of books to hide what he was doing? Why would he do that?'

'Why would he do any of it at all? I think it's quite clear that Mr Keech is a very disturbed individual who is worthy of your full attention. Who knows what bizarre motive he had for this blatant act? Perhaps it gave him some form of twisted thrill.' And the solicitor's voice softened at that, as if he were saddened by the depravity of the world.

Black was incensed. They had concocted a ridiculous defence that would surely fall apart in court, but in that instant, Black's spirits slumped because he suddenly realized the truth. Morgan was right. The head would use his impeccable record and fake outrage, along with the absurd notion that his view was obstructed, to say that Keech was able to get an extra thrill from abusing a girl in his office right in front of him while he was none the wiser. Keech had admitted pushing the girl from the roof, albeit accidentally. Was it too much of a stretch to think he might have finished her off and even taken the head's car to dispose of her body? The headteacher's lawyer would do the rest, destroying Keech's credibility along the way.

Beth also knew how court cases could go and how malleable a jury might be in the hands of the right barrister, and she was reaching the same conclusion as Black. This bastard might get off. He probably would, in fact, if Keech could be painted as the lone villain.

Black sighed. 'You could be right. We might not be able to charge your client with murder on the basis of this evidence alone. It's circumstantial and a jury might think Keech is the real killer, trying to deflect blame on to him.'

'At last,' said Morgan, and it seemed as if relief had flooded through him, 'you display a semblance of common sense. Can I go now?' The arrogance of the man and his plain disregard for the rules, which he clearly thought did not apply to him, was obvious.

'No,' said Black. 'Mr Morgan, I am arresting you on suspicion of the prevention of the lawful and decent burial of a dead body and the disposal of a corpse with intent to obstruct or prevent a coroner's inquest.'

'What?' he blustered. 'What new rubbish is this?'

'I haven't finished. I am also arresting you on suspicion of perverting the course of justice. You do not have to say anything, but it may harm your defence if you do not mention when questioned something which you later rely on in court. Anything you do say may be given in evidence.'

'Why are you doing this?' the solicitor demanded. 'You have as much chance of this stacking up as you do a murder charge. Your case will collapse.'

'It might, but I don't think it will. I'm guessing there will be traces of Alice Teale in the boot of your client's car and that this will be enough for the charges to come to court. I'll still have a possible murder charge, held in abeyance, should new evidence of wrongdoing emerge.'

'But you have no new evidence,' protested the solicitor.

'Not at the moment, we don't,' admitted Black, 'but I think that is about to change,' and Beth wondered what he was going to do that could possibly uncover some. He looked Morgan in the eye. 'You said all we had was the word of one damaged girl who no one will ever believe, but she's not the only one you and Keech have abused, is she?' The head locked eyes with Black but refused to answer. 'Now that I have placed you under arrest, journalists will be allowed to write about it, and that's when things will get really interesting. They will tell the whole country that the headteacher of Collemby School and one of his senior teachers have been arrested on suspicion of the illegal disposal of Alice Teale's body. A story like that will be picked up and run by every newspaper, radio station and TV news network in the country. Headteachers don't usually do that sort of thing, so you are about to become very famous indeed.'

'I thought that, in this country, we worked on the presumption of innocence until proven guilty,' said the head tersely, but Beth could tell he was very worried now.

'We do,' agreed Black, 'but we also have a free press which is allowed to publish details of an arrest. They may even be allowed to add that you are being questioned on suspicion of murder, but I'm sure they'll check with their lawyers first.'

'What will any of that achieve, apart from the ruination of this school?'

'You are the ruination of this school,' Beth told him, 'and you were from the day you walked into it. We're just alerting people to the threat you pose.'

'Then I shall pursue a case for wrongful arrest,' said the solicitor, but Black ignored him.

'Do you know why the police are usually happy to let journalists report when people are arrested and charged?' asked Black. 'When other victims read about something like this, they are far more likely to come forward.' He leaned forward in his chair. 'Nothing breaks down a wall of silence like an arrest. That's when people start to say, "He did it to me as well," because they know they might finally be believed. You won't be the first or the last man to be brought down by multiple accusations. How many victims have there been over the years? Remember that girl you silenced. We already have two victims who can testify that Keech abused them and one who claims you did. I don't think it will be all that hard to find others. You've been doing this for a long time, haven't you?'

Morgan lowered his head then. He looked as if his last hope of getting off the hook was gone. 'I have nothing else to say to you.' His voice cracked when he said that.

'Save it for the judge, then,' said Black, 'and the jury. You'd better hope they believe your story, or it's going to be life in prison for both you and Keech.'

He didn't protest. He didn't even lift his head or make any sound at all. He just stared at the table in front of him with a shocked expression on his face.

'Nothing to say all of a sudden?' Black chided. 'That's because you're finished, and you know it.'

53

They stood in the town square for a moment, waiting for a lorry to finish backing out of the pub after delivering kegs of beer. They had no choice because their route out of Collemby was blocked by its manoeuvring.

'He's making a pig's ear of that,' said Black as he watched the driver moving the lorry back and forth, over and over, with tiny alterations in the angle of his reversal. Each time, he had to admit defeat and try again. It wouldn't have mattered if it were not for the fact he was blocking the street and the exit to the car park. They were as trapped as he was.

A few days had passed since Black had arrested the headteacher. The response to their leak of Morgan's arrest had been a media frenzy. That afternoon, they got their first call from someone claiming to be an earlier victim of Morgan and Keech. They received a steady stream of further reports then, until the number of those willing to come forward to report one or other of the men reached a dozen.

They used the weight of this many potential victims to secure a warrant to search their houses. It took a while but, hidden in the rafters of Morgan's garage, they found a brown, leather-bound journal with Alice Teale's name written on every page. Beth read the whole thing and finally learned the full truth of Alice Teale's world. When he heard that they had found it, Morgan finally admitted his involvement in her death but stated he would plead guilty only to manslaughter on the grounds of diminished responsibility. Black's response was to charge the man with murder.

'He knows he's fucked,' Black told Beth, 'and now he's clutching at straws. We have the body, proof of traces of Alice in the boot of his car, a dozen other victims, emboldened by his arrest, willing to testify against him, and that's made even Jenny see him for what he is. Finally, we have the journal, which he has been using to put us off the scent ever since Alice went missing, selectively sending us pages that always pushed us in the wrong direction. He's even admitted he strangled her. I can't see any judge or jury in the world believing he had somehow lost his mind at that point. Morgan will die in prison.'

'Let's hope so,' said Beth wearily.

While they were waiting for the lorry she looked around the town and watched as people went about their business. 'It seems different somehow,' she said, 'like something's changed here.'

'A town doesn't really have an atmosphere, Beth. A town can't be sad, happy or evil. People can be, perhaps, or they can do evil things for selfish motives, but I don't think the town has changed just because Alice Teale's killers have been caught.'

'Think what you like,' she said, 'but look around you.'

And he did, mainly to humour her, as people went in and out of the shops, the pubs and the chippy, which was generating a wave of warm, fishy, vinegary air that escaped from its extractor fans. Black watched as people stopped to talk to one another on the street and exchange gossip, always Collemby's most popular currency, before going on their way again. He had to admit it was a more serene spectacle than on the day they had arrived here. He was snatched from his thoughts by the lorry, which revved its engines almost in triumph as the driver finally completed his manoeuvre, backing away from the pub and out into the street before heading away up the road.

'Have it your way,' he said. 'Come on, I'll buy you some chips.'

They ate them sitting on the wall as they thought about Collemby's former headteacher and the years of abuse he had been involved in.

'He had a wife,' said Beth. 'Do you think she knew?'

'We'll never know, but if you've been groomed like she was, you must know your husband has an interest in young girls. Surely you'd suspect that one day you might not be enough for him. Then there was his job. He was surrounded by hundreds of children, each and every day, and he had power over them all.'

'Did he ever love her, I wonder,' asked Beth, 'in the early years of their marriage?'

Black snorted his derision. 'He didn't marry her because he loved her.'

'He did it to shut her up, then,' offered Beth. 'To keep her sweet.'

Black shook his head. 'No. That was *a* reason, but I bet it wasn't *the* reason.'

'Why did he want her, then?'

'Camouflage,' he said quietly. 'That's what he used her

for, to blend in. Marrying her took the heat out of a bad situation and he probably did it out of necessity but, from then on, he could move freely from job to job and school to school. He was totally respectable, never under suspicion.'

'They were so careful.' She meant Keech and Morgan. 'They never did anything out in the open and chose their victims carefully. Vulnerable girls who nobody would believe.'

'They tried with Alice Teale, didn't they?' he said. 'According to her journal, but they gave up early on, before they incriminated themselves – but she knew, or at least she guessed. She sensed what was going on and her suspicions grew when she learned about the Friday-evening detentions.'

'But Alice Teale wasn't vulnerable, and she had a father.'

'An absent one,' said Black. 'He still lived in her home but he didn't take much interest in the girl, or even like her very much. Either she was out of the house or he was. They picked up on it and must have thought they could groom her, but she pushed back against it and they gave up before they stepped over the line. She didn't give up, though, did she? They misread Ronnie's disinterest in her and the effect it had on Alice, though doubtless his behaviour hurt her.'

'That's because he was convinced she wasn't his.'

'Well, that's the thing,' he said. 'Before DI Fraser left, he did some DNA tests to help ID Alice if they ever found her. I've seen the results, and they proved one thing beyond doubt. Alice Teale was definitely Ronnie Teale's daughter.'

'What? But we thought . . .'

'That she was Alex McGregor's,' said Black. 'Everyone thought that, including her own father. I think Alice thought it, too, perhaps.'

'But she even looks like him,' said Beth.

'We were seeing something that wasn't really there,' said Black. 'She also looks like her father, and he resembles Alex McGregor. I remember reading somewhere that when people have affairs they often choose lovers who are not that physically dissimilar to their partners. I think Abigail Teale had a type.'

'Tragic, isn't it?' she said. 'Ronnie Teale spent all that time hating his own daughter because he always suspected she was someone else's. He just couldn't get past that. She was a permanent reminder of a short-lived affair that ended years ago and might not even ever have been consummated. All this time, he could have just loved her, because she was his daughter.'

'And now he has to live with himself,' said Beth. 'Imagine that.'

And they did for a while, until Black asked, 'How did you get on with the journal?'

'I read every page. I found all the bits the headteacher kept back. The extracts he didn't want us to see.'

She fished into her bag and found the relevant photocopied pages then handed them to Black to read.

The Journal of Alice Teale

The moment when I first worked it out is as clear to me now as it was back then. He was walking along the corridor with her and we were going the other way, Chris and me. I don't think Chris even noticed her, but I saw this scrawny young kid on her way to the punishment block again and I wondered what on earth she could have done to deserve another session in there. So that's maybe why I looked at her a little more closely than usual, and I could see it in her face.

Not anger, not the usual fierce defiance you see when bad kids are up for their umpteenth punishment, not fear or hurt or anything. Just resignation. She was on her way to see the head, brought there by her teacher, and she just looked resigned, like this was the way it was meant to be. That wasn't the proof, though.

The proof was even less obvious than the look on her face.

When I had passed her I turned back for a second and saw it. Chris didn't, and the teacher didn't realize I was looking at them. Neither did the girl.

All it took was one little thing.

His hand on her back.

He was steering her gently through the double doors. I'd have almost described his touch as tender, if it had been anyone else, but this wasn't her boyfriend or a boy who liked her. This was her teacher, a man three times her age, and she was what – thirteen? Fourteen, at most. That hand on her back was desire, control, possession. It was all of that and more, and it triggered a memory of my own time in his class.

I had been lost in my work when the bell went and for once didn't get straight up. I wanted to finish the last paragraph of my story because I knew what I was writing was good – for my age, at least. I was dimly aware of everyone else getting up and leaving, so I had to speed up and write the final words in a flurry. They just seemed to flow from me. The class was empty and I had nearly finished, then I sensed Keech come up behind me.

I was leaning over my exercise book with my head down when it happened.

His hand on the small of my back.

It was pressing down gently but firmly, then his fingers moved, tracing up and down my spine, and I froze. I couldn't move.

'Good girl, Alice,' he said, and his voice sounded different from normal. He bent over me then, even closer, pretending to look at my work, and even at that age I knew what he wanted.

'I'm finished,' I managed, and suddenly I could move again. I got straight to my feet, grabbed my bag, closed my exercise book, then went to his desk and put it there on the pile with the rest of them. I left the classroom without looking back.

I was thirteen.

Black sighed, 'Jesus.'

'There's another bit,' she said, and Beth was about to

hand this to him, too, but his phone started to ring. Black had to fish into his jacket pocket to retrieve his mobile. He listened to the caller with little comment then finally said, 'Okay, we're on our way back.' Then he hung up, sighed and said, 'DCI Everleigh would like a word.'

HEADTEACHER HELD BY POLICE IN MURDER PROBE

A headteacher with links to politicians and senior police officers has been arrested and charged with multiple sex offences against minors, and is currently being questioned about the murder of a teenage girl in his care.

Since we first reported the arrest of John Morgan, headteacher of Collemby Comprehensive School in Northumbria, more than a dozen former pupils have come forward alleging assault against a man regularly held up as a shining light in the education system. Morgan counted local MPs, councillors and even the chief constable of Northumbria Police among his many influential friends and contacts. Now speculation is mounting that he was able to escape arrest and carry on with his alleged crimes for years due to friends in high places, an allegation strenuously denied by local police.

The alleged offences came to light following the discovery of the body of Collemby sixth-former Alice Teale, seventeen, who was found strangled near Craster on the Northumbrian coast. Morgan has also been charged with illegally disposing of her body.

54

Despite Black's default setting of extreme cynicism, Beth worried that he might have a point. They had both been called to the DCI's office and Black couldn't imagine any scenario where that joint summons could possibly end well. She needn't have worried, though. It seemed the DCI was in a generous mood.

'I have to say I'm impressed you managed to solve this,' said Everleigh.

'It was DS Black,' explained Beth. 'He remembered Alice saying something about admiring the view from the roof, he went up to see for himself and worked it all out.'

'It was DC Winter, really,' said Black. 'She was the one who realized Alice needed proof and she remembered that a camera had gone missing.'

Everleigh smiled at their modesty. 'Either way, you make such a good team I've decided to keep you together from now on.'

Beth seemed pleased at that, but Black was immediately suspicious because he had spotted something on the DCI's desk: a copy of a tabloid newspaper he'd seen that morning with an unflattering story about the headteacher and his friends in high places. Everleigh's eye seemed to move almost involuntarily to it now, a sore reminder of the embarrassment they had caused the force and their DCI by uncovering Morgan as the killer.

'Well, you certainly seem to have cracked the case,' he said, before adding: 'Not before time. Made quite a big splash in the newspapers, too.' He said this a little too brightly and Beth felt the need to intervene and defend themselves.

'It was the only way to flush out the other victims, and there were a number of them.'

'Indeed, there were.' He beamed at her then, and she wasn't sure how to react.

He clearly wasn't happy about some of the press coverage, which had accused the police of allowing Morgan to hide in plain sight for so many years. There was also an embarrassing photograph of Morgan with the chief constable at an award ceremony which came back to haunt the head of Northumbria Police when it was reproduced in several tabloids days after the headteacher's arrest.

'Well done both of you.' Was that through gritted teeth? 'In recognition of your' – he seemed to hesitate momentarily while he struggled to find the right words – 'investigative prowess, I am transferring you both to a new team.' And he turned his attention to Black. 'Along with your DI, once he returns from sick leave.'

'Thank you, sir.' This was exciting news for Beth. A new team? Some innovative task force, perhaps? An elite squad, hopefully. She noticed that Black stayed silent.

'Congratulations, both of you. Soon you'll be joining the guys at DW5.'

They were out in the car park when she said brightly, 'So it looks like you're stuck with me, albeit in a new squad.'

He realized she seemed happy about that. 'It's DW5,' he

told her. 'Have you not heard of it?' She had heard about DW5, Everleigh's miscellaneous serious-crime squad. 'People often call it DWS by mistake, because Everleigh had a logo designed for the squad and the 5 looks like an S.'

Was she supposed to understand what was going on here? 'And?'

'Do you know what DWS stands for?' he asked her. 'At least, unofficially.'

'No.'

'Dead Wood Squad,' he told her. 'DW5 isn't an elite team. It's an excuse, a sham, an elephants' graveyard, a place to send detectives to die. It's where Everleigh puts everyone in CID he has no faith in. The men and women working there are unmotivated, incompetent, alcoholic – in some cases, all three,' he explained. 'And we are about to join them.'

Beth didn't understand. 'But he said they deal with serious cases.'

'Oh, they do. We'll get cases all right.' He smiled grimly. 'The ones no one else wants. All the cold cases that are completely frozen over – every poisoned chalice, each investigation that requires huge amounts of legwork and admin will come down to us.'

'Then why don't you sound angry?'

'Because I guessed it would happen as soon as we involved the press and some of them investigated Morgan's network of pals in high places. We embarrassed them all, Beth, and people like that are very unforgiving.'

'Why not just fire us, then?'

'That would be too obvious and the press would pick

404

up on it. "Detectives fired for solving a case."' He quoted an imaginary headline. 'No, this way they get to punish us while dressing it up as a reward.'

'You mean my career is over,' she said, 'before it's even started?'

'I'm sorry,' he said.

She was bewildered. 'What are you going to do about it?'

'Do?' he asked. 'Nothing.'

'Why not?'

'What can I do?' he asked her. 'If I go over his head to complain, no one will back me. He makes DW5 sound like an elite unit. I would have to slag off everyone in it to make my point and, by the way, some of them don't even mind that they're stuck there. Time-servers see out their time, idiots don't even know they are being punished and the alkies are all in the pub that little bit sooner. It's only people like you and I that actually care. Everleigh's been very clever.'

'You don't sound as if you *do* care.'

'I do,' he snapped. 'We did the right thing. We caught the people who put Alice in her grave, and what's our reward? We've been shafted.' He let out an exasperated sigh. 'But since I can't alter the decision or affect my punishment, I will do the only thing I can do. I'm going to the pub, and I'm going to get mortal. You can come, too, if you want.' But she didn't look impressed. 'Or not.'

He turned his back on her and started to walk away. She called after him then, 'You can't alter the decision, okay? You want to get drunk tonight, then fine,' she said. 'I'm in, but when we wake up in the morning, we make each other a promise – an oath, if you like.'

'What kind of promise?'

'That we won't let him win. We join DW5 and make it work, with or without anyone else. It might not be an elite squad yet, but it could be.'

'How?' He laughed at the notion.

Beth smiled. 'Everleigh just added *us* to it,' she reminded him, 'and that's a start.'

'Well,' he said, his face softening, and he smiled at her then. 'I can't argue with that.'

The Journal of Alice Teale

How did I work it out? It wasn't just one thing. Not just the hand on a girl's back. And it was more than just a look, a touch or a comment that might have been an invitation but could easily be brushed away as something else entirely if I kicked back against it.

You had to add it all together first, then all of a sudden, I knew what was going on.

I knew it, but how can I prove it?

I can't tell Dad because he would never believe it from anyone, and certainly not from me.

My mam might think there's a tiny grain of truth here, but she wouldn't get it, not really. She'd say I have an over-active imagination, which is true, I do. I want to be a writer, so I need one, but I am not imagining this. I know I'm not. Maybe you have to have an overactive imagination to see what no one else can.

There's no use telling Daniel. He'll want to go up there and punch someone, and that will ruin everything.

Forget Chris. If I told him, he wouldn't want to do anything about it at all. He's too intimidated by the headteacher and his rules. He'd say, 'What can you do, Alice?' or 'Call the police, Alice,' as if the police would give a damn about girls like her. They have already given up on her. I know how it works. Girls like that get blamed for everything. If she was found dead in the woods, it would be her own fault. She shouldn't have gone for a walk, shouldn't have worn that skirt, had a drink, talked to that man, got in that car.

All her own fault.

Asking for it.

That's what men think.

They only see it differently when the truth is right there in front of them, if they can see it with their own eyes, become the witness to the crime. If they could look through a window and actually watch what's going on, it would make all the difference.

Well, I did look through that window and I saw what was going on.

Next time, I'll get proof.

Then we'll see.

Everybody else is just as blind as I used to be. They cannot see what is right in front of them, but I get it now and I am going to stop it.

No matter what it takes or costs.

Because doing nothing is never an option.

Acknowledgements

I would like to thank everyone at Penguin Random House for publishing *Alice Teale is Missing*. A huge thank you in particular goes to my brilliant editor, Joel Richardson, for all of his insightful ideas and unwavering support during the writing of this book. We got there in the end, Joel!

Thanks also to Maxine Hitchcock, Beth Cockeram, Olivia Thomas, Sarah Day and Beatrix McIntyre at Michael Joseph for your help at every stage of the writing process. It's been a pleasure to work with you all.

My fantastic literary agent, Phil Patterson at Marjacq, has been a constant help to me and is always a great champion of my writing. Thanks for everything, Phil. Thanks also to Sandra Sawicka at Marjacq for dealing with the foreign rights to my books.

Every author needs help, encouragement and support, and I have been lucky enough to receive a lot along the way. I'd like to thank the following people for providing it: Adam Pope, Andy Davis, Nikki Selden, Gareth Chennells, Andrew Local, Stuart Britton, David Shapiro, Peter Day, Tony Frobisher, Eva Dolan, Katie Charlton, Gemma Sealey, Emad Akhtar, Keshini Naidoo and Ion Mills.

My lovely wife, Alison, deserves a special thank you for putting up with an author in her house. Her belief and encouragement keep me going when the end of a book seems a long way off.

My wonderful daughter, Erin, brightens all of my days and that's why the writing always stops when she comes home. Thanks for inspiring me, Erin. Love you always.